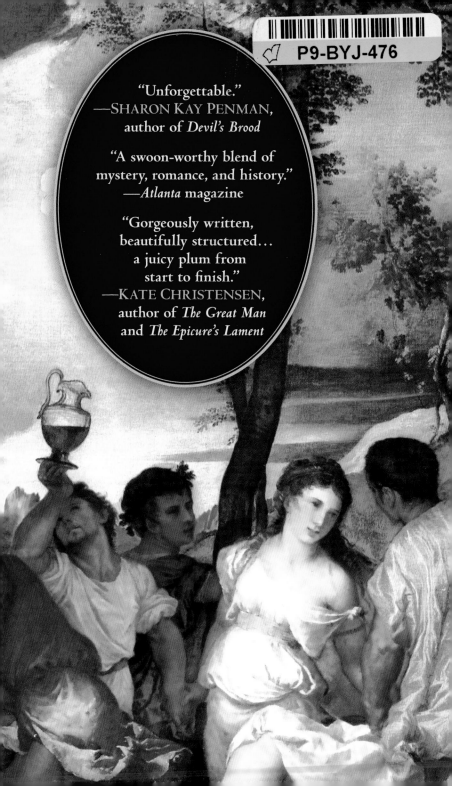

"Unforgettable."
—SHARON KAY PENMAN,
author of *Devil's Brood*

"A swoon-worthy blend of
mystery, romance, and history."
—*Atlanta* magazine

"Gorgeously written,
beautifully structured…
a juicy plum from
start to finish."
—KATE CHRISTENSEN,
author of *The Great Man*
and *The Epicure's Lament*

continued . . .

The Creation of Eve

LYNN CULLEN

BERKLEY BOOKS
New York

THE BERKLEY PUBLISHING GROUP
Published by the Penguin Group
Penguin Group (USA) Inc.
375 Hudson Street, New York, New York 10014, USA
Penguin Group (Canada), 90 Eglinton Avenue East, Suite 700, Toronto, Ontario M4P 2Y3, Canada
(a division of Pearson Penguin Canada Inc.)
Penguin Books Ltd., 80 Strand, London WC2R 0RL, England
Penguin Group Ireland, 25 St. Stephen's Green, Dublin 2, Ireland (a division of Penguin Books Ltd.)
Penguin Group (Australia), 250 Camberwell Road, Camberwell, Victoria 3124, Australia
(a division of Pearson Australia Group Pty. Ltd.)
Penguin Books India Pvt. Ltd., 11 Community Centre, Panchsheel Park, New Delhi—110 017, India
Penguin Group (NZ), 67 Apollo Drive, Rosedale, North Shore 0632, New Zealand
(a division of Pearson New Zealand Ltd.)
Penguin Books (South Africa) (Pty.) Ltd., 24 Sturdee Avenue, Rosebank, Johannesburg 2196,
South Africa

Penguin Books Ltd., Registered Offices: 80 Strand, London WC2R 0RL, England

This is a work of fiction. Names, characters, places, and incidents either are the product of the author's imagination or are used fictitiously, and any resemblance to actual persons, living or dead, business establishments, events, or locales is entirely coincidental. The publisher does not have any control over and does not assume any responsibility for author or third-party websites or their content.

Copyright © 2010 by Lynn Cullen.
"Readers Guide" copyright © by Penguin Group (USA) Inc.
Interior map by John T. Burgoyne.
Cover art: *The Andrians*, c. 1523–24 (oil on canvas); *Titian* (Tiziano Vecellio), c. 1488–1576 /
Prado, Madrid, Spain / Giraudon / The Bridgeman Art Library International.
Cover design by Lesley Worrell.

PRINTING HISTORY
G. P. Putnam's Sons hardcover edition / March 2010
Berkley trade paperback edition / February 2011

Berkley trade paperback ISBN: 978-0-425-23870-7

The Library of Congress has cataloged the G. P. Putnam's Sons hardcover edition as follows:

Cullen, Lynn.
The creation of Eve / Lynn Cullen.
    p.   cm.
  ISBN 978-0-399-15610-6
  1. Anguissola, Sofonisba, ca. 1532/33–1625—Fiction.   2. Women painters—Italy—
Fiction.   3. Élisabeth de Valois, Queen, consort of Philip II, King of Spain, 1544–1568—
Fiction.   4. Philip II, King of Spain, 1527–1598—Fiction.   5. Spain—History—Philip II,
1556–1598—Fiction.   I. Title.
PS3553.U2955C74   2010   2009036183
813'.54—dc22

PRINTED IN THE UNITED STATES OF AMERICA

10   9   8   7   6   5   4   3   2   1

For Bill Doughty's daughters,
Margaret, Jeanne, Carolyn, and Arlene

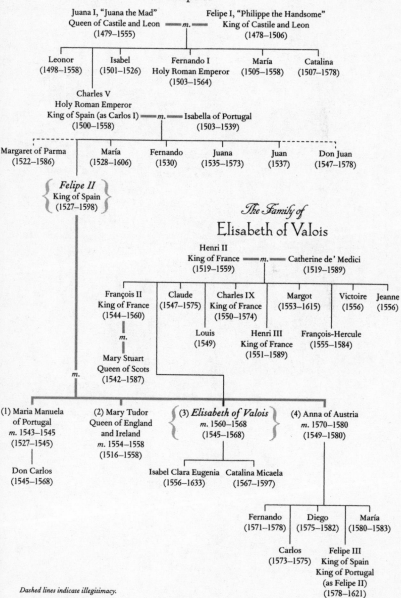

The Family of
Felipe II

Juana I, "Juana the Mad"
Queen of Castile and Leon
(1479–1555) — *m.* — Felipe I, "Philippe the Handsome"
King of Castile and Leon
(1478–1506)

Leonor (1498–1558) | Isabel (1501–1526) | Fernando I Holy Roman Emperor (1503–1564) | María (1505–1558) | Catalina (1507–1578)

Charles V
Holy Roman Emperor
King of Spain (as Carlos I) — *m.* — Isabella of Portugal
(1500–1558) (1503–1539)

Margaret of Parma (1522–1586) | María (1528–1606) | Fernando (1530) | Juana (1535–1573) | Juan (1537) | Don Juan (1547–1578)

{ *Felipe II*
King of Spain
(1527–1598) }

The Family of
Elisabeth of Valois

Henri II
King of France — *m.* — Catherine de' Medici
(1519–1559) (1519–1589)

François II King of France (1544–1560) | Claude (1547–1575) | Charles IX King of France (1550–1574) | Margot (1553–1615) | Victoire (1556) | Jeanne (1556)

Louis (1549)

Henri III King of France (1551–1589)

François-Hercule (1555–1584)

m.

Mary Stuart
Queen of Scots
(1542–1587)

m.

(1) Maria Manuela of Portugal *m.* 1543–1545 (1527–1545) | (2) Mary Tudor Queen of England and Ireland *m.* 1554–1558 (1516–1558) | { (3) *Elisabeth of Valois m.* 1560–1568 (1545–1568) } | (4) Anna of Austria *m.* 1570–1580 (1549–1580)

Don Carlos (1545–1568)

Isabel Clara Eugenia (1556–1633) | Catalina Micaela (1567–1597)

Fernando (1571–1578) | Diego (1575–1582) | María (1580–1583)

Carlos (1573–1575) | Felipe III King of Spain King of Portugal (as Felipe II) (1578–1621)

Dashed lines indicate illegitimacy.

ATLANTIC OCEAN

BAY OF BISCAY

A CORUÑA

RÍO BIDASOA

BURGOS

VALLADOLID

RÍO DUERO

Sierra de Guadarrama

PORTUGAL

SALAMANCA

SEGOVIA

VALSAÍN

EL ESCORIAL

ACALÁ de HENARES

Sierra de Gredos

MADRID

RÍO TAJO

ARANJUEZ

TOLEDO

S P A I N

CÓRDOBA

RÍO GUADALQUIVIR

SEVILLA

GRANADA

Sierra Nevada

MEDITERR

SEA

AFRICA

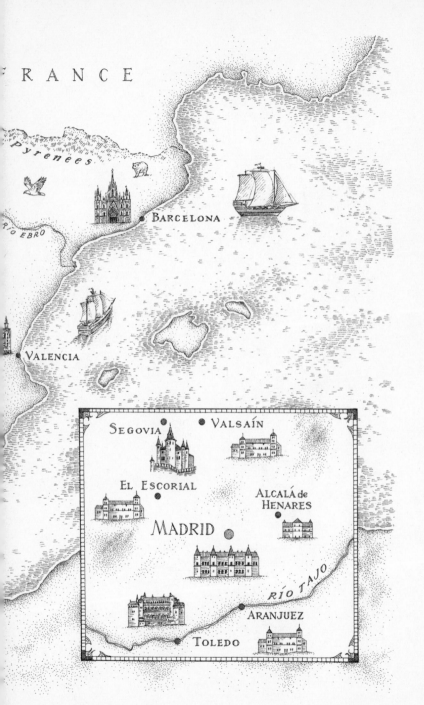

FRANCE

Pyrenees

RÍO EBRO

BARCELONA

VALENCIA

SEGOVIA   VALSAÍN

EL ESCORIAL   ALCALÁ de
                                    HENARES

MADRID

RÍO TAJO

ARANJUEZ

TOLEDO

©2008 John Blumen

The
First Notebook

In which I shall gather my impressions and observations as a painter, as well as any letters or sundry items of information that may prove useful to me and my work, as have done the great maestros Leonardo da Vinci, Albrecht Dürer, and Michelangelo Buonarroti, also known as Il Divino.

ITEM: *"Women are lustful, imperfect creatures. Nature seeks perfection in all her creatures, and would, if she could, produce nothing but men."*

—COUNT BALDASSARE CASTIGLIONE,
The Book of the Courtier

ITEM: *In painting, three things must be considered—the position of the viewer, the position of the object viewed, and the position of the light that illuminates the object.*

ITEM: *Rosemary, when its scent is inhaled, concentrates the mind.*

7 MAY 1559
Macel de' Corvi, Rome

In the time it takes to pluck a hen, I have ruined myself. I have ruined my sisters, my little brother. Papà—I have ruined Papà. My gentle, good papà, who had encouraged me to paint, when everyone in Cremona laughed. *A girl taking up a man's craft, and such a dirty one at that! Who is going to marry her now? Not that Amilcare could have scraped together a decent dowry—God knows he has already got his problems, if you know what I mean.*

Oh, I had heard people whisper. I heard them in Papà's bookshop, when they thought the groan of the printing press covered their voices. I heard them over the splashing of the fountain in the piazza outside our house, when they were strolling in the evening air, or as I waited on the church steps for Mamma to finish her prayers, always longer than everyone else's. Papà must have heard them, too, but that never stopped him from encouraging my painting. He had begun the day I'd come pattering home from Mass in my little girl's slippers, and inspired by the picture of the Madonna and Child newly hung in the Lady Chapel, borrowed his quill and paper to draw my own Nativity scene. Francesca, nursing the most recent of Mamma's babies, had been my captive model.

Hunched over the suckling infant, Francesca had glared at me under brows as thick and mobile as a man's thumbs. "You go!" she scolded in her peasant's Italian. "What you want with picture of this?"

By the time baby Minerva drained a breast, I had finished my little sketch. I ran with the results to Papà, who put aside the book he had been reading in the courtyard and held the drawing up to the afternoon sunlight. "It's Minerva and Francesca, isn't it? You even caught Francesca's frown. *Eccellente,* Sofonisba!"

My chest had swelled with pride. I was all of seven. Now I, the wondrous painting virgin from Cremona, am seven-and-twenty—and ill with fear. For my good papà, I beg the saints and martyrs to not let maestro Michelangelo talk.

Perhaps the Maestro did not see so much. It had been dark in his studio. The Angelus bell marking dusk had been ringing from the church of Santa Maria di Loreto across the piazza when Tiberio and I had run up the stairs. How could I have been so foolish as to go up to the studio alone with Tiberio? I must have been drunk, though I had had only a cup of watered wine at *cena*. But

I was drunk—on being maestro Michelangelo's chosen one. On Tiberio's choosing me, too. On the feel of Tiberio's thick fingers, rough from sculpting, around mine. I had to be drunk to do what I did.

But Tiberio said he loved me then, and he meant it, I know. His kiss did not lie. Oh, what kind of wicked she-cat am I? Even now, as black tendrils of shame seep through my heart like ink in water, I dream of his lips. I never knew a man's lips could be so soft in the flesh yet so thrillingly hard when pressed against one's own. Was it the pressure of his lips, or just the musk of his skin, that drove me to animal madness? I have never imagined such pleasure. Since the age of fourteen, my thoughts have been consumed by studying with different maestros, pleasing patrons, and painting, painting, always painting. Now thoughts of his body dance through my dazzled brain, beckoning to me like players in a lascivious masque.

It is not as if Francesca did not try to keep Tiberio and me apart. She has approached her role as a lady's companion with ferocious vigor since my first trip to visit Rome, three years ago, at maestro Michelangelo's request. Proud, then, of her recent elevation from nurse, she had at all times positioned her stocky black-clad body between me and Tiberio, who was even then Michelangelo's favorite student. No matter if Tiberio and I were tramping over the vine-covered ruins of the Palatine Hill, making sketches of the broken ancient pillars on which cows scratched their bony rumps, or watching men cart stone from the empty hulk of the Colosseum to use in the new dome of the Basilica that the Maestro was building, or just pausing in the quiet church of San Pietro in Vincoli to admire the Maestro's magnificent statue of a stern and powerful Moses—Francesca had bent every scrap of her considerable will toward creating a barrier between us.

This visit had been no different. She would have prevented all but one brief touch had she not been seized with a choking cough.

I blame the weather for her fit. It has been hot here, too hot, for May. The sun beats down from morning until night, baking the scent of the roses, now blooming from every wall, into air thick with the stench of the Tiber, wood smoke, and dung. This afternoon, as our little group made its way through the crooked streets of the old quarter in which Michelangelo lives, the filmy veil sticking to my cheeks, my tight sleeves and corset, and the lace ruff scratching my neck were but minor torments compared with Francesca's suffering in her heavy lady's-companion black. Thickly veiled and buttoned up to her chin in wool, she mopped her sweating face with a corner of her veil as she struggled to keep up with Tiberio and me. Even in her misery, had she felt the invisible threads drawing Tiberio and me together? Sweetest Holy Mary, had Michelangelo?

Perhaps the Maestro noticed nothing. He walked ahead of us, hands behind his back and head pointed down, as if searching the cobblestones for *scudi*. I tried to act properly detached toward Tiberio, coolly discussing perspective and composition and critiquing other artists' work in response to the gruff comments Michelangelo tossed over his shoulder. The Maestro was particularly harsh on the Venetian, Tiziano Vecellio, or Titian, as he is sometimes called, claiming the Venetian needed to learn how to draw, and Tiberio, echoing the Maestro in all things, cited Tiziano's painting of the myth of Danaë as a glaring example of sacrificing precision for prettiness. I did not agree. But though I wished to argue that Tiziano's failure to depict each muscle of the naked woman was more than made up for by the warmth afforded by his open brushwork and use of color, at that moment the discussion of painted flesh was too much for me, with the very real flesh of Tiberio so near. Instead I calmly (or so I thought) defended the realism in Tiziano's portrait of Pope Paul III and his two nephews, with the Venetian going so far with his honest brush as to portray the subjects as a trio of connivers.

"No wonder Tiziano abandoned the project," I said.

Michelangelo responded with a grunt.

"It's a poor artist who cannot finish a simple portrait," said Tiberio.

"It's a poor artist who would ever start one," muttered the Maestro.

"But there have been some very worthy portraits," I said. "I think of maestro Leonardo's portrait of madonna Lisa, wife of Francesco del Giocondo."

The Maestro glanced at me over his shoulder. "He overdid the *sfumato*. All his lines are too blurry, or is the picture just sprouting mold?"

I smiled at Tiberio's chuckle. "Surely, Maestro," I said, "you see merit in Raffaello's portrait of Count Baldassare Castiglione? They say it's so lifelike his dog mistook the picture for his master."

"He was full of himself," the Maestro pronounced.

"Who, Maestro?" said Tiberio. "Raffaello or Castiglione?"

"Both."

Tiberio laughed. "Raffaello did your portrait, Maestro. Are you not pleased?"

The Maestro growled.

"It's a good likeness," Tiberio told me, "the only portrait anyone has done of him. You've seen it, haven't you, in *The School of Athens* in the Vatican? Raffaello had to do it on the sly."

"Waste of time," said the Maestro.

We continued in this vein, I arguing for portraiture, the Maestro and Tiberio arguing against it. But perhaps my bold talk fooled no one. Perhaps all knew my every sense was trained upon Tiberio.

I could almost smile now at how Francesca had bustled between Tiberio and me when we arrived at the Pope's chapel in the Basilica, the chapel they call the Sistine. We had stood with our heads tipped back, all of us, silent. On the vaulted ceiling above us, over an area as large as Papà's apple orchard, hundreds of brawny, mostly naked figures writhed, bringing the stories from the Scriptures vividly to life. Their flesh, though painted, seemed as real as that of Tiberio's hands, which he placed atop his head in wonder; their painted muscles as palpable as those I could see in my side vision of Tiberio's sinuous wrists. Even Francesca, sweat rolling down her broad face as she wedged herself between Tiberio and me, gaped up at the colorful grid of scenes above us.

"I've seen this dozens of times, Maestro," said Tiberio, "and I never know what to say."

Still appraising the ceiling with a frown, the Maestro folded his arms over his barrel chest. "Not bad for a sculptor." He jerked his thumb at the mural covering the wall above the altar. "*The Last Judgment* is better. Ceilings are hell."

I stole a look at him. The maestro of maestros had a head like a cannonball, the thick, high cheekbones of a Slav, and a squashed nose. His sharp eyes were so deeply set it was impossible to determine their color. For a man of four-and-eighty, his arms were unusually muscular, contrasting oddly with his old man's white beard, and his hands were so calloused they looked to be made of the stone in which he worked. Other than his arms, and a disproportionately long torso, he was a small man. The greasy thigh-high boots of dog-skin that he wore only accentuated the shortness of his bowed legs. I smiled to myself as I returned my sights to the ceiling. The greatest living artist in the world, the creator of beauty so heavenly that he was called the Divine One, must have been quite the brawler in his youth.

"Maestro, how old were you when you finished this?" asked Tiberio.

"The ceiling? Thirty-seven. Old, I thought then. By God, I felt it, too, all that damned painting. Ha! I didn't know what old was. Old is bad bowels and trouble pissing. Makes me wonder why we fight so hard to live."

The scrape of our shoes on the marble mosaic floor was lost in the hush of the chamber. It smelled of damp and stone and incense. Outside, church bells began to clang, marking the hour.

"I wish I could paint like this," I said.

The Maestro turned on me, the folds of his coarse face deepening in a scowl. "Who says you can't? That picture you brought with you of your sisters playing chess—you're in it, too, aren't you, old lady?" he said to Francesca.

Francesca glared at the mosaics at her feet, pride and offense warring on her brow.

"It's a good start," he said to me. "I saw their souls, especially the sister turned toward the viewer."

"Lucia," I murmured, with a pang of homesickness.

"Musculature is your problem. I got no sense of it. From the neck down, your people were mannequins stuffed into clothes."

I pressed together my lips. It is difficult to improve one's understanding of muscle and the structure of the human form when, as a woman, one is not allowed to study a naked body, be it dead or alive. In truth, the only form of painting I have attempted thus far is that kind so maligned by the Maestro: portraiture. As long as I cannot learn by drawing from the nude or from the dissection of a cadaver, I will never be able to paint more than heads, hands, and gowns. I will never be able to depict scenes from the Bible or history or legend and myth, the mark of the greatest painters, and until I do, I have no chance of being considered a *maestra* by Michelangelo or anyone else.

The Maestro seemed to hear my thoughts. "Be glad you can't do dissections." He brushed a bread crumb from his beard. "There's nothing more foul in the world. No one enjoys doing them—though maybe that braggart Leonardo da Vinci did. Who'd ever guess that old peacock could cut into a dead woman's body like it was a sausage?"

Francesca rapped at my arm, signaling her demand that we leave.

"Fine talk, Maestro," Tiberio murmured.

The Maestro tipped back his head to gaze at the ceiling. "Sofonisba works in a man's world. She can take it."

Tiberio lifted his brows at me in apology, then joined the Maestro in his study of the ceiling. My face hot, I did the same. The cooing of the pigeons outside filled the awkward silence.

"Maestro," Tiberio said after a moment, "this scene of the creation of Adam—out of the dozens of other magnificent scenes to look at, the viewer's eye always goes back to this one. How did you do it?"

"It *is* in the center," the Maestro said sardonically.

Tiberio frowned at the ceiling.

"What have I taught you?" said the Maestro.

"Is it the white background? There is no greater use of white space on the entire ceiling."

The Maestro looked down to scowl at Tiberio. "What have I told you about contrasts?"

Tiberio seemed unaware of the Maestro's gaze upon him as he recited, "'In every painting, the painter must choose what he wishes the viewer to see first. Then he must put the greatest contrast between dark and light in that spot.'"

I peered at *The Creation of Adam*. Not only was there much white background in the scene, as Tiberio had said, but the white of God's robe was the brightest white on the entire ceiling. It stood out starkly against the dark band of angels swirling around Him. Once captured by this contrast, one's gaze naturally trailed from His luminescent robe to His outstretched arm, then down to the handsome, languidly awaiting Adam. From there, one could hardly move one's eyes. Never has a human been so lovingly rendered, with such sympathy and truth. How perfectly the Maestro revealed the humble spirit of the man waiting within this earthly shell.

"So," Tiberio murmured to himself, "in each of these scenes we should look for the greatest contrast if we are to know what you thought the viewer should see first."

Testing this theory, I looked from scene to scene. Starting in the direction of the door through which we'd entered, I let contrast lead my eye, from the cloak being laid over the drunken Noah by his sons, to the black cape of a fleeing mother against the lightning-lit sky in *The Flood*, to the bright yellow scales of the serpent against the dark Tree of Knowledge in *The Temptation of Eve*. In each case the drama of the scene was heightened by the eye's being sent immediately to the most important element— Noah degrading himself, the hopelessness in the fleeing mother's face, the alluring yet repulsive beauty of the serpent tempting Eve.

I stopped at *The Creation of Eve*. There, the darkest dark met the brightest light where Eve's plump pale thigh contrasted against the dark shrub below which Adam slept. My gaze slipped directly to the sweetly sleeping Adam, where it lingered on his innocent smile, his tousled reddish hair, his muscular body sprawled on the grass.

Only begrudgingly did my eye move to reconsider Eve's crouching form being raised out of Adam by God. Painted against a light blue background, her pale figure was lumpen and static, the expression on her face unreadable. The scene felt disturbingly empty.

I bumped into Tiberio. He brought down his gaze.

"Mi scusi," I whispered. My elbow tingled where it had touched the hard muscles of his belly. I could feel his gaze remain upon me as I looked back up at the ceiling. All thoughts of art fled from my mind.

We left soon after. Tiberio and I did not address each other on the walk home through the crowded neighborhoods, nor throughout an early dinner at a tavern on the Macel de' Corvi, near maestro Michelangelo's house. I picked at my stewed eel, trying my best to keep my gaze from lingering on Tiberio's lively gray-green eyes, on his hair curling over his ears in wiry wisps of gold, on his thick, veined wrists. And Sweetest Holy Mary! Was he trying not to look at me?

Too soon, *cena* was finished. We strolled back with Michelangelo to his house to pick up the drawing supplies I had left there earlier, as I was to leave for Cremona in the morning, ending my visit to Rome. At his door, the Maestro bade us good-bye, stating that he wished to continue on through the streets, as he usually does of an evening.

He had hardly stumped away, a furious bow-legged figure in dog-skin boots, when Tiberio said, "Signorina Sofonisba, before you go, would you do me the favor of looking at some drawings? They are studies for a statue I'm finishing for the Maestro."

"He gave you such a project?" I plucked at the gauzy silk of my veil, which a heated evening breeze had blown across my face. "What a compliment."

"It is a great responsibility. I have been working on it for two years now."

"*Mi scusi, signorina,* " Francesca said. "We go now."

"I would like to see these drawings. Just for a few minutes, as you gather my supplies." Then, before Francesca could respond—and shocking myself—I pushed in the heavy carved door.

Tiberio followed with a surprised grin. "How do you like my house?" Pretending to be the host, he spread his arm toward the fresco over the main stairway. "Nothing proclaims 'Welcome' like a corpse."

I pursed my lips so as not to laugh at the fresco of a coffin with a leering skeleton rising from it. "Truly inviting, *signore,*" I said.

"The old man's humor. Typical. It is getting dark. Let me get some light."

Francesca placed herself between me and the stairs as he strode up, two at a time. "*Signorina*, it no good for a maiden to be alone."

My light tone betrayed my happiness. "I am not alone. Maestro Michelangelo will be back soon, and I've got you, signore Tiberio, and who knows what other servants are around. Hello?" I called into the growing dimness. No one answered. "In any case, at my age I am hardly a dewy-eyed maiden."

"What I say about the dew eyes? I say it no good to be alone with a man."

Tiberio jogged back down the stairs with rolled-up drawings tucked under one arm. He held up a smoking lamp. "Let there be light."

"Just like in the Maestro's scene of the creation of the sun and the stars in the chapel," I said.

He laughed. "Am I convincing in the role of God?"

"Oh, yes."

He bowed. "*Grazie, signorina*. But I do not believe you."

Francesca cleared her throat.

He glanced at her, then put the drawings on the table before us, his expression growing serious. "I keep thinking about the Maestro's painting of the creation of Adam. How did he ever think to portray God bringing Adam to life through a touch of fingers? You can feel the very life force being passed from Creator to creation."

Something that had bothered me came back to mind. "It must be my failing and not the Maestro's, but I did not get that feeling in the scene of Eve's creation. It seems, almost, that the Maestro took little care in her depiction."

"Of course. That is by design. Eve is not as important as Adam."

I looked at him, wondering why this should be so.

"Trust me, the Maestro knows what he is about. That is why he is famous and we are not."

"At least not yet," I said.

His eyes warmed. "I like the way you think, Sofonisba Anguissola."

Francesca started coughing. When she did not stop, Tiberio pulled his smile from me. "Old woman, are you well?"

"*Sì, sì.*" Francesca waved him off, still coughing.

"Francesca, are you choking?"

She shook her head, whipping her shoulders with her veil. Her coughs tightened into a breathless bark.

"Go to the piazza and get yourself a drink," Tiberio ordered. "The water in that fountain comes straight from the aqueduct— good mountain water. Signorina Sofonisba won't be alone," he added when she would not budge in spite of not being able to draw breath. "I'll watch over her."

"That," she squeaked, "what give me fear."

I frowned in apology as she bent into her coughing. I had heard Tiberio's people, the Calcagnis, were a rich and powerful Florentine family. Tiberio was the one in danger of being tainted, not I. The Anguissolas may have had riches once, but our branch has been withering for generations. Papà's title as count has little land and no power behind it.

"*Signorina,* " choked Francesca, "go . . . with me."

I could stand her discomfort no longer. "Come!" I started for the door.

"You insult me, Francesca," Tiberio said quickly, "by not trusting me with your lady."

I stopped. Tiberio wished me to stay. Sweetest Holy Mary! But Francesca's cough would not stop. "For the love of God, Francesca, please! Go get yourself some water!"

Francesca, doubled over, threw me a last, desperate look, then fled.

Tiberio set the lamp on a table. "She should be fine," he said when he saw my worried expression. "The water is very soothing."

"She may need a dram of coltsfoot tea."

"You have a knowledge of herbs?"

A woman can know too much. I lowered my eyes. "Just a little."

"I should not be surprised." He rolled out the papers.

I drew in a breath. "So this is the statue?"

"Yes. The Maestro's preliminary drawings of it, at least. Once you get into removing stone from the block, plans can change."

"As in a painting."

"Similar, yes, though sculpture is the harder art to master. This is why the Maestro calls himself a sculptor, not a painter—why I chose this same path, too."

"So you think painting is not difficult to master?"

"I didn't mean to offend you—of course it is. I like to paint. The Maestro does, too, sometimes. But the Maestro says it takes a real man to endure the punishment of working in stone. You have to be brave—one mistake and you're done. Painting is much more forgiving and simple, better suited for the temperament of a woman. There is no pressure to perform."

"I see. I shall try to remember that the next time I must paint a man as a good and benevolent family man when all of Italy knows he has just poisoned his brother." I held my breath. Must I always speak my mind?

But Tiberio only grimaced and said, "Point taken." He pushed back the curling edges of the red chalk drawing. "Anyway, these are the plans. The Maestro was trying to do something here that no one else has done with success—sculpting four freestanding figures from a single block. Do you know how hard that is to do? Coaxing one body from stone is difficult enough. Four bodies— it's nearly impossible. All those arms and legs."

"I see the dying Christ." I pointed to the dominant figure, holding the sinking body. "Who is this? Joseph of Arimathea, taking him from the cross?"

"There is no cross here. This scene is later, when Christ was being prepared for the tomb. The hooded man is Nicodemus, the rich old man who wished to know Our Lord. As you remember, Nicodemus helped with the burial." He gestured to the other figures. "Here's the Virgin Mary, supporting her son, and Mary Magdalene to His other side, readying His winding cloth. If the Maestro seems preoccupied with death in this piece, it is because it is meant for his own tomb."

I gazed at the drawing, my every pore taut with arousal, but not from the rendering: Tiberio's arm was nearly touching mine.

"All had been going well with the work on the piece," he said. "Over the course of eight years, the Maestro had roughed in the Nicodemus and much of the Virgin and Mary Magdalene. Then one day, while shaping the Christ, he hit a fault in the marble."

"A fault?"

"One of the worst kinds, a vein of emery. It's so hard that sparks fly when your chisel hits it. Very difficult to shape, if you can do it at all." Tiberio shook his head. "I was in the studio at the time, though I didn't see the sparks. All I knew was, suddenly the Maestro was shouting and smashing the statue with his hammer. The three of us who were there, I, Antonio the servant, and the painter Daniele da Volterra, dropped everything and tried to hold him back."

"Did he do much damage?"

"Broke off two arms and the Christ's leg. We had to hold the old man until he cooled down and dropped the hammer. 'If you like it so much,' he shouted at me, along with a few choice Florentine curses, 'you finish it!' It turned out he was serious—he didn't care if I worked on it, as long as it was kept out of his sight." He patted the edge of the drawing. "Well, I was not letting this go. It's too beautiful, even with the missing limbs. And all that work—eight years of his hammer to the chisel, dust flying up his nose and in his eyes, chips raining down his back—for nothing. No. It took ten men to inch the unfinished block out of his studio and down the arcade to the little room the Maestro said I could use as a studio, but I was keeping it." He looked at me over his shoulder. "Would you like to see it?"

I glanced at the door.

"I will have you back downstairs before Francesca returns. No one will be the wiser."

As the Angelus bells began to clang, our eyes met.

He picked up a lamp. I do not know what possessed me: grinning like two naughty children, we ran up the stairs.

Even as he showed me into a small, dim room, its air thick with stone dust, I began to regret my actions. It was wrong for a lady, even of lowest nobility, to be alone with a gentleman. But it was for Art, I argued with myself. To learn about Art.

My thudding heart deafened me as I followed him to a hulk in the shadows. He raised his lamp, revealing the rock towering above us. From it emerged four figures, the top one, the Nicodemus, a pale hooded monster raked with the mark of chisels.

"Can you tell who the model is?" Tiberio brought the lamp closer, illuminating the full beard of the Nicodemus and its heavy scowling brow.

"The Maestro."

"Good eye. It was his idea." In the flickering yellow light, I could see Tiberio's dimples when he smiled. Sweetest Holy Mary.

"It's beautiful," I breathed.

He lowered the lamp, casting a glow upon the face of the dying Christ. "I started my work on it on my birthday two years ago. I hope to finish it by next year, when I am twenty-eight, though I am already behind schedule if I am to make as great a mark on the world as the Maestro with a piece that is completely my own. The old man was twenty-nine when he finished his *David*. I have only two years to create my own work of genius if I'm to keep up with him."

I reached for a paper on a nearby table to hide my agitation. I held it up to the dim light.

"An emblem?"

I think he might have blushed, though it was too dark to be certain. "I was working out a way to sign my work. A *T* and *C* combined with an *A* for *artista*—or *architetto*, as I become famous for my buildings. I do those, too." He grinned in his self-effacing way. "Do you think it's too much?"

Could he hear my heart beating? Grasping at a diversion, I picked up a chalk on the table. "Not unless you go so far as to call yourself a king and add the letter *R* for *re*." I did just so with the chalk.

I could hear him breathing next to me. What a fool he must think me, playing a child's game. But the closeness of his person, with his warm scent of earth, leather, and flesh, undid me. "Should there be any doubt," I heard myself say, "we might add an arm and a leg to your *T*, to form a *K*, for the English word 'King.'"

"You are an extraordinary girl, knowing English. Is there nothing you do not know? I am almost afraid of you." He took the chalk, sending a bolt of heat through my fingers. "What if that *R* is not for *re* but is truly for *ritrattista*, in honor of my friend, the brilliant lady portraitist?"

I took back the chalk just to feel his touch again—madness. "Then you must add a little leg to the *R* for the letter *L*, as in 'Lady,' as the English call their noblewomen."

He put his hand over mine before I could finish. "*Lady*, do not the two letters wish to be as one? Here is an arm, joining them." A current flowed between us as we moved the chalk in unison.

"They look good together," he said, his breath on my ear, "see?"

I could bear his closeness no longer. I turned to the statue and, trembling, touched the chill marble of the Christ's arm, draped lifelessly in the foreground. "How do you do this? How do you turn a drawing into something with three dimensions?"

"I don't. Not exactly." I felt the warmth of his body as he leaned over me to touch the statue. "Even if I have a drawing, I still must be willing to listen to the stone and change my plans if need be. The being hidden inside the block reveals itself only by degrees, like a wax figure being lifted from water. I will show you."

He put my hand to the Christ's face. My skin felt on fire as he traced my fingers over the cool polished stone. "I am removing stone, chip by chip. Something emerges: a nose. Do you feel it?"

I nodded, the back of my veil brushing against his chest.

"Yes," he said, "good. Good. And here. Here another rounding comes forth: an eye. It demands to be carved just so—the being in the stone insists. Can you feel it, Sofonisba?"

I was deafened by the roaring of my blood. "Yes," I whispered.

He slid our fingers down the ridge of the nose to the curve below, his breath caressing my ear. "And now. What is this?"

My mouth formed the word. *Lips.*

"They speak," he whispered, "if you listen. Can you hear them?"

My skirt raked the floor as he turned me toward him, my fingers still on the statue. We faced each other, the flame of the lamp licking at the silence.

"Sofonisba, you cannot deny the being within."

Slowly, he touched his lips to my exposed wrist.

I dropped my hand. "Francesca."

He went over and, softly, closed the door. "Only Michelangelo has the key."

He came back, set the lamp on the floor, then stood before me. In the golden shimmering light, he laid back my trembling veil.

"I am afraid."

"Don't be." He bent toward my mouth.

I closed my eyes as flesh met flesh, searing me wherever he kissed—lips, neck, shoulder. Our lips reunited, grateful pilgrims at journey's end, and then our kisses became urgent, desperate, until my body raged against my clothing and moans issued from the pleading creature within me.

Tiberio stopped, causing me to gasp. Gently he set me on the edge of the table and, with shaking hands, lifted my skirt.

I don't know how long the Maestro had been standing in the doorway, four thin flames wavering above his head from the pressboard cap of candles he wears when he works into the night. I don't know how I became aware of his presence. How did he get in so quietly? Or was he not so very quiet, I was just so very loud? All I know is, he was in the doorway, the candles flickering in his pressboard crown.

Tiberio straightened from the table against which we leaned, holding me loosely as my skirts slid down. He kept his back to the Maestro, shielding me from exposure as he snatched at the laces to his codpiece.

"Maestro," he said, "it is not as it seems."

The Maestro paused, his crown of candles dripping. "Signorina Sofonisba's woman is downstairs looking for her."

The shuffle of dog-skin boots receded down the hallway.

Tiberio covered his eyes with the crook of his arm, then ran it over his head before reaching out and hooking me toward him. He kissed my forehead. "Don't worry."

A wave of nausea had washed over me. Coupled with the throbbing in my nether parts, I felt faint. I sagged against him. "I am so ashamed."

"Don't be."

"But the Maestro—"

"The Maestro has a few secrets of his own."

ITEM: *Do not be swayed by those who would hurry you in preparing to paint. Before he would lift a brush, Leonardo da Vinci planned a work from its frame to its final varnish. Not even the Pope had been able to hasten him, chiding, "This man will do nothing, for he is thinking of the end before the beginning of the work."*

ITEM: *Hungary water is made of distilled rosemary and thyme infused with spirits of lavender, mint, sage, marjoram, orange blossom, and lemon. It relieves lethargy, loss of memory, dizziness, derangement, and mood-induced headaches. Drink with wine, bathe temples, or inhale from a cup.*

ITEM: *It is the law that a man who deflowers a virgin must marry her or provide funds so she may marry another or take the veil. If the maiden did not resist her seducer, his blame is less and there is no penalty.*

28 MAY 1559
Palazzo Anguissola, Cremona

I have seen firsthand the price some are willing to pay to keep honor in the family.

When I was a girl of six, Elena and I had slipped away from

Francesca, who was distracted by our younger sisters, to pick gillyflowers from the bank inside the moat surrounding the city wall, though Francesca had strongly forbidden it. "People go little way down the bank," she would warn ominously, "and— *ohimè!*—they cannot climb back up. They fall in the water and drown, just like that."

But a sweet-smelling pink carpet of the flowers grew in the stony ground in the summer, and that day we were drawn to it like bees to nectar. We had inched our way down the slope and were plucking fat handfuls when a man bolted through the city gates, pumping his arms and legs as if his tail were on fire.

Elena and I laughed and imitated his comic appearance—until three more men came bellowing out of the gate. Now Elena and I dropped our flowers to run, but before we could scramble up the bank, the three caught up and knocked the first man to the ground. We clung to each other as they kicked him, boots thudding against bone, until he no longer begged for mercy or even moved.

The men—young men, I now realized, hardly older than boys—were standing over the body, panting from their work, when a man in hooded robes propelled a sobbing girl through the stone city gates. I knew the pair instantly. It was the apothecary from our neighborhood, a red-faced hothead given to shouting when you counted out the *scudi* too slowly, and his daughter, Camilla. I knew them by Camilla's hair—a wavy yellow curtain I often admired during Mass.

Camilla's sobs became hysterical as they neared the body. "Who killed him?" shouted the apothecary. The men looked away, except for one I now recognized as the apothecary's son, Giovanni, a big-mouth who threw stones at the cats on our street.

"You fool!" the apothecary shouted. "You took away this scum's chance to make it right! He was going to pay us. Because he raped you, didn't he, Camilla?" Camilla's yellow river of hair rippled as he shook her. "He stole your virginity after you resisted him, didn't you? Didn't you?"

"*Sì*," Giovanni muttered. "Just not hard enough."

"Shut up!" the apothecary barked. Breathing hard, he turned back to Camilla, his expression becoming tender. "Yesterday I had a sweet virgin as a daughter."

"Papà—"

"Today I'm a man with a whore on his hands."

"Papà, I'm sorry."

"And you—"

Giovanni hung his head, a hank of black hair flopping in his eyes.

"You. Big shot. Brother of a whore. Where's your chance for honor now? Gone. Poof! You killed it. We're the scum now."

"You said he deserved to die!" Giovanni shouted hoarsely.

Tightening his grip on Camilla's arm, the apothecary reached for the dagger in his belt.

"Papà?" Camilla cried.

I jerked Elena to her feet. We clawed our way up the bank, dirt slicing under our nails and skinning our hands and feet. Something pelted my back. When I glanced around in terror, I saw Camilla's beautiful hair, draped in the dust where she lay.

Giovanni threw another stone. "Cunts! Don't tell!"

I didn't. I still have not, not even to Papà, to this day.

Camilla is not the only reckless virgin in the Italian states who has been sacrificed for her family's good name. But my papà? He will not even fish in the Po, because he cannot bear to stick a worm with a hook. No, I fear the opposite—that if I am exposed, Papà will go about his business, quietly letting my wantonness destroy his honor.

I cannot let this happen. This is the man who took me to a neighboring town to enroll me in painting lessons when I was twelve because he could find no artist in Cremona who would teach me. I can still see him striding beside me, his dull black gown flapping in time to the cowbells clanking in distant pastures. Insects sprang from the fields around us as I hurried to keep up, the rich stink of pig manure filling my nose.

"My stomach hurts," I said. "Let's go home." I had seen the way the last painter looked at Papà when we were leaving his studio. The disrespect in the painter's eyes toward Papà had hurt me more than his disgust toward me. *You haven't read half of the books my papà has read!* I wanted to shout. *He prints books from all over the world.* But I said nothing. It is the place of girls and women to keep their mouths shut and their gazes down, though Papà had never told me that, nor had Mamma, with her mind always occupied by prayers. I had learned it from the disapproving looks of our neighbors in the piazza when I practiced Latin or discussed Dante's *Divine Comedy* with Papà as we took our evening stroll.

With a puff, Papà blew a delicate green grasshopper from the sleeve of his gown. "Twelve is the proper age for an apprentice, Sofi. We shall find the right teacher for you."

"I don't want to paint," I said. "I want to embroider, like everyone else," though the thought of pulling a needle through stiff cloth, day in, day out, only to produce a flat image of the Virgin Mary, made my head ache.

"You are painting," said Papà. "No argument. Lucky are they who know their gift. Some people live their whole lives without learning it."

"Everyone has a gift?"

"Everyone. Though not all claim theirs. It takes great courage sometimes."

I looked up at Papà. In light of this new thought, his familiar tall figure, stooped from years of peering at books, became almost strange to me. "What is your gift?"

Papà's lips had curved within the neat gray nest of his beard. "You."

Papà, sweet Papà. He is completely oblivious of what I have done in Rome. He would never dream his good Sofi could do what I did.

I had found him in the courtyard in the shade of the poplar trees, upon my return yesterday from Rome. *"Cara mia!"* He put down his English copy of Sir Thomas More's *Utopia* and held open his arms.

He pulled back to gaze at me after we embraced. "Your sisters and brother will be so glad to see you—they are with your mother at Mass. Why, Sofi! Look at your eyes. Are you unwell?"

"It was a long trip." I kissed his grizzled cheek and breathed in his dear peppery scent.

"Sofi, are you crying?"

"It is just dust from the road."

"I do not believe you."

My breath stopped. Had Michelangelo sent a damning letter before me?

"You are completely exhausted, I can tell. That is it! I must put my foot down, you must rest at home. This trip was too much for you—first going to Milan to paint the Spanish Duke of Alba, then traveling on to Rome to study with Michelangelo. You've been gone for months! Now it is time to stay home and enjoy your gift. What is the use of having one if you can't enjoy it?"

I laughed, giddy with relief. "Oh, Papà, that is exactly what I wish to do."

He promptly ordered me to rest. At my insistence, I took to an unused servants' room on the third floor, away from my family and attendants, where without Francesca's badgering, I slept the rest of the day and well into this morning. When I rose to make water, I found I was so weak that I had to return to bed, capable only of lifting this pen to paper. Now I lie looking through the open door and the crumbling arches of the gallery beyond, to the courtyard, where sparrows flit among the tops of the poplar trees; the smell of baking rosemary bread permeates the air.

I had left without saying good-bye to Tiberio—our carriage had departed from Rome at earliest light. Will he write to Papà, asking my hand in marriage? What we had done amounted to a betrothal under the law. Indeed, my family will be within their rights to press for damages from Tiberio's family should he not come forward with a marriage proposal, as poor Camilla's family had demanded from her lover. Tiberio has taken something of great value, a maiden's virginity—worse, he has taken it from a maiden whose virginity is so treasured that she signs her paintings "Virgin."

Sofonisba Anguissola, Virgo—what a foolish idea it had been to sign my work thus. I was seventeen and full of myself when I'd begun that practice. Although I claimed it was because I wished to renounce physical pleasure to dedicate myself fully to art, in truth it was out of pride, sheer pride, that I styled myself so. *Look,* my signature proclaimed, *see what I have done that no other mere maiden has done before me! I can paint like a man!*

It seems now that I rut as well as one, too.

ITEM: *The frame upon which a canvas is stretched should never be made of green wood. It will change shape as it ages, leaving the canvas creased and the painting damaged.*

EVENING, SAME DAY

No letter yet from Tiberio. I am still hiding out in my aerie on the third floor. It is hot up here and dusty. I have only the company of a striped cat, who is more interested in the mice scurrying in the walls than in me. I yearn deeply for my sisters, but I do not seek them out, for if my sisters may come, so may Francesca, and I cannot bear her questioning looks. On our three-week journey home, she was not able to extract from me what had happened in Rome, and I will not tell her. Her opinion of me would plummet, and I could not stand for her to be one of those servants who has deference on her face and mockery in her heart.

Early this afternoon, Papà had stepped into my room with a goblet, awaking me from the troubled sleep into which I had fallen after writing the previous entry. The sparrows outside in the sunny courtyard swooped amongst the poplar trees as I sat up to receive the cup; a donkey brayed in the distance.

"Have your sisters been up to see you?" he asked.

"No, though I can hear them downstairs. Why do they not come to see me?"

"Remarkable—for once they obey me. I told them not to bother you yet. Drink this."

I took a sip from the cup. The taste of rosemary and orange spirits lingered on my tongue. Hungary water, an expensive medicine. "Papà, we can't afford this."

"Certainly we can. Besides, the apothecary extended me credit again. Why that mean-tempered man should be so generous to me all these years, I do not know, but I shall not look a gift mule in the mouth. Drink up, *cara mia*. It is good for you."

I lowered the cup. "How is Elena?"

"We don't hear much from your sister, I'm sorry to say. But a convent is not a place that encourages a lively correspondence."

I watched two sparrows squabble on a bough. I remembered when Elena, at fifteen, announced that she had chosen to take the veil. Papà had reacted with pride tempered with much puzzlement. At Elena's insistence, he had sent her with me to painting lessons soon after I had begun them, and she had shown great promise. She was excellent at drawing. Did she truly wish to put aside her talent to be a nun? Elena assured Papà she would be able to use her skills in illuminating manuscripts or embroidering vestments for the clergy, which seemed to comfort him very little. Mamma, on the other hand, was relieved by Elena's decision— she could turn her worry about Elena over to the nuns. There would be one fewer person on her endless list of prayers.

When I had questioned Elena in the weeks preceding her departure, she had responded with uncharacteristic piety about wishing to be a bride of Christ. Only on the eve before Papà was to take her in a rented carriage to the Convent of the Holy Virgins in Mantua had she come out with the truth.

We had lain in our bed in the dark, surrounded by the soft breathing of our four sleeping younger sisters: Lucia, age eleven, Minerva, eight, Europa, six, and four-year-old Anna Maria, curled up with the snoring Francesca. From our open window came the incessant sawing of crickets. "Very well," Elena said, "I shall tell, but you must not breathe a word."

"Not one," I whispered.

I heard her swallow before she began. "You know we have no money for dowries. What little Papà makes printing and selling books is given by Mamma to the Church."

I could not argue this. Though Papà tried to hide his worries, I had seen the grocer come into Papà's shop and leave with precious illuminated manuscripts in exchange for unpaid bills. The baker now owned Papà's press. Our clothes were hand-me-downs from our rich cousins in Milan. Truth is, Papà reads more books than he sells.

"Have you stopped to think what kind of man I shall attract with no money to recommend me? Some sniffling pale clerk in the magistrate's office? A butcher with pigs' entrails under his nails?"

"Elena—"

"I have not your talent, Sofi. I shall never rise above my sex and be the wonder that you are. I know what I am—a poor nobleman's second daughter. It is my fate to be claimed by some dreary Cremonese cheesemaker and made to bear his babies yearly until at last I give him his all-important son, after which time my dear husband will move on to lying with a mistress, while you, Sofi, pursue your search for Beauty and Truth in art. My only chance to search for Beauty will be in choosing a gown for Mass, and for Truth, in picking apart my spouse's lies about his mistress. Taking the veil shall be a relief in comparison."

"Papà will not let this happen."

"Which? Taking the veil or the husband?"

An owl hooted outside. Why *had* Papà not stopped her? Papà, the one who had found me a painting instructor, against all odds. My quiet tower of strength.

"Do you think he has a choice?" she whispered, parsing my thoughts. "What about our sisters? Should he settle all our money on my dowry so I might get a decent husband and leave the rest bereft? I would not have it."

"I cannot bear to lose you."

"Sofi, don't you know that you will lose me no matter what? All of us women—we are just seeds to be scattered to the winds." She had smoothed the sheets up to her neck. "At least I am choosing which wind."

"Sofi?" Papà patted my hand, startling me from my memory, and once again I was in my makeshift sick chamber. "Sofi?"

His gentle face was wrinkled with worry as he held out the goblet. "You must drink up. You are definitely not yourself."

He put the cup to my lips. I swallowed down a tingling mouthful. "Did anyone request a portrait while I was gone? Any new commissions?" If Tiberio were to come calling for me, I had to be ready with a dowry. I would not bankrupt my sisters.

"Not yet."

"Did the Duke of Alba send money for his portrait?"

Papà shook his head. "I hear he has returned to Spain."

"Why is it that the richest always pay last?" I said, wiping my mouth with my hand.

"I believe, *cara mia*, it is harder for them to let go of their ducats. We part the slowest from that which we love most."

A pain knotted in my chest. Tiberio had let me leave with Francesca after the Maestro discovered us in the small studio. He had sent no word to our place of lodging before I left for Cremona the next morning. I had tried to linger, hoping for a letter, but Francesca forced me to the carriage, asking me what I was waiting for. I had no ready answer. Neither a message nor Tiberio came. Our carriage rumbled off to the crowing of roosters. No, Tiberio had not parted with me so very reluctantly.

"Sofi, you look absolutely green." Papà kissed my hand. "Rest. But tomorrow, you must get back to your painting. That is your medicine."

It is true, painting had been my elixir. The surprising success I'd had with it had been the headiest of brews. In my early twenties I had found, to my amazement, that important persons were interested in the little portraits I had done of my sisters and myself. A family friend had sent one of these portraits—of me, reading a book—to the Duchess of Mantua, who subsequently asked me to her court to paint portraits of her children. Soon after, I received an invitation to the court at Parma. Who cared that my subjects were wan-faced little heirs and their dogs, and I was but a novelty employed to entertain the court along with the dwarfs and buffoons—Sofonisba Virgo was in demand! But the excitement of these achievements paled after Michelangelo himself had asked for me that first time, about four years ago.

The great Michelangelo Buonarroti, painter to popes and kings—Papà, that unshakable believer in my abilities, had the nerve to send *him* a sketch I'd done of Lucia laughing as she taught Francesca to read, and shockingly, Il Divino wrote back. The Maestro said that my drawing was pleasant enough, but that even a journeyman sign-painter could capture a laughing girl. How was I at showing a child cry?

I, the daughter of a Cremonese bookseller, had been challenged by the greatest artist on earth. I would not disappoint. Day after day, I watched the children on my street, searching for a unique subject. I became an expert on the different modes of in-

fant distress. I watched children fall as they toddled after their
nurses in the piazza, observed them throwing tantrums when an
older sibling wrested a ball from their hands, and weeping from
weariness as their nurses shopped at market. It was at the fish
market that I finally found my answer, when shopping for the
evening meal with Francesca. Europa had tagged along, balancing Asdrubale, then three years of age, upon her hip. Francesca
was arguing with the fishmonger over the price of a trout when I
heard Europa's guilty chuckle. I turned just as Asdrubale reached
into a basket of crabs.

Never have I been as proud as when the Maestro sent for me
after seeing the drawing of Asdrubale's tearful encounter with the
crab. Who was this virgin painter, he wrote, who captured so
much truth in a simple sketch? He invited me to come study with
him—something, I found out later from Tiberio, the Maestro
does rarely for anyone, let alone for a woman. Once I was there,
the Maestro seemed not to care if I were fish or fowl or female,
as long as I asked intelligent questions. It was then I began to
dream that I could become more than a virgin portrait painter—
I could become a *maestra*, if only I pursued my art hard enough.

Now look at me. Once mildly famous as a virgin, I am about
to be mildly famous as a whore if Tiberio does not come forward
and maestro Michelangelo brings our act to light. Papà will be
forced to press for a proposal. I cannot bear it. I would never wish
to make Tiberio marry me. I want him to want me of his own
accord. But I dream. Why would he wish to marry me? I have
overstepped my place by pursuing a man's art, I am not of high
birth, and I have not the beauty to make these things unimportant.

I have read the treatise on art by the learned monk Fra Agnolo
Firenzuola, in which he states in a nutshell what is desirable in a
woman's looks: hair soft yellow turning brown; skin fair and clear

but not pale; eyes dark brown and large, with whites a shimmering blue. No one need remind me how short I fall of that ideal. My hair is soft brown turning red; my skin pale and given to pink splotches; my eyes bright green and large, too large, unnaturally large, with an excess of whites that are shot with red, more often than not, from too much reading or paint fumes. My sisters call me the Owl, not unfairly. If forced to propose, why would Tiberio not simply laugh and point out what an eager participant I had been?

Please let Tiberio send for me. By all the saints and martyrs, I beg for him not to forget me, as undeserving as I might be.

ITEM: *The selection of the fabric of a canvas is of utmost importance. Roman linen makes for the best canvas, as it is strong, stretches well on the frame, and remains flat if a thread is broken. Cotton is the poorest choice. If a single thread is snapped, the ends will curl and split, destroying an entire picture.*

2 JUNE 1559
Palazzo Anguissola, Cremona

So that is it, then. I am to leave this place. I should be glad. But I will miss Cremona. I will miss the bells clanging so solemnly out of pitch from the tower of San Giorgio across the piazza. I will miss the carts, loaded with wheat, creaking down the cobblestone streets, hens bobbing after them in a comical parade. I will miss the servants gathered around the well in our piazza, chatting as the bucket lowers once more from its squeaking pulley. I will miss, unspeakably, my family.

Oh! See what my nerves make me do. Wretched wine—it is on my bodice, too. I thought I heard Francesca coming. She will be up here, soon enough. The moment she finishes eating the cakes Papà bought in celebration, she will come trundling through the door, asking what is wrong with me. I told Papà I had a pain again in my eyes, and he let me leave before he had finished toasting my good fortune; but it is not my eyes that hurt, and Francesca knows it.

The second day after I had returned from Rome, I awakened to my sisters surrounding my bed, informing me that they had been good long enough—now they must hear stories of my travels. After many kisses, embraces, and my own quickly hidden tears, I told them, over the cup of watered wine and piece of bread they had brought me, the news for which they hungered. I told them how even though our cousins in Milan were so rich that servants ran in front of their carriage to clear their way on streets, and that the walls of their *palazzo* were lined with gilded Moroccan leather, their place still stank of piss. I told them how in Rome women teetered around on twelve-inch-high chopines, claiming the need to keep above the mud and refuse littering the cobblestones but in truth wishing to show off the jewels encrusted on their heels. I even told them, unwisely, how I had seen a Roman woman consume at *cena* one of the world's most powerful aphrodisiacs, that strange fruit from the New World—a tomato.

"What happened after she ate it?" Europa exclaimed.

"What's an aphrodisiac?" asked Anna Maria.

"A love potion," Minerva said quickly. "Sofi, did no one warn the woman of the effects of the fruit? How did she behave?"

"She seemed unchanged." I rose. "Isn't it time we dressed for Mass?"

Lucia took my cup. "How can you tell if she was truly unchanged? People do hide their thoughts. She could be seething with desire, but unless you could see into her heart, you would have no idea."

I stared at her a moment, trying to discern if she was trying to tell me something, then dressed and fled to Mass and, afterward, my studio. There I found myself straining to listen for a messenger at the door or, please God, Tiberio's voice in the courtyard. When Papà came and saw me staring out the window, he asked if I might paint him, along with my younger sister Europa and my brother, Asdrubale, both of whom he hoped would be inspired by my talent.

It was difficult to concentrate on drawing studies for their portrait. For two days I sketched and resketched, my efforts frustratingly sophomoric and stiff. To give my composition more life, I thought of Michelangelo's trick of putting the greatest contrast between light and dark on the place where I wished the viewer's gaze to go first, though this was but a simple portrait, not a great work of art. I wanted Papà's face to be the focal point, but looking him in the eye to draw him was excruciating, especially in light of the new and terrible thought that had dawned upon me: Were my courses overdue? This afternoon, by the time I commenced upon the preliminary work on a primed canvas, I was half out of my mind.

"I cannot understand it, Sofi," Papà said. It was well after the midday meal; Papà was sitting placidly between Europa and Asdrubale in the shade of the arcade outside my little studio. Behind him, Papà's old servant from when he was a boy, Bartolomeo, waved a fan as I painted in the gray-green tones of the underpainting while calculating and recalculating the dates of my courses. "If Michelangelo was so unwell, why did he not say so? If I had known he was failing, I would have never wanted to impose on him by letting you go there."

I had just told Papà why he must not bother Michelangelo now by sending him a study I had done of Asdrubale for this new portrait. Although I was displeased with it, Papà was quite charmed by the little drawing and wished to give it to the Maestro immediately, since the Maestro had thought so highly of my earlier drawing of Asdrubale getting bitten by a crab. I could think of nothing worse than reminding the Maestro of me at this time. I silently thanked the maulstick on which I leaned for keeping my hand still. I usually do not need one, certainly not in the under-painting stage, which is meant only to establish the depth of the shading and to provide a base for the actual colors. Did Papà notice my dependence on the maulstick since my return?

"No one knows when he is to be ill, Papà. The Maestro was well when I first arrived. Things—he—took a turn for the worse."

Glad for a distraction, I shook my head at Asdrubale, who was wiggling even more than was his custom by Papà's side. Europa's lips were curled, ready as usual to laugh at her little brother's weaknesses.

"Well, I am very sorry to have burdened him," said Papà, "though I trust, *cara mia*, you behaved with your usual consideration. If you think I should not send him your work just now, I won't. But I must send him my thanks, after the great kindness he has shown to our family, inviting you to visit him not just once, but twice."

Sick with guilt, I dabbed my brush into the paint on my palette. I noticed my little brother bucking like a cat in a bag. "Asdrubale, are you well?"

"I have to make water!" he wailed. He danced in place, his little white dog nipping at his ankles in excitement.

"*Buffone!*" Europa exclaimed. "Sofi, paint him just as he is! Make people looking at this picture a hundred years from now think he has the most terrible case of fleas."

"I do have fleas!" he moaned.

Europa whooped with laughter as Papà waved a benevolent hand. "Hurry up and go, Asdrubale."

"Would you like me to keep working, Papà?" I asked pleasantly. *Sweetest Holy Mary, false monster that I am, please let me go hide my head under a pillow.*

"Of course. Bartolomeo, could you please keep fanning? Sofi looks warm."

"Must I stay?" said Europa.

"Yes," said Papà. "You'll run straight back to the cook's boy if I let you go."

"No, I won't."

"Correct," said Papà. "You will not. You are fourteen, old enough to study Latin or draw or apply yourself to some other useful exercise. Surely you do not want to waste your mind."

Europa cast down her gaze, but not before flashing him a look that announced that she would go her own way.

I drew in a deep breath. "Europa, please get back behind Papà as you were. That's right—keep your arm in alignment with his. We're trying to create a pattern of movement." I sniffed my sprig of rosemary. Let it bring me the concentration needed to keep my countenance free from incriminating looks of terror.

"I'm tired of standing so twisted," said Europa. "Do I have to?"

"Would you prefer to line up like blackbirds on a clothesline?" My light tone belied the heavy knot coiling in my belly.

She waved the posy of jasmine she was holding with the utmost boredom. "Yes."

I inhaled deeply of the rosemary. Outside, the bells of San Giorgio began their off-key clanging, marking the hour. "You remember what I told you about how the great artists give their paintings drama by having their subjects sit with their faces turned in one direction and their bodies in another, yes? And this device is called—"

She drew out each syllable with all the tragic weariness of a thwarted fourteen-year-old. "Contrapposto."

"And that word means—?"

She heaved her martyr's sigh, then assumed her position of looking over Papà's shoulder while facing away from him. "'Set against.' Truly, Sofi, I don't know why you make me stay. You've already done a study of me and you're not even doing the real painting now, just the ugly gray shadows."

Her eye caught on something behind me. Before I could move, she darted inside my studio and snatched up the oval miniature portrait drying on the table.

"What's this?" She squinted at it, then yelped as I lunged at her.

"Put it down!"

She held it behind her, out of my reach. "What do these letters mean?"

Heat poured into my face. No one was meant to see this. In a moment of foolishness, I had added the emblem Tiberio and I had devised to my own self-portrait. A grown woman of seven-and-twenty, acting like a lovesick girl.

At that moment, Francesca stumped down the arcade, a letter tied with a cream-colored ribbon raised from her man-sized hand. "Signore Amilcare! A man come, he bring you this." She gave Papà the letter, exposing the black ring of sweat under her arm, then stepped back and eagerly wiped her hands on her apron, even as old Ottavio the doorman stormed out, his sword teetering on his hip in its rusty scabbard.

"She stole it from my hands, *signore*!" Ottavio cried. "Messages, they are to be delivered by me!"

"Whose seal is this?" Papà turned the thick folded paper in his hands. "Look how large—it must be someone important."

I sagged onto the stool behind me.

Mamma sailed out onto the arcade, gripping the striped skirt of her overgown. "*Signore!* Count Broccardo was here with a band of attendants, delivering this letter. Something terrible must have happened! Have you broken the law?"

Papà distractedly lifted up Mamma, who had sunk to her knees to pray. He wagged his finger at the letter. "I know this seal. It is the King of Spain's."

"The King of Spain wrote to you?" Mamma's voice was rich with wonder.

I struggled for breath. The King of Spain? Yes, he rules this state in Italy, as he does much of Europe and the New World, but he was seldom heard from in Cremona. As rich and important as Tiberio's family is, could they have involved the King in a marriage proposal?

My other sisters ran out to us, Minerva's hands bound before her in red embroidery silks, little Anna Maria connected to her by the ball of silk that she had been winding around Minerva's hands, and Lucia holding the shears.

Minerva's fresh complexion was splotched with excitement. "Papà, have you business with the King?"

"Where's Asdrubale?" Papà said. "I want everyone to witness this. Asdrubale! Sofonisba—hand me one of your paint knives."

My brother hopped outside, his codpiece askew. "Yes, Papà?"

Papà ran my paint knife under the disc of crimson wax. The weighty paper crackled as he unfolded the letter. "Pay attention, everyone. You are about to witness a moment of great import. Not every day does a family hear from their King."

ITEM: *Of the three wives of King Felipe of Spain, his first, his cousin Princess Maria of Portugal, died at the age of seventeen from bearing him a son. His second, Queen Mary of England, died from heartbreak or a tumor in her womb, depending on who tells the tale. His third is young Elisabeth of Valois. King Felipe had asked Elizabeth of England to marry him when her half sister Queen Mary died. She refused.*

ITEM: *Remember when in Spain to address members of the Royal Family and grandees with Don or Doña before their given names. Distinguished persons of lesser rank may also be referred to as don or doña, but in the written form, the term is not capitalized.*

ITEM: *It is true, one may paint upon an unprepared canvas, but for permanent work it is a loss of effort and a waste of time.*

31 JANUARY 1560
Mendoza Palace, Guadalajara

These terrible spots of ink. It is a bad quill, but if I wait for the wine to clear from my head to cut another nib, I shall never get this record started, and I want to write of my travels to Spain. I can hear Francesca over in the bed, muttering in her peasant's

Italian. She wishes I would come to sleep so that she can rest, but this chamber is so cold, how does one slumber? They have no fireplaces in this country, only braziers burning olive pits in the center of the room. I can see my breath.

I have made no entries in my notebook since I left home. Fifteen rainy days in a coach to Genoa, nine days below deck on a caravel whose very timbers, along with one's guts, were nearly torn apart by the winter seas, eight days in Barcelona recovering from a fever in a lice-infested inn, twelve days on a teeth-rattling coach ride to Zaragoza, and sixteen days spent picking through snowy mountain passes and across high plains on a disgruntled mule are not conducive to putting pen to paper, especially in the watchful company of one's two rich cousins from Milan and their silent young wives. And no sooner had said cousins delivered Francesca and me in Madrid, their duty duly discharged and their hopes of meeting the King dashed, than I was in a conveyance again. There was no time to write, but plenty of it to chastise myself for believing as I had readied for Spain that Tiberio's betrothal letter would arrive to save me. I had never truly thought it would come to this. Fool. Now I am the King's ward and, as such, His Majesty's property to utilize as he pleases. At least my sisters may have my dowry portion.

Meanwhile, as I was making my way across treacherous terrain, the new Queen of Spain was threading through frozen mountainous passages of her own. Her journey had begun in Paris, where she had been wed by proxy to the King. They were to meet for the first time in Guadalajara, where I was required to attend their union, the beginning of my duties in my new role as one of Her Majesty's ladies.

For this reason I suffered to trundle these last two days over stony Castilian roads from Madrid, in a coach jammed with eight chattering perfumed Spanish ladies clutching their shawls and their small-bladdered dogs, with Francesca cutting her eyes accusingly at the pups each time we hit a bump. After a night four-to-a-bed with these ladies and their female companions at an inn along the way, I can assure you that the lapdog's ability to draw fleas away from its owner is highly overesteemed.

At last this morning my travels came to an end. I stood in a host of ladies lined up farthingale to farthingale in the plaza before the palace of the Duke of Mendoza, all of us straining to glimpse the new Queen. Under the four hundred blooming orange trees the duke had caused to be brought to Guadalajara from Valencia, deer and rabbits, prettily tethered to the trees for the Queen's amusement, tugged at their satin collars while trumpets played, children sang, and women laughed with joy in spite of the cold wind tearing at their veils. For even if the new Queen turned out to be ugly and dull, the people rejoiced to have her, thanks to the deal made between their King and her father, the King of France. Her marriage sealed the treaty between mortal enemies, and now war with France was lifted, and with it, crushing taxes. Isabel de la Paz—Elisabeth of the Peace—the Spanish call her.

Now this fourteen-year-old girl—a child Europa's age—eighteen years younger than her powerful new husband, rode into the plaza on a white palfrey draped in cloth of silver that was trimmed with tinkling silver bells. She looked this way and that, her dark eyes bright with excitement, the ends of her undressed brown hair slapping against her saddle. Like Europa, she seemed ready to laugh, perhaps too ready to do so, with her lips curled on the verge of a chuckle. So this was the child for whom I put aside any hope of becoming a *maestra* because the King, upon hearing about me from the Duke of Alba, thought his little bride might enjoy painting lessons.

My Lady's steed jingled to a stop before the King's dais. The silvery bells still pinging in the freezing wind, the Duke of Mendoza stepped forward and plucked the Queen from her horse, then, as unceremoniously as if she were a bag of gold, handed her to her husband. She pulled back her chin in a bashful smile.

"What are you looking at?" the King snapped. "The gray hairs in my beard?"

The musicians stopped playing. The King's men looked up from bended knees, the plumes in their hats fluttering above their frozen expressions. All of us ladies who were close at hand held our breath—at least I did, there beneath one of the flowering orange trees. It became so quiet that all you could hear was the wine splashing in the fountain in the middle of the plaza, a child crying, and the deer and rabbits, trying to shake off their satin collars.

For while the King at two-and-thirty is fair-haired and almost delicate, with exquisitely shaped brows, a small straight nose, and pink-rimmed ears, there is something vaguely terrifying about him. Perhaps it is the way he stands so rigidly upright. His thin figure nearly vibrates like a plucked guitar string from the effort. Or perhaps it is the manner in which he responds to those bold enough to address him. He pins the speaker with a coolly polite stare, not releasing the hapless creature until he or she trails off in a muddle of doubt and dismay. It could be simply the disquieting contrast his lush red lips and generous jaw present next to the rest of his refined features. He has the sensuous mouth of a voluptuary, a passionate seducer of women, not a cold and silent king. Perhaps I make too much of these things, influenced by the knowledge that insanity runs through the Spanish Royal Family like rot through a luscious apple. Madness is as much a part of the King's Hapsburg blood as his jaw and blond, now graying, hair.

But none of this seemed to bother the Queen, for an elfin grin spread over her face. She fell to her knees, dashing the pearls sewn onto her heavy brocade skirts against the paving stones. So much did I think of Europa when the little Queen snatched up the King's hand and pressed it to her lips that I almost expected her to say, "Papà, forgive me."

But this was not my little Europa. And this was not Papà in his house slippers relaxing at home after a day of printing Bibles. This was the most powerful man in the world, a serious, dangerous man, with neither the time nor the inclination for a jest.

The King pulled away his hand. "Please rise. You shall ruin your clothes."

As in a beloved lapdog that has just been kicked, surprise then confusion flashed across her young face.

The bells of the church across the plaza began to peal. The Queen stumbled to her feet, tripping on the pearl-sewn folds of her gown. The duke shot out a gloved hand to steady her.

I cannot guess how this child Queen fares in the bridal chamber tonight.

But I was writing of this day. After the meeting of the King and Queen in the morning, we all processed to Mass said by Cardinal Mendoza, the brother of the duke, and then back into the palace for introductions, then through the Moorish arches of the arcade to the dining hall on the other side of the courtyard, where whole farmyards of creatures, roasted, minced, or candied, lay upon the table, the smell of their cooked flesh mingling with the perfume of the grandees and their ladies. When the banquet was over, all I wished to do was to crawl off to a bench with my corset strings loosened. But there were speeches to hear and a play to attend (for which the scenery was cunningly painted—I must find out who did it), and always wine and more wine to drink, though the Spanish ladies hardly took a drop of it, as busy as they were with staring at the Queen's French ladies, who were daintily imbibing great vats of the wine while flirting with the gentlemen. After eyeing my unfashionable Italian dress (does no one wear striped skirts here?), neither Spanish nor French wished to interact with me. I was left alone with my frequently refilled cup and Francesca's glare boring into my back from where she stood in the servants' gallery.

Then, just when I was ready to float away on a sea of the grape, there was dancing, of the usual hopping Spanish sort, and very much of it, too, so when the King called for a galliard—a galliard, of all dances, with all its leaps!—no one had the wind to set forth.

"My Lady?" The King kissed the Queen's small hand, his eyes chillingly calm. "Do you wish to dance?"

The room fell silent.

The Queen laughed and shook her head, making the light brown wisps that peeked from under her pearl-encrusted cap stick to her cheeks with sweat. The child had been made to hop about with a stone-weight of jewels sewn upon her gown. No wonder she was hot. Her clothes alone must have weighed more than her young self, even without the pearl the size of a pigeon's egg hanging from the diamond-and-ruby brooch upon her chest. Each time she stepped it thumped her like a fist.

The King's nephew, a boy of the Queen's same age, came over to where I stood on the dance floor, noisily catching my breath.

The scarlet satin of his slashed sleeves flowed as he swept into a bow, trailing his scent of perfume and youthful sweat.

"My lady Sofonisba Anguissola." His youth's changeable voice was loud enough for all to hear. "Do you know the galliard?"

I started. Why would the King's nephew know me? I was no one, a simple painting teacher, the daughter of a threadbare count who read more books than he sold.

I lowered my eyes to lessen their similarity to an owl's great orbs. "Indeed, sir. We dance the galliard in my native town of Cremona."

There were polite murmurs of approval from the assembly.

"I know where you are from," he said as boldly as his youth's raw squawk would allow. Even at his awkward age, a boy on the cusp of manhood, he was an attractive youth, with dark ringlets and a slightly turned-up nose dusted with freckles. "Will you do me the honor of joining me?"

I glanced at the King, whose face was composed and inscrutable, then at the Queen. She smiled at me in encouragement.

"The honor is mine," I said, though my guts did turn most sharply. How would I hold up while dancing before the most formal court in the world? Knowing how to paint the hairs on a child's head is one matter, moving with grace is another.

All eyes upon us, we took to the floor, and encouraged by the sprightly sounds of the shawms, sackbut, and tambour, I began picking out the intricate hops and leaps of the galliard. I thank Papà for all of the lessons he urged upon me and my sisters under dear signore Vari, our bad-breathed dancing master. Signore Vari's instruction and breath came strongly to mind as I sailed through the air in my first great leap of the *posture*, though the memory ceased the moment I hit ground, for my partner clasped my hands and spoke.

"I am Alessandro Farnese. My mother is the King's sister, but I was born in the Italian states. I would be there still if my father had not—" He glanced at the King, then was silent. The sound of soft leather scraping the tile floor and the swish of heavy cloth accompanied our steps.

Perhaps his interest in me was due to his affection toward his native country. "Do you speak Italian, sir?"

"Like a Roman lady of the night," he answered in Italian. "I speak French and Spanish, too."

Impudent. But perhaps recent events had made me too sensitive. "In which do you dream?" I said lightly.

My partner's face was so close to mine that I could see the nutmeg-colored down of early manhood upon his upper lip. "That is easy—Italian for my dreams of home, Spanish for my nightmares, and French for the dreams that dampen my sheets."

We hopped apart, heat creeping into my face. I could ignore one bawdy reference, but two? Surely he would not have spoken so boldly to a woman of pure repute. Had word traveled across the sea? Had Tiberio betrayed me, laughing of his conquest of the Great Virgin? Had maestro Michelangelo spoken of the cat in heat he had harbored in his home? Surely I was letting my guilt get the best of me. The conduct of a lowly painting teacher would be of no import to the nephew of the King.

We commenced into the next pattern, I performing the steps and hops with difficulty, Don Alessandro grinning as if he owned the heavens. Between the wish to look my best for the occasion and my ongoing celebration of the resumption of my courses in July, I'd had Francesca tie my corset extra tight. Now gripped by anxiety and the iron stays digging into my ribs, I could scarcely draw wind.

"I hear you are an accomplished painter," he said, hopping close. "Is it true you have studied with Michelangelo Buonarroti?"

I flashed him a sidelong glance. "Yes. You have heard of him?"

"Who hasn't? He is the greatest painter of all times, is he not? My great-grandfather had him do all sorts of pictures for him."

I smiled briefly, struggling for breath. Who was this ancestor? Although I had studied a book on the King's family tree in preparation for my service, I had missed this branch.

"It was Great-grandfather who commissioned Michelangelo to paint *The Last Judgment* in the Sistine Chapel. Have you seen it?"

"Yes."

"So are the rumors true?"

We skipped our separate ways to the music, then back together, my heart rapping against my chest. "I don't know what you mean."

His dark curls bounced with his footwork. "That he loves boys."

My relief was charged with anger. "That is absurd," I said stiffly. "Maestro Michelangelo loves to work. That is the only sort of love I observed from him."

"That is not what I hear."

I was startled by a couple joining us to our left, which is not customary in the middle of a pattern. When I saw it was the Queen, I started to curtsey. I had been introduced to her that afternoon, but had certainly not been included in her exalted circle.

"Oh, please, keep dancing!" the Queen cried. "Please—we will all of us miss our steps."

I kept going, though flustered by whether or not I should have broken protocol by not stopping to acknowledge her. When I looked to Don Alessandro, he shrugged with a rustle of puffed sleeves.

I could hear the Queen's Great Pearl thudding against her flat chest as she hopped to the music. Her partner turned his face to me. "*Señorita*, be careful not to let that gentleman with you tread upon your toes."

In my panic, I had not yet taken full measure of the Queen's partner. When at last I did, I fear my double look was as broad as a mummer's in a morality play. The young man, a youth near the same age as my partner, had eyes the clear, deep blue of my rich cousin's favorite sapphire ring, their brightness set off by the fresh country pink of his cheeks. His wheaten hair, certain strands of which glinted golden in the candlelight, caught on the lace of his high collar. Though he moved with a sinuous strength and grace, he kept his chin tilted down and his eyes were friendly and alert. His was not the guarded look of an experienced courtier.

"*Perdón, señorita Sofonisba,*" said Don Alessandro, panting. "My new uncle is very rude. He should be the one watching his feet. How long have you known a galliard, Uncle?"

"I am just this minute learning it," said the young man. To the Queen he said, "How would you say I do, Your Majesty?"

The Queen, her cheeks rosy with exertion and her dark eyes snapping with excitement, lifted her pointed little chin. "Like you have been dancing it all your life."

Don Alessandro made a scoffing sound. "How else is she to answer your question, Don Juan? Her Majesty is much too kind to say that you have the feet of an ox and the gait of a pig."

Don Juan smiled apologetically, then raised the Queen's hand to the music. As he whirled her away, I saw her lips curl into a laugh.

The King saw, too, from his throne at the edge of the dance floor.

The music played faster, hurrying my feet and making me laugh as I abandoned all thoughts of impropriety and Rome and Michelangelo. My heartbeat pounding in my ears, I leapt toward Don Alessandro in the final *posture*, but before I could land, he grabbed me by the waist and lifted me in the air.

Shocked, I did as my brain commanded: I raised my arms as if flying. The crowd broke out in a roar as Don Alessandro turned me above his head, and for six long beats, six long beats, I soared like a bird. And there on high, the crowd's applause and my own ragged breath ringing in my ears, I looked down upon Don Juan. I saw his look into the Queen's eyes and her returned questioning gaze.

And then I was back to the earth again.

Too soon, the dance was over. When the music stopped, everyone turned and bowed to the Queen and Don Juan, then to young Don Alessandro and me in approbation.

"Well done," said Don Alessandro. He kissed my hand. "If you paint as well as you dance, you must be Michelangelo's match."

"You flatter me," I murmured.

Soon afterward all we ladies and lords of the court escorted the King and Queen to the bridal chamber, and after both were bedded in their shifts of finest linen, the Queen laughing, the King alternating between scowls at his men and sidelong frowns at his bride, we withdrew to find our lodgings.

Still glowing from the congratulations of many on my galliard, I retired with Francesca to our lodgings in the palace, to a room I was made to share with an older lady from Sevilla, doña Elvira de Herrera y da Silva. After receiving this lady's kind words of praise, I asked her a question that had been on my mind.

"*Señora*, who was the Queen's partner in the galliard? Don Alessandro called him his 'new uncle.'"

"Don Juan de Austria?" said doña Elvira. "'Newly discovered' is more the term." She shrugged off her gold-stitched black bodice with the help of her maid, a young woman with the dark complexion of a Portuguese.

Francesca unlaced the back of my own bodice, the upturned knob of her chin raised in a frown. "I do not understand," I said.

"Don Juan did not know he was the King's brother until only recently," said doña Elvira. "He was brought up as a common country boy."

"How could that be? Ah, thank you, Francesca, that feels better."

Francesca folded my discarded garment. "If the *signorina* did not throw herself around so much . . ." she muttered.

"His father was the Emperor, like Our King," doña Elvira said, "but his mother— Maria, please, can you not undo these laces any more quickly?" She raised her arms as her maid finished her unlacing and lifted off her corset. "He is a comely boy. I would not look for him to be at court too long. The King is used to being the only cock in the roost. He cannot take too kindly to this golden youth showing up in his middle age, in spite of their common blood—indeed, perhaps because of it."

"But who is Don Juan's mother?" I asked.

Massaging her ribs, which, if like my own, bore the aching impressions of her recently removed corset upon them, doña Elvira dropped onto the narrow bed in her shift and, without answering my question, almost immediately began to snore. Such is the effect on the body of much feasting and dancing.

So now, with Francesca stirring in the bed and my robe upon my shoulders and the frail light of the moon seeping in through the thick round panes of the window, I try to record my thoughts, though my head swims in the dimness. It is no use. I can write no more. It is not the dark nor the grape nor this wretched quill that stills me, but the cold. I cannot feel my toes! Where are all the fireplaces in this country?

To the Very Magnificent Signorina Sofonisba,
In the Court of the Spanish King

*Congratulations on your appointment to serve Her Sacred
Majesty Elisabeth, Queen of Spain, as Painter to the Queen.
How pleased I was for you when maestro Michelangelo, upon
receiving your father's letter, told me you were afforded this
honor. You must be very proud, painting the portraits of such
important personages. My work on the Maestro's broken statue
must seem like child's play in comparison. Still, I am
satisfied. I have reattached the two arms. After I polished the
seams, you cannot tell where they had been struck off. It is
odd—I have not found the vein of emery which had so
enraged the Maestro. The flaw he struck must have been very
small, but he is such a perfectionist even the smallest
imperfection will cause him to abandon a work. I certainly
cannot ask him about it. He falls into a hostile silence if I
merely mention the piece. But I will keep working on it. In my
small way, I am honored to be a part of what I think will be
his most important work when it is finished.*

*Again, my congratulations. I am humbled to say that I
know you.*

From Rome,
21st January, 1560

Your servant,
Tiberio Calcagni

ITEM: *The King's grandmother is said to have gone mad from loving her husband, Philippe the Handsome, too much. Queen Juana attacked her husband's mistress with scissors, chopping off the woman's long hair. The Queen shrieked from the battlements of the castle at La Mota when not allowed to follow her husband to Flanders. She dismissed all her ladies, to prevent her husband from dallying with them. When he died, she wandered with the wagon carrying his coffin over mountains and plains, peeking in each night to see if he was still there.*

ITEM: *To size a canvas, one must scrape on a thin solution of rabbit-skin glue and powdered white chalk. The glue must not taste sour or salty when moistened; putrefied glue has little adhesive power.*

ITEM: *"A woman needs be graceful, mannerly, clever, prudent, and beautiful to excel at court."*

—COUNT BALDASSARE CASTIGLIONE,
The Book of the Courtier

13 FEBRUARY 1560
El Alcázar, Toledo

There was a play at the bishop's palace last night at which I cried overmuch when the shepherdess died, though I could tell the shepherdess was truly a shepherd and her swain was so drunk that he thrice forgot his lines. When I left the performance with the Queen and her other ladies, I wept again when I saw a *caballero* steal away from the window grate at which he'd been wooing a lady. This morning, on the way to the Cathedral with Her Majesty, the mere sight of a husband bowing before his wife as she stepped from her carriage made my eyes fill to overflowing. It seems I will weep at anything.

I can see the worry on Francesca's face. Perhaps she thinks I will go mad like the King's grandmother Juana the Mad. Perhaps I shall. For since receiving Tiberio's letter yesterday, I am unbalanced.

Did Papà tell maestro Michelangelo my position here was greater than it is? If so, his boasting has undone me, for Tiberio seems to believe that I think I am above him. If he ever had thoughts of wedding me, he does not have them now.

What cruel irony! I am less of a person here now at court than I was in Cremona. At least in Cremona I could still nurse my wild hope of becoming a *maestra*—as long as the truth of my transgression in Rome remained secret. Now, here in Toledo, I watch the last wisps of my dream melt away like honey in water. At best, I am a useless, not particularly attractive, ornament of the court; at worst, a novelty akin to a white crow or singing cow. Courtiers peer at me in curiosity as I sketch scenes of court life while I stand in wait for the girl Queen to let me teach her colors. In the fortnight since my arrival, she did not acknowledge my purpose until just last night, when we were in Her Majesty's heavily perfumed chambers, dancing for her as she waited for the King to arrive for his nuptial duties.

I was resting between measures, fretting about Tiberio's letter and desiring more wine but receiving only water from Francesca. Several of Her Majesty's French ladies, led by madame de Clermont, a young blonde beauty with long, hooded eyes and an aq-uiline nose, were complaining in broken Castilian to the Queen's Spanish ladies that their trunks had not yet arrived from Paris. It seems the poor ladies had been made to dress in the same tired clothing they had worn since they had entered Spain, a trial they could scarcely endure.

Though the Queen's Spanish ladies murmured their sympathy, I saw their smirks behind their handkerchiefs. I was drinking my cursed water and idly wondering if the Spanish ladies might have had anything to do with the delay of the trunks, when the Queen's chief Spanish lady-in-waiting, doña María de la Cueva, condesa de Urueña, a gaunt, thin-skinned, proud woman of perhaps fifty years, stalked up to me in her stiff black gown. Hanging from her girdle was a silver pomander the size of a lime, from which ex-uded the musky scent of civet. She now lifted it to her nose as if warding off a bad smell.

"I do not think we have met," she said, though we had, in fact, several times. "I am the condesa de Urueña."

She stopped sniffing long enough to watch my curtsey, judging its length and style.

"I have seen your sketches," she said.

I lowered my eyes as I rose. "Yes, my lady."

She took another draught. "I have heard you do little portraits."

"Yes, my lady."

"As I am the Queen's first lady, it would behoove you to paint my portrait before all others at court, should you try your hand at such."

My heart sank. How was I to portray this woman, with her small black eyes, pinched nose, and furred lip? It would be like painting a ferret in a dress.

"My lady, I will remember that."

"How soon can you do one?" she demanded. "I should like to have it before Easter."

Less than two months! I could not prepare the canvas and pigments, draw her likeness and plan the composition, and then carry out the scheme through successive layers of paint—let alone make the woman look agreeable—in this amount of time. "Of course, my lady," I said. Did she ever put down that pomander?

The Queen spoke up from where she was sitting on a bench, drinking a cooling draught. In her soft, girlish voice, she said, "Doña Sofonisba is here to instruct *me*."

The condesa de Urueña dropped her pomander. It bounced from the end of its chain around her waist as everyone turned to look at the Queen. Even the Queen herself seemed surprised, her eyes widening as if she were not used to speaking up, let alone to having her way.

The condesa recovered first. "Of course, Your Majesty." She retrieved her pomander and sniffed with a pleasant smile. "My portrait shall come after your lessons are complete."

"No." The Queen held up her little chin. "I mean she shall be busy enough instructing me, for I intend to get quite good. Then, if she has time, she shall paint me—if that is agreeable to you, doña Sofonisba."

I curtseyed. "Certainly, Your Majesty."

The condesa drew deeply from her pomander. "Your Majesty, I believe you already have someone to paint your portrait. The King has appointed a renowned painter from the Low Countries, Anthonis Mor, in that capacity. He awaits you in Madrid."

The Queen shrugged her thin shoulders, rustling the thick gold brocade of her robe. "Then doña Sofonisba can assist him."

The condesa leveled me a cold gaze. At that moment, my goblet appeared before my eyes. I looked up. Francesca flashed me a look of warning as she held out my water.

"Where are you staying now?" the Queen asked me.

"Me, Your Majesty? In the Posada de la Sangre on the Plaza de Zocodover, with my serving lady. His Majesty's chamberlain has kindly found us a place there."

"Both of you shall move into my quarters in the palace. Doña María, can you find them a room near yours?"

"Of course," the condesa de Urueña said sourly.

The Queen ducked her head in a shy smile. "You must keep near to me if you are to do my likeness someday."

"Yes, Your Majesty," I said. "Thank you."

I did not have to meet Francesca's frown to know that I had made a new enemy in the condesa. But the Queen had made one, too, and it was not wise to displease the condesa, who could damage her deeply with one dark word of innuendo or gossip. And to risk this over something as trivial as drawing lessons, the impetuous child. Even I, the daughter of lower nobility, knew that dangerous undercurrents flowed beneath the surface of tranquillity at every court. One misstep and a person could be washed away on a tide of disfavor, even a Queen. It had happened in my papà's youth at the English court of King Henry. All the world knows that King Henry's wife Anne Boleyn had lost her head because the King had turned against her. King Henry had been mad for her, ignoring all who spoke of her unsuitability as Queen, but when the scales had fallen away from his eyes, aided by vicious court gossip, he was ruthless. Only producing a son could have kept her head on her shoulders. With that lesson in mind, this headstrong little French Queen should take great care. For her Spanish ladies whisper she has not yet had her monthly courses.

There is no possibility of a son to buffer her should the winds commence to blow the wrong way.

This afternoon at the running of the bulls, my young mistress again unwittingly put herself in a vulnerable position as she watched the proceedings with her husband the King. It was before the third running, just before the bull was loosed. We were on the balcony of a nobleman's palace overlooking the Plaza de Zodocover. The Queen stood with the King, and the condesa de Urueña and the French blonde beauty, madame de Clermont, were just behind them, with me and several other ladies completing the row. Just inside, Francesca elbowed her way for position among the crowd of servants. The Queen was gazing out over the stone balustrade, toying with the Great Pearl hanging from its brooch upon her narrow chest, when the King's son, Don Carlos, reeking of perfume and medicinal camphor, spilled onto the balcony with my dancing partner, Don Alessandro, and the King's comely "new" brother, Don Juan.

Swords a-swing at their hips, the young gallants made their way through the gathered grandees to greet His Majesty and the Queen. This was my first glimpse of Don Carlos, the King's fourteen-year-old son by his first wife, the Princess of Portugal. Illness had kept the Prince abed for the previous days of the wedding festivities—it appeared he should be there still. The skin upon his sunken cheeks was so pale as to be bluish, and his white-lashed, protuberant eyes were glossily feverish. But ailing or not, this fair-haired wisp of a youth was now being released from his father's affectionate embrace to be introduced to the Queen.

Don Carlos stared at her, dumbstruck. He crossed and re-crossed his arms, thin sticks within the confines of his tight golden sleeves. Only after the King whispered into his ear did he take the Queen's hand into his shaky grip.

The Queen smiled. "So you are the one I have heard of since I was a babe in the cradle. I am glad to meet you at last."

Scarlet splotches crept up the hollows of Don Carlos's cheeks. "You are—you are even more beautiful than your pictures."

"We told you so," said Don Alessandro.

The Queen laughed as Don Alessandro kissed her hand. "Ah, the famous dancer," she said.

"You do me great honor, My Lady, though it was my partner who made me look good." Don Alessandro nodded over the Queen's shoulder at me. "I think she sails on angels' wings."

"A nice compliment," she said to me.

I blushed like a *buffone*.

Don Juan took his turn at her hand. "Your Majesty Doña Elisabeth, thank you for teaching me to dance. I hope your toes survived my lesson."

"My toes fare well." She poked the tip of a slipper from the voluminous hem of her skirt. "Thank you for inquiring about them, Your Majesty."

"'Your Excellency,'" said the King, correcting her.

She pulled back her foot. Everyone turned in surprise. Indeed, for a moment, even I had forgotten the most important man in the world.

The King patted his son's shoulder as he gazed coolly at the Queen.

The condesa de Urueña stepped forward and whispered to the Queen, "Your Majesty, the proper address for Don Juan is 'Your Excellency.'"

"Why, My Lord?" the Queen said to her husband. "Don Juan is your brother. Why is he not 'Your Majesty' or 'Your Highness' like the rest of the Royal Family?"

The King studied her dispassionately as Don Juan looked between them, the color heightening in his face. A silence descended over the balcony, punctuated by the sound of the King's pennants snapping in the wind.

Who did not compare the two brothers, standing so close to each other? Almost twenty years apart and the sons of different mothers, the two favored each other remarkably, though on Don Juan, the King's blue eyes were brightened with dark lashes, His Majesty's fair skin livened with fresh rosiness, his cropped and graying curls smoothed into flowing honey. But the brothers truly differed in one regard: whereas the King bore the jutting Hapsburg jaw, Don Juan was graced with a handsome dimpled chin. How it must rankle the King to be subjected to this young, improved version of himself.

"The bull enters!" Don Alessandro cried. All eyes turned to the plaza below, where a flock of youths scrambled on the cobblestones before a charging bull. Though the King observed the hilarity with the cool serenity the Spanish call *sosiego*, I could see the muscles twitch in his jaw.

I fear young Don Juan will have to take care. As will the headstrong Queen.

To Tiberio Calcagni in Rome

Thank you for your kind letter. I must admit I was surprised to receive it. I had thought by your long silence since I had departed from Rome that our association had ended. Perhaps this gap can be explained by your work with maestro Michelangelo. I recognize the importance of this work and applaud the effort you put into it.

I fear you misconstrue my position here at Court. While I am honored to serve His Sacred Majesty as a lady to his Queen, I am but her teaching instructor. I am not allowed to paint her portrait. A Netherlander named Anthonis Mor has that privilege and right as Painter to the King. So you must see how I look back on my studies in Rome with particular fondness. I know now that they were the most important days of my life.

I hope your efforts on the unfinished Pietà continue at a satisfactory rate. It is truly excruciating not to be able to bring unfinished business to fruition.

From Toledo,
this 15th day of February, 1560

Sofonisba Anguissola

ITEM: *Some hold that inhaling the scent of a pomander is an effective deterrent from disease. This is yet to be proven. If one insists upon its usage, the recipe for filling it follows: Take two ounces of labdanum and benjamin, of storax one ounce, musk from a male musk deer, six grains, civet six grains, ambergris six grains, and of* Calamus aromaticus *and* Lignum aloes, *each the weight of a* maravedí. *Beat all these in a hot mortar with a hot pestle till they come to paste. Then wet your hand with rose water and roll up the paste. Place in the sections of a pomander.*

ITEM: *Several of the sisters serving the ill at the Hospital de Cardinal Tavera here in Toledo are fallen women who have renounced their sins and taken the veil.*

ITEM: *Over the canvas primed with glue and chalk, apply a thin layer of white lead ground into linseed oil and diluted with essence of turpentine. Let dry. Repeat.*

20 FEBRUARY 1560
El Alcázar, Toledo

The Queen fell ill last night. The Small Pox, it is feared. Her household is frantic. Ladies pace the halls and wring their hand-

kerchiefs, then sob into their veils when the physician strides by
with a flask of Her Majesty's urine. Her young pages, the beautiful
sons of the mighty, cower against the wall, abashed by the out-
pouring of feminine anguish. Servants huddle together in watchful
knots; messengers stand agape with their letters unread; tutors
clutch closed books; dressmakers hold wound bolts of silk; musicians dangle silent instruments; cooks' boys balance unopened
tureens smelling of chicken. Among this crush of stunned attendants, lapdogs wrestle and bark and squat, mindless of the small,
still figure on the red-draped bed of state. For in spite of all the
orders given in regard to the primping, educating, and feeding of
this precious commodity, no one has been assigned merely to hold
the Queen's hand.

Who could have imagined this scene yesterday morn? It
had begun so promisingly, cold and windy but clear. The skies
were that hard, brilliant blue particular to Spain—particular, too,
to the eyes of young Don Juan—as we ladies of the court took to
mule-drawn litters after Mass and a light meal. I peeked out of the
crimson brocade curtains of our conveyance as we passed under
the carved stone towers of the Bisagra city gates, frightening a
boy on a donkey. Apparently ladies do not often pop their heads
out of luxurious conveyances.

On the seat across from me, the condesa de Urueña, irritable
for having been excluded from the Queen's litter in favor of Her
Majesty's French ladies, frowned as I watched our descent to the
dusty plain on the only side of Toledo not bounded by the river
Tajo.

"What are those?" I asked as we joggled past a scattering of
stone arches among weedy drifts of rosemary. The smell of the
woody plants permeated the dry air.

"Ruins from Roman times. A coliseum." The condesa lodged her pomander, with its attendant reek of civet, into her nostril. "Please close the curtains."

I sat back with a pang. I remembered Tiberio and me, notebooks and charcoal in hand, sketching the ruins on the Palatine Hill on my first visit to Rome, four years ago. Cows were cropping weeds around the fallen stones as I worked.

"Well done," Tiberio had said, looking over my shoulder. He backed away as Francesca inserted herself between us. "Clever how you portray Time reducing the great to rubble, *signorina*. I can feel the sadness in the air." His gray-green eyes lit in a smile. "The Maestro will love it. He is the King of Melancholia."

"I don't understand it," I said. "He is the most beloved and respected painter and sculptor in the world. Popes, dukes, everyone sings his praises. If I were he, I would be insufferably joyous."

Tiberio shrugged before Francesca blocked him from my view.

Now the mules stopped, jolting me back to the present and the condesa's watchful frown. We had come to the playing field for one of the cane tourneys of which the Spanish are so fond, where the gentlemen form teams and challenge each other on horseback, throwing darts made of river canes at each other. It was the first of such events since Her Majesty's arrival. Curious to see at last this uniquely Spanish spectacle, I let Her Majesty's page hand me down from the litter and escort me to my place among the lesser ladies lined up to either side of the Queen at the edge of the tourney field.

The wind tugged at the voluminous veil I wore in the style of the women of this country. Unless given permission by her husband or father, a lady never goes abroad in public without one. How I wished to cast off the bothersome thing, itself a castoff from the condesa—it smelled of her, like old fur, masking the pleasant weedy scent of the field and the aroma of horse and leather. But good manners and Francesca, free of the servants' wagon and tottering my way, kept me wrapped in my cocoon.

The gentlemen lined up to parade before us. They looked so very manly on their prancing steeds, their armor shining in the brilliant winter sun, the tails and bright trappings of their horses blowing in the wind. I peered down the row of ladies and toward the Queen, expecting to glimpse her enjoyment of the *caballeros*, but saw instead that she was biting her gloved fingers under her veil and fidgeting with the Great Pearl she wore then as on all occasions.

Then I remembered: Not yet eight months before, the Queen's father, Henri II of France, had died at a tournament celebrating her wedding by proxy in Paris, though it had been a different sort of tourney from the one here. It was the kind where men rode at the lists, trying to unseat each other with their lances. A splinter from a breaking lance had shot through the French King's visor and pierced him through the eye, resulting, ten days later, in his death. All of Europe had been in shock that so powerful a man had been felled in his prime, all in the name of sport.

I looked around. Had no one thought how disturbing even a cane tourney might be for the Queen? Though the condesa de Urueña and her ever-present pomander stuck to Her Majesty's left side like sealing wax, and the Queen's chief French lady, the beautiful madame de Clermont, attached herself with equal persistence to Her Majesty's right, both seemed more aware of each other than of their distressed Lady. The Queen's other French ladies were busy, too, still voicing their humiliation and outrage over having to wear the same tired clothes day after day since their trunks had not arrived, while the Spanish ladies were occupied with arranging their veils just so, as to attract the attention of the gentlemen. Francesca, allowed only as far as the huddle of servants at the end of the row of ladies, met my worried gaze.

As the eldest of our family, I am accustomed to giving comfort. With six girls, a boy, and only one nurse, there is often need for another hand at it. But this was the Queen of Spain, not Europa crying because Count Broccardo's daughter had snubbed her.

The line of noble horsemen paraded before us, led by the King in black armor chased with swirls of gold. His helmet under his arm, he bowed briefly from his saddle to the Queen, then forced his black steed into a show of sidesteps to the crowd's wild applause.

The ladies were still calling their approval when into the King's wake clattered Don Carlos, Don Juan, and Don Alessandro. Despite their fine horses and armor, they fought like a pack of eager puppies to position themselves before the Queen.

"You must choose one, Your Majesty," the condesa de Urueña told the Queen. "They each wish for you to be their liege lady."

Even from down the line of swaying skirts, I could see the Queen's nervousness evaporate as she considered the young bloods jostling before her. The King turned on his horse to watch.

My Lady held out her handkerchief to Don Carlos. "For the one who is like a brother to me."

Don Carlos, a pale worm within a golden shell, reached with a clank of armor for the handkerchief, nearly falling from his horse. He caught himself just in time, clutching the frothy lace cloth to his breastplate. Even from where I stood, I could see his watery eyes shining with gratitude through his open visor. Equally visible was the King, leaning back in his saddle, taking it all in.

With a satisfied nod, the King swung back around. I followed his line of vision until it came to rest upon his sister, Doña Juana,

Crown Princess of Portugal. I had seen Doña Juana at many of the events celebrating the arrival of the Queen. With perfect skin, shrewd blue eyes framed by white lashes, and a rounded brow that she lowers like a battering ram when she speaks, she is a beautiful woman in a formidable way. A person with any sense would not argue with her, though she is a young woman, near my years in age. Widow of the Portuguese Crown Prince, she had come back to Spain six years ago at her father the Emperor's request, leaving behind her infant son. Busy waging war in France, the Emperor had chosen her to rule as his regent in Spain, since Felipe, then Prince, had gone to England to wed Mary Tudor. She quickly earned a reputation for stern efficiency and an unblinking commitment to enforcing the law. But now even the woman known as the Iron Princess was chuckling as her nephew, Don Carlos, galloped off whirling the Queen's handkerchief aloft, his page racing after him, calling him back.

The flash of a jewel caught my attention. I looked again to the King's sister, then to the lady-in-waiting next to her, a beauty whose dark uncovered hair shone blue-black in the sun. She toyed with a large diamond brooch as she stared at the King, and he, I did realize, was staring back at her.

That evening, at a masque given by the Archbishop of Toledo, I watched this lady closely. While the performers sang to the music of viol, lute, and harp, she did nothing more than carry Doña Juana's train, fetch her mistress goblets of water, and stand back while the Princess voiced her many irrefutable opinions. The only time I took my eyes from the lady in the space of the first hour was to lift my empty cup to the pages circulating through the chamber with wine, while Francesca shook her head *no* from the servants' gallery.

But even after the performance had ended and a dance had

begun, not once did the lady look at the King nor he at her, and no movement between them would have gone undetected. My attention was not divided, as was the other ladies' in the Queen's household, by the little war gaining momentum between the Spanish ladies and the French, ever since a French lady had overheard a Spanish lady complain to a gentleman that the French women were dirty. I had just decided that perhaps the connection between Doña Juana's lady and the King was a figment of my imagination when the three young Royal *caballeros*, Don Carlos, Don Alessandro, and Don Juan, sauntered into the hall.

They made their way first to kiss the hand of the King, as was proper, then the Queen's, though Don Alessandro had to push Don Carlos forward to her, as newly shy as the Prince was from her attention to him at the cane tourney. When Don Carlos brushed her hand with his lips, then stammered the standard "I kiss Your Majesty's hands and feet," the little Queen, as spirited as always, responded by asking him to dance.

The King watched them make their way to the floor, his brother Don Juan beside him. Although the King's expression was calm and aloof, beneath crossed arms his thumbs twitched against his forefingers.

Cold air seeped through the shuttered windows, stirring the fringe of the tapestries covering the walls and bending the flames of the candles studding the great wheels of the candelabra overhead. As the Queen and Don Carlos stepped into a somber pavane, I studied the King and his brother. They did not speak to each other, even when in close proximity.

"Will you gape at them all night?"

I turned to find Don Alessandro at my elbow. Quickly, I averted my eyes. "I was studying His Majesty. I hope to do his portrait someday."

"Is that so?"

I paused as if being torn from deep painterly thoughts, but Don Alessandro led me onto the dance floor to the sweet sawing of the viol. In truth, I had never entertained the possibility of painting the King. A lady drawing teacher was hardly a likely candidate ever to do so. As we commenced into the hesitating march of the pavane, I could smell Don Alessandro's curls, fresh-washed in scented water, though a faint, boyish odor of dirt clung to him, reminding me he was but a new-grown man.

"So tell me more about the great Michelangelo," he said.

I flinched.

"Does he paint all the time?" he asked.

"Not anymore."

"As good as he is? Why not?"

"He is over eighty years of age now. At any rate, sculpting is his preference." I forced a carefree laugh. "I think spending seven years on his back, painting the ceiling of the Sistine Chapel in Rome, soured him toward the brush."

"H'm. Being on one's back usually has a happy effect."

Did he reserve his impertinence for me, or did he speak this disrespectfully to every woman? "Maestro Michelangelo says painting is all artifice," I said, my voice cool with formality, "an illusion. It is merely a trick, compared with the solid reality of sculpted stone." I drew in a breath, hearing in my mind Tiberio arguing for the superiority of sculpting. I could see him bent over the red chalk drawing of the unfinished statue in Michelangelo's house, the planes of his cheekbones sharp with seriousness as he proclaimed sculpture to be the harder art to master. Sweetest Holy Mary, had I misspoken in my letter to him? Should I have assuaged his pride more? Let my own hurt show less?

"I must like being tricked, then, because I like paintings better than statues. Besides, aren't portraits a form of reality?" Don Alessandro peered at me as he raised my hand at a pause. "Are you well?"

"Yes. Of course." I lifted my chin. "In Francisco de Holanda's famous treatise on portraits, he defines them as 'the *contrived* likeness of any prominent person of high standing, whose image should rightly be preserved for centuries to come.'"

"Well," he said as we resumed our footwork, "I would like you to contrive my likeness. And make it good—I wish to be known to history as a handsome devil."

The King's nephew or not, he had a terrible way of asking for a portrait. Even if I were not obliged to instruct the Queen only, I have my pride. I took a few more steps before speaking. "I see Don Carlos wears Her Majesty's handkerchief from the tourney."

He glanced at me, then laughed. "Oh, you have noticed? Poor idiot, you cannot take it off him."

"Like the Queen and her Great Pearl."

He turned me slowly to the music. "What do you know of the pearl?"

"Nothing—why do you make that face?"

He gave me a conspiratorial smile. "The King gave it to her."

We processed together in the opposite direction. "Is that unusual?" I said. "I understand it is the best of the Spanish crown jewels. It is the largest perfectly shaped pearl in the world."

"He gave it to his previous wife."

"Don Carlos's mother, the Portuguese Princess."

"No, his second wife."

"The English Queen Mary?"

He nodded. "Like our Queen, she never took it from her

person. Bloody Mary convinced herself that the pearl was a token of his great affection—if she couldn't have the King, at least she had it."

"How sad. Even in Cremona, it was known that he did not love her."

He leaned close to whisper. "She died alone, with the pearl upon her breast. They say they had to pry it from her cold, stiff hands."

A chill prickled my scalp. Ahead, the Queen chatted brightly with Don Carlos as they stepped. Although the Prince hung his head, I could see his radiant smile.

"Why has not anyone told her?" I said.

Don Alessandro laughed. "Whom would you suggest? Her Spanish ladies will not tell her because they enjoy knowing something she does not. The French ladies will not tell her because they are afraid to make her unhappy—or the Spanish ladies happy at seeing her unhappy."

"For one so young, you notice much."

Don Alessandro shrugged. "I have lived all my life in courts. First my father's"—his brow clouded as he glanced at the King— "now here. Someday I shall have one of my own as Duke, not that I want one."

"Every man wants his own court, does he not?"

"Not I. I shall be sick of people asking me for favors all day. When *I* have a court, I will be tough like my great-grandfather. He was the Pope who had to fix the Church after Luther made his mess. Had a few handsome bastards, too."

Luther. Who would have known that one man could tear all of Europe apart by suggesting that people did not need the Pope or priests to get to God? Such a simple idea. And such an intolerable one, especially to popes—and kings—whose position and power come from being God's anointed representatives on earth.

Don Alessandro nodded ahead, to where Don Juan had just broken in to dance with the Queen. Don Carlos was standing aside, his pasty jaw ajar in shock.

"He still has not gotten over it," Don Alessandro whispered. He turned me around again.

"Over what, *señor?*"

"He was betrothed to her at one time, you know."

"Don Carlos? To the Queen?" It was hard to imagine the poor wisp of a youth as anyone's bridegroom.

"From the cradle, nearly. When the King was married to the English Queen Mary, Don Carlos was pledged to Elisabeth. Why do you look surprised—they are nearly the same age. You should have seen Don Carlos when the English Mary died and the King promptly announced that *he* would marry the French Princess himself. Don Carlos threw a chair out the window of the palace in Madrid."

"I would not think he had the strength."

Don Alessandro raised my hand to the music. "Truly? You have never seen the power of anger?"

Not long after, the dance concluded and the condesa de Urueña, madame de Clermont, and several other of Her Majesty's ladies were in the Queen's chamber, preparing her for bed as our own servants hovered in the background. The little Queen drooped, her face and neck flushed with exhaustion, as madame de Clermont unpinned the Great Pearl and handed it to me, heavy as a plum in my hand. As the condesa waited nearby with a fresh chemise, madame removed the Queen's robes and unlaced her tight bodice. She then pulled away the stiff cage of sumptuous cloth binding Her Majesty's thin chest. When she drew off the Queen's shift to remove the corset underneath, she gasped.

The Queen looked up heavily, her arms folded over the peaked buds of her breasts. Seeing madame's face, she gazed down at her groin. A cluster of angry red pustules dotted her downy girl's mound.

"My Lady," madame said with haste, "it is nothing."

I turned to Francesca, standing along the wall. Sweetest Holy Mary, was it the Small Pox?

The condesa stepped forward to slip the clean chemise over the Queen's head, then without a word briskly left the room. Her voice rang harshly from the arcade outside. "Doctor Hernández! Send for doctor Hernández!"

Meek as a babe in a cradle, Her Majesty let madame de Clermont lay her in her bed. "Do not let the King come tonight," she whispered.

Anger flamed within me. Poor young thing, having to worry about a husband when her greatest concern should have been which of her lapdogs to take to bed. If it was the Small Pox, she would soon be battling for her life.

"Do not let him see me!" the Queen cried.

"Of course we won't, My Lady," said madame.

"Make certain!"

When the King did come, he scowled at madame de Clermont's anxious whisperings, then shouldered his way past her to where the Queen lay very still, her eyes closed tight. Only doctor Hernández's arrival and his subsequent dire warnings about contagion forced the King from the bedside.

No sooner had his departing footsteps stopped ringing from the cold stone walls than the ladies resumed huddling in their panicked knots. They wrung their hands and sniffed back tears, though whether their distress was driven by fear of exposure to the pox or the possible demise of My Lady, it is hard to say.

Now the dazed crowd lingers in the halls, waiting to see which way Fortune's wheel will turn. Heaven help this girl who lies on the damask bed of state. She is the slender branch upon which the peace between two kingdoms hangs.

ITEM: *The Small Pox should not be confused with the Great Pox. The Small Pox is characterized by a rash of pimples that become fluid-filled pustules by the sixth day. The pustules are found on the face and extremities, less commonly on the trunk, leaving lasting scars should the patient survive. The Great Pox covers the patient's body from the head to the knees, resulting in some instances in the flesh falling from the face. Bleeding is the recommended treatment for the Small Pox. The Great Pox may be relieved by the application of mercury to the skin, thus the saying, "A night in the arms of Venus results in a lifetime on Mercury." The Small Pox cannot be passed to a child at birth by an infected mother. The Great Pox can, though the infant may not show symptoms until later in childhood. These symptoms include rashes, fevers, and weakness.*

ITEM: *The best oil for mixing with pigments is achieved by cooking linseed oil over a very low flame for two turnings of an hourglass or until it is reduced by one half. It is good to keep an infusion of willow bark on hand for the resulting headache.*

22 FEBRUARY 1560

El Alcázar, Toledo

The doctors have pronounced My Lady's malady indeed to be the Small Pox. The Queen has been quarantined with her ladies, who check themselves hourly for signs of infection. But after just two days, Her Majesty's fever has ebbed, leaving her with just a sprinkling of pustules, the most of which are centered, oddly enough, around her groin. There is, however, a single large pimple upon her forehead and a rash upon her cheeks.

None of this was enough to keep our little patient in her bed this afternoon. Nor was she daunted by the dried egg-white and lead mixture cracking upon her face—a recipe to keep her from scarring, recommended by her mother, Catherine de' Medici, in instructions in case of afflictions of the flesh, sent with My Lady to Spain.

"Come away from the window, Your Majesty," the condesa de Urueña said from behind her pomander. "Do you want your subjects to see you like this?"

The condesa was even more implacable than usual, perhaps because of her exclusion from the ceremony at which the lords of the realm were to swear allegiance to Don Carlos today. By King's Order she was to remain in the Queen's quarters, robbed of the chance to dress in her finest garb and show off her high position at court. How she smiled when it was announced that none of the French ladies were to go to the ceremony, either.

The Queen looked over her shoulder, her chin tucked back in a girlish grin. "Do you fear I might be mistaken for a unicorn?" She raised her fingers to the white-crusted pustule on her forehead.

"Do not touch!" shouted the condesa.

The Queen lowered her hand.

"Until your mother hears of your illness and its progress and allows us to discontinue the treatment she had expressly ordered, you must remain out of sight," said the condesa. "It is hardly attractive."

Her Majesty's chief French lady, madame de Clermont, sat on a pillow, languidly leafing through the brightly illustrated pages of her Book of Hours. "We are thankful Her Majesty's mother, the Most Serene Queen Mother of France, had the foresight to send such an efficacious remedy," she recited in the bored voice of someone toeing the official line.

"Her case is light and she probably would not have scarred anyway," said the condesa. "In fact, I wonder if it is the Small Pox at all."

The Queen blinked. "What is it, then?"

"A foreign rash."

Madame de Clermont looked up from her book and frowned as if wondering if she had been insulted somehow. The Queen turned quickly to the window.

"Whatever it is," said the condesa, careful not to return madame's gaze, "you can still catch a chill, Your Majesty. Come away from that window."

The Queen tossed her hair, which without a headdress hung in tight fawn-brown waves to her waist. "I think I shall die if I stay cooped up in this room!"

She leaned out the window, then laughed when a passing priest looked up and gasped.

"See what a spectacle you make of yourself!" the condesa exclaimed. "I shall tell the King I have no part in it." She strode over to her pillow, puffing on her pomander.

"Sofonisba, you join me," said the Queen.

I looked up from where I had been adding depth to the shadows in one of the drawings I'd done of her while she had been abed.

The Queen smiled sweetly at the condesa. "She's supposed to teach me to draw. My husband says."

I went to Her Majesty, ignoring the condesa's scowl and Francesca loudly clearing her throat from where she sewed with the other servants at the far end of the chamber. As pigeons strutted on the nearby ledges, My Lady and I looked out over the huddle of yellow and gray stone buildings from our position atop the highest hill in the city. Here and there a brick Moorish tower, pierced with pointed horseshoe-shaped windows, or a Flemish bell tower, recognizable by its four-sided pointed top, jutted above the red-tiled roofs. Dwarfing them all was the massive gray-slated dome of the Cathedral. With all the shapes and angles, the scene would make an interesting sketch.

But it seems my mind is drawn to portraying people. It is a thrill to capture in paint something so elusive that we seldom see it even when it is before our very eyes—the inner self. I had done so before, once, in the painting of my sisters playing chess, with Francesca watching them in the background. A glimmer of each one of their dear souls had peeked out from the canvas. Even Michelangelo had remarked upon it. But limning one's sisters and nurse well hardly made one a *maestra*.

"Your Majesty," I said to the Queen, "perhaps we ought to step back."

The Queen glanced at the condesa, now loudly haranguing one of the lesser French ladies, which served to embroil madame de Clermont in an argument. "I don't care if she has been at this court since she was a child," the Queen whispered, "and the King wants me to learn Spanish ways from her. I won't give in to her. She is just like my mother."

A trumpeting and shouting arose from below. A cavalcade issued forth from the side of the palace—the great lords of the land were riding to the ceremony.

The condesa rushed to the window. "Come away, Your Majesty!"

"Do you see him?" The Queen's hair tumbled over her shoulders as she strained to distinguish among the riders.

"Who?" I asked over the condesa's frantic bleats.

At that moment, Don Carlos, his slight figure wrapped to his crown in fur of ermine, trotted into view on a white charger housed in trappings of gold. Behind him rode Don Alessandro, in a cape of lynx, then Don Juan, his blond hair free in the wind.

The young bloods pulled aside their horses. The King came galloping through, his jeweled hands gripping the reins of his black stallion, his cape flowing over the horse's muscular haunches.

"There is your King!" the condesa cried. "Does he not look magnificent?"

The Queen shrank back inside.

"Shame!" The condesa drew the mullioned windows closed with a bang. "Heaven knows who saw you in such a state!"

The Queen said nothing, but went over to her embroidery frame, called her little spaniel to her lap, and listlessly began to stitch. I withdrew to my table and took up my chalk and paper. Before me, the German clock the King had given the Queen ticked on like Time itself, its golden parts spinning and whirling.

The Queen fell into a nap, her dog snoring in its nest in her skirts. Around the chamber the other ladies slumped on their pillows in various positions of slumber. Only Francesca remained awake, now plunging, now pulling her needle through the torn lace of my chemise. I scratched wanly with my chalk, my thoughts drifting to where they should not go—to Tiberio.

If only I could touch his arms again. From wielding his sculptor's chisel with Michelangelo, they are roped with veins and as hard as the stone he hews. Just the memory of their feel stirs me. But as firm and thrilling as are his arms, it is the skin on the undersides of them that I most crave to touch. It is as soft and smooth as an infant's cheek.

With a sigh, I closed my eyes.

I woke to the sound of muffled voices outside, and the Queen easing open the window. I slipped to her side as the cavalcade, all flapping banners and capes and clashing hooves, poured through the street below.

The Queen wrested some crumbling plaster from the window frame. She searched the stream of riders and then, when Don Carlos approached with Don Juan, flung the plaster hard. It smashed on the stones next to Don Carlos, unnoticed.

She scrabbled at the frame again. When it yielded no more grit, she scanned her own person, seized a black pearl from the clasp of her robe, and hurled it with a grunt. It bounced off the hilt of Don Carlos's sword with a bright ping.

He looked up.

"Hey!" A grin swallowed his pasty face as he pointed at her window. "You!"

The Queen laughed and ducked inside even as the condesa sailed toward us with all the fury of a gale sweeping across the Toledan plain. I tugged at the windows as the King cantered up behind the young gentlemen. I could see his long jaw lift from the folds of his ruff as he looked up.

I drew back, heart lurching. The condesa was waiting for me when I turned.

"Do you think you are doing her a favor, letting her lessen herself in the eyes of Our Lord and King? Do not think he will not hear about this. He hears all. He has eyes and ears everywhere. Your Majesty, you have erred!"

"You cannot chastise the daughter of the Queen of France!" said madame de Clermont, up from her pillow now. "Where is your respect?"

The condesa rounded on her. "You are aware of how the King spent his time with her in the nuptial bed before her illness. Do you think her mother would approve of the King dozing away the night instead of trying to beget a child upon her?"

I glanced at the Queen. She hung her head like Europa caught stealing sweets.

I did not know he had not been bedding her. My heart went out to my little Lady. "Her Majesty has not yet had her courses," I said. "Perhaps he is being kind until she matures."

The condesa fixed me with a look of disdain. "Unless you wish to see Her Majesty sent home to her mother due to breach of contract, I would think you would want to aid our Queen in gaining the King's favor. I suggest that you stick to your chalks and leave matters of the Queen's comportment to me."

Over in her corner, Francesca's square peasant face took on an even grimmer set than was usual. Slights to me are taken doubly hard by her. But insulting or not, the condesa's concern rang true. What man has ever been "kind," when he has a chance to bed a maiden? Not even Tiberio had kept me at arm's length when I had proved to be willing.

ITEM: *The King's great-great-grandmother Isabella of Portugal suffered from derangement. Her daughter, Queen Isabel of Castilla, was forced to lock her mother in the Monastery of Miraflores, in the wilds outside Burgos. There Isabella of Portugal spent her last twenty years, wandering amongst the beautifully carved cloisters, unable to harm herself or anyone else.*

ITEM: *The King's great-great-great-great-grandmother was not mad, but perfectly sane and very stout. Cymburga of Masovia was so strong she could crack walnuts with her fingers and pound a nail into a board with her clenched fist. It is said she would not brook comments on her jaw, which jutted out as powerfully as a thrust elbow.*

ITEM: *That most useful of pigments, white lead, is the better the more it is ground.*

28 FEBRUARY 1560
El Alcázar, Toledo

Although the talk at court may be of the frost that has nipped the buds of the almond trees, and of the continuing mystery of the

disappearance of the French ladies' wardrobe trunks, and of
the word from Genoa that a virulent strain of the Great Pox is
renewing its rounds among the men there, all thoughts here now
are truly of when the King will tumble at last in the Queen's
bosom. Although he visits her chambers each evening, the sheets
are not sullied when we come to dress the Queen in the morn.
What will become of our little Lady if he continues to reject her
in bed? Indeed, why does he bother to visit her each night?

Perhaps the King simply awaits the Queen's complete recovery. There are still vestiges of the great pimple upon her forehead
and the sores on her nether-quarters, though they are fading fast
and the King discontinued My Lady's treatment without consulting her mother. Indeed, the ailment that now plagues Her Majesty
most is boredom, a malady compounded by the condesa de Urueña's hectoring to maintain proper Spanish decorum even in the
sickroom.

Among the court rules:

Her Majesty is not to allow servants to speak to her first.

She is to insist that everyone curtsey to her before addressing her.

She is not to use anything a commoner has touched, even if it
is something she herself has dropped. Thus, if she should drop a
handkerchief before the cook's boy and he should pick it up, it
would become of no use to her. Only one of her ladies or someone of the Blood can retrieve it. I saw Her Majesty lose a perfectly
good glove this way, a rose-colored kid one perfumed with civet.
The goldsmith the Queen had brought with her from France retrieved the glove she had dropped when trying on a new ring.
How the condesa smiled with grim approval when the Queen
reluctantly let the glove go, telling the goldsmith to keep it,

though it had been a present from her brother the King of France and was dear to her.

Doctor Hernández has ruled that Her Majesty is still too weak for me to teach her painting. It is too great a strain, he says, on her woman's brain. The only antidote to her boredom that I can offer her is to sketch her in various poses and then show her the results, though I swear the condesa looks for ways to outlaw even this. Why she takes such enjoyment in irritating Our Queen, I do not know, but irritate her she does, like a burr in one's chemise.

The Queen was sitting in one of these positions for me to sketch this afternoon, with her hand to her chin as if thinking, when she broke her pose to examine my progress. "Do I really look like this, Sofonisba?"

"To me you do, My Lady."

"But I look like I am full of—"

A male voice broke in. "—secrets?"

Her Majesty and I turned in surprise as the King made his way across the room to us, the Queen's ladies falling into curtseys beside their embroidery frames as he passed, his sword swinging at his side.

The Queen's chin receded in a smile as he kissed her hand, something he'd not shrunk from doing after doctor Hernández had pronounced her free of contagion. "I was going to say 'laughter,'" she said in French.

He smiled as if not quite certain what she said. His Majesty knows little French, so the Queen must always converse with him in Spanish. Although the King is a renowned scholar in many other fields, he is not gifted in tongues, and being King, others must accommodate him, not he make allowances for them. It was a surprise, therefore, when he said in halting French, "Are you comfortable, My Lady?"

The Queen's face lit up. In rapid French, she launched into a young girl's complaint of being restrained indoors due to her illness as the King looked on helplessly.

"I am sorry, My Lord," said the Queen, switching to Spanish when she saw his incomprehension. She laughed. "It was a rambling best unheard. As my mother says, 'If you cannot say anything good, then say nothing at all.'"

"A wise woman," the King said in his own tongue. He rested his hand on the pommel of his sword, as if waiting for her to continue.

The Queen gripped together her hands in thought. She wore the Great Pearl pinned to her day robes, giving her the air of a child playing dress-up in her mother's clothes. "And how fares your son the Prince Don Carlos? I hear he has taken ill. I hope he is better now."

"Yes," said the King, and nothing more. He cast his gaze about the chamber. Madame de Clermont smiled at him from behind her embroidery frame; the condesa nodded. I myself made a show of drawing, though I was only adding crosshatching to a shadow.

"Doña Sofonisba."

I nearly jumped from my skin. I put down my pen to curtsey.

"No, don't stop," he said.

I hesitated, then resumed my appearance of drawing.

He stood over me, close enough that I could catch his scent of cinnamon and hair pomade. "I see you are keeping company with the Queen, as I had hoped. Have you taught her to draw?"

"Doctor Hernández wishes the Queen to regain her strength before she takes on a new endeavor, Your Majesty."

"I see."

He glanced at the Queen as if he wished to speak with her. A lady coughed quietly into her hand; my pen scratched against the rough paper.

The King drew in a silent breath, then looked down again at me. "I understand that you were a great favorite of the artist Michelangelo."

My heart missed a beat. "He allowed me to study with him briefly. Very briefly." I tried to keep drawing. In my side vision I could see madame de Clermont slowly edging her way over to My Lady in a tortoise's race with the condesa de Urueña.

"He must be an interesting individual," said the King, still watching me, "so favored by God with an otherworldly talent. I would say he is the most revered artist alive."

"Yes, Your Majesty."

The condesa spoke up, having reached the Queen first. "Your Majesty," she said to the King, "they say in Michelangelo's painting of the Last Judgment, he outstripped even himself in portraying the punishment for those who have not lived well. The demons he imagines pulling the sinners into Hell are quite horrific."

"I have seen copies of the painting." I could feel the King's cool gaze move from me to the condesa. "I would say the true terror comes from how well Michelangelo understands the sinners' agony. He captures their fear of having to pay for what they have done." Behind me I heard the rustle of the King's voluminous sleeves as he crossed his arms. "I am pleased that my wife should receive instruction—when she is well—from someone who has learned at his feet."

The Queen swallowed. "Sofi," she said in the shrill voice of a child trying to please, "show the King your other drawings."

I got up to retrieve the other papers on the table across the room, my scalp prickling with the awareness that he was watching me.

"Do you like art, My Lady?" the King asked the Queen.

"Oh, yes."

He cleared his throat. "And which artists did your father prefer?"

Over my shoulder I saw the Queen look at madame de Clermont. "Clouet," madame whispered to the Queen.

"Clouet," the Queen said.

A silence ensued in which I was painfully aware of the scuffling noise I made in gathering up my sketches. If this was how they conversed in the bedchamber, no wonder there was so little tumbling done in bosoms.

"Oh!" The Queen brightened. "And Leonardo da Vinci. Grandfather had him stay in one of our manors. Monsieur Leonardo died there, in fact. He left behind a curious picture of a lady with a mysterious smile on her face. You cannot tell what she is thinking, yet her eyes follow you everywhere. It is most eerie."

I looked up—she was speaking of *La Gioconda*, the portrait I had championed to Michelangelo. Her family had that painting in their possession? Oh, to be a queen!

"I see." The King cleared his throat. "Well. Has your father any Flemish work?"

"Flemish, My Lord?"

"My grandfather was Flemish. Philippe the Handsome—I am named after him. 'Felipe' is 'Philippe' in the Castilian tongue." He stopped, frowning.

I groaned inwardly as Her Majesty blinked at her husband.

Flatter him, My Lady. Tell him he was well named, that he is Felipe the Handsome, too. Do not let this opportunity to ingratiate yourself to him get away.

Her Majesty's German clock ticked and whirred on the table. At last the King said, "I rather like the work of a man named El Bosco. A Fleming. Bosch, he is called in his own country. Hieronymus Bosch."

"Oh!" said the Queen.

Madame de Clermont smiled broadly at the King, as if her mistress had just explained the Mystery of Life.

I held my breath, my arms full of sketches. In a voice both desperate and hopeful, the Queen asked, "Does he draw dogs?"

"Dogs?" the King said.

"I like dogs," she said, her voice small. She picked up her spaniel, who had been nibbling at its rear leg.

The King stroked his pointed beard. "Well . . . I do believe there are two dogs in the piece by El Bosco I have just acquired. It is a tabletop painting."

"Two dogs!" The Queen's voice was full of gratitude. "Are they adorable, My Lord?"

"Well, I do not know about that. They are acting out the Flemish proverb 'Two dogs with one bone seldom reach agreement.' The painting is of the Seven Deadly Sins."

"Envy," the condesa said, as if explaining to an infant. "There are two dogs fighting over one bone, representing envy."

The King frowned at the condesa before turning back to the Queen. "So you like dogs, My Lady?"

"Yes!" exclaimed the Queen, visibly cheered by the King's defense. "Very much. I like animals of all kinds."

"Then perhaps you would enjoy the collection I have put together in my animal house in Madrid. Among various other beasts, I have an elephant, an ostrich, and some camels, and I just received a rhinoceros."

"A rhinoceros! I should love to see it. My mother has an animal house in Paris, but we have no rhinoceros. Does it not have a great wicked horn?"

"Indeed." A smile nudged at the corners of his mouth. "The wickedest." He adjusted the clock's position on the table, then regarded her thoughtfully. "What amazes me is that from one Heavenly Hand comes the rhinoceros, the snake, and the ostrich. Such diversity, but to what purpose?"

"I had not thought upon that," said the Queen.

"I often wonder," said the King. "Why did He create thousands of creatures instead of twenty? Why did He think we needed them all?"

My Lady gazed at him, her admiration real. "You are wise to ponder it, My Lord."

His Majesty glanced away quickly, his hand straying to his chin.

"Doña Sofonisba," he said gruffly. "Are we not going to see your drawings?"

With a jolt, I stepped forward, then, curtseying, offered the King the sheets of paper. He began to turn through them, revealing my portrayal of Her Majesty looking out the window, of her sleeping, of her reading her Book of Hours.

"These are good," the King said. "Quite good. You capture her essence, *señorita*, her"—he looked up at the Queen—"sweetness."

The Queen smiled shyly.

The King handed me the drawings. "Pack them up. Doctor Hernández says the Queen will soon be well enough to travel, and we will go to Madrid for Lent."

"Oh, I should like that!" the Queen exclaimed. She caught the King's gaze. "My Lord," she said softly, "I should like to be with you."

They regarded each other in silence. Between them, the workings of the golden clock clicked and whirled in their continual rounds.

A voice came from across the room. "Then perhaps you will want this when you go."

I cannot say who was the most surprised to find Don Juan standing at the door, but I can say who seemed least glad.

"*Señor,*" the King said icily. "What brings you here?"

Don Juan bowed, then asked the Queen, "May I enter, My Lady?"

"Certainly—if my husband permits it."

"Of course," the King said.

Don Juan's young countenance was lit with a friendly smile as he approached. "I did not mean to interrupt, Your Majesty. I am here as a favor to His Majesty the Prince Don Carlos."

The King drew an irritated breath. "What does my son want?"

"I am sorry to say that Don Carlos's fever has risen this afternoon, and the only way any of us could convince him to return to bed was to promise to give you this, My Lady."

"Something from Don Carlos?" said the Queen.

Don Juan opened his hand, revealing the black pearl the Queen had ripped from her dress to throw at the Prince.

"He said to tell you that it fell from Heaven," Don Juan said in rapid French.

"Perhaps an angel sent it," the Queen said in the same tongue.

"Yes." Don Juan's smile was genuine. "I believe one did."

The Queen turned pink.

"What is it?" snapped the King. His face was so hard it was difficult to imagine I'd seen a gentle creature in it only moments before.

"Nothing," said the Queen. "A pearl that had fallen from my dress." She reached for it quickly.

"You may not take it."

She stopped, her hand above the pearl.

"It has left your person," the King said. "It cannot be returned by common hands."

"But My Lord," said the Queen, "your son Don Carlos picked it up. He is family."

The King's chill gaze went to Don Juan.

An edge of incredulousness crept into the Queen's voice. "And so is Don Juan." She took the pearl.

The King lifted the Queen's hand, the pearl still clasped within it. "Keep better watch over your things, my dear." He kissed her hand and left.

When he was gone, Don Juan said in the Queen's language, "I did not mean to interrupt, Your Majesty."

"How can you interrupt when there was nothing to interrupt?" she said lightly in French.

With a quick brush of his lips to her hand, he left immediately, the very model of decorum.

So why do I feel that I was a witness to wrongdoing, when no one has committed a wrong?

My Dearest Daughter,

I am glad to hear you are faring well in spite of the many bull runs you are forced to witness. Do not judge the Spanish too harshly. The grisly spectacle you describe is no more gruesome than the bear-baiting preferred by the Cremonese, and at least it is economical in that it provides meat at the end of the ordeal. Just be grateful that the bulls' terror is short-lived and that soon they are in God's hands as are all His beloved creatures in the end.

My own beloved creatures do well here. Lucia has completed a portrait of your mother that captures her delicate beauty. Gazing upon it gives your mother a moment's respite from her worries, which is a relief to me as well, for the poor woman's anxieties grow greater by the day. Her prayers are so endless she will barely eat or sleep, for she feels that if she stops, something terrible will befall the family. The weight she must feel! But you must not think it is all gloom and sorrow here. On the contrary, Asdrubale still charms us with his clowning as does Anna Maria with her sweetness and Europa with the predictability of her willfulness. Minerva is working on drawing, inspired by your having told her how messer Michelango said the basis of all good painting is to master drawing first.

By the way, I did not tell messer Michelangelo that you were the Painter to the Queen. Why did you ask me about that in your last letter? In the note I wrote thanking messer Michelangelo for his kind attention to you in Rome, I *mentioned that you were now serving as a lady to the Queen, as the King wished for you to teach Her Majesty her colors. Have Their Majesties asked you to be their painter? If they have not yet, I am certain they will. Show them your work— they will clamor for their own likenesses to be done, I promise.*

From Cremona,
this 1st day of March, 1560

With deepest love and affection,
Your Father

ITEM: *The pearl called La Peregrina, which means "The Wanderer" or "The Pilgrim," came from the shores of Panama in the New World. It was given by a conquistador to Isabel of Castilla, who in turn gave it to her daughter Juana the Mad. Juana's son the Emperor Charles took La Peregrina from his mother, assuming she would not want to waste such a precious thing, locked within her tower.*

ITEM: *Grind bone black for half an hour, an hour, or as much as you please. If you were to grind it a year it would be the better for it. Ochre, ground for ten years, would only be improved. Of vermilion, it cannot be said twenty years of grinding would be too much.*

23 MARCH 1560
El Alcázar, Toledo

The dull winter days of Lent, unmitigated by parties or meat or warm sunshine, have fallen upon us. I have been allowed to begin to teach the Queen to draw, which has raised her interest in art to the point that she has asked for her portrait to be made. I leapt at the opportunity, only to be shot down by the condesa, who insisted that the Queen employ the official court painter, the Netherlander Anthonis Mor, not a mere lady-in-waiting. The condesa did find it in her heart to allow me to accompany the

Queen to her sittings. But now I fear I have alienated myself with maestro Mor.

I had only been curious. At his insistence, I had been completely silent as he worked on Her Majesty's painting. Other than myself and his assistant, Alonso Sánchez Coello, a painter Doña Juana had brought with her from Portugal, all attendants had been banished from the chamber—musicians, too, save for one boy, who was bidden to play a single melancholic melody unrelentingly on a shawm. During the first few sittings, as the shawm squawked and señor Sánchez Coello mixed pigments and the Maestro flicked the tip of his tongue in concentration as he worked, the Queen had darted amused looks at me from where she sat by the window opened for the light, though her teeth did chatter with cold. I cringed, fearing she would burst into laughter, for I could just imagine the Maestro, a wiry man with a rat's shining eyes and a sharply forked beard, furiously smashing into splinters the wood panel upon which he worked. But the droning shawm and stinking linseed-oil fumes eventually dulled My Lady's spirit, until at last she lapsed into silent stares, entertaining what thoughts I did not know, as the glowing mound of charcoal, heaped up against the chill of the open window, groaned in the big brass brazier. Reduced to standing to the side, I was painfully reminded of the irony that Tiberio should think I was Painter to the Queen. Papà had not told Michelangelo that was my role here—why had the Maestro told Tiberio such a thing?

Finally, as maestro Mor painstakingly painted the bluish shadows under Her Majesty's worried eyes, I blurted out a question that had nagged me since he had begun laying in the greenish-gray shapes of the underpainting, three weeks ago.

"*Signore*, I beg your pardon, but do you always prefer painting on wood?"

The shawmist looked up, though he kept up his dreary bleating. Maestro Mor stepped back from his easel, his fist bristling with five different brushes. Under his floppy Flemish cap, his small black eyes flashed fire. "Excuse me?"

Señor Sánchez Coello, a thin-faced fellow with sad dark eyes, shook his head from where he cleaned brushes behind the Maestro.

"*Signore.*" I curtseyed. "I am so sorry to have interrupted."

He readjusted the square palette, loaded with uniform dabs of paint, that was hooked on his thumb. "Well, you have now, so spit it out. What?"

"Wood, *signore*—do you always paint on it?"

"What else would you suggest?"

His tone of voice did not invite suggestion. I rephrased the thought that was needling me. "I notice you use softer brushes than I am familiar with."

"Not surprising, with your limited experience." He gazed at the smallest brush, from which a thin bundle of hairs sprang from the goose-quill ferrule. "This little beauty is of finest miniver tail. She has caressed the likenesses of two kings, three queens, and I cannot count how many princesses—too many."

Her Majesty's whalebone stays crunched as she raised her arms to stretch. "Is there such thing as an excess of princesses?"

Maestro Mor pointed the forks of his beard at her in a prideful smile. "There is when they demand the impossible. Even I cannot make a mare look like a filly, though I did try my best with Mary of England. H'm, though she was a Queen then, was she not, not a princess."

The Queen looked more lively than she had in days. "Do you mean Mary, my husband's previous wife?"

I curtseyed at the Maestro, feeling my chance for resolving my question slipping away. "*Signore,*" I said quickly, "I have been taught in the Venetian style, which is to paint upon canvas with stiff hog-bristle brushes. In practicing this technique, I have observed"—he frowned in dismissal, so I sped up my words—"that using stiff-bristle brushes on rough canvas results in softer edges than using soft brushes on wood."

"Yes, that is the disadvantage of using stiff brushes on canvas." He stepped back up to the easel. "Your Majesty, forgive me for referring to the King's former wife so disrespectfully."

"*Signore,*" I said, "begging your pardon, but can it not sometimes be an advantage to have soft edges? If most edges in a painting are soft, then if there are a few edges that are harder, would these few not be more noticeable? If one wished to call attention to a certain feature, say the eyes or a gem, a softer brush and finer strokes could be used to harden the edge and thus direct the viewer to that item, as one uses the contrast of dark against light. Otherwise, how does the viewer know where to look in a painting, if every detail has equal importance?"

"Whatever do you mean, girl? Everything upon which the viewer's eye falls should be a delight and a wonder." He nodded at the Queen, tacitly ordering her to resume her pose.

"Did she really have a voice like a man's?" the Queen asked. "Had she a man's beard as well?"

"Your Majesty, to answer your questions, yes and no."

"*Signore,* but how do you get across what is unique about your sitter? What is it you wish to say about"—I lifted my palm to the painting—"our Queen? What is your message?"

He laughed. "Message? That this painting is perfect and beautiful." He moved forward from the easel to take the Queen's hand. "As is My Lady." Her Majesty scratched her nose as maestro Mor kissed the Royal knuckles.

"What you learned is lazy painting," he said to me. "I would expect that of those in the Italian states, pleasure-seekers that they are. What I do is give my patrons an accurate portrayal of their features illuminated in strong light, so that their subjects—and history—may know their face. It has been an agreeable enough method for most of the crowned heads of Europe."

"But their personalities—"

"Stick to drawing pictures with Our Lady the Queen—you are good enough at that, yes?"

Señor Sánchez Coello grimaced in sympathy.

After that, I left the shawm to its squawking and the Maestro to his painting. But maestro Mor made me think about the use of both hard and soft edges in a picture, to control what one wanted to say about the sitter. I would have to work on a painting with this concept firmly in mind, and since I had no other model, I would have to use the only available subject—me.

But even as my spirits lift in the undertaking of a new project, I do notice the Queen's spirits sink deeper. For the day after Don Juan had returned the Queen's pearl, the King had chosen to go hunting with his men instead of joining her at the Shrove Tuesday entertainments. He then rode to Madrid without her, where he had gone into retreat for Lent at the Monastery of San Jerónimo, never leaving her word of his whereabouts. She had to learn them from Doña Juana, who was only too happy to demonstrate her superior relationship to the King. Now, several weeks into his absence, the Queen's countenance grows a little more glum each day, made more so by the letters that pour across the border from France at an ever-increasing rate. Word has reached Paris that the King has found My Lady unsuitable for bedding, and her Most Serene Majesty, Catherine de' Medici, Queen Mother of France, does not plan to tolerate it.

Like Spain, France sits upon a religious powder keg. But unlike the Spanish empire, where war threatens to break out only in its far-flung holdings, the unrest between the Roman Catholics and the Protestant Huguenots seethes within the very heart of France. When alive, King Felipe's father, the Emperor Charles, made it clear to his son that he believed allowing dissenters to hold their services within his realms only spread their discontentment. The Emperor thought it kinder to squelch Protestant dissention before it got started than to fight a full-fledged civil war. Thus the dirty work of the Inquisition that commenced under King Felipe's great-grandparents the Catholic monarchs Isabel and Fernando, to root out Moors and Jews, has now made its chief quarry Protestant heretics. Yet the French Queen Mother Catherine allows both the Inquisition to secretly prosecute Protestants *and* for Protestants to hold their services. The result is murder and mayhem and barely contained war. Thus Queen Catherine counted on her daughter's ability to pleasure the King into helping France should a full-fledged civil war erupt. And to date, My Lady has accomplished very little in this way.

The most recent of the French Queen Mother's missives to My Lady came two days ago. I was in my chambers, a small suite of rooms just below the Queen's on the second floor, boiling down rabbit skins to make glue for sizing the canvas for my self-portrait, when My Lady appeared at my door. The condesa, madame, and Her Majesty's other French and Spanish ladies were in tow.

Francesca dropped the sticks of wood she had been feeding into the fire and sank into a curtsey. "Don't," said the Queen, when I stopped stirring and hastened to join Francesca. "You are busy." She peered over my shoulder at the pot. "Is this part of preparing for a painting?"

"We could smell the stench upstairs." The condesa's voice was muffled by her firmly applied pomander. "Her Majesty insisted upon coming down to see what you were doing."

"I am making glue for sizing a canvas, Your Majesty." I glanced around at the pots scattered about the floor, at the canvas, stretched upon the wood frame and flung upon my bed, and at the stoppered flasks of cooked linseed oil on my toilet table. "I'm afraid it does smell most terrible."

"Most terrible indeed," said the condesa.

"You do right to make it," said the Queen. "I would like to know all the parts of the painting process, even the basest ones. That way I might appreciate a painting more. Go," she told the condesa. She waved at the other ladies. "All of you. You need not endure this stink."

"It is hardly right for a Queen—" the condesa began.

The sizing boiled up, spilling over the sides of the cauldron and into the fire with malodorous effect.

Snapping out a few last admonishments, the condesa left, taking the other ladies with her. When they were gone, Her Majesty peeked into my cookpot, listening to my explanation of what was in the evil brew and why I was cooking it, then sank down upon a bench with a handkerchief to her nose. She bade me to continue as she drew a letter from her bodice. She was poring over it, worrying the Great Pearl on its pendant as she read, as I took back the stirring stick I had given Francesca.

"Almost done, *signorina*," Francesca murmured. She wiped her hands on her apron, which was spotless as usual.

I prodded the skins, immediately splashing some of the milky brew just below my apron onto my skirt. Already my overgown was spotted with food, though each night Francesca, clucking, brushes my clothes as if killing them. Through no fault of hers, both of my overgowns are irreparably stained.

With a loud sigh, the Queen dropped her letter in her lap. "How am I to catch the King's heart when he thinks I am just a child? My mother insists that I make more progress with him. As if I had a shred of control over anything he does!"

I stirred quietly, uncomfortable with being taken into her confidence. I did not need the condesa to tell me it was not appropriate for me to comment on my betters.

The Queen picked up her letter and read on, her young face unhappy. "She says that I must get him to turn away from his lovers. How does she know he has lovers? I do not know that he has lovers. Does he, doña Sofonisba?"

I recalled the warm gaze that bound him to his sister's lady at the running of the bulls. I glanced at Francesca. She had told me she had heard from the other serving women that doña Eufrasia de Guzmán, Princess Juana's chief lady-in-waiting, was the King's lover before his marriage to the Queen, and that their affair still burned bright.

"I see your looks," cried the Queen. "I knew it—he does have a lover! Oh!"

"Is not the King in retreat for Lent, Your Majesty?" I asked cautiously. "In a monastery in Madrid?" I hoped Her Majesty had not heard tales like the ones Francesca told me about the secret improprieties carried on within the monasteries around that city, how men had assignations with women and even nuns in them. The King, it is said, indulges in these forbidden pleasures as much as anybody.

The Queen crossed her arms, the emeralds and rubies on her yellow sleeves rattling against each other. "I am not so easily fooled. Growing up in my father's court, I always knew who ruled my father's heart, and it was not my mother."

Francesca cut me a look.

"I can face the truth, you know," the Queen said. "My mother was wed to my father just as I was married to the King, to seal an alliance—in Mother's case, between the Medici pope Clement and my grandfather François I. She was only fourteen, just like me, though my father was her age, not an old man like my husband."

"Your Majesty," I said, "forgive me for saying so, but His Majesty is hardly old."

She waved her letter in dismissal. "Father was fourteen, and he already had a mistress—Diane de Poitiers. Why would my husband not have one, with all his years to do so?"

"Your Majesty, excuse me, but you do not know this for certain."

"How well I know the signs from my parents' own arrangement. My father's polite treatment of my mother in public and his cold tolerance of her in private—it is happening to me now." She bit her nail, then snatched her hand away from her mouth. "Why won't the King touch me at night? He lies next to me until he thinks I am asleep, then watches me as I pretend to slumber. Am I that wretched?"

I gazed at her heart-shaped face, illuminated by the shining yellow of her satin bodice. She looked so fresh and bright with the bloom of youth, yet so full of heartrending doubt. "Your Majesty," I said, my voice thick with conviction, "you are nothing but beautiful."

A girl's grin warmed her worried countenance. "I am?"

"Yes, Your Majesty. You are indeed."

Her smile fell. "Have you seen that diamond doña Eufrasia

wears? Do you think I do not know what it means when jewels only a king could afford appear on one of the court ladies?"

I kept stirring the pot.

She lifted the Great Pearl from her bodice front. "See this? It is La Peregrina, the pearl they call the Wanderer—the biggest oval pearl in the world. It may be worn only by the Queen of Spain, not that the King's black-haired wench will care. But I care. I know who is Queen. And I hope each time the King sees this, he recalls who his Queen is, too."

I could feel Francesca's dark gaze boring into me. I had told her the story associated with the Pearl and Bloody Mary, and of the King's lack of regard for both.

"This sizing can cook on its own." I laid the stirring stick, still dripping, across the top of the pot. "Your Majesty, would you like to practice sketching? We need to work on hands. I must show you a copy of a drawing the great German maestro Dürer did of hands clasped in prayer."

The Queen shuddered with a sigh. "Not that my mother's being Queen mattered one *soupçon* to my father. Against Mother's wishes, he made his mistress head of the Royal Nursery." She grimly noted my look of surprise. "That is correct—he had his mistress take care of the children he so coldly got upon my mother. Could he have wounded my mother any more deeply?"

"Oh, My Lady."

"And I, without knowing it, served perfectly as an instrument of his torture. For I loved Diane de Poitiers. I admit it—I loved her deeply. I love her still. How can I help it? She was kind to me when no one else was, even though I was but a pale shadow of my cousin Mary Stuart. Madame Diane paid attention to me in spite of my own father's insistence that Mary be put above me, as Mary was to wed my brother when she grew older and become the

Queen of France. To Father, I was nothing, but to madame Diane—she believed in me. It was she who insisted that I learn Latin, Greek, Italian, and Spanish. Oh, I may act silly before the King—he flusters me so!—but because of madame Diane, I know philosophy, literature, mathematics, and history. I suppose I am the only woman for a thousand miles who can quote Ovid: *'Hic ego qui iaceo tenerorum lusor amorum / Ingenio perii, Naso poeta, meo . . .'"*

I picked at the glue on my skirt. "'Here I lie, Naso the poet, playful writer of tender loves, perished by my own talent.' A very doleful self-epitaph, that."

The Queen looked at me in surprise. ". . . or am the only woman who knows which beasts of burden Hannibal took over the Alps in winter to win a surprise victory over Rome . . ."

"Elephants." I smiled. "*Pardon*, Your Majesty, I could not help myself. We were barely off the breast before my papà taught us of Hannibal. He is Papà's ancestor— Papà is inordinately proud of it."

She raised her brows. ". . . or is familiar with all of Boccaccio's tales in *The Decameron* . . ."

"All one hundred of them? Well done, My Lady. In Italian?"

"'*Umana cosa è aver compassione degli afflitti . . .'"*

"'. . . and so compassion is especially demanded of those who have had need of comfort and have found it in others . . .'"

The Queen tucked in her chin and broke into laughter. "Doña Sofonisba, I had no idea! Wouldn't the condesa just burst to hear us spouting our learning like men?"

"I have never understood why women should not."

She clapped her hands in delight. "That is just what madame Diane used to say! You do remind me of her, doña Sofonisba. Greatly. The King was right to give you to me."

I drew in a breath. Well, she was correct, wasn't she? No matter how well trained my brain, I will never be anything more than chattel to be owned—just as, now that I think on it, is she. Be a woman queen, lady, or servant, in this world of men, all women are the same—disposable, should we fall.

My Lady sighed. "You would have loved madame Diane. I wish that you could have met her. She called me her *petite chouchou* and took me on visits to her palace of Chenonceau. We used to float down the river under umbrellas, eating sugared almonds and reading Aesop's fables to each other in Latin."

"I am sorry, Your Majesty—has she left this world?"

She smiled ruefully. "Only Mother's. Mother chased her from court the moment Father was laid to rest. Mother owns Chenonceau now. She keeps her soothsayers there."

She got up slowly. "How my love for madame Diane must have salted my mother's wounds. I used to take madame's side against her, but why wouldn't I? My mother, so squat and harsh compared with the elegant madame, had little time for me, obsessed as she was with gaining my father's attention. So while Mother was scouring the world for soothsayers to portend Diane's downfall, and sorcerers to charm Father into her arms, her own daughter was running to the other woman. How I wished to be Diane, so calm, so beloved. And now here I am—as desperate as my mother."

I gazed at my glue-spattered apron. I wanted to help the Queen in her quest to win the King. But even if I had the slightest notion of how to succeed at love, who was I but a painting instructor, born of minor nobility?

The jewels on her yellow skirt clicked on the bench as she plopped down next to Francesca. "You two shall know the worst of it: I was terrible that first night when the King came to our wedding bed. I didn't know what to do with my hands. They lay at my side like two dead things until he pushed inside me. Then I used them to push him away." She covered her face. "He has left me alone since."

Gingerly, Francesca put her arm around the Queen. "Shhh. Shhh." She glared at me, demanding me to produce words of comfort.

"Show him that you want him," I blurted. "A man cannot resist a woman who wants him."

The Queen raised her head from Francesca's breast. "Do you think?"

The memory of Tiberio, of our night together, rushed into my mind, transporting me to the Maestro's upper room, where the lamplight flickered in air thick with stone dust and desire. Carefully, tenderly, Tiberio was folding back my veil. He brought my mouth to his; our sweet kisses turned to fire. When I thought I should cry out with the agony of containment, he sat me on the edge of the table, where I watched, my lips throbbing from his kiss, as with shaking hands he lifted my skirt, pushed back my petticoats, then groaned, low and lost, at the sight of me.

Now I drew in a shuddering breath. "Let him feel you tremble, My Lady, and feel his trembling, too."

I felt Francesca's questioning gaze upon my face. "*The Decameron*," I said.

"Which tale?" said the Queen. "I remember nothing about trembling."

I would not look at Francesca. "My Lady, is not the shared vulnerability between husband and wife the essence that brings them together? At least—at least that is what I would guess."

The Queen sighed. "Felipe does not seem very vulnerable when he stares down at me in bed."

I stirred the thickening sizing. "Perhaps, then," I said quietly, "we can catch His Majesty's eye with your talent. Let us work some more on drawing hands."

"Oh, what cares a man for talent!"

The Queen lolled back onto Francesca's breast. Francesca smoothed her hair, the murmur of her shushing in peasant Italian blending soothingly with the bubbling glue.

ITEM: *"The Courtier should use his eyes to carry faithfully the message written in his heart, because they often communicate hidden feelings more effectively than anything else, including the tongue and the written word."*

—COUNT BALDASSARE CASTIGLIONE,
The Book of the Courtier

ITEM: *To purify vermilion before mixing it in oil, take the vermilion lump and grind it on the stone, first dry, and then with pure water. Then you must put it on a shell and place it on warm ashes, to evaporate the moisture. When dry, put it in a horn of glass, throw in strong gum water, stir it with a stick, then let it settle. Drain off the water. Repeat all steps three times.*

27 MARCH 1560
El Alcázar, Toledo

Four days have passed since I have last written. I have begun work on my self-portrait. Having prepared my canvas and oils, I am working on a study of my face in ink. I wish to portray myself at the clavichord, for which I have set up a large mirror between the instrument and my easel to look upon myself.

It is not such an easy thing, trying to find oneself in one's reflection. I see two large eyes, pink-lidded from lack of sleep; thick though silky brows; a turned-up nose; stubbornly set lips. If I can beautifully execute the details of these features, Anthonis Mor would say I would have an accurate portrayal. But will that truly be me? Am I not more than just flesh and peaked cartilage and the shining surface of eyes?

Thoughts like these do help turn my thoughts from Tiberio, who has not yet replied though there has been sufficient time for him to have done so. How I wish My Lady had a similar diversion to keep her mind from her failure with the King. When the invitation came for the conde de Benavente's Lenten Feast, I welcomed it, thinking it would do the Queen much good.

Indeed, it cheered me to see Her Majesty at the head table, enjoying herself like the girl of nearly fifteen years that she is. On her right was Don Carlos, hanging on to her every word, and on the left, Don Juan, looking on quietly, as, with a flourish of trumpets, kitchen boys brought forth magnificent dishes designed to circumvent the dietary rules of Lent. The air was rich with the smell of cloves and cooked fruit and toasting almonds as boy after liveried boy ushered forth with glorious dishes of confections, fruits, and fish—with not a speck of meat in any of them—until at last, four boys struggled in under a platter the size of a door. Upon this platter, on a bed of winter greens, lay a trout the size of a suckling pig. How the Queen clapped as it was placed before her, wafting its succulent aroma of fish fried with lemon, olive oil, and sea salt. Her approbation was exceeded only by that of Don Carlos, who roared like a bear cub when he turned from gazing upon the Queen and saw the magnificent fish.

It was touching to see how My Lady pampered the King's son, the poor awkward thing, crooning at him to get him to eat, teasing him when he burped, giving him the attention he has not received, I do guess, from a lady his whole young life, as his mother died when he was born. He sat up proud as a cock when she dabbed his mouth with her napkin.

"What about me?" said Don Alessandro, on the other side of Don Carlos. He pointed to the corner of his own mouth. "Do I not need a little tidying up?"

"None that I can afford you, *monsieur*," said the Queen.

"Am I that filthy?" said Don Alessandro. "What about my uncle?" He nodded toward Don Juan.

The Queen turned to look at Don Juan, whom she had been scrupulously ignoring though he was sitting next to her. She turned back around. "I know not where to begin."

"See, Uncle," said Don Alessandro. "Our Lady finds fault with you. Did they not teach you to wash in the mountains?"

"Quite well." Don Juan dabbed his mouth with his napkin. My table, adjacent to theirs, was not so far that I could not help noticing the V of downy golden beard trailing from below his lip into the dimple of his chin. "The sheep and I were bathed in the spring whether we needed it or not."

"And I thought the smell at table was of the fish," said the Queen.

"Oho!" said Don Alessandro. "She stung you there!"

Don Juan grinned. The Queen tucked in her chin with her winsome manner. "Where in the country did you grow up?" she asked shyly.

"Born in a stable," said Don Carlos, taking a draught, "no doubt."

"Just like Our Lord Jesus Christ," said Don Alessandro.

"Hardly," said Don Juan. "I spent my first years in the countryside near Toledo, My Lady, then outside Valladolid, and later in the Sierra de Gredos, in a village so small you could spit from one end to the other."

"Which you probably did," said Don Alessandro.

"You cannot tell me," said Don Carlos, "that in all that time you had no idea my grandfather the Emperor was your true father."

Don Juan shook his head. "I did not. I thought my parents were dead. I was just a typical country boy, raised by a foster mother."

"Who wouldn't tell him the name of his father," said Don Carlos, his mouth full. "Isn't that what you said, Don Juan?"

Don Juan shrugged.

Don Alessandro laughed. "Unknown father, born in a manger—you really *were* the Christ Child."

Don Juan scratched at his neck with one finger. "Don Alessandro, I think that lady over there does look at you."

Don Alessandro peered at my table. I blushed to think they had caught me staring, then saw he was looking at a French lady younger than myself, seated a few persons away. *Buffone!* Of course they would never notice me. To them I am a woman past Youth's first blush, dressed in odd and spotty Italian clothes. I have not been able to swallow my pride to ask My Lady for new ones, though as the King's ward I am entitled to them.

When I glanced back at the head table to see if they were still admiring the lady, Don Juan was looking into the eyes of the Queen. She turned away quickly.

"Must I feed you dessert, too, Brother?" she said to Don Carlos.

The Prince opened his mouth wide.

The Queen laughed stoutly. "Look at you with your mouth open—you look like a little toad! That is what I shall call you— my Toad. Shall I put in a fly, Toady?"

"Yes." He grinned. "Do."

That was yesterday. Today Don Carlos brought the Queen a ruby the size of a cherry. He said it was his mother's. When Her Majesty said Don Carlos should save it for his bride, he said nothing, just turned and stalked away.

It is good only a short time remains of Lent and the King will then leave his retreat at the monastery to resume his relations with the Queen. For surely the Prince does grow to love the Queen too much.

ITEM: *The Seven Deadly Sins and the colors associated with them in painting:*

Pride—*Violet*
Envy—*Green*
Anger—*Red*
Sloth—*Light Blue*
Greed—*Yellow*
Gluttony—*Orange*
Lust—*Blue*

21 MAY 1560
The Palace, Aranjuez

A war rages between Her Majesty's French ladies and her Spanish, although the Spanish ladies have won a partial victory by getting the King to send most of the French ladies back home. The remainder of the French ladies never did get the clothes that had been sent ahead when they had first traveled over the Pyrenees to Spain. Francesca tells me the maid of one of the Spanish ladies brags that some trunks with French labels on them can be found in a stable in Cáceres, at the family seat of her mistress.

But hardened by battle, the surviving French ladies do fight back. They scramble for the seats closest to My Lady at bull runs and fiestas. New trunks from Paris have arrived, from which they introduce décolleté gowns in rose and emerald and tangerine that make the Spanish ladies, with their penchant for stiff, black, high-collared garb, look like fusty old nuns. The French ladies choose the richest of the Spanish men for their affairs of the heart, and win them handily. Although dressed in the most exquisite French gowns of all, the Queen seems scarcely aware of the *petit* dramas around her. She has troubles of her own. As do I.

Today we celebrated the King's birthday, his thirty-third. Last week, he had decided he would like to mark this day by having a family picnic at Aranjuez, his country estate a day's ride east of Toledo. Those of us who attend the Queen were crowded into coaches, farthingale crushing farthingale, the French refusing to speak to the Spanish and the Spanish to the French. Each faction gossips amongst itself, excluding me, an Italian and of lower rank than any of them, excepting their maids. We trundled through the dun-colored hills with the household servants, the kitchen servants, the tapestry makers, the embroideresses, the jewelers, the doctors, the musicians, the stable boys, and all the rest of the twelve hundred essential household attendants rattling in the wagons behind us. As I gazed out the leather-curtained windows at the ranks of twisted gray olive trees rolling by, I could not help remembering my first trip to see the Queen, when she had gone to meet the King. Although it was not five months ago, how much younger she had looked then, so lively, a little girl ready to play the Queen.

Now, just turned fifteen, she has already begun to change. Her beauty has grown even in this short period of time, with her face ripening and her cheekbones gaining more prominence. She still plucks her brows and hairline in the French manner, though her face would be pretty without it, as it would be without the thin coating of lead-white powder that her mother insists that she wear. Yet in spite of her growing beauty, she acts less sure of

herself, with no small part of her unhappiness caused by a certain
lady riding two coaches behind us, in the suite of the King's sister
Doña Juana.

For the Queen knows beyond certainty now of the King's affair with doña Eufrasia. The condesa de Urueña finally informed
her with great relish disguised as sympathy, though publicly no
one acknowledges it, especially the King. He visits Her Majesty's
chamber after lunch each day, to ask after her health. He sends
small gifts of fruit and flowers, perhaps a length of lustrous blue
cloth, a new prayer book. But he has stopped even making the
appearance of visiting their marital bed in the evening, though
she waits each night behind the crimson brocade bed-hangings,
dressed in a gossamer shift, while I toss and stir in my own bed,
hating myself for opening my person to Tiberio's scorn by writing
him back. It has been nearly five months since I have written, and
he still has not replied.

What a beautiful afternoon in May it was today, with the birds
singing in the woods and the sun sparkling through the spring-
green leaves, as a band of musicians strummed their guitars on
the banks of the river. A breeze, scented with the milky green
water of the Tajo and the fresh-scythed grass of the lawn, ruffled
the lace at our cuffs and the feathers on the hats of the gentlemen.

"Sit with me," the King said to My Lady, who was hesitating
near the blanket on which he reclined. Her page rushed forth with
a pillow. Upon helping her to settle, the lad seated the condesa de
Urueña and madame de Clermont next to her, as was their due.

The Queen's voice was high with nervousness. "Doña Sofonisba, please, sit with us, too."

Under the scowling gaze of the condesa de Urueña, I found a
corner of the blanket as Francesca retreated to stand in the shade
at the edge of the woods with the other servants.

Pages sallied forth with baskets piled with hams, strawberries, and asparagus. I was enjoying the smell of the cut grass and the river and the music of the guitars when the King asked the Queen, "So how go your drawing lessons, My Lady?"

The Queen pulled her attention from the King's sister's blanket, upon which doña Eufrasia had alighted and was neatly arranging her skirts. The Queen looked down upon the front of her own green velvet bodice, which had been slashed in vertical strips across her bosom, with puffs of yellow satin pulled through to give the illusion of curves where she has none. She wears a new gown every day, always cut cleverly to enhance her slim figure as only her French dressmaker can do.

"They go well, My Lord."

"Indeed?" He leaned out to look at me.

"Yes, Your Majesty." I dashed my gaze to the blanket, though I could see him take a strawberry from a basket and offer it to the Queen.

He watched her as she took it wordlessly. Since the afternoon she had come when I had been making glue, the Queen has come most days to my chambers or I to hers, to work on her drawing technique. Why did she not tell him how she has learned how to shade, taking into account the distance the object is from the viewer and the source of light when deciding upon the depth of the shadow? She has watched me enlarge my drawing for my self-portrait with the use of a grid to create a cartoon. She has seen how I then placed a transparent paper over the cartoon to prick the holes of an outline, and how when this in turn was placed over the canvas and chalk blown over the pinpricks, an outline was left. Why does she not explain this to him? The King is interested in painting. She might impress him in this way.

"Will she be painting soon?" the King asked me.

"Your Majesty, yes. She is a natural." I did not add that My Lady had applied her lessons in chalks on a drawing of the woods of her husband's beloved Aranjuez. It was to be a surprise birthday present, and was not a bad piece for someone with her limited experience.

"Good," he said. He held out a plate of strawberries to the condesa, madame de Clermont, and me.

The Queen put down her strawberry and looked up determinedly. "I have examined the tabletop painting in the palace in Madrid by the artist El Bosco, My Lord. The one of which you had spoken, with the two dogs fighting over a bone."

After we ladies had chosen a fruit, the King took a strawberry for himself. "*The Seven Deadly Sins*—you remembered."

"Yes, My Lord. But actually, there are three bones in the painting, not one—two on the ground and the man holds one. Yet is the saying not 'two dogs fighting over one bone'?"

The condesa, who had been quietly sniffing her strawberry, spoke up. "If I may explain, My Lady. Although the dogs already have a large bone each, they still crave the bone held by their master. Their sin is in having all they need yet desiring what someone else might get. Is that not what the artist intends, Your Majesty?"

"Yes. I believe that is the crux of envy." He inclined his head toward the Queen. "I commend your interest in art."

"Learning to draw has helped my understanding, My Lord."

The King closed his mouth over a berry, then pulled away the naked green stem. "I had thought," he said to the Queen, swallowing down the remains of the fruit, "to install a small grove of mulberry trees near the palace here. I thought it might give you something to do, My Lady, in tending the silkworms. My mother had such a grove in Valladolid when I was a boy."

"Worms," the Queen murmured. "Thank you, My Lord."

"One of my earliest memories of my mother is of her tending her garden."

"That is where you must have gotten your love for growing things," said the condesa. She smiled proudly at his nod.

The Queen's gaze drifted over to doña Eufrasia, who was taking a plate of strawberries from a page. Under the pale blue gauze of her veil, doña Eufrasia's long black hair lay like a glossy sheet upon her narrow back.

I spoke up, startling even myself. "Your Majesty, your love for nature is apparent. You have made Aranjuez a beautiful place." I glanced down quickly at my edge of blanket, heat coming to my scalp.

"I have put in two thousand and forty trees this year," said the King, "from France and from the Low Countries—from the New World, as well." He granted me a slight smile when I looked up.

"Which of the trees are from your far western lands, Your Majesty?" I asked. My Lady still gazed at doña Eufrasia. Why would she not look away and join the conversation?

The King nodded to one of the alleys of saplings leading from the meadow. "Elms. I am told by doctor Hernández that the New World elms will grow to great height, much greater than the ones from France. How beautiful that part of my woods will be when they have grown."

"Will it be many years, Your Majesty?" I asked. "Before they are tall, I mean?"

"Yes, but I am a patient man. Time and I can take on any two others."

"That is your motto, Your Majesty," said the condesa. She sniffed happily when he agreed.

"The elms will be tall when our sons are grown," said the Queen.

The King looked at her in surprise. "Yes," he said. "Indeed they will."

The condesa took a smug whiff upon her purple-enameled pomander, punctuating the thought that circulated unspoken amongst us: It is difficult to get a son without the benefit of monthly courses, let alone to do so without lovemaking.

Checked by our thoughts, our group ate quietly as others chatted on their surrounding blankets—or laughed loudly, as in the case of Don Carlos, dining nearby with Don Juan and Don Alessandro. Though the tender slivers of *ibérico* ham melted on my tongue, I could not savor them in a silence that diminished the Queen. With Francesca firmly cordoned in the woods, I drank more wine to embolden myself.

"Your Majesty," I said after a long draught, "I have heard that doctor Hernández has much knowledge about the plants of the New World. He says the plants are different there from ours, and hold great medicinal powers."

The King took a bit of bread. "He wishes for me to send him on an expedition there. But I cannot spare him, not with . . . things being as they are."

I glanced at the neighboring blanket, upon which Don Carlos and his *caballeros* sat stuffing their mouths with ham and bread, then washing it down with wine. Only last week Don Carlos had been abed again with the fever that racked him more often than not. And though she appears to be much more robust than the Prince, the Queen has endured her share of fevers and rashes, too. As physician to the Royal Family, doctor Hernández was indeed kept busy at court.

"You are quiet," the King said to the Queen.

"I apologize, My Lord."

He gave a short nod, then crossed and recrossed his arms. "It is no use," he burst out. "I am no good at holding a secret."

The Queen stiffened. The fine black wool of the condesa's habit swished, as did madame de Clermont's veils when the ladies turned abruptly.

The King pulled a folded sheaf of papers from his doublet and handed it to the Queen. She took it, then with an audible swallow laid open the sheaf.

She looked at it, blinking.

"Read it aloud," he said.

She squinted at him before beginning to read. "'On the Diversity of Animals. Our Lord'"—she cleared her throat—"'Our Lord, in his infinite wisdom, has created for us a wondrous variety of animals—'" She broke off. "You wrote about animals?"

"For you, My Lady," said the King, "and for my God. During my retreat, I have been cataloguing the varieties of creatures as I know them. I thought you might have an interest . . . with your love of animals."

Her hand flew to her Pearl. "I thought you were going to send me—I—" She laughed out loud. "Oh, Your Majesty, it is only about animals?"

His expression cooled.

"No! What I mean is, I did not expect—I—oh, My Lord, thank you so much." She clasped the papers to her breast. "I shall cherish it."

But the damage had been done. "Put the papers aside," he said.

Red-faced, she tucked the treatise next to her skirt.

The King peered into the woods. "I see my new gardener from Ghent. Excuse me."

"Of course." The Queen smiled meekly while he strode across the lawn. A hush fell over the picnickers as all eyes shuttled between Her Majesty and doña Eufrasia, watching to see if the King would acknowledge his lover when he passed and how the Queen would react if he did.

"How thoughtful of the King to write a treatise on animals for you," I said loudly. Heads turned.

The Queen drew in a shuddering breath. "Yes."

But only when the King had gained the woods and had begun to speak with a man leaning upon a shovel amongst the trees did the buzz of speech resume.

An olive landed on the blanket near His Majesty's treatise.

With a sad countenance, the Queen looked over her shoulder.

Don Carlos's pasty face lit up with a grin. He raised his goblet, a vessel the size of his head. "Did you get my present?" he called.

All diners paused on their blankets to listen.

"This?" The Queen flicked the olive. It hit the condesa de Urueña on the arm.

"*Excusez-moi, madame!*" the Queen cried as the condesa brushed at her sleeve.

The condesa returned her pomander to her nose and took an extra-deep draught to recover from her injury.

"Thank you very much," the Queen mouthed to Don Carlos.

Don Carlos shook his head, setting a-flutter the orange-dyed plume on his hat that dwarfed his delicate face. "Not that," he shouted from his blanket. He shoved his goblet into the hands of his page, then scrambled over to the Queen as we courtiers pretended not to watch. "I mean the emerald that I sent."

The Queen shaded her eyes to look up at him. "I received it."

"And did you like it?"

"Yes, very much. But Toad, you really should not have sent it. It is too much for me."

"Nothing is too much for you, My Lady."

"Should you not have sent it to Anne of Austria?"

"I am not betrothed to her yet, nor to anyone, for that matter. I do not know why they bother. There is no one I wish to marry."

"Not even my sister? My mother wishes you would marry her, and I can assure you that she is quite sweet—sweeter than I."

Don Carlos grabbed her hand, startling her. "No one is sweeter than you, Doña Elisabeth."

"Your Majesty!" the condesa de Urueña hissed. "People do watch."

"Let them!" Don Carlos cried. "Doña Elisabeth, if I had known how—how kind you are, I would have done everything in my power to—"

"Would you like an olive?" Don Juan thrust a plate before Don Carlos.

Don Carlos looked up angrily. "I was talking here!"

"Maybe you are thirsty, Your Majesty." Don Juan shook the wineskin he carried.

Don Carlos pushed away the wine. "Do not toy with me, Juan."

The wind lifted a page of the King's treatise. The Queen clamped it to the blanket as Don Alessandro sauntered up.

He nudged Don Juan with the toe of his boot. "Look at you, Uncle, bothering the ladies. Do you country folk not know how to hold your wine?"

"Only in our bellies." Don Juan nodded in apology to the condesa, who looked away with a scowl.

Don Alessandro took the wineskin from him and squirted himself a draught, spilling two drops onto the red flowers embroidered on his black silk doublet. "Do you know that Uncle Juan talks to animals, My Lady?" He wiped his mouth. "You should see him carrying on a one-sided conversation with his hound. I think he expects it to speak."

"Your hound does not?" said Don Juan.

"You both mock me with your talk," Don Carlos said, though with less heat now. "Your Majesty, you have not told me—will you wear the emerald?"

"Of course I will." She drew his hand to her lips and kissed it. "And will think of my own good brother."

"No," he said, "I beg of you, wear it instead of that pearl. It hurts me to see that thing upon you."

The Queen took up the great pear-shaped bauble hanging as usual from her neck. "My pearl from the King?"

Don Juan took Don Carlos's arm. "I think I hear our hounds barking. Let us go have a word with them."

Don Carlos shrugged free. "My Lady, don't you know that pearl is a jest? It is a castoff from ugly old Bloody Mary—it means nothing to Father. It is just a signal of his wealth, nothing more. He doesn't even like it. You might as well wear a bag of gold around your neck."

The Queen gazed down at the gem.

"Wear my emerald." Don Carlos's thin voice broke. "Please, My Lady. It would make me so happy."

"Your Highness," hissed the condesa, "what are you thinking? Saying such things to the King's own wife."

"Shhh!" Madame de Clermont flashed her eyes toward the woods, where the King was just then leaving its leafy shelter. His cheerful look cooled when he saw the *caballeros* gathered around the Queen, and the guilty gazes of the courtiers on the nearby blankets.

"*Feliz cumpleaños*, Your Majesty!" Don Alessandro called.

"What is going on here?" The King stood over the Queen.

My Lady tucked in her chin as she gazed up at him. "Did the gardener please you, My Lord?" she asked, timidly.

"Well enough."

Don Alessandro stepped in front of Don Carlos, who was either too smitten or too foolish to wipe the love-struck look from his pale face. "Uncle Juan was just convincing us of his ability to chat with dogs, My Lord."

The King turned to his brother. "Oh, can you now?"

"I am sorry, Your Majesty," said Don Juan. "Don Alessandro exaggerates greatly."

"He *can* speak to them," said Don Carlos. "Or communicates with them somehow. Dogs go mad for him."

The King smiled with disdain. "So your calling is in the kennel, Brother. Father would be so pleased."

Don Juan's own smile faded into a wary stare.

Don Carlos started when Don Alessandro flung his arm around him. "Come, my illustrious Prince, let's go riding. Coming, Uncle Juan? Many happy wishes on your birthday, Your Majesty."

Don Carlos let himself be led away as Don Juan bowed rigidly to the King. "Enjoy your birthday, my brother." He lifted the Queen's hand, then kissed it. "*Señora.*"

She cradled her hand in her lap as he crossed the lawn to join his compatriots.

The wind snatched the King's treatise from the edge of the Queen's skirt and blew it across the lawn. Several gentlemen jumped to retrieve it.

"Let it go," the King ordered.

The papers tumbled across the grass, then down the banks and into the river. One by one they sailed off, a paper flotilla, upon the milky water.

Later that night, the Queen lay in her bed, waiting for the King. The hour was late, past compline. The moon had long drifted to its post at the top of the heavens; frogs screamed from their hiding spots along the river. The Queen had banished everyone from her chamber but me, to the condesa's consternation, and though I knew that Francesca had readied my own bed in our chamber nearby, sprinkling it with lavender for its soothing smell and rue to kill the fleas, it would have to wait. The Queen had need of me.

"I think the King liked it when I gave him my drawing of Aranjuez tonight," she said.

"It was a very good drawing." I turned from the window at which I had stood watching the full moon spread its thin silver path over the river. My Lady lay with her covers up to her chin. I thought of Europa when she was younger, requesting a bedtime story.

"I think it made up for my blunder of not praising his treatise of animals, don't you?"

I turned back to the window, then closed my eyes. "Surely."

Unbidden, the image of Tiberio overtook my mind. I could hear the Maestro's footsteps recede down the arcade as Tiberio covered his eyes with the crook of his arm. Seeing my stricken face, he reached out and hooked me toward him. He kissed my forehead. "Don't worry."

I felt sick. "I am so ashamed."

"Don't be."

"But the Maestro——"

"The Maestro has a few secrets of his own." When he saw that I was not comforted, he touched my cheek. "My love, we've done nothing wrong. Not compared with what the Maestro has done, at least not from what I have heard."

"Sofi?" The Queen's soft girl's voice brought me back to the present.

I opened my eyes.

"Why did you not tell me about the Great Pearl?"

I turned around quickly.

But there was wonder on the Queen's face, not anger. "I just made sense of something," she said. "It used to wound me how my mother let my father wear Diane's colors to his ceremonies. She allowed Diane's initials to be carved with his on the cathedrals and palaces he had built. She even publicly praised the poems he wrote for Diane. How this made me hate my mother! I thought she was a fool, letting Father scorn her. I was furious with her when she let him fly Diane's black and white at the tournament at which he died, bringing Mother's own private shame to my wedding celebration. It was Diane's black and white scarf that they tore from Father's helmet to give him air."

"My Lady——"

"But I understand now. I understand why she allowed this. It is far better to know and bear the truth than to look the hoodwinked fool."

I nodded. I knew how it felt to be played the fool. I had never meant to hurt My Lady.

"If there should ever be something I should know, will you promise you won't spare me? Please don't look like that—it is what I want. Will you promise me? Please, Sofi? There is no one else I can count on here."

"If it is truly what you desire . . ."

"It is, truly."

"Then I promise."

She studied me until satisfied of my word. Then, with a sigh, she gathered her covers closer. "He did not even look at that woman at the picnic today. Did you notice?"

"No, he didn't, did he?"

"Once he tires of her for good, I will not tolerate her at court, whether she is part of Doña Juana's household or not. Whore."

Some could call me that, giving myself so freely to Tiberio. But it had seemed so right. I had seen his true spirit trembling and he had seen mine. "No, My Lady."

"My mother did not suffer fallen ladies in her court. When she found that mademoiselle de Rohan had lost her maidenhead to one of Father's men, she dragged the slut from her lover's arms and marched her before Father and the Cardinal of Lorraine. Though I was just a little girl, I shall never forget the sound of mademoiselle de Rohan's sobs echoing down the halls when she was sent packing."

I forced a smile of agreement. "What did she expect when she broke the laws of God and man?"

"I cannot wait until I can banish doña Eufrasia." She settled her head into her pillow and folded her hands over her neck. "I think he will come to me tonight."

I turned my burning face to the window. A movement in the garden to the left caught my eye. A fox in His Majesty's roses?

"Don't you think he will come, Sofi?"

I swallowed. "I hope so, Your Majesty."

A deer broke from the cover and with tentative steps, leaned to nibble a rose overhanging from a bower. The animal, its glossy hide silvered by the moon, ate its fill, twitching its great soft ears.

I could hear the rustle of the covers behind me as the Queen stirred beneath them. "Doña Sofi, I have been meaning to ask: Could a person get with child before she first bled? Could she be ripe without her knowing it?"

"I don't know. Perhaps."

Below, the deer raised its head and, ears pricked, stilled its jaw. With a flick of its tail, it turned and sprang deeper into the garden as two shadowy figures emerged from the other side of the palace, a man and a woman, walking along the river. I peered closer just as the man looked up. I jerked back, but not before I saw his long chin jutting over his ruff.

I turned back to the Queen, humming as she picked at a swirl in the red brocade on her covers. For once her high forehead was unlined with worry; the corners of her mouth turned up with the impishness that had marked her when she first came to court.

She smiled when she saw me looking. "What is it?"

Should the truth always be told, even when it damages one's hope or one's reputation? Are there not circumstances in which it should be withheld? What kind of Hell would we live in if we all revealed our secrets?

"Nothing, My Lady."

Dearest Daughter,

Good news! A writer from Florence named Giorgio Vasari has come to our home, looking for you. It seems messer Vasari is working on a second edition of a book he has written on the lives of the Great Painters. His first edition includes Leonardo, Botticelli, Raffaello, Michelangelo, and other well-known maestros, but he wishes to expand the book to include more painters who have made their unique contributions to art. He would like to speak with YOU, having heard your praises sung in the courts of Mantua and Milan and in Rome. I explained to him that you were serving Her Sacred Majesty, Elisabeth, Queen of Spain, which seemed to interest him much. I then showed him your painting of Lucia and Minerva playing chess, for which he had much admiration, and the portrait you had done of Asdrubale, Europa, and me before you left. He asked about your visit to messer Michelangelo four years ago, telling me how singular it was for Michelangelo to invite anyone to study with him, let alone a woman (apparently he knows Michelangelo well), and I corrected him, telling him there were actually two visits, the most recent one just last year. I told him he should ask messer Michelangelo himself about it, to which messer Vasari said indeed he would, as he was on his way to Rome before returning to his home in Florence. Is that not excellent news? I gave him the miniature self-portrait you had done, the one with the curious emblem you devised, so he would have a token of you while he wrote his book. I hope you do not mind.

All are well here. I must finish this quickly, as we are in the midst of printing a book about the animals of the New World. Know that every one of us thinks of you each day.

> *From Cremona,*
> *this 2nd of September, 1560*

> *With all my love,*
> *Your Father*

ITEM: *A recipe overheard during a gathering of ladies: To simulate virginity, on the morning of the wedding day apply a large leech to the maidenhead. The leeches' sucking will raise blisters of blood, which will burst upon the bridegroom's gallant doings on the wedding night, giving ample evidence of the bride's maidenhood.*

But what becomes of the leech?

ITEM: *Before the first line is drawn for a picture, you must look past the subject to the spirit of the pose.*

27 SEPTEMBER 1560
El Alcázar, Toledo

Papà, Papà, you know not what a Pandora's box you opened, sending this Vasari fellow to Michelangelo. Sweetest Holy Mary, what would Michelangelo say if anyone should ask about me? That for a virgin, I certainly like to rut? And for Papà to give this writer the miniature—what if Tiberio sees it and our emblem that I have painted on it? Architect, Portraitist, Lady, and King, indeed. He will know that I have doted on him overmuch.

I must not think about this. I must think about something else—something—anything—the storks flying outside my window. Look at them, five, flying low in the evening sky, their white bellies lit orange by the last of the setting sun. They are leaving in flocks for Africa. Fall is on its way, marked by the leathery orbs swelling on the pomegranate trees in the courtyard below. A cat with a kink in its tail slinks under withered grapevines plucked clean by beak and human hand. The cat, being black, had its tail broken as a kitten to remove the Devil's claim upon it—someone believes in witchcraft. Many do, including the Queen's mother in France. She sends My Lady a new amulet by post each week, thinking to conjure a child into my little Queen's womb if she cannot pray one in. In this past month alone, she has sent My Lady the finger of a fetus born two months before its time, the blood of a hare mixed with sheep urine, and the left hind paw of a weasel, soaked in vinegar. Just last week she sent My Lady a girdle made of goat's hair and soaked in the milk of a she-donkey—an itchy, smelly affair. My Lady wore it two days before demanding it be burnt. But whatever the potency of these charms, none of them will work if the Queen does not persuade the King to approach her. Still he comes not to her bed.

Each night the Queen's ladies tuck her in bed, dressed in her pretty shift and shriveling amulets. Each morning we find her in her bed, shift and amulets undisturbed, her mouth turned down. I fear her mouth will grow that way, spoiling the beauty she was meant to have. I try to cajole her into good spirits as I dress her by singing the silly songs I taught my little sisters or by telling her humorous stories, such as the one I told her yesterday at her toilet, about how I had come across the King sitting in a chair on a landing of stairs in the palace here. Surprised to find His Majesty in such an odd place, I had fallen into a curtsey and was waiting for him to release me, when a passing servant advised me, chuckling, that the "King" was merely a mannequin dressed in His Majesty's clothes and topped with a false head. The mannequin is for use when the King is too busy to oversee the countless ceremonial processions that parade under his balcony.

"Even the curls upon the King's head," I said, "had been faithfully cast in silver and painted by the sculptor Leone Leoni—all in all a most convincing reproduction." I thought surely the Queen would laugh.

But the Queen just held up her face so I could wash it as the condesa de Urueña stood back with My Lady's shift. "I told him that I welcomed him."

"Leone Leoni, Your Majesty?" I asked.

"The King," she said.

"Oh." Had she heard a word I said? I scrubbed her cheek. "Perhaps he wants to be certain none of your ladies are about. You know how he has taken an aversion to us."

My Lady glanced at the condesa, who had turned away to scold one of the French ladies. "Not you, Sofi. It is the squabbling between the others he doesn't like. But everyone left early last night, before the nightjars had begun to call. You know that." She turned her head as I washed each ear—dear little shells that stuck out slightly like a country boy's.

I lifted her heavy hair from her neck, revealing the thin red string knotted at the top of her spine. From it hung a walnut-sized amulet.

She followed my gaze. "Dried bullfrog. Mother says it will bring me a male child."

I could not meet her eyes. There could be no child, male or female, without coupling.

"I tried again to do as you said once," she whispered. "I trembled as he looked down upon me."

"Did it . . . work?"

"He asked me if I was chilled. I felt so foolish, I said yes, so he covered me up to my chin and left. What *did* you mean by that, Sofi? Let him see you tremble. I don't understand."

"Boccaccio," I murmured. Who was I to give her advice? For though I may know Leonardo da Vinci's theory on the Proportions of Man or how long to cook linseed oil before mixing it with pigment or the names of the constellations in the heavens, it is apparent I know nothing of men. I had thought Tiberio loved me. Like the greenest young milkmaid seduced by a cowherd, I had mistaken his lust for love. Now, if I am exposed by Michelangelo, it is too late for me to claim that Tiberio seduced me—a true victim would have cried foul sooner. I would look like a whore trying to put a good face on things. Still, I am glad that I had not tried to force myself upon him since then. Because you cannot make someone love you.

Witness the Queen. She who can have anything that can be bought in this world—jewels, palaces, painting instructors—cannot have her man. The King's recalcitrance takes its toll on her. When he is not around, she is quiet and wan, or, when in the presence of doña Eufrasia, cold and hurt. When the King is present, she laughs extra loud at the antics of his favorite female dwarf, Magdalena Ruiz. Magdalena merely has to steal the condesa's wine or to fall, sputtering, on her rounded bottom and the Queen shrieks with laughter, a move that assuredly does not impress our austere King. If we are with Doña Juana, My Lady speaks extra loudly, trying, like a child, to get him to look at her and not at doña Eufrasia. There is only one circumstance in which Her Majesty's true vivacious and sweet nature still shows itself—when she receives Don Carlos and his *caballeros*.

Yesterday afternoon Don Carlos had stormed into the Queen's

chambers, where she and her dozen or so ladies were working on their embroidery. He threw himself on some pillows near her feet.

"He says I cannot go to the Netherlands!" he exclaimed.

Don Alessandro strayed in, his lightly freckled face crooked in its characteristic playful smirk. "Don Carlos offered his services to rule there," he explained as he kissed the Queen's hand. "The King turned him down."

"And he wonders why the people there are in revolt!" Don Carlos cried from his pillows. "They want a true ruler governing them, not some woman who is not even Queen—sorry, Don Alessandro. I know your mother does the best that she can as the regent there."

Don Alessandro leaned against a wall. "No offense taken. I am deeply honored by every bone your father throws my family's way."

Don Carlos cocked his head as if deciding whether there was mockery in his cousin's voice, then went on. "The Dutch need a Prince who will love them and respect them, and will let them have their religion. I do not care if they are Protestant—not if they would love me back."

From her pillow at her embroidery frame, the condesa began, "One's subjects are not always the best judge of what is good for—"

"Of course they would love you, Toad," said the Queen, breaking in. "You would rule with your heart." My Lady, who had been crying over the death the previous day of the spaniel she had brought with her from France, wiped her eyes and pulled her needle through the linen stretched on a frame before her. It was to be a covering for a kneeler in the convent of the Descalzas Reales, where the King's sister Doña Juana lives when in Madrid.

I could not help wondering if the Queen took some pleasure in stabbing her needle into the cloth on which doña Eufrasia might someday kneel.

Don Carlos rolled onto his back and rearranged the pillows to gaze up at her. "I would let the Dutch keep the profits they made from working their land."

"That would be just like you," she said. "So kind and so good."

Madame de Clermont murmured in agreement.

He warmed to their encouragement. "And I would provide alms to the needy among them."

"I know you would, Toad."

"And I would—"

"—guarantee a hen in every Dutch peasant's stewing pot?" Don Alessandro grinned from his position against the wall. "I will tell my mother to try that."

One of the French ladies laughed.

Don Carlos's rapturous smile twisted into a frown. "This is nothing to laugh about."

The French lady lowered her head. The Queen started to soothe him, but her words were cut off by the twelve-o'clock bells clanging from their tower above the Cathedral. As we waited for their incessant tolling to finish, I thought of the King's motto: "Time and I can take on any two others." Only the most powerful man in the world would dare claim Time as his personal ally. Most humans are mercifully unconscious of Time slipping through their fingers at every moment—certainly not conscious of it often enough to think of yoking it to their own purpose. For others of us, Time is a torture, spinning itself out in maddening fits and starts while we wait for our true lives to begin.

"Doña Sofonisba," Don Alessandro said when the bells had stilled, "I like the picture you did of yourself." He nodded to the

canvas brought from my chamber and hung on the Queen's wall
at her request.

All heads turned to where I sat at my customary place by the
window, sketching the Queen, then to the portrait. I could feel
my cheeks color. Although in response to maestro Mor's painting
I had carefully considered when to use hard edges, employing
them only on my eyes to give them what I hoped would be a look
of intelligence, the portrait had not been a success, at least not to
me. It lacked the vitality I had envisioned as I worked, resulting
in little more life to it than maestro Mor's soulless portrait of the
Queen. For all my good intentions, I had not been able to find the
spirit behind my own face.

"When are you going to paint me?" asked Don Alessandro.

"Thank you for your interest, Your Highness, but maestro
Mor is the court painter."

"Not any longer." He laughed. "Mor is no more."

I said I did not understand.

"You had not heard?" he said. "Señor Mor left very suddenly
the night before last, without a single good-bye. The details are
not yet clear, but it seems Mor made the mistake of bragging to
Doña Juana about all the heads of state he has painted when she
was sitting for a portrait. When Doña Juana asked him to list
these personages, among them were several German princes
known to be sympathetic to Luther. Doña Juana then inquired—
quite nicely, she told me—about the books maestro Mor has read.
She had heard there might be Protestant books circulating behind
closed doors at court, not that he would know of them, of course.
He was gone the next day, the unfinished painting of Doña Juana
still on his easel. Word has it that he is on a ship to England."

"If Sofonisba's painting pictures now," Don Carlos said from
the pillows at the Queen's feet, "she had better paint me first!"

I was too stunned by how quickly Mor had been ousted to respond. No matter. The condesa was only too pleased to speak for me. "Doña Sofonisba is here to give instruction to the Queen. Not to paint sundry portraits."

Don Carlos sat up, puffing out his sunken chest. "Mind whom you speak to, woman. I am the heir to the Spanish Empire."

The condesa took up her pomander in consternation.

"Don't worry, Toad," the Queen said mildly, "I would make an exception for you."

"You would?"

"Please excuse me, My Lady," said the condesa, "but you said if doña Sofonisba were to paint portraits, they should be of you alone."

"I made that rule," said the Queen, "I can break it. Sofi, would you mind?"

"Of course not." I straightened my pile of paper, panicking at the thought of making this willowy wisp of a youth appear as a stout limb of the Spanish family tree. Is this how the great Leonardo had felt, when pressured by Isabella d'Este, Duchess of Mantua, to do her portrait? For years, it is said, the duchess badgered maestro Leonardo to paint her. The most he could ever produce was a sketch of her profile, painful in its portrayal of her thin lips and large nose. On the other hand, there are subjects so beautiful the artist finds himself portraying them over and over, as maestro Michelangelo had painted his secretary, Tommaso Cavalieri, when signore Tommaso had been young. I had seen study after study of signore Tommaso in the Maestro's house. I even recognized him in the fresco of the Last Judgment in the Sistine Chapel—arrows in hand, he is the handsomely pensive Saint Sebastian.

Don Carlos pressed an exuberant kiss on the Queen's hand.

"Thank you, My Lady!" He clambered over and knelt before me on one knee. "Could you paint me soon, doña Sofonisba?"

"I can start whenever Her Majesty wishes me to."

"I should like you to start now."

The Queen nodded at me, her chin tucked back in amused affection.

"Now? Truly?" Don Carlos raked his fingers through his thistledown hair. "How should I stand?"

Don Alessandro stopped the page bringing in fruit on a blue and yellow ceramic tray. "You ought to hold the Rod of Office," he said, taking some grapes.

"Like thus?" Don Carlos struck a pose with his hands clenching an imaginary staff.

I saw the Queen hide her smile.

"I do believe you appear to be shimmying up a pole," said Don Alessandro.

"Or milking a cow." Don Juan entered the chamber with a playful grin on that fresh country face so like the King's yet so different. "A very noble cow, of course."

"Your words do not hurt me," Don Carlos said, though he dropped his hands to his side.

The Queen sat up, her cheeks suddenly bright.

"Perhaps it would be best if you just continued talking with the Queen, Your Majesty," I suggested to the Prince. "I can sketch informally, to get a measure of your face. It will take me some time to plan a painting. Usually I do several studies first."

The Queen shook her head at madame de Clermont, who offered to get her fruit. "Meanwhile, we shall have a sketching party."

"Sounds entertaining." Don Alessandro dangled some grapes over his mouth. "Though poor 'Sofi' will be doing all the work."

"You forget," said the Queen. "I can draw, too."

"You are talented *and* beautiful," said Don Alessandro, munching. "I think I shall die of love."

"Shut your mouth," Don Carlos growled.

Don Juan petted the little spaniel that had jumped down from madame de Clermont's lap to run to him. The little dog turned its head in pleasure as Don Juan scratched its back. "My Lady, I am sorry to hear that you lost your dear pet," he said to the Queen.

She nodded, tears welling in her eyes.

"How do your drawing lessons go?" he asked gently. "Is she a good student?" he asked me.

"The best," I said.

Don Alessandro cut me a look. "As excellent a student as you were with maestro Michelangelo?"

I fumbled with my box of chalks. "The Queen excels me."

"Of course," he said.

Don Juan gave madame's little spaniel one last pat. "Your Majesty," he asked the Queen, "would you like to practice your sketching on me?"

Don Alessandro looked between the two of them, wiping his mouth. "Yes. Do start with Uncle."

The Queen's sadness disappeared as quickly as it had come. "I *am* going to start with Don Juan," she said, "because he asked me nicely."

"Is that why?" said Don Alessandro.

The Queen rose from her embroidery frame. "Sofi, do you have a chalk and paper I can use?"

At the Queen's bidding, and with sarcastic laughter from Don Alessandro, Don Carlos and Don Juan struck poses on the pillows before us, Don Juan rather tentatively, Don Carlos proud as a dog with a new bone. The Queen settled next to me at the window. We began by holding out our chalks, to take measurement of our subject's heads, to transfer the proportion to our paper.

The Queen made a few marks, then stopped to watch me. "I am sorry, Don Juan, my sketch will not be as good as Sofi's."

"That wouldn't be your fault," said Don Juan. "You are hampered by poor subject matter."

"Now that's the truth," Don Alessandro said over his mouthful of grapes. "Can't they do any better than you, Uncle, out there in the country?"

"What ails you today, Don Alessandro?" said the Queen. "You are as bitter as spoiled wine."

He smiled and crossed his arms. "You wouldn't say such a thing to Don Juan."

"I would not need to." The Queen squinted at her upheld chalk to gauge another measurement. She lowered her arm. "Has anyone told you how much you look like the King, Don Juan? You have the same forehead and brows. You can tell that you are brothers."

"Except that whereas the King's mother was a queen," said Don Alessandro, "Don Juan's mother was a whore."

I winced. The ladies glanced at one another before resuming their sewing.

Don Alessandro laughed. "What is wrong with everybody? I merely speak the facts. You don't take offense, do you, Uncle?"

Don Juan did not answer.

"Dear Alessandro," the Queen scolded, "the rules of courtesy apply even to the Royal Family. You should apologize."

Madame's little spaniel jumped in Don Juan's lap. He smoothed the dog's fur over the bony knob at the top of its head. "It does not matter."

"No." The Queen put down her chalk. "He should."

"This is ridiculous," said Don Alessandro.

"I don't care if your father is the Duke of Parma and your mother the regent of the Netherlands," said the Queen. "Do you know what happened to an heir to the throne of France when he thought he was above common sense?"

Don Alessandro made a face of weary annoyance. "No."

"This is a true story. It is about my father's brother."

"Oh, good—a story!" Don Carlos crawled forward, then sprawled at her feet. "Tell me, My Lady."

"Are you sure you are comfortable, Toad? The floor looks very hard."

He knocked a green-and-orange-glazed tile. "Not so bad. Please, tell me!"

"Very well, then. For you, Toady, I will." The Queen spread her skirts over her knees. I sat back, too, unable to work with Don Carlos out of position.

"Not so very long ago, before my father was King, his younger brother went riding to war with his friends somewhere in northern France. There were three or four of them, all of them young and full of high spirits and mischief, for they were going to join a real battle, not just jousting and riding at the lists."

Don Carlos nodded vigorously.

"They rode along," said the Queen, "running their horses into each other and throwing chestnuts, and calling each other names. And then, in the midst of their merriment, they came to a village. There they went from house to house, thinking to demand food, but all the cottages were empty. For you see, the plague had freshly struck."

"Oh, no," Don Alessandro groaned. "Not a plague story."

"Shh!" said Don Carlos. "*I'm* listening, My Lady."

"Thank you, Toad. Well, the young men staggered from cottage to vacant cottage, drinking, singing, and carousing, becoming more and more rambunctious as they went. By the time they stumbled into the last cottage, they were overturning tables and smashing the crockery. Suddenly, one of them had a brilliant idea: 'Why don't we slash the mattresses with our swords?'"

Don Carlos's eyes brightened.

"Oh," said the Queen, "that was great, good fun, indeed, destroying all those mattresses. And then, when there were no more mattresses to slash, they had a merry pillow fight. The down was still fluttering onto the shoulders of my father's brother when he cried out, 'No son of the King of France has ever died of the plague! I could wrap myself in these sheets and never fall prey to it.' One of his friends said, 'Would you like to bet?' And my father's brother said, *'Oui!'* So they placed their drunken wagers and he rolled in the empty sheets."

"Fool!" Don Carlos shouted.

"This is my uncle," the Queen reminded him.

Don Carlos frowned in contrition. *"Lo siento."*

"Apology accepted," said the Queen, then continued. "Later that evening, when he joined his father the King at camp, my father's brother began to vomit. Soon his body burned with fever. His arms and legs shook like reeds in the wind. Priests were called, doctors consulted, and surgeons put to work with their lancets and leeches."

The Queen gazed over her audience: The ladies held their breath, hands frozen over their embroidery; Don Alessandro stood with arms crossed; Don Carlos chewed at his drooping lip. Only Don Juan looked away.

"Three days later," the Queen said quietly, "twenty-three-year-old Charles d'Orléans was dead."

Don Carlos leaned forward and kissed the hem of her gown. "I would never roll in plaguey sheets, My Lady!"

The Queen smiled fondly upon him. "I know you wouldn't, Toad."

"Good story." Don Alessandro popped a grape into his mouth. "But I have been wanting to ask you, Uncle—just who was your mother, anyhow?"

I stopped sketching.

"Don Alessandro," the Queen said in warning.

Don Juan stroked the spaniel's silky ears. "It does not bother me. I know only what I've been told. She was from Austria, a minor nobleman's daughter."

"So not a common whore," said Don Alessandro. "I apologize, Uncle."

Don Carlos rolled over to look at Don Juan. "Don Luis never told you much, did he?"

"Don Luis was your foster father?" the Queen said.

"Yes, My Lady, don Luis Quijada," said Don Juan. "He was the vice-chamberlain of His Majesty the Emperor—he has retired to his estate in Villagarcía."

"Villagarcía—near Valladolid?" said Don Carlos. He gazed around to see if anyone noticed his knowledge of the kingdom.

"Yes," said Don Juan. "His Majesty the Emperor chose well when he picked don Luis to raise me. I could not have had a kinder, wiser father. But kind as he was, don Luis did seem to have a sense of mystery."

The Queen commenced again on her sketching. "Please hold your face to the right, Don Juan."

"Until the moment I met my brother the King," he said, doing as told, "don Luis would not tell me who my father was, though don Luis treated me with such care that I imagined—at least I truly hoped—I was his own illegitimate son. I thought that if I were just good enough, don Luis would finally admit I was his flesh and blood."

"Perhaps you should turn your head back like you had it a moment ago," said the Queen.

"Like this?"

She nodded solemnly, the undressed ends of her hair swishing against her back.

"Go on with your story about don Luis," said Don Carlos. "Should I get back into position as well, doña Sofonisba?"

I nodded.

"Where was I?" said Don Juan.

"You weren't good enough," said Don Alessandro.

Don Juan gave Don Alessandro a long look before continuing. "I think don Luis's wife suspected I was his love child, yet she was kind to me, even though she believed her husband was making her raise his mistress's son. Imagine her relief when she found out whose son I really was."

"I don't think I could be so good if I thought I was raising the child of my husband's mistress," said the Queen.

"Oh, you would be," the condesa muttered, over at her embroidery frame, "if you had to be."

Don Alessandro went over and plucked an orange off the platter. He tossed it to Don Juan. "Well, if you must be a bastard, Uncle, you might as well be a Royal one."

Don Juan handed the orange to Don Carlos. "I suppose, though I was happy enough imagining I was don Luis's secret son."

Sharp footsteps sounded in the hall. The King entered, followed by his secretary. Rosary beads clicked amongst rustling skirts as all of us hastened into curtseys. The King quickly waved us up as he walked over to the Queen. "I am taking a break from my paperwork," he said in his cold voice. "How do you fare, My Lady?" He raised her up and kissed her hand.

When he gazed in my direction, I rushed forward to pay my respects. He nodded at the drawings at which the Queen and I had been working, as I put my lips to his cool perfume-scented skin.

"We are sketching, My Lord," the Queen said. "Don Carlos and Don Juan."

"I see." He embraced Don Carlos, then let Don Juan kiss his hand.

"We were listening to Don Juan's hilarious story, Father," Don Carlos said, "about how as an orphan, his fondest wish was to be the real son of the country squire who raised him. Whoever would have guessed he was not just a gentleman's son, but the true son of the Emperor?"

"Yes," said the King. "Whoever would have."

"You've never told me, Father," said Don Carlos, "how did you and Don Juan first meet?"

The King pressed his lips together. "I do not remember. It was not important."

"It was in a field," said Don Juan.

Rich fabrics rustled as everyone turned to listen.

"A field?" said Don Carlos. "Not in a palace or such? That is odd, Father."

"His Majesty was hunting," said Don Juan. "In the country-side outside Segovia." He looked at the King.

The ladies made busy with their needlework, as I did with my chalk. No one wished to be made party to a confrontation with the King.

In this atmosphere of sudden busyness, the Queen put down her chalk and held up her chin. "Please go on, Don Juan. I want to hear."

The King turned his countenance upon her. "Yes, Juan. Please do."

Don Juan paused as if weighing the consequences of his words. "I was brought to the King by don Luis. My foster father and I were made to wait and watch as His Majesty shot a deer."

"A deer?" The Queen frowned at her husband.

"A buck—it had a long white scar on one of its shoulders." Don Juan gazed at the King. "His Majesty's beaters had driven it from its cover and toward the King. When the buck was down and they were carving out its heart, the King came over and told me who my father was."

"You have a good memory," the King said grimly.

"At times, Your Majesty."

The King looked between Don Juan and the Queen. "I had a better memory when I was not so burdened with matters of state. Being King of most of the world since I was eighteen years of age interferes with remembering all my little hunts." His Majesty nodded at my sketch. "Finish that quickly. My son should be with his tutors, not dallying away his day in idle pastimes."

Is it a surprise that His Majesty did not come to My Lady's chamber last night?

Now a page has come, announcing that the Queen has sent for me. I must hide my notebook and join her in this place where the thorny canes of discord spread in the tranquil shade of civility.

To My Very Magnificent Signorina Sofonisba,
In the Court of the Spanish King

Imagine my happiness and my dismay when I returned to
Rome this day and found the letter you sent in February.
Happiness, because I have heard from you. Dismay, because
your letter has gone unanswered all this time. I have been in
Florence on a mission for maestro Michelangelo, to present his
designs for a church to Duke Cosimo de' Medici. My trip far
exceeded my expectations. The Duke commended the Maestro
for the drawings and me for my presentation of them. He then
bade me to make a clay model based on the drawings, and,
approving that, bade me to make a wooden model. All this
took time, and the receptions and dinners that the Duke
requested that I attend both as his distant kinsman and as the
Maestro's representative did nothing to speed along my work,
though I did enjoy the food. A man there named Suria
makes pig's livers so succulent they melt on your tongue.
Do they know the galliard called "Kick to the Tassel"
in the Spanish court? I had never seen it before. It was all they
wished to dance in Florence. There is much pirouetting and
kicking and jiggling of ladies' flesh.

The Maestro asks how you fare. Be flattered. He usually
asks after no one, caring for few beyond his nephew, Lionardo,
whom he writes faithfully, though he gives Lionardo a verbal
cuffing in most of his letters. I still have my studio in the old
man's home, but it is possible that will not be the case much
longer. I fear for some reason he does not care much for me

anymore. *He looked the other way when I greeted him upon returning from Florence; then he walked away before I finished speaking to him. Yet no sooner than I had gone up to my studio to gaze upon the unfinished Pietà, he came in and plunked a rough bust of a Caesar on the table and said, Here. Finish it.*

I grow weary now, having just returned to my lodging, but when I saw your letter I did not wish to keep you waiting another moment. A boy walks under my window—let me catch him to post this letter.

Please grant me the favor, great lady, of excusing me for the delay.

From Rome,
This 4th day of September, 1560

Your servant,
Tiberio Calcagni

ITEM: *When drawing, which is more difficult to perfect—the lines, or capturing light and shade?*

1 OCTOBER 1560
El Alcázar, Toledo

Excuse him? I care not where he has been. He could have been to Cathay and back for all the difference that makes. It is his lack of acknowledgment of what went on between us that stings. Do I mean so little to him that he feels he owes me no explanation of his feelings toward me? Does he think I gave up my most private self to him just to become his prattling correspondent from over the seas? What a good secretary I have become, dutifully keeping copies of both my letters and his in this notebook, as if there were any value to them.

I cannot think on this now, not after what has happened here. Indeed, just moving this quill against paper is painful. Yesterday morning, two days after his latest confrontation with Don Juan, the King entered the Queen's chambers while I was dressing her. As I had received Tiberio's letter the day before, I was distracted by my emotions, and the Queen, watchful girl that she is, picked up on my discomfort and tried to wheedle out of me the cause of it.

"My most serious Sofi," she had said as I braided her hair, "you do stare into space like the King's silver-headed dummy. What is it? Do you think of a new picture?"

I crossed one handful of wavy dark hair over the other. "If only I had time for that."

"Then is it because you miss your family?"

"I always miss my family."

She held up her mirror and blinked at me, as if it were a novel idea that someone other than she had a family that was deeply missed. "H'm. Well. If that is not it, then you must be thinking of a man."

"A man," I scoffed. "What men do I see besides doctor Hernández and the King's Painter señor Alonso Sánchez Coello?" I put in the first comb. "And both of them are married."

"How I love my good and proper Sofi. Only you would be deterred by a man having a wife."

The Queen's laughter stilled as the King walked into the chamber, his hand in his doublet, his demeanor more grave than usual. My distraction solidified into apprehension. Did he have orders in his pocket to send My Lady packing? It happens. Think of Anne of Cleves and Henry of England in Papà's time. That good lady had done nothing but not to be to King Henry's taste. Now My Lady seems not to be to our King's, not with his reluctance to know her carnally. Worse, her constant defense of Don Juan provokes the King like salt in a festering wound. The most powerful man in the world has no obligation to tolerate it.

"May I come in?" he said.

I quickly stuck the last comb into the Queen's hair and withdrew three steps behind her. None of the other ladies had yet arrived. Over by the bed, Francesca folded the Queen's night robes.

"Pardon me for coming so early," the King told the Queen. He shifted his feet as if uncomfortable, as well he should be if he was breaking his alliance with France. The French Queen Mother would make it hot for him.

The Queen rose. "You are always welcome here, My Lord." Although she kissed his hand gracefully, her nerves showed in her voice. She, too, knew that her failure to please could not go on.

"I have brought you something." He glanced at me and frowned before digging inside his doublet. What he produced was not a document but a handful of white fluff with black button eyes.

"For me?" the Queen gasped. "Oh, My Lord!" She rushed to retrieve the pup.

A smile pushed at the corners of the King's lips as she cradled it in her arms. "It came from France. I believe they call these white dogs *chiens de Lyon*." He crossed his arms. "You do like dogs, do you not?"

"You know I do," she said. "And from France! Thank you, My Lord."

The King recrossed his arms, scowling as the Queen kissed the puppy and crooned to it in French.

"See how he nibbles upon my fingers, My Lord!"

The King held up his first two fingers, revealing a set of tiny red toothmarks on the ends of them. "The pup does teethe. His teeth are needle-sharp. You must pet him on the back of his head, where he cannot bite on you." He reached out to show her how to stroke the dog.

In a flash of her old impetuous self, the Queen grasped the King's nibbled-upon fingers and kissed them. "Poor you! Do they hurt?"

He gazed at her as she held on to his fingers. "Not any longer."

The Queen looked at their joined hands, then slowly met his eyes. Cupping her head with his hand, he pulled her to him and softly kissed her.

Her mouth parted as he withdrew.

"I have been waiting to do that," he said quietly.

"Why, My Lord? Why have you waited? I have been waiting for you."

"You do not find me—?"

"What, My Lord?"

I could feel his glance upon me. I made as if pondering upon the spots of blue light cast by the leaded glass of the window onto the floor.

"I have never had to force myself on a woman," he said to her in a low voice. "Women have always wanted me. I have only had to choose from them."

"I know, My Lord."

"My first two wives—well, I was a young buck then, vainly proud of my thick hair and strong muscles. But you—" He drew in a quiet breath. "I am older now, and you were commanded to accept me. I was not your choice."

She laid her hand on his arm, her head thrust forward in earnestness. "But you are, Your Majesty. You are my choice."

He looked into her eyes as if to see if this was true, then smiled ruefully. "You are so young."

"I am old enough, My Lord," she said stoutly.

At that moment, the condesa flounced into the room, followed by an angry madame de Clermont and her ladies. Their argument stopped short when they discovered the King and Queen.

The Queen held up the puppy. "See what My Lord has brought me? A dog from France!"

The Queen's high spirits continued all that morning through Mass and breakfast, and then through distributing prayer books to the former church on the Calle de los Reyes that Cardinal Siliceo has made into a refuge for penitent women, during all of which she carried her new pup. I myself stayed behind in the litter at the refuge, made uncomfortable by the downcast looks on the faces of the penitent women.

But in spite of my own unhappiness, it was with a genuine bright countenance that I accompanied the Queen to the rooms of the King's sister that afternoon. For how many times has My Lady entered Doña Juana's quarters with her tail between her legs, aware, with all the rest of the court, of the presence of the King's favorite?

It is not as if My Lady had no reason to approach Doña Juana with caution. Doña Juana never seeks to lessen the Queen's discomfort—indeed she seems to revel in it, insisting that doña Eufrasia sit near the Queen at Mass or hold the Queen's train as My Lady and her sister-in-law stroll around the courtyard of the palace. Doña Juana seems to wish to draw everyone's attention, and particularly that of the King, to the difference between doña Eufrasia's mature dark-haired beauty and the girlish ways of the Queen. Francesca has even heard it told that it is Doña Juana who arranges for the coach in which doña Eufrasia steals away at night and returns at dawn with the curtains drawn.

Still, I wonder if Doña Juana's machinations are meant solely to wound the Queen. She had encouraged the affair before the Queen had come to Spain. Perhaps more than anything Doña Juana savors the power she derives in controlling the King. It is but a small thing compared with controlling all of Spain as she did while he was wed to the English Queen Mary, but one takes what one can get.

But yesterday, confident for once, the Queen flounced into the chamber where Doña Juana was having her fingernails clipped by doña Eufrasia. "See what the King has got me!" the Queen announced before the last of us ladies had filed into the chamber.

Over by the window, a lutist was tuning his instrument. Doña

Juana exchanged amused smiles with doña Eufrasia as she withdrew her hand. "How precious," she said sarcastically. "A little dog."

Doña Eufrasia rose and brushed the clippings from her skirt. "What did you name him, Your Majesty?" she asked, her voice as velvety as her skin.

"Cher-Ami," said the Queen. "'Dear Friend' it means, in French."

"How nice that my brother has given you a little friend," said Doña Juana. With a flash of bone-colored lashes, she shifted her gaze to the large diamond hanging from doña Eufrasia's neck.

The Queen followed her line of vision. "The King knows my heart. He knows he could not have given me a better gift. What care I for gems and fine stuffs—I have had plenty of them my whole life."

Doña Juana smiled smugly. "For someone who has no regard for jewels, you certainly seemed to enjoy the Great Pearl. Where is that big gob these days? I have not seen you wear it recently."

Hurt flicked through the Queen's eyes, then was quickly replaced by a look of haughtiness that, alas, even with her pointed chin held high, was not entirely believable. "It was the first gift the King sent me. I cherish it."

"Oh, yes. It has been a much-cherished piece, hasn't it?"

The Queen stared at Doña Juana.

"You mustn't listen to those who say such a small breed of dog is useless," Doña Juana said. "They have their purpose as comforters. I have heard that when borne in the bosom of a diseased person, they can draw out the sickness by the exchange of their bodily heat."

The Queen opened her mouth, then closed it firmly. "I would not need a dog for that."

"Of course not." Doña Juana smiled archly. She signaled for the lutist to begin his playing. He commenced into an English folk tune.

"Why do you wish me such ill?" the Queen exclaimed.

Doña Juana straightened the lace at her cuffs. "Why would you think that? You are dear to me, Sister. When I ruled our empire when my brother was in England, how I wished I had had my sister María with me—ruling half the world is lonely business, but you wouldn't know that. But María was in Vienna, wed to the Prince there at my father's wishes, and I was all alone, with not even my child to give me comfort. I gave up everything that was precious to me to do Father's bidding, and now Felipe is back, and I have nothing to do but go to Mass. How nice that I can do that now with such a sweet little kinswoman."

I may be only a painting instructor, but I could not bear to let Doña Juana defeat My Lady with her words. I leaned around the condesa to address the Queen. "Your Majesty, I beg your pardon, but did you not say you wished to take a ride into the countryside?"

I could see the condesa stiffen. My own heart pounded with my boldness. Doña Juana was not a person to trifle with. But a country jaunt was sure to boost My Lady's spirits, for the people of Toledo never fail to cheer for her when we go out by open litter to the various churches and convents in town, the only places she is allowed to visit unescorted by the King. Folk shout their blessings and fall to their knees, and when she has passed, they run off bragging, "I have had the luck of seeing the Queen today!" For though she may be belittled by Doña Juana and not bedded by the King, the Spanish people love their Queen, and have loved her ever since that day she first rode into Guadalajara, looking brightly at the crowds.

My Lady was confused for only the briefest of moments. "Yes, doña Sofonisba," she said, seeking my eye. "Thank you for reminding me."

Outside, it was a perfect day in late September, the kind when the golden stone buildings of Toledo stand out crisply against the heartbreakingly blue sky. The Queen ordered that coaches be made ready for all her ladies, and Doña Juana begrudgingly agreed to join her. Soon we were preparing to take our places in the coaches lined up in the courtyard, where flocks of birds chattered noisily from the lime trees as they gathered to make their fall pilgrimage to Africa.

"It is unseasonably warm today," complained the condesa de Urueña, who had joined us for the jaunt. She plucked the black robe of her widow's habit away from her body as we stood behind the Queen, now being handed by her coachman into her coach. "We should be indoors, resting. Your Majesty, do you think it wise to go out in the hot sun?"

The Queen had stopped to answer the condesa when her gaze fell upon a red-and-yellow-painted open sporting conveyance, the sort designed for a lady driver and a companion, propped nearby on its empty leads. "Whose chariot is that?" she asked her man.

"Her Majesty the King's sister, My Lady," said the coachman.

"Why is it out?"

"Her Majesty had use of it last night." He glanced at doña Eufrasia, now being handed into the coach of the King's sister directly behind us, then quickly lowered his eyes.

The Queen set her mouth when she saw where the coachman had looked. "Hitch it up," she told him.

"The chariot?"

"Yes. Now. Please."

The coachman called to a stableboy, who ran to find a horse.

"Your Majesty!" cried the condesa. "Do you think it safe to ride in a chariot in court clothes? You are not dressed for such."

"I should like some light exercise."

"But your train! The back of the chariot is completely open. Your train could slip onto the wheels."

"I shall keep it wrapped around my arm."

"Even if you could secure your dress, Your Majesty," said the condesa, "the chariot holds only two, and I am not attired for driving, nor is madame de Clermont."

Madame de Clermont glared most unlovingly at the condesa. "The Queen should be able to ride if she wishes."

"I do wish to drive," said the Queen. "And Sofi will help me. You aren't afraid, are you, Sofi, to ride in a little chariot?"

I was careful not to look at the other ladies. They already felt that the Queen spent too much time with a mere painting instructor, when they were daughters of dukes and marquises. "As you wish, Your Majesty."

A horse was found to hitch to the chariot. The Queen handed her pup to madame de Clermont, grabbed the reins, and off we jostled, with the Queen shaking the reins and laughing, and me gripping the brow of the chariot, the Queen's train wound around my arm.

We started out at a sedate clip-clop, the coaches rumbling close behind us. Folk rushed to their doors to shout blessings for the Queen—there were no such cheers for Doña Juana. But as soon as we left the dun-colored walls of the city, the Queen urged our horse into a trot and struck out across the stony plain, leaving the line of lumbering carriages in our ochre cloud of dust.

"Thank you," she said, her raised voice vibrating from the

rough ride. She saw my questioning expression. "For releasing me from that old dragon's clutches."

"Most happy to help."

"I don't know what I'd do without you, Sofi."

We bumped along, my veil slipping to the side of my head. Though it was almost fall, heat radiated from the plain. To the west, mountains rose, silent and hazy blue against the stark sapphire sky.

My Lady shook off her veil and let her hair whip in the wind.

"Your Majesty is feeling bold today!" I shouted.

"I am!"

She looked behind and gasped. I followed her gaze to three riders, galloping from the city gate. They streaked toward us, raising a plume of yellow on the baking plain.

"It's Don Carlos and his *caballeros*!" I shouted.

The Queen cracked our horse's reins.

I gripped the chariot, my teeth rattling with the bouncing wheels. "They try to catch us!"

She snapped the reins again. "I know!"

Behind us, the condesa leaned out of her carriage, her shouts lost in the thudding of our wheels.

My arm muscles burned as I clung to the bouncing chariot. The *caballeros* drew closer, leaning over their horses. The tails of their animals flew straight out behind them.

My veil blew from my head. I snatched at it, too late, causing the slippery cloth of Her Majesty's train to slither down my front. Clinging one-handed to the chariot, I reeled in her train before it could drop beneath the base and catch in the wheels.

At that moment, Don Juan urged his horse before the others. He galloped abreast, then snatched our horse's bridle.

The chariot ground to a bumpy halt.

The Queen laughed and coughed as she waved off the cloud of dust. "Why did you do that?"

Don Juan said nothing, just jumped down and stroked the nose of our horse, whose nostrils flared with exhaustion. Its graceful neck was slick with sweat.

Don Carlos galloped up with Don Alessandro. "Why did you run from us, My Lady?" the Prince said in an injured voice.

The wind tugged at the Queen's skirts and at the lengths of her silk train that I juggled in my arms. "I was racing you," she said. "I was beating you, too!"

"You had a head start," said Don Alessandro. "We would have caught up."

"You shouldn't have run from us," said Don Carlos.

The Queen pulled back her chin and smiled. "I was just playing, Toad."

The wind had torn the tails of Don Juan's white shirt from his breeches, exposing his taut belly as he whispered to our horse, his lips brushing her ears. Still blowing hard, the animal rolled her gaze at him, exposing the whites of her eyes.

The Queen tapped her fingers on the brow of the chariot. "Well, Don Juan, how go the wedding plans? Now that you are fifteen, won't you claim your wife?"

Don Juan kissed the white velvet of the blaze on our horse's nose, then gazed at the Queen. "What wedding plans?"

"With my sister. Oh, I know about them. I got my mother's letter yesterday. She says the King is considering her offer."

"I do what I am told."

"Oh, you do, now? Well, congratulations. Her dowry will make you one of the richest men in Spain."

They studied each other as if the rest of us were not there. She pushed her hair out of her eyes with the back of her hand. "So when is the wedding?"

"Here comes the rest of your party," said Don Alessandro.

The Queen turned toward the carriages, of which the lead was now close enough that we could see the sun glinting from the condesa's silver pomander just inside the window. Before anyone could react, the Queen tugged the reins from Don Juan and snapped our horse into a trot.

I snatched at the chariot to keep from falling as it bounced forward. In doing so, I dropped the Queen's train. Frantically I fumbled at the slippery silk even as a length slid onto the turning wheel and caught on the axle. In one sickening jolt, the train ripped from the Queen's shoulders and the chariot flipped.

I hit the ground with a bone-jarring thud.

Later, inside the palace, into which the bleeding Queen had been carried in the arms of Don Juan and I in the arms of Don Alessandro, the King paced in the reception room outside the Queen's bedchamber. Don Juan, Don Carlos, Don Alessandro, the condesa, madame, and I stood in a miserable row before him. My right shoulder throbbed. I could not move it without searing pain. What if I could not paint?

The King's face was tight with contempt. "How could you have let this happen?" he said to us. "It is your duty to keep the Queen from doing foolish things. She is only a child. It is your place to protect her."

"You, *señora*," he said to the condesa, "I gave you my full trust. You have disappointed me, and I shall not forget it."

Although she held her head high, the condesa's eyes brimmed with tears.

"And you, *señorita*." He turned to me. "What will your father say when he hears that it was in your company the Queen received her injury?"

I held my hurt arm and tried not to cry. Francesca's frightened scolding when I'd returned to the palace was but the buzzing of a fly compared with the thought of disappointing Papà. Even without the revelation of my deed in Rome, I will have managed to bring shame to him and my family.

"Are you injured?" the King asked.

I curled my scraped palms upon themselves. In addition to damaging my shoulder, my left leg stung where the skin had been laid bare, my hip ached, and somewhere out on the plain lay my veil and one of my shoes. "No, Your Majesty. Thank you."

He blew a breath from his nose, then turned to the *caballeros*. "And you. *Brother.*"

Don Juan looked up. Though his hair had fallen over his eyes and his face was streaked with dirt, his anguish was undisguised.

"Is this how you repay our father who has lifted you so high? By encouraging my wife to act rashly? My son says you were holding her horse's reins when she made to get away. Be glad that our father is dead, and cannot see what you have done."

"Papá," Don Carlos groaned. "Tell us how she fares."

The King took in his son in one dismissive gaze. "I have no words for you. Begone. Before I say something I regret."

Before Don Carlos could move, doctor Hernández came from the Queen's chamber. The condesa stiffened.

"Doctor!" Don Carlos cried. "How is she?"

The doctor scanned our wretched group as he pulled the heavy carved door behind him. His long face, with its skin as pitted as a lichen-covered boulder, was impassive. "Your Majesty," he told

Don Carlos, "she has a bump to the head and wounds to the flesh
of her shoulder, hip, and ankle, but all are superficial."

"I saw blood running down her leg," the King said. "A great
deal of it. Should you not consult a surgeon?"

"Your Majesty, may I have a private word?"

That was yesterday afternoon. It was only this morning that
I learned from Francesca, who learned it from the Queen's
laundress, the source of the Queen's blood. At last, at the age of
fifteen, Her Majesty's courses have begun.

The King has not left her bedside. He tends to her himself, having sent all of her attendants from her chamber. It is just the King,
the Queen, and her little Cher-Ami. I believe she will recover, and
pray that I will too, though it hurts each time I lift my arm.

But I am troubled by what I heard in those few moments during which I had lain on the dusty plain with the Queen as the
overturned chariot, dragged by our frightened horse, receded
into the distance in a cloud of dirt. As I rolled onto my back, with
grit in my mouth and my hair in my eyes and the ground trembling from the *caballeros'* approaching horses, I could hear her
whisper.

"Juan."

The

Second Notebook

ITEM: *In times two centuries past, a lady threw herself on her knees before the Spanish King Alfonso, begging justice. She pleaded for relief from her husband, with whom she was made to lie thirty-two times in the course of a day and night. The King sent for the husband, who admitted the fact, claiming he did no wrong—were not his rights to his wife unlimited? After consulting his counselors, King Alfonso decreed that the husband must limit himself to six embraces in the twenty-four hours. At the same time, the King expressed a twofold astonishment: firstly at the extraordinary heat and potency of the man; secondly at the extraordinary coldness and continence of the woman, so contrary to the nature of her sex, for usually the woman is on her knees beseeching her husband or lover to give her more pleasure.*

ITEM: *In painting, darkness imbues everything with its hue. The more an item is removed from darkness, the more it shows its true color.*

20 DECEMBER 1560
El Alcázar, Toledo

It makes me blush to think what a pair of spring rabbits the King and Queen have become. The Queen herself is delighted. Even in these dark days of December, when icy gusts of wind buffet blackbirds in flight and send roof tiles smashing to the cobble-

stones, she sings to herself and smiles in her mirror or teases the
condesa de Urueña until the old lemon retreats to the solace of
her pomander. This morning the dawn blew in on icy winds that
whistled through the shuttered windows. Yet when I entered the
Queen's chamber with the page whose job it is to replenish
the charcoal in the brazier, and pushed back the hangings round
the Queen's bed, I found My Lady on her side, dangling the ties
of her chemise over her puppy and humming a nursery tune.

"Good morning, Sofi!" she sang out.

Because of the King's distaste for the bickering among the
Queen's other ladies, and the Queen's embarrassing but satisfying preference for me, I am the only lady now allowed to help her
rise each morning. Today the King was not there but must not
have been gone long. The bed smelled strongly of man.

I could not look her in the eye. "My Lady," I said, tying a bed-
hanging up out of the way, "would you like to rise and dress
now?" I pulled her bed-warmer from under the covers by its long
wooden handle and handed it to the page, who gave the charcoal
in the brazier a last jab, then shot out of the room. The Queen
threw back her covers. I could not help noticing there was a stain
on the sheets. She smiled demurely when she saw my gaze.

I looked away. The Queen's sixteen-year-old brother, the
King of France, died two weeks ago, and the Queen, as merrily
as she now carries herself, is officially in mourning. Indeed, she
has been given to tears in fits and starts since she first received
word of his death—even more so than since her courses began
and, with them, brief periods of melancholia—though her demeanor at the moment belied any sort of grief.

Francesca waited in the doorway with a clean white chemise
embroidered with black-work, along with the black robes of
mourning.

"Do you wish to just stand there, Francesca?" I said, completely unnecessarily. If Francesca is zealous in her care of me, she is doubly zealous in her care of the Queen.

Francesca rushed forward. Her dark look at me changed to a worried smile for the Queen. "Madonna Elisabetta, are you well?"

"Why would I not be?" The Queen scooted to the edge of her bed and hopped off before I could help her, leaving her pup to burrow in the covers. "Though someone awoke foul-tempered," she said to me.

I fussed with the towels on her dressing table as she retired to her close stool. "I am not foul-tempered, My Lady."

"Oh, yes you are," she said from behind the screen. "The very air bristles with your prickliness. Do you know what I think? I think you are uncomfortable with the idea of a man and a woman coupling."

I folded then refolded the towel.

"It is because you are a virgin," she said. "You did not jest when you signed it on your paintings." She came over to where I stood waiting with the pitcher and bowl. "'Sofonisba Anguissola, Virgo.' Shh, Cher-Ami—you bark too much."

I could feel the fiery furnace of my face as I poured water over her hands. It was enough of a farce that I had to pretend I was a virgin. The irony was doubly compounded by the fact that as a lady to the Queen, I can no longer sign my name, with its false appendage or not, to anything that I paint. A Queen's lady may not broadcast her skills like an artisan seeking work, and now, more than ever, as high as I have risen in the Queen's household, my efforts at painting must appear like a genteel game. My drawings may amuse, but to excel at painting—that is best left to the hands of a male expert.

Francesca stepped forward with a clean chemise.

"See how Sofi blushes," the Queen said.

Francesca would not look at me. *"Sì."*

Gooseflesh rose on the Queen's skin as she raised her arms for me to lift off her chemise and slip the clean one upon her. "Hurry, Sofi. I should not catch a chill if I am with child."

"No, indeed, we must keep Your Majesty warm and snug." I tugged her chemise into place.

"Would that I were carrying the King's heir," said the Queen. "Then maybe Mother would quit writing to me each night and day. I cannot believe there is a courier left alive between here and Paris."

I finished tying the black-work strings of Her Majesty's chemise and took her robe from Francesca. "Your mother means well."

"You know she does not. All she cares about is getting her clutches firmly into Spain now that France is falling apart."

It is true that trouble hounds the French Queen Mother from all sides. She herself had written to My Lady upon her son the King's death that she was left with three little children and a divided kingdom in which there was not one man whom she could trust. The great noble family of Guise have positioned themselves against the Bourbons; the Huguenots have lined up against the Catholics; none of them has love for the Medici Queen. No wonder she was more frantic than ever to cinch her tie to Spain.

The Queen let me help her into her robe, then lifted her chin as I fastened it. "Sofi, I want you to paint my portrait."

She noticed my look of surprise. "I liked what you did with Don Carlos's picture, and now it's time that you did me. If we wait much longer, I will be with child, and the smell of paint might make me sick. My mother said when she was with child, odors were the death of her. She especially could not stomach the smell of cooking meat." She put her dog on the floor. It immediately went to a corner and pissed.

"As you wish, Your Majesty," I said, knowing the job would go to Alonso Sánchez Coello, and even if it did not, señor Sánchez Coello would get the credit.

I do not invent this result. It had happened in the case of my portrait of Don Carlos, a picture that was, out of necessity, mostly gorgeous tawny lynx-fur cape and golden quilted doublet, and very little of the fragile youth peeping warily from within. I had solved the problem of portraying My Lady's dear Toad as a beloved prince by painting him in another creature's beautiful skin and then bathing the painting in gold. Not a single sharp line disturbed the tranquillity of the painting—it was all softness, warmth, and mellow gold. For once, Don Carlos was the golden child he always wished to be.

But when the picture was unveiled last week before the King, Doña Juana had asked if I had done the picture alone, and when I replied that I had, with my thanks to señor Sánchez Coello, who had lent me several of his brushes, a knowing smile had grown on her face. After that, even though señor Sánchez Coello protested that he had not contributed to the work in any way, some at court thought he was merely being gallant—and the more he protested, the more gallant he appeared. At least the Queen believed in me.

The Queen sat at her table. I began to brush her hair.

"Are you still stewing about being a virgin? I'll have the King get you a husband—you will still be able to serve me."

"No!"

She raised her hand mirror to look at me. "No?"

The brush made a rich scraping sound as I stroked her hair. "No, thank you, Your Majesty."

"Why?"

I pulled the brush twice down the length of her hair. "I do not wish to be like a mare in the King's stable, with His Majesty pondering my bloodlines and temperament in considering a suitable match."

She laughed. "Dear Sofi, must you be such a bore?" She picked up the ruby necklace the King had sent her and shuffled it from hand to hand. "Trust me, having a husband is not all bad." She put the jewel to her lips and closed her eyes. "Oh, Sofi, if you could only imagine how divine it feels to be with a man. I could lie with the King five times a day." She opened her eyes. "How many times do you think a pair could couple in a day?" She smiled privately, rocking the ruby against her lips.

"There is more to a relationship than coupling, is there not?"

The Queen pulled away from the hairbrush. "You're hurting me."

"Pardon, My Lady." I had not realized I was brushing hard. I lightened my strokes. "You might educate yourself on the King's interests so you may share them with him."

"Oh, I think I know his interests."

The condesa's sharp voice rang out. "I said no!" She entered the chamber with madame de Clermont, arguing as usual, even at that early hour of the day. "I do not care that mademoiselle Noailles's father has become a duke. He is French. This is Spain. She may not move up her place at the table. Doña Teresa is to stay exactly where she is."

For once, I was grateful for their rancor. We finished the

Queen's toilet, then accompanied My Lady to Mass. From there we went to Doña Juana's quarters, where the King wishes that we go each day now that Don Carlos no longer visits us. The King had ordered Don Carlos and his *caballeros* to attend university at Alcalá shortly after the Queen's accident in Doña Juana's chariot. It has been two months since we have seen them—I'd had to finish Don Carlos's portrait without him.

How much happier Doña Juana had been when the Queen had been a scorned and malleable child. Now that the Queen is favored by the King, the friction between her and Doña Juana is unbearable. So it is with held breath that I enter Doña Juana's heavily perfumed quarters of late, but today was particularly disturbing. For sitting on a folding leather chair next to the brazier, his ample belly resting on his lap like a full sack of gold, was the head of the Inquisition in Spain, Inquisitor-General Valdés.

The Queen and her ladies exchanged stiff kisses with Doña Juana and her attendants, including doña Eufrasia, who has looked uncharacteristically wan in recent weeks. We kissed the hand of Inquisitor-General Valdés, who then beamed upon us, his hands folded over his gut like a benevolent saint.

"How are you feeling, My Lady?" he asked Her Majesty in his jolly voice. "Have we produced a new champion for the Church of Rome?"

The Queen raised her chin. "I expect a son soon, Your Holiness."

"Are you pregnant?" Doña Juana asked sharply.

"I shall be," said the Queen, "if I am not."

The Inquisitor-General patted the Queen's arm as doña Eufrasia looked away. "Excellent, excellent. I shall call God's blessing upon you. The Church needs a new prince to root out heresy."

The Queen's smile was all teeth. Last month, she had been required to go to an *auto-de-fé* to watch the burning of a tailor who refused to recant his support of Luther's Protestant edicts. As the fire crackled from the fagots at the tailor's feet, the Queen gazed in disbelief between the King and his sister, marking the King's expressionless countenance and Doña Juana's grim smile of satisfaction. Afterward, the Queen had flung herself weeping onto her bed, vowing that nothing could force her to attend another burning. She had wondered aloud how anyone could be so cruel as to enjoy it. But to say such a thing to the Inquisitor-General—or to his supporters—was to risk having his attention turned upon her. As the Protestant Elizabeth was finding out in England, not even queens are exempt from the wrath of the Church should they rebel against it. Now that Queen Elizabeth has broken with Rome, it is just a matter of time before the Pope openly calls for her removal. Then she would be forced to suppress the Catholics in her lands, and fires might rage under the feet of Catholics as frequently as they burn under Protestants' here. Who knows where this madness will end?

"My deepest condolences on the death of your brother, Your Majesty," said the Inquisitor-General. "He was a soldier for the Church of Rome, a great crusader against heresy, as is his widow, your sister-in-law and cousin, Mary Stuart. The Church has no greater friend than Mary Stuart. All queens could learn a lesson in comportment from her."

My Lady kept her lips raised above her teeth. "Truly."

My poor Lady. All her life, from her father during her childhood, to the Inquisitor-General now, she has been held up unfavorably to Mary Stuart. Yet to her credit, she took no pleasure in hearing from Paris that upon the death of her brother the King, her mother had stripped Mary Stuart clean of the Royal jewels, leaving Mary in a plain dark dress in a plain dark room in the palace at Orléans, alone.

My Lady reached for a prayer book in the neat stack of them upon Doña Juana's dressing table and began to turn its colorful pages. "How beautifully this is illuminated," she murmured.

"Inquisitor-General Valdés brought them," said Doña Juana. "Do take one."

"The art was done by the friars of the Monastery of San Jerónimo in Madrid," said Inquisitor-General Valdés. "I prefer the work of the clergy to lay painters. I believe the lay painter's impurity taints his art—your work excluded, my dear," he said to me.

Gooseflesh rose on my arms. I knew who he was—I had seen him presiding over the burning at the *auto-de-fé*—but I did not expect him to know me.

"I think the work of a virgin is the most God-given and pure of all," he said. "Think of the Blessed Virgin. Just as she was the vessel to bear our Christ, you, with no stain of sin upon you, are a vessel to bear God's Beauty."

I curtseyed, my skin prickling.

"How your work shines brightly in contrast with the work of your master." He chuckled when he saw my surprise. "Oh, I know you studied with Michelangelo Buonarroti. It is my business to know everything."

Doña Juana offered the Inquisitor-General a tray of marzipan. He leaned forward, the leather of his chair groaning, and, pinky raised, chose a piece shaped like a cross. He settled back with his treat. "I know there are many who esteem Michelangelo's work, but *I* find it ugly and obscene. No number of sculptures of the Blessed Virgin holding her crucified Son can make up for the naked men your Italian friend exults in carving. Does he think persons do not notice? And his paintings—his women look like men! Why is that so, Sofonisba Anguissola?" He popped the sweetmeat into his mouth and smiled kindly.

A shout preceded the sound of footsteps outside the chamber. The Inquisitor-General, breathing through his mouth as he munched, turned heavily as the King's guards stood aside at the door for the King to enter.

"Inquisitor-General Valdés," said the King. "A pleasure." He offered his hand for the Inquisitor to kiss, embraced his sister, and then his wife. I saw the Queen's triumphant glance at doña Eufrasia when the King kept his arm around her.

"We were just having a discussion about art," said Inquisitor-General Valdés. "I have asked doña Sofonisba to explain why her friend Michelangelo paints his women to look like men."

The King half frowned at me. "What's this?"

"The virgins, the sybils, Eve," said the Inquisitor. "All the women in the paintings in the Sistine Chapel look like men. The female attributes have been attached to them as if a filthy afterthought."

A cold knot squeezed in my chest. Where was this leading?

Doña Juana murmured her disgust. "Oh, yes," said Inquisitor-General Valdés. "I have had accurate copies of these paintings brought before us. So why do you think he does this, doña Sofonisba?"

"Your Grace," I said, nauseated, "I do not know."

The King stroked the Queen's arm. "It is easily explainable, Your Grace."

His breath whistling through his spongy nose, the Inquisitor-General revolved slowly toward the King. "Yes?"

"I assume Michelangelo uses only male models."

"With all due respect, Your Majesty," said the Inquisitor, "this does not fully account for it. *All* male artists use only male models. Women cannot stand for a male artist unless it is for a portrait— I need to hear of it, if they do."

Doña Juana put down the tray and plucked up her own piece of marzipan. She aimed her rounded brow at me, her eyes icy blue beneath her dust-colored lashes. "We are investigating accusations that have been made. Is there anything you can tell Inquisitor-General Valdés, Sofonisba, anything improper you noticed while studying with Michelangelo?"

I stopped breathing.

"My dearest Sister!" The King smiled and tightened his arm protectively around the Queen. "Doesn't the Inquisitor have enough on his hands, protecting Spain from religious wars, without pursuing an elderly artist in Rome?" The King took up his sister's hand and kissed it before she could speak further. "I regret that I must cut this visit short, Juana, but I am using this break from my paperwork to steal away the Queen for a little moment. Will you please pardon us?"

"But of course, Your Majesty." The Inquisitor-General beckoned for a page to bring him the tray of marzipan.

My ears rang with fear. How would I bear up to the questions of the Inquisitor-General and Doña Juana when left alone with them?

"My Lord," said the Queen, "I need someone to hold my train if I am not to stumble. Sofi, will you come?"

I took her train, my hands shaking. Outside Doña Juana's chamber, the Queen asked, "Are you well?"

"A touch of indigestion," I said. "That is all."

Though the Queen and King were but three ells of velvet brocade away, it was several minutes before my heart had calmed enough for me to hear their speech as they strolled across the tiled floor of the receiving chamber.

She playfully pushed into his shoulder. "You have not told me where we are going, My Lord."

"It is a surprise."

She tucked in her chin. "If it is to your bed that you take me, Your Majesty, it will hardly be a surprise."

Amusement played upon his lips, threatening to break his cool expression. "I am not taking you to my bed."

"You are not?"

I could feel the King ascertaining if I was listening. He lowered his voice. "I cannot bed you every moment, My Lady. Too much sex can kill a man."

She burst out laughing.

"You laugh," he said, bemused. "I speak the truth. My father warned me of it. His great-uncle died after six months of unbridled coupling with his bride. He was but nineteen."

She laughed even harder, the fringe on her turban jiggling.

"You find such tragedy humorous?" said the King, though his eyes were merry. "You laugh at the death of the son of Their Sacred Majesties Isabel and Fernando?"

"I envy him! What an excellent way to go."

"Good point, my dear." He nestled her hand under his arm.

Though it had not fully unclenched the fist of fear knotted within my gut, to see My Lady and this most somber of kings so lighthearted did help to calm my mind. For the King, for all his austerity, was proving to be a gentle husband, even making allowances when My Lady fell into her spells of quiet sadness during their new season of conjugal joy. He weathered these brief bouts with watchful patience, attributing her lapses, he told me, to her tender years.

"My Lord," the Queen said, "I do suppose there is some truth to your father's warning, but not for men. It is women who pay the price for happy coupling—in the childbed. Do not worry," she said quickly, when she saw his pained face. "I am not afraid. I shall have scores and scores of babies—you'll see."

"Like your mother, My Lady."

She pulled away from him. "Not like my mother."

He gathered her back in. "I am sorry, my darling. Forget that I mentioned her."

We walked on, our footsteps echoing from the intricately carved and coffered wooden ceiling high overhead. The room, though now empty, kept its smell of candle wax; there was the odor, too, of stone and musty timber.

A screeching burst forth above. A blackbird beat against the ceiling, its cries frantic and pitiful.

The Queen leaned away from the King. "Oh, My Lord, it is trapped!"

"It will find its way out."

"But all the windows are closed."

The King stroked her arm. "I shall send someone to help it."

"You will?"

"Of course."

She winced at the bird's screams. "Do not forget."

He drew her closer. "I never forget."

"If you promise, then." The Queen sighed, then mustered a faltering smile. "Tell me another piece of your father's advice."

"Well, let me see," said the King. "In truth, he gave me a great deal of it. When I was sixteen, he put much of it in a letter."

The bird flew to a window on the far side of the room and rested on the top of the frame. The Queen lowered her shoulders, visibly relaxing as the bird quieted.

"To start with," said the King, "he said to avoid flatterers."

She cocked her head, her turban fringe dangling, to gaze into his face. "Did I tell you what beautiful eyes you have?"

He gave her arm an affectionate shake. "He also said to find time to go among and talk to the people."

"I like that."

"As you should. The people adore you, My Lady."

"Do you think?"

He kissed her hand in acknowledgment, then laid it on his chest. "Yes."

They resumed walking. "Well, let's see what else," said the King. "Father said to keep myself from anger, and do nothing in anger."

"That is not a problem for you, My Lord. You do not get angry."

He opened his mouth to speak, then seemed to think better of it.

"I have not seen you angry," she said, persisting.

After a moment he said, "He also said it would not hurt for me to learn a bit of French."

She laughed. "I see you did not mind all his rules."

"I speak French."

"Like a toddling child."

"You catch me out." He patted her hand on his chest. "Well, for the most part, I tried to take his advice. As you see, he was very wise."

"Except about the coupling."

"Excepting that, yes."

They walked along. "It must have been a terribly long letter," said the Queen.

"I still have it. He was leaving for the Low Countries again, and I was distraught. As a boy, I saw far too little of him. He was always off fighting wars in his lands."

"My father did not travel, but I hardly saw him, either. He was always with—"

The King stopped to listen.

"Nobody."

He gently rearranged a dark tendril that had escaped from her turban. "You can tell me."

She looked away from his eyes. "His mistress. Please do not misunderstand, madame Diane was good to me and I was fond, very fond, of her, but—"

He laced his fingers through hers, then kissed her fingertips. "You know what else was in that letter?"

She looked up.

"Once married, I must not go with other women."

"I think I like that letter very much," she whispered.

"You should." He kissed her tenderly, then glancing at me, drew her toward a window overlooking the stable courtyard. "Now," he said, his voice more brisk, "you must not look until I say."

She darted forward, nearly ripping the train from my hands. The King blocked her way. "Not until I say."

"I will look!"

They got in a loving tussle, me clinging absurdly to her train like a dog to a stick in play. Sweetest Holy Mary, give me the order to let go!

The Queen broke free of him and put her nose to the wavy glass of the window. "Is it a—? My Lord, it's a new chariot!"

"In which two can ride . . . *safely*." He nodded at me to go, then put his arms around her from behind as I receded. "It is for you and me," he said, kissing her neck, "once the weather warms."

I walked back to my chambers, the blackbird's renewed cries of fright ringing in my ears. I should be glad for the Queen and her happiness, yet I felt unsettled. Why were Doña Juana and the Inquistor-General so intent upon probing into any improprieties on Michelangelo's part? What if they dug so deep they unearthed the truth about me?

Francesca looked up from mending the hem of my skirt as I entered the room. She frowned when she saw my expression. "*Signorina,* you keep your face that way, and it will stay, just like that. What trouble you?"

I shook my head.

She spat onto the coals. They hissed; then all was silent save for the almost imperceptible groan of the thread being drawn through the thick brocade cloth. She glanced at me, then frowned at her work. "You are not the only one, *signorina*. Every heart, it have its own ache."

ITEM: *A certain Raimond Lully, governor of the isle of Mallorca and the possessor of a rich and noble heritage, became enamored of a fair and honest lady. He wooed her long and ardently, pressing for her to bestow her love on him, for she, he said, was the most beautiful woman he had ever beheld. After two years, she relented and gave him an assignation, at which time she appeared before him more radiant than ever and dressed in finest clothes. But just as he thought he was about to enter Paradise, she bared herself, showing herself to be covered with a dozen plasters. One by one, she tore them off and threw them to the ground, then, pointing to her sores, demanded of him whether he still thought she was beautiful. He left her straightaway, commended the fair lady to God in her affliction, gave up his office, and became a hermit.*

ITEM: *The greatest art conceals art.*

8 JANUARY 1561
El Alcázar, Toledo

The Queen has the Small Pox.

It is strange, since she already had a case and usually the contagion passes over previous victims. Could her earlier affliction have been something else? But there is no denying the cause of the bubbling pustules that have arisen from her cream-white skin.

It is clearly the Small Pox. We know not if she will live or die. I should sleep, but how can I, knowing My Lady is struggling for her life in the next room?

The situation has become dire since I was first called by the King's man eight days ago. I had been in my chamber, reading about a superior new red pigment obtained from a beetle from the New World, when he rapped upon my door. Upon hearing that the Queen had fallen ill, I dropped my book and followed the King's man to My Lady's chamber, with Francesca churning behind me, rubbing her hands and moaning. The King was at My Lady's bedside, looking pale and stern in the torchlight.

I dropped to a crouch next to the Queen. She stirred in her sweat-dampened sheets.

"My Lady?"

"She was well when I saw her after dinner," the King snapped.

I touched My Lady's forehead, then jerked back my hand as from a hot kettle. She watched me with glassy eyes.

"You are her favorite—where were you today?" he demanded. "What did she eat?"

"Just here, My Lord, and at the refuge for penitent women, delivering bread." I did not mention that I stayed in the coach as usual when we went on that errand, so I had not observed her in that place. "She ate nothing out of the ordinary for dinner—roast hen, figs, some marzipan. All was prepared by the palace cooks."

"Who tasted it for poison?" He looked past me at Francesca. "You?"

"No one did," I said. I felt ill. "We had not thought it necessary."

"Half the world is at war, fighting the Church. Fighting me. And you think it not necessary? Send for our cooks," the King ordered his man. "All of them. I shall see them in the anteroom."

"I shall send for doctor Hernández, too, My Lord," I said.

THE CREATION OF EVE   189

"He is coming. If you want to be of use, get her some more water."

It has been eight days since then, eight long days filled with My Lady's moans and sobs and cries of pain, until her fever broke and hundreds of pustules rose all over her face and body, marking her affliction as the Small Pox. She is unconscious now, not waking even when doctor Hernández bleeds her, her blood trickling into his cup just as surely as her life force. The King does not leave her, though his advisors beg him to stay away. Do not risk your own health, they say. Think of Spain. Think of your subjects.

But His Majesty just shakes his head and pushes away the chalices or bread or blankets that are brought to him. He says nothing, just paces by her bed, his dagger slapping against his breeches, and asks the doctor for a sign, any sign, of the return of her health.

Once, a few days ago, in the dark of night, when I had fallen asleep on the floor of her chamber after struggling with Her Majesty to keep her hands from her wounds, I woke to the sound of a man murmuring. I lay there with my nose buried in a silk-covered pillow, the sweet rotten scent of silkworms filling my head as I strained to remember where I was and why I was there.

"Heavenly Father, forgive me." The King's anguished voice clarified my wits.

I squeezed my eyes shut and tried not to breathe. I could not let him know I heard his prayers. Such was the domain of his confessor, not his wife's companion.

"Forgive me, Father. This poor girl. This lively little sprite. She touched me with her spirit—and I have ruined her, for what? For a moment's pleasure? Father warned me how too much sex weakens a body, but I gave in to her, to our lust, though I knew she was a child and I had to be strong for the both of us. This poor child, sent to me by her parents like a tun of French wine. No one has ever cherished her properly, and I am as bad as the rest, letting my unbridled desire overrule my will to take care of her. It is not her fault, Father. Let her live. I beg of you, let my sprite live."

His choking swallow wrenched my heart. "Father," he groaned, "it is right that you punish me for the sins I have committed in the past. They are most grievous. I should burn in Hell for them—both you and I know what they are. But Father, I beg you, do not punish this girl for my own wickedness."

Footsteps rasped against the rush matting as someone entered the room.

"Your Majesty." I recognized the voice of doctor Hernández. "How fares our patient?"

The King's voice turned cold and low. "Just get her well, doctor. Her mother will have my hide if not." I held my breath as I heard him leave the room.

"*¿Qué es esto?*" cried doctor Hernández, nearly tripping over me where I lay.

The light of the doctor's lantern shone on my face. Behind him stood the condesa, her frown framed by her white wimple.

"We nearly fell upon you there," she said. "Get up and go to your chamber. You do no good for her there."

Reluctantly, I returned to my chamber, to the relief of Francesca, who hurried to remove my bodice, corset, and skirt. As I lay shivering in my shift under unwarmed covers, I could not help wondering: What were the King's most grievous sins?

ITEM: *All colors, no matter their original brightness, when in shadow look to be equally dark.*

27 FEBRUARY 1561
El Alcázar, Toledo

After all these weeks, during two of which we despaired each day for her life, the Queen has survived her case of the Small Pox. Her vision, which for a time was lost, has been restored, but she is still very weak, and covered from head to toe in slowly fading red wounds. Once it was clear that she should live, the King reluctantly returned to his office to conduct the business of holding together his far-flung lands, and let the French Queen Mother take over her daughter's care from afar.

Upon the Queen Mother's orders, My Lady's frail body was bathed twice daily in asses' milk, greased with a yellow ointment relayed to us by couriers from France, and swaddled in silk gauze. I do not know what is in the ointment, but knowing the Queen Mother's penchant for magic and the gruesome ingredients in the charms of the Black Arts, I do not wish to ask. I will say only that it smells of stale human urine and scythed grass combined, and of tar. The Queen's chamber does reek of this mixture and soured asses' milk, and Francesca complains that I reek of it as well.

But the results are encouraging, though the Queen's skin remains reddened and her lovely hair has thinned to the point that you can glimpse her scalp in places.

Late in the Queen's illness, when her vision began to return, the condesa ordered that all mirrors be removed from Her Majesty's chambers, to spare My Lady shock at her appearance. The condesa remains firm in this notion, even though the Queen's imagination has begun to work and she fears she must be a dreadful monster indeed if the condesa forbids even a glimpse.

Yesterday, we were peeling the linens from the Queen's face, when again My Lady pleaded for a mirror.

"Wait just a little longer, Your Majesty," said the condesa, unrolling a strip of gauze from around Her Majesty's head, "until your recovery is complete."

"If I am going to be ugly," said the Queen, "I must begin to get used to it."

"Surely you'd rather wait to see yourself at your best," said the condesa.

I took the ball of used gauze from the condesa as she started upon another piece. I swear the condesa enjoys frightening Our Lady. "You are not ugly, Your Majesty. You bear the marks of your suffering, but they are not so deep as to be permanent."

"Thank you for telling me the truth, Sofi. I can always depend on you. So Mother's stinking ointment has worked?"

"Wonderfully," I said. "In fact, in my opinion, you might think to discontinue it. Perhaps your skin only needs now but to breathe."

"Then let us stop it!" the Queen exclaimed. "How wonderful to be rid of this stench up my nose! I fear I shall go on smelling it forever. How does madame de Clermont fare with it? Has she been using the ointment I've sent?"

I winced. Although a month had passed, I could still hear the sweet-natured French lady's gasp when she discovered that first pustule upon her hand. And I could still see her rushing to a mirror and pushing back the top of her bodice, revealing another watery wound bubbling up from the tender skin of her breast.

"You are kind to think of madame, My Lady," said the condesa, "though I know not how she fares. She is still recovering in her rooms."

I drew in a breath. Madame had not fared well. I had promised My Lady to always tell her the truth, but how did I break such troubling news?

"Your Majesty," the condesa said, "do you think discontinuing your treatment is wise? Do you not want to look your very best?"

"Sofi," said the Queen, "call for doctor Hernández. We shall let him judge."

I summoned a page. He ran off before the condesa could stop him.

When doctor Hernández came, he did indeed pronounce Her Majesty's skin to be healed enough to discontinue the malodorous balm. Influenced by the Queen's fervent pleading, he even allowed her to leave her bed to sit in a chair by the brazier. This morning, she was feeling well enough for us to wash her hair. No sooner than we had rinsed the last of the soap away with rose-scented water, attired her in a robe of black velvet lined with sable, and seated her near the warmth of the brazier with her hair spread down the back of the chair, did we hear a shouting from the rooms below.

Footsteps pounded on the stairs; the heavy door flew open. In rushed Don Carlos, clutching a fistful of drooping snowdrops to his gaunt chest.

"My Lady—I heard you are well! I rushed home from university to see you."

The Queen's hair rippled down the chair back as she turned slowly, her hand to her wounded face.

Don Carlos gasped. "Oh, My Lady!"

She smiled sadly. "Am I that wretched?"

Tears welled in his pale-lashed eyes. "I knew that your illness was grievous, but—"

A gentle tapping sounded on the doorjamb. Don Juan leaned in the doorway with his hat in his hands; Don Alessandro stood behind him. "May we come in?"

Don Carlos dropped to his knees and pressed the Queen's hand to his cheek. "I prayed! I begged God to take my life for yours—"

"And it seems that He has spared you both." Don Juan entered quietly. "No need for tears, Carlos."

But Don Carlos was too deep within his grief to pay him mind. "Oh My Lady, your beautiful hair is so thin now, and your pretty skin—"

The Queen gazed down upon the hand still captive to Don Carlos. "Ah, well, so much for my need of a mirror now. I suppose I've received my report."

The Prince looked up, tears streaming down his pasty face. "Did anyone tell you how hard I prayed for you? That I sent my love to you each day?"

"Yes, my dear Toad," she said gently, "and it helped me. I thank you for your kind wishes."

"They were not just kind wishes, My Lady! I desire only your greatest happiness. I—"

"Come," said Don Juan. "We need to allow her to rest."

Don Carlos leaned away from Don Juan. "You don't know how I feel! She is nothing to you." He looked up beseechingly at the Queen. "He has not shed a single tear, while I have wept myself sick!" Recalling his misery, he laid his face in her lap and sobbed.

The Queen stroked his hair. Slowly, she raised her head, until her gaze was met by Don Juan.

Don Alessandro looked between them. A crooked smile crossed his freckled face. "Perhaps not everyone needs to cry."

"What?" Don Carlos lifted his head, sniffing. Seeing Don Alessandro's pointed look, he peered at the pair. His attention was broken by noise in the corridor.

The King stormed into the chamber.

"Carlos! Why do you weep? Get up. I could hear your whimpering down the stairs."

Don Carlos released the Queen's hand and struggled to his feet. "Father—"

"Quiet yourself! Do you think you help her this way?"

"But I think only of her welfare."

"Do you? Or do you think only of yourself?"

"Father!" Don Carlos's voice cracked with brokenhearted wonder. "You have never spoken to me thus."

The King knotted his fists at his side, thumbs twitching against forefingers. "Just—pull yourself together."

Don Carlos nodded, his pale eyes watery with tears. To my surprise, the Queen's eyes were full, too.

"Too much crying around here." The King's cold voice belied the emotion etched on his brow. He has never been anything but protective of his son, even when others would have lost patience. I felt my own throat clog with tears as the King fought to master his countenance. Disconcertingly, I sensed that someone in the room did not share in the heartbreak of this scene. Over by the window, Don Alessandro slouched against the wall.

He straightened when he saw me, and composed that freckle-dusted face, so charmingly framed by dark ringlets, into an expression so deeply sympathetic that I wondered if I only imagined the smirk I had seen just the moment before.

ITEM: *The Queen's grandfather François I was celebrated for his love for the ladies. He formed his own personal group of maids of honor, La Petite Bande—twenty-seven young beauties chosen for their looks and wit. He dressed them to his taste and bade them to follow him everywhere, even to his bed. Beyond these ladies, his conquests were many, though he also begot seven children upon his wife.*

ITEM: *In preparation for transferring a drawing to a canvas, take care not to overfill your pounce bag with charcoal dust, for patting an overfull bag to the canvas will send dust into your eyes. As a preventative measure, it is best to keep on hand the eyewash solution made in the following manner: Steep one ounce of dried chamomile flowers in a glass horn of boiling water for ten minutes. Strain and use when cool. Also soothing for eyes swollen by an excess of tears.*

13 OCTOBER 1561
El Alcázar, Madrid

Almost eight months have passed since I last wrote. Once the Queen regained her strength, court was moved from Toledo to the recently refurbished El Alcázar in Madrid, the palace the King wishes to establish as his seat of power. To this effect, he has added towers and chapels and gardens to the old Moorish fortress.

Shopkeepers have set up stalls in the courtyard; courtiers build their palaces nearby; international merchants and ambassadors stride through the streets. Overnight the sleepy town has become a bustling place of commerce and influence. But more has changed here than the scenery.

"Why, Sofi?" the Queen lamented to me yesterday morning as I helped her into her robe of sheer black silk embroidered with gold-work leaves. Francesca hovered in the background, folding the Queen's night garb. The condesa and madame de Clermont were busy discussing who would receive the Queen's garments from the previous day, since Her Majesty does not wear the same clothing twice. Meanwhile, over in a corner, little Cher-Ami chewed on a lady's calfskin slipper he had dragged in from another chamber. "Why does the King come no more?" said the Queen. "Is it my reddened skin? My thin hair? My weak vision?"

"You know none of that is true," I said. "You have made a complete recovery from your illness. Your skin heals by the day, and your hair"—I twisted a lush hank of it away from the upright edge of her wire-stiffened collar—"is thicker than ever. Darker, too."

"So are my eyebrows," she said. "Pluck them, Sofi. I look like a bear. Mamma would think me a fright."

"Has My Lady thought of letting them grow in the Spanish fashion? They would only accent your lovely dark eyes. But regardless of any of this—you cannot say the King does not come to you."

She made a pouting face. "Oh, he comes—every Tuesday and Thursday and Saturday after vespers—he did not even make an exception for my birthday. You could set a clock by him. Indeed I think I shall. Where is that annoying buzzing piece of

German frippery he gave me? I shall melt it down to a lump of gold."

"What is your complaint, My Lady?" asked the condesa, who was now listening in.

The Queen folded her arms over her chest as I began braiding her hair. "Nothing."

The condesa cleared her throat. "*Perdón*, My Lady, but did you not wish for madame de Clermont to have your gown from yesterday?"

Poor madame. She fared less favorably than My Lady in her battle with the pox. She was so disfigured she has taken to wearing veils over her face, even now, when it is warm, and indoors, in the company of ladies. It is a shame. She was a beautiful woman, in the French way, with her pale blond hair, long nose, and hooded eyes. Now that madame is less a source of jealousy, the condesa smothers her with kindness, forcing the Queen's cast-off clothes upon her, allowing her to take the place directly behind the Queen when we venture out in public. Unless I can manage to slip back farther in the pack, I am third now, behind the condesa, who tips up her head so high Francesca hopes she will trip over a mule pile.

Now madame's eyes closed wearily in the slit between her veils. "I am drowning in used gowns, condesa. Please, take this one or I shall scream."

I clung to the Queen's hair as she shook her head with impatience. "Give it to Sofi."

"My Lady," I said, "the King has already been too generous, giving me five new gowns since Michaelmas."

"Give it to Sofi's Francesca, then."

Francesca looked up, startled. A smile grew on her square

peasant's face. She was still smiling when the Queen excused her to take the gown to our chamber.

Then the Queen shooed madame and the condesa from the room and picked up her hand mirror as she waited for everyone to leave, save me.

"I am so bored," she told my reflection when they were gone. "He comes to me now as if to an appointment with his ministers. Bedding me has become a duty he must perform."

"That cannot be true, My Lady. He loves you. Do you not see the pleasure he takes in you? How he smiled when you sang for the Dutch Lord Egmont after supper last night!" I fought to keep the irritation from my voice. I grow weary of reassuring her by the hour. She has the eye of the most important man in the world and finds no joy in it.

"The King was laughing at my stumbling over the words." She scrunched her nose, which has lost all vestiges of its childish stubbiness. "Thank you for covering for my blunders on your clavichord. You play far better than I sing."

"That is not true," I murmured. Stray wisps sprang free of her braid to curl at the nape of her neck. I wished I could seize my paintbrush and capture their sweetness on canvas. I have done so little painting since Her Majesty's illness.

The Queen saw my averted eyes. "So you do think he has lost delight in me!"

"Your Majesty! Any fool can see his love for you. He is just being careful with you, as his father advised."

She put down her mirror. "You remember that stupid letter? Ridiculous, telling Felipe to curb his desire. Why should he heed such poor advice? He didn't heed the part about learning French. Why should he obey the part that is boring?"

"My Lady, it is because he cannot bear to lose you. Your illness impressed that fear upon him. Can you not see how much he cares for you?"

"He cannot keep me like a vase on a shelf, Sofi. I am sixteen and alive." She raised her mirror to smile at me ruefully. "You would not know what it is like, never having been awakened as a woman to a man, but believe me, once you've known carnal pleasure, it eats at you night and day if you don't get it. You become a seething mass of need, just burning for—" She blew out a breath. "I cannot think about it."

I pushed a comb into her braid.

"I am sorry, Sofi, I should not speak out so crudely. But he is cruel to put me off. It makes me look foolish, an unwanted ugly hag, like Anne of Cleves, rejected by my godfather King Henry when she came to his wedding bed."

"But the King does not reject you." Not as I have been rejected by Tiberio. My silence since his letter a year ago has not provoked even his curiosity, let alone his dismay; he has not bothered to write.

"Father said my godfather Henry called the poor dame the Flanders Mare. Sofi—oh! Does the King call me the French Mare? You must tell me! I will go into hiding."

"My Lady—please. You know better."

"I know people talk. Even my mother in Paris knows of his lack of interest. She badgers me in her letters more shrilly than ever. How am I ever to get with child, she demands, when he takes me only on occasion?"

I tucked in the last comb, pretending I did not hear the unspoken thought vibrating in the air between us: The blame for the Queen's inability to bear children could not be placed solely on the King's alleged lack of desire. His fertility was proven; he had fathered Don Carlos. Even on his regimented schedule for lovemaking, they should have coupled enough by now for her to conceive.

"There now," I said, "your hair is done." Though I grew impatient with her, even I wondered if the King's great love would be never-ending for a wife who proved to be barren.

To My Most Magnificent Signorina Sofonisba,
In the Court of the Spanish King

From your silence since my letter of September past, I fear I
have offended you. I had hoped you would understand that I
had been away in Florence when you last wrote, and I replied
as quickly as I could. I would cherish hearing back from you. I
treasure our association and had never thought it would end so
abruptly.

Meanwhile, my work here continues to consume me. As the
representative of the Maestro, I am overseeing the building of
two new churches here in Rome. While I am glad to do this
for the old man, it is my work on the unfinished Pietà that
intrigues me. For every step forward I take on it, a new
problem presents itself and I must go backward. I cannot seek
the Maestro's help with it. Even if he did not hold a particular
grudge against this piece, I would not approach him on it, for
he has grown more difficult than ever. His habit of walking in
the evening in all weathers particularly alarms me. He is now
seven-and-eighty, not young! but each night after supper he
tramps off as if in a rage. When I bid him to at least put on a
cape, he glares at me as if I had called his mother a whore.
Although he has now offered me a room in his home as well as
a studio, he has remained distant toward me since my return
from Florence, or if not distant, agitated. I will admit this
hurts me. Does he think I wish to take his mantle of the
Greatest Artist in the World? I am hardly up to that. When I
present his designs to patrons, I am careful to make it clear the

designs are his and not mine. I know oh too well who the true Maestro is. Perhaps he has just grown weary from his many detractors. No man of his stature goes without acquiring his fair share of them. But in this current atmosphere of reform, with the Pope so anxious to give no one grounds to find fault with the Church, the Maestro's critics grow more shrill about his work not being sufficiently rooted in the Scriptures. They complain particularly about the naked figures in the frescoes in the Sistine Chapel, questioning their appropriateness in a place of worship. He has heard it all before. Those jealous of his talent have attacked the frescoes since they were completed decades ago, with that loudmouth Aretino increasing the noise about five years ago, but the outcry has grown more serious of late. I fear time, now, is not on his side. The constant condemnation of his work wears him down, and I am laid low myself by seeing him thus. How a letter from you would bring me cheer, though the Maestro warns me that with your duties at court you will not have time to write one. I hope he is wrong, though I do understand if he is right.

From Rome,
this 12th day of March, 1562

Your servant,
Tiberio Calcagni

ITEM: *You should have your subject sit for a portrait at the hour of the fall of the evening, for the light is perfect then, especially if it is cloudy or misty. Or have a courtyard fitted up with walls painted black and with the roof projecting forward for the subject to sit beneath. Strong light does not agree with beauty.*

ITEM: *As is said by Ovid in* The Metamorphoses, *the marten conceives and gives birth via the ear, thus enjoying its own form of an immaculate conception. Therefore it is considered to be fortuitous to include a marten in the painting of a woman who wishes to conceive.*

6 APRIL 1562

The Palace, Aranjuez

Tiberio writes, and to what end? To discuss the health of the Maestro? I have too much on my mind to add him to it. He is bold to think that I care about him now.

It being spring, we are at the country palace of Aranjuez. After walks in the woods and gardens by day, I work on the Queen's portrait in the evening. It had been the Queen's decision for me to commence upon the studies for her picture in February; her idea, too, to wear the Great Pearl in it. Mary Tudor's beloved trophy dangles like a trifling trinket from My Lady's jaunty velvet cap: her idea of a jest. It was her intention to jab at her enemies, too, by holding a fur meant to catch fleas.

"It will show how I am beset by pests," she had said last night. "And I do not mean just fleas." She wagged the gold-encrusted head of the marten whose pelt made up the accessory. "'Go, condesa!' she squeaked, as if making it speak. 'Go, Doña Juana! Shoo!'"

As I dabbed at the canvas, adding depth to the shadow of her browbone, I could not help looking over my shoulder for either of these ladies. In these past six months, as if reacting to the King's prudence in his bedding of her, My Lady has been wildly imprudent. Besides purchasing jewels and exquisite manuscripts and lavishly decorated carriages for herself, she is extravagant in her show of preference for me, awarding me with jewels, bolts of fine cloth, even, in secret, knowing my interest, books on the workings of the human body, forbidden for women by the Church. She does not think of the havoc her favor wreaks with the other ladies higher than I in rank. I am forever appeasing them, slipping farther down the row from My Lady at processions in town so that they might reap the glory of being seen with her in public, offering them the choicest dishes at dinner, dashing off flattering sketches of them, or, in Doña Juana's case, sketches of the Virgin Mary weeping. All the while, I must not show ingratitude to the Queen for lifting me up so high. It is a fine line that I walk.

"The condesa means well," I had said, dabbing at the Queen's portrait.

The Queen wrapped the flea fur around her arm, letting the thick gold chain that hung from the gilded mouth of the marten dangle down her heavy black skirt. "You always say that of people who mean not well at all."

"She does serve you faithfully."

"Why, I must ask? Do you think she does it to win the King's favor? Do you notice how she fights to get his attention? Sofi, I do think she lusts after him—imagine!"

"No, thank you."

The Queen had laughed, affording me the chance to note the way her eyes lit when amused and to quickly record it.

But I am not happy with the portrait as I near its completion. Even though I may not get credit if it is a success, for my own satisfaction, I want it to be right. Yes, I did capture her skin color—its pallor, I should say, for she has been slow in regaining her natural color since her illness. Her expression is true, too—the alert way she holds her head and her barely contained smile are just right. I am pleased with how I was able to create a sense of her liveliness by repeating the same diagonal angle of her cap, her ruff, her arm, even the decorative slashings in her sleeve, thus affording her the illusion of motion. Interesting how establishing a pattern on the diagonal works in that way. But even after adding the sharpest point of white to highlight her black pupils, I failed to catch the spirit behind her eyes. I sense that she did not want me to. The more I tried to connect with her, to plumb her true feelings, the more skittish she became, darting her gaze to her flea fur, to her dog, to the tapestry hanging behind me. It is as if she bears a secret she wishes not to reveal, and no use of sharp lines against soft, of pattern, of splashes of red on her ruby, her lips, and her sleeves to communicate her vitality, will coax it out.

Others have not seemed to see this weakness in the Queen's portrait as I work on it. After viewing the studies for it at Easter, Don Alessandro insisted that I paint his portrait—from memory, no less—now that he has returned to university. At least he believes in my work. The studies have been much praised by others, too, including by Alonso Sánchez Coello, who as Painter to

the King must now be addressed "don." On the basis of the studies, the King requested that don Alonso paint his own versions of
the Queen's portrait for His Majesty's country homes at Valsaín,
El Pardo, and here at Aranjuez. Journeymen painters have seen
the studies, too, and have in turn churned out their own rough
drawings for the price of a jug of wine. When My Lady and the
King left Madrid for Aranjuez, people clutched their crude likenesses of the Queen and held up their children to see her as she
passed, pushing and shoving to get a better glimpse. "My Lady!
My Lady!" they cried, so caught up in their eagerness that they
forgot to cheer the King.

Older courtiers whisper that His Majesty cannot bear for other
men to look upon his wife, that the King they know would put to
death any man who stared too long. That black legend is not borne
out by His Majesty's actions. I, who see him daily, have seen only
how proudly he smiles when others gaze at her with admiration in
their eyes. I have seen him basking contentedly in the reflection of
her glamour before turning back to his mountains of paperwork
and the business of ruling. He even insists that she go without a
veil when she travels amongst her people in his company. It is with
his encouragement that she wears new raiment every day and buys
herself whatever jewels she pleases, though he draws the Royal
purse strings ever tighter for other expenditures, skimping on the
pay of his troops in the Netherlands and selling off viceroyalties
in the New World. For while the expense of maintaining order in
two worlds is great, the cost of satisfying an impetuous young wife
has its own painfully dear price.

Very well. Very well. *Very well*. I cannot bear pretending I
don't care a moment longer. I will write to Tiberio, if that is what
he wants. But he may not like what I have to say.

To Tiberio Calcagni in Rome

Please forgive my silence. It was the silence of confusion. For even though you may have forgotten what transpired that evening in Michelangelo's house, I have not. In my duties of serving the Queen in her happy marriage to the King, I am reminded of it constantly. Indeed, I would not be serving Her Majesty at all if it had not been for that night. It was not my dream to teach a young queen her colors. I would have turned down the position and continued to pursue my studies, but fear of bringing shame to my family forced me to this court. I am blunt now because I have put away all hope of a happy resolution to that evening. I have accepted my fate and wish you well in your work with maestro Michelangelo. Please give him my fond regards. He has been nothing but kind to me.

From Madrid,
this 9th day of April, 1562

Sofonisba Anguissola

ITEM: *The Stork is a mute bird except for when it returns to its nest in April. Then the male and female, who have been separated all winter, throw back their heads and make a loud, prolonged clattering with their beaks when at last they see each other again.*

ITEM: *A bag of buttercups worn around the neck is said to cure insanity.*

ITEM: *One's attention must be given over entirely to perfecting the drawing and modeling in the monochromatic grays of the underpainting before one begins to consider the top layers of color.*

30 APRIL 1562
The Palace, Aranjuez

Her Majesty was in one of her silent moods today, a state I fear more than her spells of open complaining. As she herself had told me, her mother often fell into weeks of grim silence during the years she endured the French King's preference for another woman. I could not bear for this lively girl to become a dour ghost as had her mother, especially over disappointment in a husband who truly cares for her, albeit not in the manner of her dreams.

Yes, the King can be rigid and sometimes distant and even frightening, especially if one grasps the limitlessness of his power, but My Lady should enjoy his favor while she has it. If anyone has just cause to be glum, it is I, having rashly revealed myself to Tiberio by my letter a fortnight ago. So to cheer us this day, I suggested a walk in the woods after Mass, it being a fresh, bright day. She shrugged but made no objection.

The smell of incense from Mass still clung to our clothes as we strolled over the bridge and into the woodlands beyond the river. It was a typical fine morning in late April, with a damp breeze full of the green perfume of new leaves and the awakening earth as we tramped through the woods, our skirts dragging along the sandy trails, little Cher-Ami scampering ahead of us. The Queen and I were alone—madame de Clermont had returned to her bed as she so often does these days. The condesa said she would join us shortly; she wished to take advantage of madame's absence to chide the French ladies, no doubt. I had sent Francesca back to the palace to find us a snack—perhaps some cheese, or some fruit, or some honey-and-almond pastries. It was just the Queen and me, picking wildflowers, at least I was—the Queen could have been making a bouquet of nettles, for all the care she paid to her gathering.

I had brought along drawing materials in case inspiration should strike. With my sketchbook under my arm and my string-wrapped chalk gingerly pressed between my lips, I was tucking some buttercups into my handful when I spied doctor Hernández in a clearing on a sunny slope, on his knees inspecting the leaves of one of perhaps twenty low plants growing in a row. Next to him knelt a man dressed in a countryman's tunic and leather leggings. I understood from his clean-shaven face that he was not Spanish. The Spaniards do love their mustaches and beards.

I took my chalk from my mouth. "Doctor Hernández!" I called out, seizing upon a possible diversion for My Lady. I had no compunction in addressing the doctor freely. He is a married man, quite devoted to his wife, and he treats me as he would a daughter, protective of my imagined virginity. We had gotten quite familiar with each other while bringing the Queen through her terrible illness, and through the frequent fleeting fevers and skin eruptions to which Her Majesty is prone. Over our many hours in each other's company, I had become acquainted with the doctor's interest in plants from the New World, and in his hope of discovering their medicinal properties.

"Doctor Hernández!" I called. "Have you a new specimen there?"

He sat back on his knees. When he saw the Queen and me, he dropped his measuring stick and stood, the other man doing the same behind him.

The Queen smiled, pulling in her chin, which is sharper these days with the flesh of childhood gone from it. "Doctor Hernández," she said.

He kissed her hand, his craggy face somber. "Your Majesty. Picking clover?"

She looked at the sad little bouquet in her other hand. "I have simple tastes in flowers." Her laugh was a tonic to my ears.

"Your Majesty, you look a little pale," he said. "Have you been taking the roots of the plant I sent to you?"

"Sofi had them boiled into a tea for me."

"Francesca does it." I let the buttercups fall from my hand and readjusted my sketchbook, smudging the edges with yellow fingerprints.

"Very good." Doctor Hernández nodded to me with what

would be deemed a grimace in another man, though those of us who know him would understand it to be a smile. "And? Do you feel stronger, Your Majesty?"

"They really are foul-tasting, *monsieur*."

"You are not consuming them daily?" He saw from my expression this was true. "Your Majesty, how are you to benefit from their goodness if you do not take them each morning?"

"They are terribly hard to get down."

"Do you mix the brew with honey and mint?" asked the other man.

"'*Your Majesty*,'" doctor Hernández whispered with a frown.

The Queen waved her hand. "We are not standing on ceremony now. The condesa is not here."

"Your Majesty, this is doctor Debruyne," said doctor Hernández. "He comes to me from Bruges. He, too, has a great interest in the medicinal plants of the New World."

A long-boned man with hair and eyes of the same rich brown, doctor Debruyne stepped forward to kiss first the Queen's hand and then mine, the tassels of the white shirt he wore under his tunic dangling before him. "You must forgive me. I can be a bit of a root granny. I will spout off remedies without thinking."

"You must get along well with doctor Hernández," said the Queen.

"I never thought of myself as a 'root granny,'" doctor Hernández said stiffly. "A scientist, yes. Grandmother, no."

"I meant that you knew so many remedies, *monsieur*, not that you were a granny. Oh—Cher-Ami!" The Queen dropped her weeds to scoop up the pup, who was watering the leather water bucket near doctor Hernández's feet.

Doctor Debruyne flashed a good-natured smile as she scolded

her dog in French. I found that I could not take my gaze from his teeth. They were straight and white, with just a hint of a gap between the front two.

"Actually," he said, "it was my grandmother who got me interested in plants and their properties, though she never dreamed of there being a land beyond the sea when she was a girl. How she itches to go to the Indies now, to dig up new and exciting roots, though she is in her ninetieth year."

"No more than do I," said doctor Hernández. "Doctor Debruyne has offered to draw the plants for my catalogue when I sail, though I regretfully must refuse his generous offer. I need him to assume my studies here. It is a pity, though. He is a gifted artist as well as a physician." He turned to doctor Debruyne. "You would be interested to hear that doña Sofonisba has a gift for drawing, too." He nodded at my sketchbook as if providing evidence. "She studied under the great Michelangelo."

Doctor Debruyne pushed back the hank of hair that had fallen into his eyes. "Did you? How extraordinary."

I looked down quickly. I could see the sandy gray soil of Aranjuez under the nails of his long fingers.

"I would be honored to see your work," he said.

"Perhaps you already have," said doctor Hernández. "Her drawing of a boy being bitten by a crab has been copied all around Europe. In fact, it was the great Michelangelo who first commissioned it from her."

"The Queen has done her own drawing in the same vein." I kept my gaze lowered. "Only it is her little dog there who is the surprised victim. It is really very good."

"And you are really very bad," the Queen said, scolding Cher-Ami as she put him down. He tottered off, tail a-wag, bits of leaf litter clinging to his white fur.

"I am familiar with Michelangelo's work," said doctor Debruyne. "I have seen copies of the cartoons for the Sistine Chapel.
I find them to be exquisite, though I understand that there has
been some question—"

"Being from Bruges, you must know the work of Memling and
van Eyck," I said.

"Yes, of course, but I am particularly intrigued by Michelangelo's—"

"The King is fond of the Flemish painter Hieronymus Bosch,"
I said. "Here he is called El Bosco."

"Oh," said the Queen, "El Bosco—he is the one who likes to
paint about sin."

I stole an upward glance. Doctor Debruyne was watching me,
puzzled. I shifted my paper under my arm as inwardly I cringed.
What must he think of my awkward conversation? But I could
brook no further talk of maestro Michelangelo.

Doctor Hernández bowed to the Queen, then turned to pluck
a leaf from the plant at his feet. "Your Majesty," he said, rising,
"have you had your headaches of late?"

The Queen pulled her gaze from the woods. "I'm sorry—I
thought I heard someone out there. *Excusez-moi?*"

"Have you had headaches?"

"Yes. Always."

"I see." Doctor Hernández glanced at doctor Debruyne.

Doctor Debruyne nodded at the oval-shaped leaf doctor
Hernández twirled between his fingers. "My colleague here has
something from the New World that allegedly cures them."

Doctor Hernández stilled the leaf. "We aren't sure—"

"A cure for headaches?" said the Queen. "What is it?"

"The conquistadors called it the miracle plant," said doctor
Debruyne. "The people of the Indies chew its leaves to relieve

their aches and pains. Imagine the good we could do with it here if we can get it to grow."

"We cannot count on that," said doctor Hernández. "It is a miracle that the rooted plants sent to me from the New World last fall have survived their travels. That they are still alive is a credit to doctor Debruyne."

The doctor bowed, his glossy forelock slipping into his eyes.

"It will help my headaches?" The Queen held out her hand. Reluctantly, doctor Hernández laid the leaf across her palm.

"What is this plant?" she asked.

Doctor Debruyne smiled. "Coca."

"Please excuse my excess of zeal, Your Majesty," said doctor Hernández. "We should not have spoken of this so soon. You must wait until after we have carefully measured its properties before you can try it. As of now, we are relying on hearsay from the Indian people—accidents can happen if we rush into application." He frowned at doctor Debruyne.

"Accidents?" said the Queen.

Just then Don Alessandro and Don Juan appeared in the bend of the path leading from the palace, Don Alessandro whacking the undergrowth with his sword, Don Juan gazing up into dappled light sparkling through the trees. When Cher-Ami bounded for the *caballeros*, yapping, Don Alessandro raised his sword in jest. Don Juan plucked up the dog and tucked him under his arm.

"Your Majesty." Don Alessandro sheathed his sword with the *shish* of metal upon metal and took the Queen's hand. He turned and opened it. "A leaf?"

She dropped it, her cheeks bright pink. "Where have you been? You did not even say good-bye to me at Easter. I am much offended."

Her lips quivered with an ill-hid smile as first Don Alessandro kissed her hand and then Don Juan, who handed her the pup. I, too, was glad to see them. The palace was dull without them now that they were at university. How rarely they'd been home since the Queen's riding accident a year and a half before.

Don Alessandro grinned. He had matured into manhood over these past two years, though with his dark curls and darting eyes, he still had the mischievous air of a grown cherub. "Do not look on us with such ill favor, My Lady. We would have come sooner if our tutors had let us escape. Security has been tightened since Don Carlos's adventure." There was an uncomfortable silence, acknowledging the tragic event to which Don Alessandro had so flippantly referred. Last October in Alcalá, during the dead of night, Don Carlos had fallen down the stairs of his lodgings and dashed his head against a stone step. He had teetered on the brink of death for eight days, until, in desperation, the doctor called in from the Netherlands had ordered a hole to be drilled through his skull. From this surgery, Don Carlos developed a fever so high that only prayer and the intervention of Saint Isidro the Laborer, whose bones had been laid next to him in his sickbed, could have saved his life. Only after it was clear that Don Carlos was going to live did Don Juan come forward with the story that the Prince had been sneaking off to see the daughter of their porter. But when Don Alessandro retold this tale in the Prince's presence when we first saw them again at Easter, Don Carlos was furious. He flashed the Queen a lovelorn look and said that it was to another lady he had been stealing.

"It is because of Don Carlos we are here," said Don Juan. "He sent us to look for you, Your Majesty."

"He would have come himself," said Don Alessandro, "but he has a tremendous headache, though we are not to tell you that. Doña Sofonisba, have you started on my portrait?"

I confessed that I had not.

"You've got your paper there. Why not sketch me now?"

"Perhaps Don Carlos would benefit from your coca leaves," the Queen said to doctor Hernández.

Doctor Hernández grimaced. "I regret they aren't ready to test."

"As his physician at court, *señor*, you should be informed," said Don Juan. "Don Carlos has not gone a day without pain since his fall."

"He is lucky he's alive," Don Alessandro muttered, "hard as he cracked his head."

"How much pain would you say he was in?" asked doctor Hernández.

"He does not complain of his suffering," said Don Juan, "but it is apparent in his behavior. His moods are dark, and he is provoked into violence by the smallest thing, which is not within his character. You know what a gentle soul he has."

I lowered my gaze. Don Juan was most generous. Even before his accident, Don Carlos was unstable and easily upset. I shuddered to think how difficult he must be now.

"Please beg my pardon for interrupting," doctor Debruyne said to his colleague, "but this is why we must learn more about this coca, to ease the suffering in cases like this."

"Yes," said doctor Hernández, scowling, "but—"

"Please, doctors," said the Queen, "you must not let us stop you, not if this could help Don Carlos. Please get on with your work."

We bade the physicians good-bye and began down the path taken by Don Juan and Don Alessandro. The low heels of my slippers sank into the sandy soil as I padded along next to Don Alessandro, who had resumed his sport of whacking the trailside vegetation with his sword. I could smell the muddy river through the trees, though I could not see it from our path. Ahead of us, the Queen walked with Don Juan, her hands folded over her belly. The King's young brother has also matured since going to university. The top of My Lady's head now reaches only to his shoulder. And though his complexion is still as fresh and rosy as when he was a youth straight from the country, his former open friendliness has been tempered with reserve.

"It is good of you to be concerned about Don Carlos," the Queen said to him. She looked not at Don Juan's face, but at little Cher-Ami trotting on the trail before her.

"I am worried about him, My Lady," he said. "He is definitely not himself."

"I have heard ugly rumors," said the Queen. "It was all over Madrid—is it true that he forced a cobbler to eat the boots he had made because Don Carlos did not like their fit?"

Next to me, Don Alessandro kept slashing. "Until the old man vomited them up, he did," he called to them.

Don Juan turned on him. "Why do you say such things? People will believe you."

"Don't get so hot," said Don Alessandro. "You know I only jest."

"You underestimate the power of the spoken word, my friend. Already My Lady has heard in Madrid the jest you started in Alcalá—which, by the way, I did not find humorous even the first time you told it. Should that not convince you how far a few dropped words can travel?"

"I find it rather gratifying that my joke has carried so far," said Don Alessandro. He grinned. "No harm done. No one truly believes our soft-hearted Prince would order such a thing."

There was a short silence.

"*Señor,*" I asked, "how fares your Latin? Both of you, with your noses so much in the books these days—you must be veritable Virgils."

"My Latin is miserable," said Don Alessandro. "I can no more speak it than can a turtle. However, we have learned the art of debate, have we not, Don Juan?"

"Not so well," said Don Juan. He threw Cher-Ami a stick.

Don Alessandro poked at a yellow tree fungus with his sword point. "We have the most important topics to debate. The subject this week: Did God replace the rib he took from Adam to make Eve with another rib, or did He just pack a bit of flesh in its place?"

The Queen glanced at Don Juan, then waited for Don Alessandro to catch up. "And which position did you take?" she asked Don Alessandro.

"I, *señora*, went with the flesh."

"And did you win the debate?"

Don Alessandro smiled but did not answer.

"Oh, he won, in his fashion," said Don Juan, with disapproval in his voice. "In the end."

Don Alessandro twirled his sword. "My opponent saw my point, so to speak."

We walked along, Cher-Ami now darting, now pouncing upon invisible creatures on the sandy path. "Back in France, the ladies had debates, too," said the Queen, "among themselves."

"Oh, the old how-many-angels-dance-upon-a-pinhead argument?" said Don Alessandro.

"No." The Queen took a few more steps, her skirts brushing the bracken sprawling into the trail. "We debated which is better in love: fulfillment or desire."

"Oho," said Don Alessandro, "not the sort of thing our professors debate. Which did you argue, My Lady?"

"I was a child," she said lightly. "I didn't know which to champion."

"And now?" he said.

"Now, *monsieur*, I know better than to deliberate this with you."

He whacked at a fern. "You hurt me, My Lady."

She twitched her skirt from the vegetation upon which it had snagged. "Don Juan, my mother writes that not only have you discontinued your pursuit of my sister's hand, but that you dropped your hunt for the hand of my cousin Mary Stuart."

"I think," said Don Juan, "it was more a case of them dropping me. Apparently I was not an eager enough suitor. Both had been your mother's idea for me to wed, not mine."

Don Alessandro sent a toad hopping at swordpoint. "Just be glad your brother the King feels your blood is not rich enough for ones of their high rank, or you would be in France just now, 'eating peaches,' as they say."

Don Juan cut him a look of warning.

The Queen's frown did not hide her good cheer. "You wouldn't want them, anyhow. My sister is but a child and not suited for you at all, and Mary Stuart—I must tell you, she would be the worst shrew of a wife."

"A shrew?" Don Alessandro cried in mock horror.

"She was always bossing me around the nursery. Father made me bow to her in all things, as it was known since she was an infant that she was to wed my brother and be the Queen of France as well as Scotland. It made her insufferable. Oh, she acted demure and sweet around Father—sweet to me, too, as long as she got her way. But if crossed, how she would roar . . . until Father came. Then she was a meek little puss again."

"I would not like a two-faced woman," said Don Juan.

"Ah, so Uncle does know what he wants in a woman," said

Don Alessandro. "I suppose this comes with all the experience he is having with the ladies these days."

The Queen drew in a breath. "Is this true?"

"No."

"Goat feathers," said Don Alessandro. "You know the ladies love you. I'm sick of picking up the gloves they 'accidentally' drop near you. Why don't you just pick them up yourself?"

Don Juan shrugged. "They're throwing them at you."

"You know they're not." Don Alessandro snorted in disgust. "I don't understand. Why is it that those who try the least are always the most generously rewarded? Uncle dreams of being a modest gentleman's child, then finds he is the Emperor's son. He gives his books the briefest glance, then gets the highest praise from our *profesores*. He pays more attention to his dog than to the pretty *señoritas,* and the women throw their clothing at him."

"You exaggerate," Don Juan muttered.

An awkward silence fell over our group, amplifying the swish of skirts and breeches as we walked. At last we turned a corner under the spreading branches of an oak. Ahead, before a fountain in which water splashed down the green mossy face of a stone lion, stood the King. He was leaning on an arquebus, its wooden stock sunk into the sandy soil, as he spoke to his sister Doña Juana and doña Eufrasia, whose little dogs snuffled through a drift of leaves near their skirts, oblivious of the King's pair of mastiffs being restrained at leash a short distance away by one of the King's men. It appeared to be an innocent encounter between siblings with their attendants. Perhaps that is all it was.

The Queen's pup scampered forward, then rolled on its back as the other ladies' dogs rushed to meet it. The smile that lit the King's eyes when he saw the Queen dimmed when he took in the presence of Don Juan.

"My dear." He hung his gun over his arm to kiss the Queen's hand.

He let Don Juan and Don Alessandro kiss his ring. "I heard you were here," he said to the *caballeros*. "Why are you not at university?"

"We came to celebrate El Sotillo," said Don Alessandro.

"Didn't you overshoot your mark?" said the King. He smiled slightly at his sister's chuckle. "The festival is in Madrid."

"Your son the Prince wanted to come here first, Your Majesty," said Don Alessandro.

"Have you seen him?" said Don Juan.

A hint of worry shadowed the King's cool face. "No."

"I fear his headaches grow worse," said Don Juan. "I mentioned it to doctor Hernández just now."

The King beheld his brother dispassionately. With the two standing together, I could not help noticing the growing inequality between the brothers, a phenomenon only increasing with time. It made me wince for the King to see how much more handsome their shared features were in Don Juan.

"Thank you for your concern for my son," said the King, "but I am keeping an eye on the situation."

"Of course," said Don Juan.

"How are your studies coming along?" Doña Juana asked the two *caballeros*.

The Queen spoke up loudly, as if wishing to assert her place. "They are debating whether God replaced Adam's rib with a fresh rib or with flesh after giving it to Eve. Don Alessandro thinks it was just flesh."

The King stood his gun back on the ground, causing one of his mastiffs to start forward. Its handler jerked him back.

"What did you argue, little brother?" Doña Juana asked with

a brittle smile. She picked up her dog, leaving doña Eufrasia's pet and Cher-Ami to snuffle companionably in the leaves. "About the rib?"

Don Juan opened his mouth, then settled into himself with a frown. "I think trying to understand God's mysteries is a waste of time."

"Oh?" said the King. "You wish not to know Our Lord?"

"I think that we cannot know the workings of a being greater than ourselves, Your Majesty. To think that we can is to give ourselves more credit than we deserve."

"Well spoken," said the Queen.

The King swung his gaze at her, then readdressed Don Juan. "So you think Scripture study is unnecessary?"

"I am not saying that at all. I am saying only that time is better spent on problems we can solve for the good of the living than on theoretical questions we can never answer."

The King's lips formed a thin red crescent in his beard. "Are you sure that is not just lazy thinking?"

"Dear little brother," said Doña Juana, "I would not recommend speaking of this too loudly before Inquisitor-General Valdés. He has a poor sense of humor these days, with the Protestants renewing their rioting in France and emboldening heretics here."

"Who is joking?" said Don Juan.

"You are," said Doña Juana. "If you are smart." She turned to me with a smile. "Doña Sofonisba. I have been meaning to tell you—Inquisitor-General Valdés says some poetry written by your Michelangelo to young men has recently come to light. There has been talk of his wickedness before, but his friends have always managed to hush it. Would you know of a young gentleman named—"

One of the King's mastiffs rushed out and bit Cher-Ami, who

had just snatched something from the pile of leaves. Cher-Ami screamed sorely as the handler yanked away the mastiff, with Cher-Ami's trophy—a dead canary—now in its own jaws.

The Queen clutched her pet to her breast.

"Is he hurt?" said the King.

Don Juan stepped over to examine the pup, who licked him fearfully as Don Juan gently manipulated his leg. "Try setting him down," he told the Queen.

She placed him on the ground. Cher-Ami yelped, then scuttled under his mistress's skirts.

"He moves well," said Don Juan. "I think he is more afraid than hurt."

"Who are you, Uncle?" Don Alessandro said with a laugh. "Saint Francis?"

The Queen scooped up her dog. *"Merci, monsieur,"* she said gratefully.

"Juan didn't do anything," said the King. "The dog was unharmed."

Francesca appeared, winded and sweating and mumbling in Italian as she struggled along the path with a basket the size of a soup kettle. She gasped when she looked up and saw us with the new members to our party. She dropped the basket and scuttled forward to kiss the King's hand and curtsey to Doña Juana. The King bade us to repair to our picnic, and we did so, though without Don Juan, who did not want to leave Don Carlos waiting at the palace. Our smaller group picnicked on the banks of the river, eating cheese and ham and the famous strawberries of Aranjuez, as diving ducks popped up from the water, drops rolling off their curled tails, and shiny green dragonflies poked among the bulrushes. Don Alessandro entertained the Queen and me with humorous stories about his life as a student at Alcalá while I sketched him, though I fear we were not the most appreciative of audiences, for the Queen's gaze did rove toward the palace and mine toward the sunny slope on the other side of the woods. Even as I thought of doctor Debruyne kneeling in the soil, tending his miraculous coca, I wondered: To whom had the Maestro addressed his poems?

ITEM: *In Rome, as in Spain, the penalty for sodomy is death, or five years' rowing in the King's galleys, which is the same as death.*

1 MAY 1562

The Palace, Aranjuez

Francesca has been more irritable of late. True, that is like saying that vinegar grows tart. But this morning, as I readied to go to Madrid for El Sotillo, the festival of Saint James the Green, you would have thought Francesca would be pleased by the prospect of having a few days at her disposal, and would be in a light (for her) mood. And I especially needed her benevolence just then— Doña Juana's accusation that the Maestro wrote poetry to young men unsettled me.

But no. Instead of attending me in a cheerful (for her) manner after she roused me before dawn, she tied my bodice as if strangling it. She plopped the rolls that pad my skirts onto my hips like a pair of saddlebags onto a mule, then jerked the strings of my skirt as if intending to rip them in two. When she braided my hair, she tugged it so hard that my scalp still tingled as I hurried down the corridor to the Queen's chamber.

"Your face, you cover it in the sun," she ordered, stumping behind me.

"I will," I said. "But I doubt if I will get out of the carriage at the parade grounds. I hear that Their Majesties do not."

"You stay in the carriage, then."

"You need not worry. When am I not a perfect lady?"

She clapped her hand to her jaw and scowled.

"Did you want to say something?"

She shook her head.

I tried to laugh it off. "You are just sad that you're not going."

"Bah!"

I did not believe her. The Queen's Spanish ladies are all astir about the festival. They say that everyone—from grand ladies and gentlemen in their mule-drawn carriages, to shopkeepers and their wives walking with their little ones gamboling between them, to servant boys, released for the day and loping along in freedom—wishes to go to the banks of the Manzanares for El Sotillo, so named for its location in a shaded grove near the Toledo bridge. The Queen, who has been too ill in past years to attend, is especially eager to see the crowd and to witness the custom unique to this festival: be they old or young, rich or poor, infirm or well, every last subject turns away when Royalty first passes by.

"I am sorry there's no room in the carriage," I said.

"With the King and Madonna Elisabetta? With the Prince and Signore Juan? Bah! You not get me in that wagon." She spat. *"Fratelli, flagelli."*

"Francesca! The wrath of brothers is not the wrath of devils. Not these brothers. The eyes of the world are upon them."

She shook her stubby finger. "You mark my words."

Hours later, joggling to and fro on the seat next to the Queen, I could still see Francesca's sour face as our carriage trundled along the stony road to Madrid. I tried to get her dire warning out of my mind as Don Carlos chattered merrily to the Queen.

Happiness lit the translucent flesh of his face, illuminating the webbing of thin blue veins within. "It is the most curious custom, My Lady," he said in an animated tone. "As soon as we arrive, the people will turn away from us. If they are in carriages, they will close their curtains. If on foot, they will turn their backs. Even their horses are turned away. We can see our people but they must not see us."

"Truly?" The plume in the Queen's turban wafted as we joggled along. She glanced at Don Juan, staring out the window next to Don Carlos. "It makes no sense. Why do they do this?"

Don Carlos shrugged cheerfully. "Tradition."

"And here I wore my best gown—for nothing."

"Oh, not for nothing," Don Carlos said reverently.

I glanced at the King, sitting on the other side of Don Carlos. The sunlight beaming through the carriage window caught the clear curvature of his eye as he studied the barren landscape. I wondered how I might catch that transparency in paint.

"Your Majesty," the Queen asked him, "how did this custom come about?"

The King rolled his gaze across the carriage interior. Dust motes danced in the shaft of light between us as he considered the question.

"It has always been," he said.

"Did they do it in Grandfather's time?" Don Carlos asked.

"Yes. They did. My father and I went together, once, when I was twelve."

"Once!" cried Don Carlos. "Why just once?"

"My father was in Spain for only two years altogether during the time he ruled," said the King. "And when he was here, he had too much business to conduct to go to little parties. Our lands were not won by attending *fiestas*."

I stole a glance at Don Juan. He would not have been born if the Emperor had not spent so much time outside Spain. I wondered if he was thinking this, too.

"What good is being King if you cannot enjoy it?" Don Carlos exclaimed.

"When my father turned his kingdoms over to me," said the King, "he was a tired old man, far older than his fifty-six years. Believe me, my son, you should enjoy this time when you do not feel the weight of the crown upon your head."

"I will not mind being King when my time comes. I will be a good one. But I have to have some practice, Father. How am I to know how to rule without experience?" He looked away, exposing the side of his head where the hole had been cut to save his life. Though it had been nearly six months, the scar in his temple was still an angry shade of red. He turned back to the King. "I don't understand why you won't send me to the Netherlands as your representative."

The King drew a breath as if bracing himself for a familiar battle. "Carlos, you are too young."

"Too young! I am almost eighteen—you were sixteen when your father sent you to see our kingdoms."

"Times are different now. Then, the monk Luther was but a thorn in the side of the Church. Now bands of his followers wish to overturn our rule. The Low Countries in particular require an experienced person's statesmanship, influenced as they have been by rioters. Any false move could tip the balance and we could lose our grip."

"Why do we need to grip? Why can we not hold on gently?"

"If only it were that simple."

"It is that simple! The Dutch deserve someone young and full of ideas, a new way of going about things. They don't want boring old men like Cardinal de Granvelle, and they certainly don't want Don Alessandro's mother, an old meddler with a mustache on her lip. Why don't you give me a chance to show you?"

"His mother proved her loyalty to me, doing what I had asked of her when her husband had fought my rule in Parma. Her sacrifice was long ago—Alessandro was only seven—but I do not forget."

"That was then—this is now!"

The King sighed deeply. He glanced at me, then sat up as if glad to find a diversion from their argument. "Doña Sofonisba, my sister has asked that you might do her portrait. She insists that don Alonso will not do."

I was so startled I am afraid I simply stared.

"You will be able to spare her?" he asked the Queen.

"It's not fair!" Don Carlos blurted. "I am almost as old as you were when your father abdicated and gave you the world. All I ask for is the Netherlands!"

We swayed in uncomfortable silence, I in shock from hearing that Doña Juana admired my painting, the others on edge from the discord in the air. The carriage rolled along, its traces jangling and its wooden body creaking.

Don Juan leaned forward. "I think I see the city walls."

He pulled back so the rest of us could peer out the window, though the King, I noticed, only closed his eyes.

Don Carlos clapped with eagerness, forgetting his fury as quickly as a child. "Look, My Lady! See the riverbanks? There's a line of carriages."

"Oh! Now I do." The Queen pulled me by the arm. "Sofi— look very hard, you can see the people. Will they turn their backs on us the whole day, Don Carlos?"

"Only when we first pass by." He crossed his arms, causing the ermine-trimmed sleeves of his cape to pool on his puffed velvet breeches. "I don't know if the rule applies to you, Uncle, since you are not full-blooded."

"Don Carlos!" the Queen exclaimed.

"I can't help that he is a bastard."

"Don Carlos!"

He shrugged. "Don Juan knows I mean nothing. Don Alessandro's mother is a bastard, too, and I don't think the people would have to turn away from him, either, if he were here. He's not purest Royalty, since she is not." He saw my poorly concealed look of surprise. "What? Did you not know? Doña Margarita's mother was—I don't know, some nobody—but Grandfather was her father, just like he was Don Juan's. I thought everyone knew. That is why Grandfather married her so highly to the Duke of Parma, who turned out to be a crook. But she did what Father asked of her, and for that alone he lets her rule the Netherlands." He cut the King a pointed look. "Even though I would be much better at it."

But the King did not pick up his challenge, and the excitement of arriving at El Sotillo dissolved any remaining ill feeling in the air. The mules' hooves rang out sharply against stone as our carriage rattled over the Toledo bridge. The heralds riding before us announced our presence with their trumpets; the coachmen shouted; the carriage wheels ground into the dust. Even as I drew back the curtain, the people processing on foot began to turn away. One by one, they rotated on the crowded path along the river until, to a person, they stood with their backs toward us, the plumes in the men's hats and the tasseled edges of the women's shawls fluttering in the wind. Only the cry of an infant broke the odd hush.

"It is a marvel!" the Queen whispered. "Just as you say, Don Carlos."

"These people know who their master is." He leaned over Don Juan and banged on the door. "Open up!"

"Carlos, let them be." The King spoke quietly so as to keep his words from the wall of humanity just outside our window. "The people turn away as a show of their respect."

Sunlight poured into our carriage as the door opened, framing in the doorway the coachman in his crested helmet. "Yes, Your Majesty?"

Don Carlos clambered over Don Juan, pushed past the coachman, and spilled outside. Before anyone could react, he picked himself up and rushed to an ancient *caballero* garbed in the long robes of the previous century.

"*¡Buenos días!*"

The old man pointed his white beard as far away as he could, but the Prince thrust his face into the elderly gentleman's view, forcing him to hobble in a circle.

"I said hello, old man!"

The Queen shrank back next to me. "What is he doing?"

Don Juan sprang from the carriage and to Don Carlos's side. "Your Majesty," he said, swinging his arm around Don Carlos, "look at how this gentleman turns away. How he must love and respect you."

"He does, doesn't he?" Don Carlos peered into the open carriage to see if the Queen was watching.

"Carlos." The King's jaw was rigid with mortification. "Come back here now!"

Don Carlos's happy expression faded. He shrugged off Don Juan's arm, then threw himself before a one-legged soldier. "You there!"

The soldier pivoted on his crutch, but Don Carlos would not let him escape. "*¡Buenos días!* It is your Prince! Speak to me!"

"He shames himself," the Queen whispered to the King, her eyes full of tears. "You must do something!"

In a low voice, the King told the coachman, "Bring him here. *Now*."

But before the coachman could move, Don Carlos sidled up to a toddling girl whose mother could not tug her away fast enough. He stuck his face before the child, a girl so young as to have only a few pale wisps for hair. "Boo!"

The child pulled back.

He galumphed closer, his pasty face lit in a goblin's grin. "I'm going to gobble you up!"

The child broke into tears.

Don Carlos stood up, hands on hips. "Mother, get your child. She cries like a baby."

"She *is* a baby, Carlos." Don Juan got down on his knee to comfort the child.

The King nodded at the coachman and a herald. They snatched Don Carlos by the arms.

"What are you doing!" He writhed as they wrestled him toward the carriage. "Let go of me! Let go!"

The men pushed Don Carlos inside the carriage and slammed the door. The Queen flinched with each blow as he kicked the walls.

"To the palace," the King told the driver. "Quickly."

The carriage bounced as the driver swung onto his post at the front of the vehicle.

"You make a fool of me!" Don Carlos cried. "I was only playing!"

With a whip-crack and a shout, we jerked to a hurried start.

"You shouldn't have done this!" Don Carlos sobbed. "What will everybody think? I'll never forgive you. Never!"

Rocking in the thundering carriage, I caught one last glimpse of the riverbank, where Don Juan still knelt next to the child as he spoke to her mother.

Except for the mother, whose shyness was evident in her posture even as she receded in the distance, the people surrounding Don Juan kept firmly turned away.

ITEM: *To beautify your face: Soften white beans in white wine for nine days, then pound them and return to the wine. Take the milk of a goat, whole barley, and boil them until the barley is broken. Mix these things together and add six egg whites. Distill for two weeks, then use to wash the face.*

ITEM: *While extracting the tooth is the most efficacious cure for toothache, it has been suggested that one might hold a candle close to the offending tooth so that the smoke might flush out the worm causing the pain. A cure might also be found in touching a dead man's tooth.*

4 MAY 1562

The Palace, Aranjuez

I shall not mince words. The trip to Madrid was a disaster. The blow to Don Carlos's head has altered him completely. While he is not the cruel beast of Don Alessandro's jest, forcing cobblers to eat their boots, he is completely unpredictable. It is as if his injury has robbed him of his self-control. At dinner that night in Madrid, he spit his soup all over his page when he deemed it too hot. The next day, he threw an apple (which hit the condesa) at a bullfight, after he had taken a bite and found a worm. He shouted something vulgar during a play. These were but a few of his eruptions. In the space of three days, there were too many, and it is too painful to recount them all here. The King deals with his son's aberrant behavior by determinedly pretending the problem doesn't exist; the Queen is tense and watchful. It tears my heart to pieces.

This is why I was particularly susceptible to upset when I arrived back in Aranjuez this afternoon and Francesca wasn't there to greet me. I searched the palace only to find her outside, pacing in the stable yard.

"What are you doing here?" I asked tiredly. "I looked everywhere for you. I would have never found you if madame's woman had not told me you'd gone out-of-doors."

She kept walking, her head down. Next to the stable yard, horses cropped grass in the pasture. The place smelled of straw and manure.

"At least you could say hello."

"Buongiorno."

I trudged toward the palace. A horse nickered from the pasture. I stopped and looked behind me. "Are you not coming?"

"Go. I catch up."

"What is the matter with you?"

"Tooth."

I stopped to frown at her.

She touched her left jaw and winced.

"Francesca!" I rushed to her side. "Why did you not tell me? How long have you been suffering?"

"Six day. Today, yesterday—the worst."

"Oh, dear Francesca! I am so sorry. What have you done for it?"

"I put the clove on the tooth, but it no good. Then I try holding the candle to it. The worms, they no fall out."

Tenderly, I turned her sallow face by her chin. "Your left side is swollen. Why don't you go back to bed?"

"No. *Grazie.* I want to walk."

I had no choice but to leave her to stump along in the stable yard, a sturdy bowed figure with her hands knotted at her chest, her hair scraped into an iron-gray bun. The Queen expected my attendance as soon as I could manage, for I'd left her in the care of the condesa and madame de Clermont. The two fared worse than ever of late, with the condesa's condescending pity only fueling madame's distaste for her rival. Indeed, their present hostile silence was even more discomfiting than their former bickering had been.

Later that afternoon, I was walking with the Queen and her other ladies in the King's woods, scarcely listening to a silly argument between the condesa and madame about which is best, French wine or Spanish. (Neither—it is Italian.) The Queen herself was quiet, as she had been since our trip to Madrid, upset, I assume, from her new awareness of the extent of the damage Don Carlos had suffered in his injury. My mind was shuttling like a startled hen between worrying about Francesca's tooth and painting Doña Juana, when we came upon a gardener in a countryman's smock and boots, digging under an elm tree. Cher-Ami scuttled over to greet him.

"Why, hello, little one," he said, petting the dog. He stood as soon as he saw the Queen. I drew in my breath. It was doctor Debruyne.

He kissed the Queen's hand, then that of the condesa. He waited, smiling, for madame de Clermont to gingerly offer up her pox-scarred hand from the depths of her veils, then kissed it gently before taking mine. I must confess my heart pounded like a foolish child's as he released me.

"And how fares your grandmother?" the Queen said.

"How kind of you to ask of her," he said with his warm smile.

THE CREATION OF EVE

"She's fine, I assume. I believe her herbal teas will keep her going forever."

I don't know what possessed me. My lips did move of their own volition—

"Might she take the coca plant for her health?"

He turned his disconcerting smile upon me. I meant to hold my ground, but its warmth undid me. I dashed a frown to my feet.

"The coca plant," he said. "You remembered. I wish that I could send her some. She would find all sorts of uses for it."

Though I kept my eyes downcast, I could feel the condesa's appraising gaze upon me. "Doctor Debruyne has been growing this plant from the New World," I explained to the leaves in the path. "It is supposed to have great medicinal powers." A curse on his beautiful teeth. I am thirty, not some silly girl.

"We hope to try it as a painkiller," the doctor explained. "It is reported that the people of the New World have endless energy and feel little pain when they chew its leaves. They chew it before working in the silver mines in Peru."

"If it is so good, why do you not use it?" asked the condesa.

The doctor smiled with regret. "If only it were that easy."

"My maid," I stammered.

Doctor Debruyne raised his brows pleasantly at me as I looked up. "Pardon?"

"She has a terrible toothache, and neither cloves nor smoke seem to help her. I wonder if this coca . . ." I felt myself blushing like a child. A wry smile crooked the corner of the condesa's mouth.

"I'm sorry," I said, "it is a foolish idea."

He regarded me soberly. "Actually, *juffrouw*, that is a most intriguing application. But there is the problem of testing it first."

"What is the problem?" said the Queen.

He made as if to speak, then crossed his arms with a frown.

"I am sorry," I said. "I should not have spoken out."

"No," he said. "I admire your thinking."

I turned away, hating myself for the smile that threatened to overcome my face.

Mercifully, the topic turned to herbal remedies for the condesa's bunions. After a few more pleasantries, doctor Debruyne took his leave. But even the Queen seemed to respond to his refreshing manner, for her step seemed less burdened as we continued deeper into the woods, the birds flitting in the tangle of boughs above us, Cher-Ami snuffling off the trail just ahead.

A shot rang out.

We stopped. The condesa dropped her pomander. It rolled off the path, into some leaves.

Madame de Clermont patted the Queen's arm. "Perhaps you shall see your King now," she said, which was indeed the logical explanation behind the shot. Only the King and his family were allowed to hunt in these woods.

"Yes," said the Queen. Madame and I hurried to smooth the Queen's skirts and hair to prepare her for His presence.

Cher-Ami yapped ferociously as Don Carlos broke through the cover of the woods, his arquebus pointed at us, with Don Alessandro tramping close behind.

The Queen's gaze darted behind them. The look of disappointment that flitted across her face disappeared as quickly as it had come.

"Toad!" she said stoutly. "Do you wish to kill me?"

He rushed forward and fervently kissed her hand. "Sweetest Elisabeth, I would never hurt a hair on your head! Tell me I did not truly frighten you!"

"Hush, Toad, I am fine." The Queen looked over Don Alessandro's shoulder as he took his turn at her hand. "What are you two doing out here? I thought you went back to university."

"School," scoffed Don Carlos. "What need have I for that?"

Don Juan stepped from the woods, though he carried no gun.

"There you are!" said Don Carlos. "He ruins our hunt, moving fast when he should move slow, and slow when he should move fast. You would think he is trying to make us miss all our shots."

Don Juan quickly kissed the Queen's hand. She drew it back as if burnt.

"Now that I have further damaged your hunt," she said lightly to Don Carlos, "will you walk with us?"

"You can never damage anything, My Lady." Don Carlos fell in step beside her, his arquebus on his shoulder.

You could feel the tension in the air as the rest of us took our places according to rank. Although the Prince behaved himself now, who knew what would provoke him and how he would respond? I found myself behind Don Juan and the condesa, and next to madame and Don Alessandro, who shouldered his own gun then pantomimed painting, with a questioning grin at me.

The group walked along, our silence amplified by the rustling of skirts and the crunch of footsteps upon the sandy trail. Wood doves cooed loudly from their nests in the crooks of the trees; a fly buzzed among us. The Queen scooped up Cher-Ami, who had stopped to smell something, then twirled around to face Don Juan.

"Do you truly understand dogs?" she said, walking backward.

Don Juan pulled back, surprised at being addressed so suddenly.

"Don Alessandro said once that you understood what they said," she explained.

"Oh, that."

She held up Cher-Ami, exposing his naked pink belly. "Tell me what he says."

Don Juan smiled crookedly. "He thanks you for taking him with you on this beautiful day."

"Oh, brilliant, Nostradamus," Don Alessandro muttered.

Don Carlos brayed with laughter.

The Queen kept up her backward tread. "Do you not truly talk to dogs, *señor?*"

"No," said Don Juan. "That was just someone's idea of a jest. In truth, it is the dogs who are the clever ones."

"How so?"

I frowned at the Queen from where I walked with Don Alessandro. I wished she would turn around before she fell.

"If they see you are trying to understand them," said Don Juan, "they give it their best to understand you. How well do you understand your dog, My Lady?"

"I don't," she said with a laugh.

"Yet you will find that as he grows older, he will perfectly understand you."

The Queen kissed Cher-Ami on the top of the head. "Very smart, for an animal."

"Very smart, period. We are all of us animals."

"Don Juan," said the condesa, "please. We are hardly animals. God gave us dominion over the beasts. It says so in the Holy Scriptures."

"You must pardon me, *señora,*" said Don Juan, "but why should we have dominion? Are we better than the dog that stays by a master who forgets to notice him? Than the cat who lays the mouse at your door when she is hungry and could have eaten it herself? Than a horse who will keep galloping to please you until its lungs have given out?"

The Queen stumbled in her backward walk. He reached out to steady her.

"They teach us about devotion," he said, holding onto her wrist.

The Queen glanced away, blushing.

He let go.

Don Alessandro called up from beside me, "You would be proud of us, My Lady. We were just practicing the art of debate among ourselves, without the bother and boredom of sitting around with a pack of tutors. Don Carlos, in particular, needs no tutor to help him to frame and argue his point."

Don Carlos's face flushed the red of a ripe pomegranate. "Our discussion was private!"

Don Juan flashed Don Alessandro a look of warning.

"Did I say something that was untrue, Uncle?" said Don Alessandro. "My Lady, I had told the Prince of your debate in the French court, about which is best in love, desire or fulfillment."

"*Señor!*" the condesa said sharply. "This is not the French court."

"And what is so wrong with the French court?" the Queen said, laughing. "I should like to hear of your debate, *monsieurs*."

"You don't want to hear," said Don Carlos.

"Truly, I would, Toad."

I drew in a breath. The Queen should not provoke him this way. "Has anyone seen don Alonso Sánchez Coello?" I asked stoutly. "Doña Juana has asked me to paint her—has don Alonso left the King's service? I cannot think why she would ask me when he is the King's Painter."

Don Carlos had no ears for me. "Since Don Alessandro told me of your debate, My Lady, I have been thinking about it much." He lifted his chin. "I have decided upon my position."

The Queen paused, arresting our whole assembly. "Which is?"

"Desire is best in love. It burns all impurities from the heart."

"Oh, Toad, that is sweet." She began to stroll again.

He stood in place, fists clenched at his side. "No, My Lady. It is not sweet."

Everyone stopped, breath held.

"My Lady, desire is a burning Hell that keeps you awake at night and fills your days with misery. It never leaves you in peace, but keeps gnawing, gnawing, gnawing, sucking the joy from everything. I would not wish it upon a dog. I"—he hung his head—"hate it."

Don Alessandro spoke up from beside me. "Forgive me, My Lady, but I must debate him."

Don Carlos looked up, his pasty face wrenched with pain.

"As our Prince says," said Don Alessandro, "desire hurts like Hell. For this reason I argue that fulfillment has to be the more satisfactory of the two."

"That is quite enough," said the condesa. For once, I agreed with her.

"What have you ever desired, Don Alessandro?" Don Carlos snapped. "The porter's daughter in Alcalá? What would you know about love?"

"Never mind about me." Don Alessandro poked Don Juan with his gun. "What about you, Friend to the Animals? What is your position?"

"Truly," said the condesa. "We must stop this."

"Such a beautiful day!" I exclaimed. "Your Majesty—"

"I want to hear him!" Don Carlos exclaimed. "Speak, Uncle, before I thrash you!"

Don Juan nodded to the condesa as if to assure her this was the last remark. "Both desire and fulfillment are painful."

"Always taking the middle ground," said Don Alessandro. "That's our Uncle."

"Sometimes it is the only ground one can take," said Don Juan.

The Queen glanced at him over her shoulder. "Are you sure it is not the way of the coward?"

"Ouch!" crowed Don Carlos. "She burns you!"

Don Alessandro made a scoffing sound. "She is right, Uncle. Truly, would it kill you to take a position for once?"

"Tell us! Tell us!" chanted Don Carlos. He rocked his head in growing agitation. "Tell us tell us tell us!"

I clenched my jaw.

Quietly, Don Juan said, "Desire, then."

"What?" said Don Alessandro.

"He said desire!" sang out Don Carlos.

"Toad." The Queen touched Don Carlos's arm to settle him. "And why do you say desire?" she asked Don Juan lightly.

"I really must put an end to this!" the condesa exclaimed.

"No." The Queen stopped our progress. She gazed into Don Juan's eyes. "Speak."

A squirrel scrabbled up a tree, sending bits of bark flying as we stood, waiting.

"I have never experienced fulfillment," Don Juan said simply.

"Pobrecito," said Don Alessandro. "Seventeen years old and never fulfilled at love. My heart bleeds."

Don Carlos shouldered his gun, and before anyone could act, discharged it into a tree. A wood dove flew off, its wings whistling.

"You bagged a branch," Don Alessandro called after the Prince as he stalked off.

"*Señor,*" the condesa scolded, "you really must not provoke him."

Don Alessandro hitched his own gun up under his arm. "He's harmless."

He found no accord amongst the furled brows and pursed lips in our group.

ITEM: *In Madrid, a woman whose only crime was to look especially beautiful dressed in her gown for Mass was gouged on the cheeks by her husband, his weapon being his fingernails. Her husband was found not guilty of any wrongdoing. She bears the scars on her face to this day.*

6 MAY 1562

The Palace, Aranjuez

It has been a night of little sleep. My gut does churn with anxiety; the hollow roar of the river outside the palace window makes my temples pound. At least Francesca rests, the pain of her toothache abated, though at what price did her ease come?

What have I done now?

The day was strange from the start, when I had been jolted from my sleep by the scream of fighting cats. Francesca, groaning from the pain of her tooth, then dressed me, and we went directly to the Queen, though my heart did ache to see Francesca in such misery.

My Lady was suffering in her own manner. We found her in an agitated state, picking threads from the tufts of her brocade covers. She spoke little and, when she did, often did not complete her thoughts. She fidgeted through her toilet and then Mass, popping up from her knees as soon as the priest had eaten the Host. The other ladies and I genuflected like jack-in-the-boxes before the altar and caught up with her outside the chapel.

"I cannot sit another moment." She held up her skirts as she strode into the arcade surrounding the courtyard. "I must go outdoors, or I will suffocate."

We passed finches cheeping from cages hung in the arches of the arcade. A charwoman scrubbed the bright blue and green tiles of the floor; the sharp odor of her lye soap mixed with the mossy scent of the river flowing outside the palace walls. I picked up Cher-Ami so he would not get the caustic soap on his paws.

"Should I send word to the King to meet you in the garden?" I asked.

"No!" The Queen glanced over her shoulder, the small veil suspended from her cap swishing. "No. He will not want to be bothered. He has his work." As indeed he did. It is not without reason he is called the Paper King. Now that rebellion mounts in his far-flung lands, each day when he could be out pursuing pleasure, His Majesty is at work instead, answering the myriad documents brought to him in dust-covered courier bags that have traveled across land and sea. He holds his far-flung lands together with a pen instead of a sword, writing away the hours of his life.

Our footsteps echoed from the vaults of the arcade. "Would you like to go riding in the little chariot he bought for you?" I asked. "You have not used that conveyance this spring, and the King had it sent all the way from Toledo."

"No. Not today."

"I could ask the King if he would like to ride with you." It could not be healthy for their union for them to spend as little time together as they did of late. Surely he'd want to spare her an hour.

"Sofi," she said, "no."

"Let Her Majesty be," said the condesa. "If she does not want to see the King, we must respect her wishes."

I glanced at Francesca, who was so miserable that she did not catch my look. It was not the condesa's way to bow to the Queen's wishes. But I could do little except to follow briskly in the Queen's wake, leaving the arcade for the passageway that led out of the palace and into the riverside gardens. It was a fresh, green day in May, though I was so dismayed by the Queen's erratic behavior and Francesca's misery that it was hard to savor it. Two by two we sailed through the fragrant beds of roses and other exotic flowers the King had caused to be planted in his riverside gardens, with Cher-Ami running ahead, and Francesca trailing behind, her hand to her swollen jaw.

"Shall I order your barge, My Lady?" asked the condesa.

"No!" exclaimed the Queen. "I just wish to walk. I need to clear my head. I— Oh!" Doctor Debruyne rose from behind an arbor. "You frightened me!"

Cher-Ami barked while the doctor kissed the Queen's hand. "I am so sorry, Your Majesty. I did not mean to disturb you. I was checking on the progress of this specimen sent to His Majesty."

"What is it?" she asked, trying to regain her composure.

I scooped up Cher-Ami as doctor Debruyne plucked a pale pink blossom and held it up to the Queen. "Tobacco, My Lady."

"Pretty," she said, hardly looking at it.

"It is more than pretty. When burnt, the leaves are supposed to relax the patient and bring comfort when the smoke is inhaled."

The preposterousness of this remedy overcame my restraint. "You hold its smoke in your lungs?"

The condesa looked disdainfully over her shoulder. "You misunderstand him."

Doctor Debruyne laughed then bowed before me, winning no points with the condesa. "It does sound mad. Leave it to the English to embrace such boldness. I understand that they have gotten their hands upon it and already puff away with great enthusiasm. But you know my good colleague, doctor Hernández—he must test its properties thoroughly before recommending it to the King.

"Fortunately," he said, addressing the Queen, "your husband possesses a keen scientific mind and is as curious about the potential of these herbs from the New World as we are."

The Queen smiled, then glanced across the river at the woods.

Doctor Debruyne's eye fell upon Francesca at the back of our group, her face cast down.

"Is this the servant with the aching tooth, juffrouw Sofonisba?" he asked me.

I caught my breath, surprised that he should remember anything about me or Francesca. I nodded and put down Cher-Ami, who had been wiggling to be released.

Doctor Debruyne leaned past me to speak to Francesca. "Is it grieving you greatly, *mevrouw*?"

The knobs of Francesca's cheeks flushed red when we turned to look. She shook her head then winced.

"It seems a shame," he murmured, "when I have found that—"

The Queen interrupted as if unaware that he was speaking. "Good luck with your work, *monsieur*. Ladies?"

I ducked my head in apology as we left the doctor to his tobacco plants. His warm brown gaze remained in my mind as we slowly wound our way back to the palace.

At midday dinner, the Queen listlessly picked through her food. I myself tried to savor the first course, as the simple soup, *sopa castellana*, with its morsels of ham, bread, and poached eggs in garlic broth, is among my favorite dishes, but it was hard to take pleasure in food when Francesca was unable to eat a single bite. It mattered little. My Lady jumped up before I had finished my bowl.

"Where do you go, My Lady?" I waved off the page offering me watered wine.

"I must walk."

With a last, longing look at the earthen bowl containing the remains of my soup, I rose with a scrape of bench against tile, even as the condesa made to rise next to me. What must she think of the Queen, wishing to dash for the woods at every chance she got?

"It is the heat that makes you so agitated, My Lady," I said.

"Everyone, stay." The Queen picked up Cher-Ami, who'd been snuffling under the table. "Please. The guards will watch over me."

"That is not done!" the condesa exclaimed. "His Majesty—"

"Very well!" the Queen exclaimed curtly. "Then Sofi, you come—Francesca, you too."

Francesca struggled up from her bench at the servants' table. She would accompany the Queen even if every last tooth in her square old jaw throbbed.

The condesa drew back in perturbed silence as we passed. "At least take your shawls to cover yourselves!" she shouted after us.

I sighed as we once more made our way through the arcade, the finches chirping in their golden cages, Cher-Ami scampering before us, the smell of the lye soap still lingering though the char-woman was gone. "You should not let the condesa see you this way," I said.

The Queen stopped. Her breathing echoed under the vaulted arches as she regarded me. "In which way is that, Sofi?"

We stared at each other, Francesca with head bowed behind us. And in this moment, as the finches cheeped and Cher-Ami's nails clicked on the tile, it occurred to me with heartbreaking clarity that I did not know this young woman. Oh, I bathed her, I dressed her, I groomed her. I knew the smell of her skin in the morn. But even knowing all this and so much more, I saw that she was closed to me, and ever would be, as all of us are closed to one another. I would never truly know her secrets. And she would never truly know mine.

"Nothing, Your Majesty."

We spoke no more, even after we had crossed the bridge and were following along the river across from the stable yards, with Cher-Ami bounding before us, and Francesca plodding behind. We had left the sound of whinnying horses and the voices of the groomsmen and had come to a stand of willows, Francesca trailing out of sight, when the Queen wheeled around.

"I think I shall burst!"

I drew back. "Your Majesty."

"I am stuck in the stuffiest court in the world, in the most boring little palace, where my every single movement is dictated by the King. One unapproved move and his fist will come smashing down on me, as will my mother's, from a thousand miles away."

"Of what do you speak? There have been no 'unapproved moves.'" Had there?

"He does not even desire me!"

"The King? How can you say that? You have what every woman wishes, a husband who esteems her."

She tore off her veiled cap and flung it to the ground. "Would that I got a single thing I ever wished for!"

I gazed, dumbfounded, at the fallen cap, to which Cher-Ami had returned to sniff, and then at the Queen. She ripped a pearl-studded comb from her braids. "Here, *chéri*!" she called, then tossed it to the dog. "Catch!"

"Your Majesty!"

The Queen plucked out the remaining ornaments, then shook out her hair. "There. Better now."

My skirts and farthingale billowed up as I crouched down to beat Cher-Ami to the combs. Unescorted by her husband, it was not proper for a married woman to go out in public with her hair unbound, let alone for the Queen of Spain to do so, and in the woods no less. The condesa would be livid.

"Take off your cap, Sofi. See how wonderful it feels."

"I cannot."

"Oh, drop those things and do as I say. You must, for your own sake."

"It is not proper, Your Majesty."

"Are you starting to wish for a pomander? Go on, Sofi, off with it. In the name of Spain, I command you—there, now will you do it?"

Francesca caught up with us. *"No, signorina!"* she cried, cradling her jaw. "Madonna Elisabetta, your hair! I fix."

A man's voice called from behind Francesca: "Your Majesty! *Hallo!*"

Our clothes swished as we turned in alarm. Cher-Ami bolted to charge the intruder.

Doctor Debruyne approached, a small leather pouch hanging from each of his wrists.

"I am sorry," he said over Cher-Ami's yapping, "I did not mean to sneak up on you. Your Majesty, may I speak to you for a moment?" He just then seemed to notice our uncovered heads, for he stopped abruptly. "Perhaps this should wait."

"Cher-Ami—hush!" The Queen smiled, obviously enjoying the doctor's discomfort. "As my physician's colleague, please do speak. Surely you have seen the uncovered heads of your women patients before."

The boughs of the willow trees shimmered in the wind while doctor Debruyne frowned good-naturedly as if trying to understand. "Well, in truth, I am here as a physician and not a man." He caught Francesca's piercing look. "Is that permissible?"

Francesca's threatening stare was cut short by a wince.

Doctor Debruyne bent down and held out his hand for Cher-Ami to sniff. "Actually, *mevrouw*," he said to Francesca, "it is for you I have come. Your Majesty, will you permit me to speak?"

"What do you have there?" asked the Queen.

He stood and held out his arms to display the pouches at his wrists. "Coca."

I fear my mouth did ease open. "Coca? For her tooth?"

He nodded.

This herb might bring Francesca relief. My wonder overtook my shyness. "*Señor*, you have had good results with your experiments?"

Doctor Debruyne paused before answering. "I must tell you the truth. The experiments have been limited."

"But there were good results, yes?"

He drew in a breath. "Well, at least I can personally attest to the results." He smiled apologetically. "I tried it on myself, yesterday after we had met."

The Queen laughed.

"I had no choice, Your Majesty," he said. "The coca is flourishing, your woman's woman is in pain, and the plant has a reputation of bringing relief to all misery. With these things in place, it seemed wrong to wait any longer. I could not wait for doctor Hernández to agree to the expediency of a trial."

"Why had you to wait?" I asked. "Doctor Hernández is a man of learning. Surely he would readily agree to your experiment."

Doctor Debruyne brushed back the hank of shining dark hair that the wind had blown into his eyes. "I should explain. Not long ago, one of our colleagues tried a root from Peru touted by the Indians to be a nutritious meal in itself. As doctor Hernández and I watched, our colleague eagerly ate one of these roots raw, complaining only as he consumed it of its plain taste. Twenty-five minutes later, he reported a pain in his belly. Within an hour, he was vomiting uncontrollably. By the morning, I am most grieved to say, he was dead."

The Queen gasped.

"Did he get a bad piece of this Peruvian root?" I asked. "How did he come to be poisoned by something that was reported to be so beneficial?"

Doctor Debruyne regarded me with regret. "It was only later, in questioning an Indian newly brought from Potosí, that we learned the vegetable should be cooked before consumption. If the skin is still green, the uncooked root can be lethal if eaten unpeeled. So you see why doctor Hernández is now rightly cautious. Even plants that are beneficial can have a poisonous nature if not handled correctly." He sighed. "And we had so much hope for the potato."

"Well," the Queen said to doctor Debruyne, "at least you know this coca does not kill. You say you tried it on yourself, and you have obviously lived to tell us."

The slight gap between his teeth showed as he grinned. "Not just lived, Your Majesty, thrived. After chewing an ounce of coca leaves, I was able to single-handedly dig a new herb garden in an hour. I felt no pain whatsoever in my limbs and back."

"It afforded you energy?" I asked.

"If you think it will help Francesca," the Queen said abruptly, "then do give her some. I would like to walk along the river while the day is still fair."

He gazed at the Queen as if trying to ascertain whether he had offended her somehow, then asked Francesca, "Would you like to try it, *mevrouw*? Do you want a chance to be rid of your pain?"

"I not always get what I want." She sighed deeply. "*Bene, bene*. But go fast. Madonna Elisabetta want to walk."

Doctor Debruyne nodded, then opened one of his pouches and drew out a pinch of pointed, oval-shaped green leaves. "Hold out your hand." He laid the leaves on her palm, then drew out another pinch.

"I will accompany you," he said, "to assure you of its safety."

Francesca scowled at the greenery on her hand. "What this do?"

"What I found when I tried it is that it first numbs the mouth, which in your case is just what you want. Then I found it eased my brain and made me feel quite fine all over, not just in my mouth."

"How I use?" she said gruffly.

The doctor rolled his own small pile of leaves into a wad. "Please do likewise, *mevrouw*."

As Francesca prepared a little bundle, he slipped his own plug between his gum and cheek. Watching him, she did the same. Their lower cheeks bulged as do goats' when feasting on refuse.

The Queen laughed as she threw a stick for Cher-Ami. "Oh, most attractive."

Francesca made to remove her wad. I could not bear for her to lose this chance.

"Doctor Debruyne," I said, "please—let me try it, too."

He looked at me in surprise.

I blinked, astonished at myself. But if my taking of the herb would convince Francesca to try it, I would.

"Please. I would really like to."

"I am afraid I cannot allow it," he said, thick-tongued. He pushed on his cheek, readjusting his wad. "It is not a matter of emergency, and you are a woman, and—"

"Would you let me try it if I were a man?"

He paused, his fingers at his jaw.

"I'll have you know I have had a man's training in science. Black bile, phlegm, blood, yellow bile—of which of the four humors would you like me to speak? A patient with melancholy is suffering from too much black bile. Convulsions are the result of an excess of phlegm—the body is trying to rid itself of the obstruction. Persons with fevers obviously have too much blood and should have it let, the volume commensurate with the degree of heat, until balance is restored. The pulse music should then be—"

"I believe you, I believe you!" he exclaimed. "Where did you receive your training?" He laughed. "I should not act so surprised. Well I know the abilities of an intelligent woman—my grandmother holds a pharmacopoeia in her mind."

"Oh," the Queen cried, "for the love of God, just let her try it! I can hardly bear to stand here. Go on, I order you."

I put out my hand more bravely than I felt.

He drew in a breath. "This really is not a good idea."

I reached closer. "Please."

Shaking his head, he drew out another pinch.

I sniffed the leaves upon my hand. They smelled of new-mown hay. I touched them to my tongue. There was little taste, just . . . leaves.

I loaded my bundle into my cheek until my lip bulged as if tumorous. If he ever found me even slightly attractive, I promise, he no longer did so.

"I don't feel anything," I said with my new fool's lisp.

"You won't," he said in his own muffled tone. "Not without the secret ingredient."

He searched the ground for a small twig, wet the tip of it on his tongue, then dabbed the damp twig inside the other pouch.

"What is that?" I asked.

He smiled, making the lump rise under his lip, affording him an idiot's grin. "Lye."

I drew back. "Lye?"

"I took some from the woman who scrubs the palace floors. The coca cannot be activated without an alkali. You have to put it in once your wad is in your lip."

Opening his mouth, he carefully poked the lye-laden twig into the center of his wad. He readjusted the bundle with his fingers, then retrieved another trace of lye from his pouch for first Francesca, then me. I opened my mouth like a new-hatched bird to let him perform his operation.

He painstakingly touched the lye to my leaves. "You don't want to get this on your tongue." When he was done, he closed my mouth and patted my jaw as one would pat one's donkey, for good service.

"When should we feel something?" I said, muffle-voiced.

At that very moment, a smile spread over his face. I looked to Francesca. Her eyes were widening just as something wonderful began to blossom forth in my mouth.

It was odd. Odd and marvelous. It seemed as if my mouth had turned into a butterfly—no, it was my entire head—and it was taking wing, floating softly, serenely, on the warm spring breeze.

I grinned up into the trees, at the languidly waving branches. If only there were stairs to the treetops, I would skip right up them.

I looked down from my tree-gazing and found doctor De-bruyne, beaming at my face. I laughed when I saw him, then he laughed, and then Francesca laughed, the three of us chuckling at everything and nothing.

"It appears to be working," said the Queen, making us laugh even harder.

"Good," she said. "Enjoy yourselves. I am taking my walk. Just watch Cher-Ami, would you? Cher-Ami, stay. *Stay*."

"We follow," said Francesca, then sat down, giggling like a maiden.

I picked up Cher-Ami and sat down beside her. "You know, Francesca, I believe I have never heard you giggle."

Her dark eyes narrowed into a frown. Then, with a shrug, she giggled again.

"How is your tooth?" asked doctor Debruyne, grinning.

"My tooth?" Francesca felt at her swollen jaw, then smiled with bliss. Green drool trickled from one corner of her mouth. "What tooth?"

"You're leaking," I said, pointing.

She pointed back. "So you."

I felt around my lips. When I brought back my hand, it was wet with green saliva. I had not even felt it.

Doctor Debruyne wiped his own dripping mouth on the back of his hand. "Salivation is hard to control when you're numb."

"I see." I wiped my fingers on my skirt so I would not get my mess on Cher-Ami.

"Take out the tooth," Francesca said, suddenly.

Doctor Debruyne pulled back in surprise.

"Take it out. You know how, *dottore*. Do it now."

"H'm." He tucked his hands under his arms. "Might not be a bad idea."

"Then get the pliers, *signore*. Go! While I feel good. I sit here and wait." She lay back into a tall clump of grass.

"You know, I believe I will. Ladies, if you will excuse me."

"Good-bye," Francesca said from her clump of grass.

I watched him sprint off like a youth, then lay back with Francesca, Cher-Ami still tucked under my arm. I admired the wind playing in the trees and amused myself by snatching at bits of poplar fluff as it wafted by.

"Where is Madonna Elisabetta?" Francesca said from our bed of grass.

"Oh, I don't know." Cher-Ami buried his moist snout behind my neck. A breeze picked up, twirling the silver-backed leaves of the trees. How I would like to paint them now, flashes of green, yellow, black, and white.

"*Signorina?*"

"Yes?"

"Did that student, that one of the Michelangelo—did he make you a promise?"

I turned my head to look at her, grass crunching in my ear. "What?"

The knob of her chin quivered as she stared up at the trees. "Oh, *signorina*, I know how the woman can give herself to the passion—oh, *signorina*, I know. Have you never ask yourself, how can Francesca have milk for all the babies in your family? Where her baby, to start her to make milk?"

I sat up. "Francesca, do you have a child?"

"This *scultore*, this Tiberio"—she reached over and stroked

Cher-Ami, still lying in the grass—"do he promise himself to you?"

My heart pounded, from the herb or guilt or astonishment. "Where is your baby, Francesca?"

She kept her gaze on Cher-Ami. "I left her at the door of the convent outside my village. She is the nun now. No men to cause her trouble. Happy"—she looked up, then drew in a breath—"I hope."

We stared at each other. I marveled at the enlarged size of her shining pupils—an effect of the coca?—at the smooth olive skin of her face. How little I knew about this woman with whom I'd spent nearly every moment of my life.

A man spoke in the distance. Cher-Ami lifted his head.

Francesca struggled to sit. *"Madonna."*

"I shall get her." I sprang up before she could get to her feet. "Keep Cher-Ami."

Unbothered by the tightness of my corset, I strode along the riverside path that the Queen had taken, my body powered with energy, my mind in a confused twist. Francesca had a child out of wedlock? Why did she speak of Tiberio?

The man's voice came again, closer now. I heard the Queen laugh.

The path ended abruptly at a stand of reeds. The only way past them was to wade along the shoreline. I looked behind me. Had I missed a fork in the path?

I leaned forward. I could hear the Queen speaking. She did not sound afraid.

I parted the sharp-edged reeds with my elbow.

On the other side of the reeds, the course of the river curved sharply to the right. Ancient alder trees leaned from both banks,

forming a green tunnel down which the call of birds echoed and
fluffy stars of poplar down twitched. There, in the tunnel, sat the
Queen, on a rock at the river's edge. Don Juan stood above her,
his foot upon the rock. They looked like Adam and Eve, content
in their earthly Paradise.

I batted away an insect darting for my eyes. If I barely breathed,
I could hear Don Juan.

"We should go back," he said.

The Queen nodded to the pair of swans meandering farther
down the verdant tunnel. "Tell the swans to stop. I don't want
them to go away. You can tell them, can't you?"

"You listen too much to Alessandro," said Don Juan. "I have
no power over swans or anything else."

"That is not true." The Queen waved away the fluff floating
around her face. "You have a good effect on Don Carlos."

"Be still."

He moved his hand to her sleeve, where a blue-black dragonfly
sat, rhythmically lifting its shiny tail. Carefully, he eased his finger under its glistening black legs, then brought the insect, still
raising and lowering its tail, to the back of her hand.

"*El caballito del diablo,*" he said quietly.

They gazed at their joined hands. "The little horse of the
devil," she repeated.

"He likes you," he said. "It is you who has the way with the
beasts."

The dragonfly flew off. Don Juan withdrew his hand.

The Queen drew in a sigh, then plucked up a blade of grass
growing by the rock. "What was it like? Your childhood, I mean."

He pushed away from the rock. "Like any country boy's, at
least at first." The swans drifted forward as he started out over a
chain of low stones that crossed the river. "I'm sorry," he said,

balancing himself, "you would not know what that is like, would you? Well, let's just say I got in trouble throwing apples in a farmer's orchard."

"You? In trouble?"

He stepped to the next stone. "I rode every animal I could get my hands on—I cannot recommend cows, in case you ever wonder. I raced the other boys in donkey carts. I broke my arm falling out of a cypress tree, returning a bird to its nest. It was a terrible tree for climbing. Too prickly."

The swans watched warily, strumming the water with their thick black feet, as the Queen arose and stood, wavering, on the closest stone to the shore, her balance hampered by her voluminous skirts. "So that is a country boyhood."

"It was mine, at least."

"It sounds heavenly."

I smiled from my viewing point as she picked ahead carefully.

"Oh, it had its duller moments," said Don Juan. "It could get very lonely at times. My foster father was always gone, serving the Emperor Charles—" He stopped, letting her work her way closer. "Serving my father, I mean. That still sounds impossible."

He waited for the Queen to hop to the next stone. "Don't misunderstand. I loved my foster mother—I still love her. She was good to me, but I could always feel a distance. I tried to bridge it by being the perfect son. What I would do to see her smile! When I got older, I realized she was sad because she thought I was don Luis's unacknowledged love child. How that shamed me, to know that my very existence hurt her."

"You said once that you wanted to be don Luis's son."

"Yes. It would have been easier if I had been." He swiped his arm over his face. I, too, was warm there behind my screen of rushes—sweat trickled down my back. "When I got older, don

Luis made me wear well-cut clothes, too fine for a country boy. He gave me my own pony, a piebald with white stockings—I loved that horse! He also made the mistake of telling the teachers in my school to treat me with deference—without explaining why. The boys in my school just laughed. The teachers found new reasons to beat me. Who was I, a bastard not loved enough by don Luis for him to legally claim me, to put on such airs? I got tired of fighting every boy in the school who wished to knock me down a notch, so I was relieved at first when we moved to Cuacos de Yuste when I was eleven. Don Luis was to serve the Emperor in his retirement to the monastery there. But whenever I visited the Emperor at my foster father's heels, the great man stared at me with a strange smile on his face. I was sure there was something horribly wrong with me."

"Oh!" She slipped into the water with a splash. The swans scuttled off.

He came back to steady her. "Your gown," he said.

She held up her dripping skirts. The bottom ten inches were dark and sagging.

"Did you hurt yourself?" he asked her, his hand upon her arm.

They stood face-to-face in the muddy water, the poplar down twitching aimlessly around them as in a dream.

She sighed. "I wish—"

He put his finger on her lips. "No."

She closed her eyes. When she opened them again, he drew his finger slowly down her lips. "No."

She stared at him through the meandering down. A breeze stirred the trees, setting the leaves whispering in silvery tongues.

"Just tell me that you feel this, too. That I am not going mad."

He would not answer her.

"Tell me, Juan, please, then I shall go if you wish."

I must have made some kind of sigh, for at that moment, they parted and turned in my direction. She saw me first.

"Sofi?"

Her chest rose, then fell in a sigh.

"Sofi," she said loudly now. "Perhaps you overheard me." She squared off before Don Juan. "I was asking the gentleman this: *Monsieur, s'il vous plaît*, would you be so good as to tell me"—she kicked at the river, showering his doublet—*"do you like the water?"*

He stood there, dripping.

"Can you not decide, *monsieur?* Here, perhaps you need just a *soupçon* more." She splashed him again.

Sorrow and gratitude passed over his face like the shadows of clouds upon the river. "*Madame,* please. Allow me to return the favor."

He smacked the surface of the water.

"Oh!" Drops glittered in the Queen's loose hair. "Oh, you did not just splash me!"

"Oh," he said, "but it seems that I did."

"Beast!"

A war of splashing erupted between them. Their insults and shrieks of laughter ringing in the air, I grabbed up my skirts and turned . . . directly into the King.

I drew back from His Majesty's grim visage as would a mouse trapped by a cat. All good sensations drained instantly from my person, leaving behind a shell of horror.

Cher-Ami wriggling in his arms, the King eyed my bulging jaw then my chest. I looked down. A green trail of coca juice led down my rumpled bodice.

"Doña Sofonisba," he said, "would you be so kind as to explain what is happening?" Behind him, Francesca wrung her hands, her face ashen.

The same breeze that poured over my burning face ruffled the plume in the King's hat as he stepped past me to the riverbank.

Don Juan was bending down to paddle water at My Lady when he saw the King. He received a faceful before the Queen saw the object of his stare.

Immediately, she slogged through the water to her husband, the ropes of her hair catching on her sodden sleeves and back. Her shocked smile spoke more of her guilt than would have a gale of tears.

She gained the King's side. "My Lord," she said, breathless, "it is nothing."

The King cast a cold look at Don Juan, still standing in the river, and then upon the Queen, now pressing his Royal hand to her wet lips.

He pulled away his hand. "My Lady, I assure you, it is not."

ITEM: *Don Pedro, the two-year-old son of the Spanish King Pedro the Cruel, fell to his death from the north tower of the castle at Segovia, where he was playing with his brothers and sisters. Understanding her fate, the nurse in whose charge he had been threw herself immediately from the place where he had fallen.*

20 MAY 1562

The Palace, Aranjuez

I have heard the English Queen, Kathryn Howard, had been feeding her dogs bits of boiled chicken when King Henry's men came and took her screaming down the halls of Hampton Court. Within days, her young head parted ways with her neck, leaving the dogs without a mistress and England without a Queen. It seems she had been carrying on a flirtation with her cousin, and her aging husband could not abide his young wife's taste for a virile kinsman. Not a soul in Europe had felt sorry for her. She should have known better. For when a King wishes to punish his wife for an indiscretion, it is not called murder.

This was the dark thought on my mind at supper in the Queen's chambers last night, when Cher-Ami suddenly sprang up barking from his basket and caused My Lady to burst into tears. The page whose entrance had set off the dog was bewildered to find My Lady crying when he offered her some pears.

The condesa lowered her spoon and knife. "Are you well, Your Majesty?"

"Yes. Yes, of course." The blue-black rings etched into the tender skin under her eyes said otherwise. She took a pear from the tray, then put it down, forgotten, before the page had bowed and backed away.

My poor Lady. It is my fault that she has suffered in purgatory these past fourteen days. If I had been in my right mind, I would never have let her wander off with Don Juan. Why, oh why, did I take the coca from doctor Debruyne? Me and my pride, pretending to be a scholar! I thought I could partake in the experiment of a learned man—ha! I am no scientist.

The condesa frowned at the Queen. "You have not a new rash, have you? Does your throat hurt?"

My Lady shook her head.

The condesa blinked in thought. "Well, your courses are due next week."

The Queen's forlorn expression lifted into one of hope. "I could be with child, couldn't I?"

The condesa knows nothing about the incident at the river. No one does. After Francesca and I had braided Her Majesty's hair and straightened her wet attire, the King had made our guilty trio return to the palace without him. Don Juan had been ordered to depart on the spot. The Queen and I had slipped in through the kitchen. No one saw us enter, not the condesa, nor madame, nor even doctor Debruyne, since we had left before he could return with the extractors. He had to do the job on Francesca's tooth later that night, after the effects of the coca had worn off. Poor Francesca had to pay for my misjudgment, too.

Now I grasped at the hope that the Queen could be pregnant. If she was carrying the King's child, her splashing game with Don

Juan might well be forgiven. These past fourteen days would be soon forgotten, fourteen terrible days in which I would be sorting through My Lady's combs or kneeling in Mass or spooning in a mouthful of soup, and be gripped by a sudden chill, knowing that at any moment one of His Majesty's fierce German bodyguards could storm in and drag my little Queen—and me—away.

For even though I know the Queen and Don Juan did nothing more than play in the water like children, it must have looked bad to the King. What must he think of his wife, bare-headed and wet, frolicking unattended with his brother? An unfaithful wife was never tolerated, and now, during these tumultuous times, especially when many in the Low Countries wished to throw off the yoke of his rule, the King could not afford to meekly don the shameful horns of a cuckold. If his seventeen-year-old wife could undo him, others would be encouraged to do so, too. If implicated in her misdeed, I could be taken with her. What would become of us? The Spanish do not behead their queens, that is not the Spanish way. No, the Spanish lock their errant queens in towers and lose the key, as they did to Queen Juana the Mad, the King's grandmother and rightful heir to the crown, whose only crime was to be so deranged that she kept the body of her dead husband with her. If a son could lock up his mother, as the King's father, the Emperor Charles, had done to Queen Juana, what would a husband do to a wife who had dishonored him?

Tomorrow is the King's thirty-fifth birthday. I cannot think how he will wish to celebrate.

ITEM: *The King's ancestor Alfonso XI was known as the Avenger, because of his taste for having his enemies' backs to be broken, or having them hanged and dragged at horse's tail, or causing them to be brought to the stake and burnt. Even his court whispered that his efforts to impose authority had strayed from justice to rigor.*

21 MAY 1562
The Palace, Aranjuez

The King has had his revenge.

This morning, instead of ordering that his wife be seized and me along with her, the King ordered for his Royal barge to be fetched and for his wife and all the court to go picnicking down-river with him. A feast was promptly packed, and the court assembled after Mass; then we boarded the boats according to our rank while serenaded by Moorish guitarists. The King insisted that I ride with the Queen on his barge—a great honor. Why should he do so? How could he have forgiven me for letting his wife run wild? I could not forgive myself.

I entered the craft in the privileged company of the King and Queen. But I was too nervous to admire the barge's wondrous prow, carved like a sea serpent, or its gleaming sides of wood. As the guitarists played a soothing melody, I left the King at the entrance and followed the Queen past the rowers sitting at their oars. We ducked under the cloth-of-gold canopy emblazoned with the King's and Queen's intertwining letters to join the King's sister Doña Juana, with her lady doña Eufrasia, sitting on a divan with their hands upon their laps.

"There you are, sister," said Doña Juana. She remained seated while exchanging kisses with the Queen. "I have not seen you this past fortnight. The condesa de Urueña reports that you have been ill. With child, I hope?" She smiled coldly as My Lady blushed.

"I pray so," murmured the Queen.

"I suppose your care for your mistress accounts for why you have not come to paint me, Sofonisba—my brother did tell you that I wished for my portrait to be done?"

A murmur of delight rippled through the crowd on the landing. I looked around in time to see the King holding out his hand for Don Juan to kiss. The Queen and I exchanged miserable glances.

My Lady had not been unfaithful, not technically. What was the harm in splashing a little water? And even that small wrong was known by no one but the King.

The guitar players switched to a gay gypsy tune as Don Juan boarded the barge. The Queen and I settled on the couch beside Doña Juana and her lady. As I smoothed Her Majesty's skirts, the King took his place on the divan across from us.

"Brother," he said to Don Juan. "Sit by me."

He sat, stiffly. Doña Juana whispered something to doña Eufrasia as the oarsmen bent to their work.

"Go slowly," the King told the captain standing just beyond the golden fringe of the canopy. "I wish to smell the flowers."

We sailed by the rose garden with its velvety sweet scent, by the beds of exotic specimens arranged in formal knots, by fountains splashing in mossy scallop-shaped basins. On the other bank, wood doves cooed from their nests in the crooks of the elms planted in perfect rows by order of the King. I gazed down one of the rows, hoping, foolishly, to catch sight of doctor Debruyne.

"Felipe," said Doña Juana, "do you like the painting I gave you for your birthday?" Her strident voice carried easily over the hushed splash of the rowers' oars. The closest boat of celebrants to join us was still at the landing—their speech and the gypsy music were but a distant pleasant hum.

The King leaned around to speak to his sister. "The new van Eyck? You were most generous."

"I wish to turn your taste away from those odd paintings by that mad Fleming, El Bosco, which you insist upon acquiring." She lowered her formidable brow. "Your new one, *The Garden of Earthly Delights,* is the worst. All those naked bodies, committing sins. How can you think the painting isn't heretical?"

"They are allegories." He flicked a glance toward the Queen. "We are to be reminded of our weaknesses and think what happens when we fall prey to them."

"Just because El Bosco's paintings are couched in religious themes," said Doña Juana, "does not absolve them. I am reminded of something Inquisitor-General Valdés was telling doña Eufrasia and me about your Michelangelo, Sofonisba."

Sweetest Holy Mary. Always she must refer to him as "my" Michelangelo. I composed myself. "My Lady?"

"Have you seen the ceiling of the Sistine Chapel in Rome?" she asked.

I stared at her warily, as in my mind's eye a field of muscular bodies writhed overhead. In the center of this panoply of flesh, beautiful Adam reached forth to receive the touch of life. The work was a wonder, no, a miracle of painting, and on a ceiling, no less, but the Maestro has done many more paintings and many other famous statues. Why did she bring up this work again? "Yes, Your Majesty. I have had that privilege."

"I refer specifically to the twenty nude youths sitting above the cornices throughout the painting." Her beige-lashed eyes were pleasant beneath her broad brow. "What are they called, doña Eufrasia?"

Doña Eufrasia lowered her gaze. "*Ignudi*, Your Majesty."

"There are hundreds of figures in the fresco, Your Majesty," I said. "I cannot remember them all."

"You might remember these. Some are accompanied by acorns, either in sheaves upon their backs or in great bunches upon which they sit."

"Acorns?" said the King.

"Yes, Felipe. A certain large-headed kind. They have a name." Doña Juana grimaced as if sorry she had to speak of such.

I kept my silence, not rising to her bait.

"It is a coarse name, in Tuscan slang. *Testa di cazzo.*" She pressed her fingers to her puffy lips in innocence. "There, I said it. Could you translate it for us, Sofonisba?"

She frowned when I said nothing. "Are you not Italian? Go on, tell us what it means."

"I cannot say."

"Oh, please. Do not act as if you don't know it."

I saw that she would not rest until I said it. I drew in a breath. "Prickhead."

The King turned to look at me.

I sank into a curtsey. "I beg your pardon, Your Majesty, and the pardon of all who are here."

Doña Juana shook her head. "There are bunches of these, these *acorns*, sheaves of them, in what is supposed to be a holy painting. I cannot see the reason for them. Nor are the youths who carry them necessary to the painting. The naked louts are just there, with their . . . seed-heads."

"Juana," said the King. "Enough."

"But I am not done. Inquisitor-General Valdés and I have discussed this matter and cannot come up with a reason for their inclusion in the painting other than to please the artist's own despicable tastes. Perhaps there is another reason for this. Perhaps you could explain his thinking for us, Sofonisba, since you know him so well."

"I was only his student."

Doña Juana drew back. "Perhaps you should think about this. The mood in Rome is very serious these days about art. Protestant mobs protesting symbols of the Catholic faith have been tearing down religious works in churches across Northern Europe. Pious work. Holy work. Centuries-old pieces of great value. Our bishops will not stand for it. They have called for an examination of all paintings for any possible seductive charm, perversion, or lasciviousness, to destroy them before the wicked hordes have an excuse to wreak their wanton destruction on holy pieces. All work in the Church must be pure beyond doubt." She smiled. "So you see, I am not just making indecorous conversation."

The King stood. He waved away a bit of meandering poplar fluff as he cleared his throat. "I wish to make an announcement."

Doña Juana lowered her brow in displeasure at being interrupted. The Queen's hand sidled to mine.

"Don Juan," said the King. "Please rise."

Don Juan stood. He lifted his chin, revealing the hollows under his eyes. These past two weeks must have been a nightmare for him, too.

The King slid his hand to the back of Don Juan's neck. "I want to announce within the circle of family what will soon be made public."

A breeze stirred, rippling the fringe of the canopy. "Do you love the Church, Brother?" asked the King.

The light under the canopy turned green as we passed into a tunnel of trees. I glanced at the riverbank, then drew in a sharp breath. We had come to the place where the King had discovered us.

"I love my God," said Don Juan.

"Your God. That is good. Your private God." The King smiled slightly. "Congratulations, my brother. You shall leave for Rome tomorrow. When you come back, in several years' time, you shall be wedded to your God as a cardinal."

ITEM: *"Painted figures must be done in such a way that the spectators are able with ease to recognize through their attitudes the thoughts of their minds."*

—MAESTRO LEONARDO DA VINCI

22 JUNE 1562
El Alcázar, Madrid

We returned to Madrid after the King's birthday. The Queen has been quiet and given to fevers. I have had to leave her in the care of Francesca while I work on studies for Doña Juana's portrait, for Doña Juana will brook no excuses for me not to go forward with her picture. But even in this drawing stage, the process is made painful by her constant disapproval. "My brow is so prominent that it looks like a smith could hammer a rod upon it," she said yesterday, and the day before, "Those are a man's thick lips!" These are but two of the myriad complaints that have issued from her pursed mouth nearly every afternoon over the past month as she has stood before me in her severe black dress. She spares me exactly one turning of the hourglass, always in her chamber, and always with doña Eufrasia reading out loud to her from her Book of Hours. There is no conversation, not even about maestro Michelangelo—a blessing, though this makes it clear she thinks little more of me than as an instrument to needle My Lady, saving her pointed remarks about the Maestro for when we are in the presence of the Queen. Indeed, I have come to believe she wishes me to do her portrait only to deprive the Queen of my company.

Today, after her usual moaning, she struck upon the idea of borrowing the little daughter of one of her ladies to "enliven" the picture, since I was obviously on the way to producing a dull portrait. I was enthusiastic. The music of a child's voice would have been a relief in that dreary chamber, heavy with the sounds of Doña Juana's stern breathing, doña Eufrasia's halting reading of the Scriptures, and the hiss of the sand dwindling in the hourglass. But no such music was to be heard. Once Doña Juana clamped her jeweled hand upon the girl's thin shoulder, the child was terrified into silence.

I was holding out my chalk, visually taking measurements of the poor little girl to record on my paper, when doña Eufrasia's soft voice caught my attention. She was reading a lesson from John in her Book of Hours when I heard the word "Nicodemus." I paused. Nicodemus was the character from the Bible whom the Maestro had chosen to depict as himself in his unfinished statue.

"What is it, Sofonisba?" said Doña Juana.

I marked where the top of the child's head came against Doña Juana's skirt on my study. "Just measuring, My Lady."

"Have you a special interest in Nicodemus?"

"Do not we all, My Lady?" I said quickly. "He is a worthy figure."

"Is he? As a leader of the Jews, he was so afraid of his people's bad opinion that he came to Christ only at night, when no one would see him. He was a coward who would have no one know his faith."

I thought of the statue. These three years after seeing it, I could still remember how even in its unfinished state, the Maestro, depicted as Nicodemus, lovingly looked down upon the dying Christ. "But he did come to Our Lord, Your Majesty."

"Did he? After Our Lord told him he must leave everything and be born again in the faith, Nicodemus asked how it could be possible. How could a man be born when he was old?"

I pictured the Nicodemus of Michelangelo, laying the Christ to rest. "He must have done so, My Lady, because he was there when Christ was buried."

"Again, a safe thing to do. Who saw him at the grave? No one, besides Mary Magdalene and the Blessed Virgin. Show me in the Scriptures where we see Nicodemus proclaiming his faith to others." She watched with satisfaction as I marked measurements in silence. "That is correct. Nowhere. You've made no remarks on doña Eufrasia's other readings. Why this interest in the cowardly Nicodemus, he who hid his faith from the world?"

Why had maestro Michelangelo chosen the ambivalent Nicodemus to represent him on his own grave? He could have chosen anyone—Peter, Paul, John the Baptist—any of the saints.

But I said nothing more, and soon the sands ran out, releasing me from Doña Juana's inquisitive eye. This assignment cannot be done quickly enough. I shall start the painting tomorrow, if my studies are ready or not.

To Sofonisba Anguissola,
In the Court of the Spanish King

With immeasurable pride, I enclose a commemorative medal of the most worthy of subjects: you, my dear. It was done by a Leone Leoni, a most famous worker of metals in Milan. Have you ever heard of him? The medal is being circulated all around Lombardy, Rome, and Florence, perhaps in Venice, too. Its existence came as a complete surprise to me—Count Broccardo brought me one. He says your friend Michelangelo commissioned it and drew the study for it, though this I do not know for certain. That the likeness is so true to you that it must have been supplied by an expert who knows you does lend credence to this conjecture. But all I know is that Broccardo is gathering up as many as he can get his hands on, boasting of the close friendship he shares with the most famous person Cremona has ever produced. All this is too wondrous for me to contemplate. I am just your father—how proud this must make you feel!

All is well here, though your mother prays too hard. It is as if she does not trust God to answer her. If only she could stop praying long enough to rejoice in all He has given us. We have so much. You are aware, I think, of my most blessed gift. Although you are so very far away, I thank Our Heavenly Father for you each and every day.

From Cremona,
this 9th day of October, 1562

Your loving Father

ITEM: *"Tiẓiano Vecellio can go hang himself, for the portrait that he has painted resembles Her Serenity as much as a wolf does an ass."*

—THE DUKE OF MANTUA,

upon receiving his wife's painfully accurate portrait

ITEM: *Let not your flesh color freeẓe. Let it not be too cold or purple. Vermilion makes even the coldest flesh warm. Use yellow ochre with the vermilion chiefly on peasants, shepherds, or mariners.*

10 JANUARY 1563

El Alcáẓar, Madrid

I have not written in this notebook for six months. Much of my energy has been sucked out of me in working on Doña Juana's portrait. Bearing in mind Francisco de Holanda's admonishment that the image of a person of high standing must be contrived in order to leave a portrait worthy for centuries to come, I have tried to cast her in a favorable light. I have softened every line in the picture to reduce the formidableness of the subject, I have painted her cold countenance in a friendly shade of pink, I have cast the brightest light in the painting on the child's innocent face and little yellow gown to coax the eye to safer ground, but still the result remains the same: It is a chilling portrait of a woman with a taste for control.

I had sought out don Alonso Sánchez Coello for advice.

"How do I breathe some warmth into this?" I plunked down the mostly finished canvas on an easel in his studio. It was an afternoon in late October, and raining, hard, as it is wont to do in that month in Madrid.

In his typical slow and deliberate fashion, he turned his drooping gaze away from the Tiziano he was copying for the King and to the portrait. His palette still hooked to his thumb, he carefully looked it up and down.

"Good usage of color, doña Sofonisba. And I like how you've softened the lines. Here now——" He pointed with the maulstick he had been using. "Here I believe you are striving for detail, but perhaps it might be too much?"

I frowned at the sharp widow's peak slicing an auburn V into the bulge of her brow. Avoiding Doña Juana's threatening gaze, I had spent much time on her hair. Indeed, I had delineated each hair coming out of its shaft where it met her forehead.

"Look at this Tiziano," he said.

The work don Alonso had been copying for another of the King's palaces was Tiziano's painting *Venus and the Organ Player with Cupid*. When I bent to study it, instantly my eye went to the place of greatest contrast: the dark fork where Venus's torso met her thighs. That the organist's gaze led in a direct line to this place only reinforced its central importance in the painting. I glanced toward the arcade. I was glad I had made Francesca wait outside.

Don Alonso broke into a mournful smile. "I apologize for the subject."

"Do not apologize. I am an artist." Or at least I was.

"I hoped you would understand. I find this fascinating. He got you to look exactly where he wished you to look, yet what did you see? Darkness. Nothing. A smudge. Yet you saw everything, or at least all you needed to, all by suggestion."

"Yes, I do see what you mean. But I don't know how this may bring warmth to my painting."

"If only you could suggest warmth."

But I couldn't, not in Doña Juana's case. Even after much smudging, her portrait was hard and forbidding. It was as if the creature staring from within her cool eyes wished me to fail and I did.

The painting now hangs in the entrance hall of the convent in which Doña Juana lives, the Monasterio de las Descalzas Reales, the small palace near to El Alcázar in Madrid that she has made into a well-feathered nest for her and a select group of noble-women who have become nuns. There Doña Juana's grim image challenges all visitors, reminding those with the temerity to enter who is in control of the house.

At least she does not suggest now that don Alonso carried out the painting. She does toss me that scrap of respect, though she will not have any medals struck to honor my work. That Michel-angelo or any other person would want to commemorate me, as Papà had written, is astonishing. Does Michelangelo honor all his students this way?

The King has been gone from Madrid during much of this time. His most recent journey was to Aragón in September, put-ting down the unrest there. The nobles of that court have chal-lenged the King's authority, as indeed people all across Europe are challenging any authority, be it of kings or emperors or popes, encouraged by their claim to self-determination unleashed by Luther. His Majesty returned only seventeen days ago, just in time for Christmas.

He arrived on a quiet afternoon soon after the Queen's siesta, while some of the ladies were still sleeping. Her Majesty, an expert now with the chalk—and fairly skilled with the brush, if I prepare the canvas and pigments and set her palette—had been chuckling and sketching Cher-Ami as he chewed on the pomander that had rolled upon the floor while its owner slept. I was admiring the texture of the dog's fur in Her Majesty's drawing when the King strode into the chamber and flung off his hat.

The condesa woke with a start as he scooped the Queen into his arms and kissed her on the neck while a page ran after His Majesty's hat.

"I have been dreaming of you," the King said.

The Queen turned away her head. "You came straight from the road."

"I must smell. I am sorry."

The Queen put her arms around his neck and leaned back, her train falling prettily from her shoulders. "You were good to come to me first." She kissed his dusty cheek.

The King placed the Queen away from him. "I will bathe, then come back. Ladies—" The row of us dipped in curtseys like keys plunked on a clavichord. "Ladies, attend to her needs as she wishes, then please leave her in her chamber."

I dined with Francesca that night on ham and bread, alone in our chamber. For the King did claim his marital rights, as he has done every night that he has been home since his birthday last year, when he sent away Don Juan. It seems he has put aside his vow of physical temperance. Still, there is no child.

I found My Lady in bed that next morning, making Cher-Ami

dance by holding his front paws. "There you are, Sofi!" she cried as I entered, Francesca stumping behind. "How are you this morning?" The question was asked more as an announcement of her own high spirits than as an inquiry about my own.

"I am well, Your Majesty."

"Just 'well'?" The Queen stretched and yawned luxuriously.

"Well enough."

"You lie." She patted her chin for Cher-Ami to lick it. "We really must find you a husband."

"But I do not wish for a husband," I said lightly. Inwardly, I cringed. I have not heard from Tiberio since laying my soul bare to him. But what other result did I expect?

"Another lie. Everyone wants a husband. Even doña Eufrasia. At least that is what I told the King. And at last, he says he has found her one—the Prince of Ascoli."

I tied back the bed-hangings. "Doña Eufrasia is to marry?"

"Oh, Cher-Ami, what terrible breath you have," she said, then to me: "Yes, immediately. The King arranged it while he was gone. Heaven knows how much he had to pay Ascoli to take the simpering whore."

"Indeed."

"Well," said the Queen, "I say good riddance, though the King should not have wasted a prince on her, and a handsome one at that. A rat catcher would have been more suitable—a loutish, hairy, stinking one. At least Ascoli will take her to his own palace, far away from here."

"Congratulations, Your Majesty."

"Thank you," she said with a grin. "You are next. I will ask the King today." She smiled to herself. "I think this morning I could ask anything of him."

She put down her dog and hopped out of bed before I could

object to her plan. It little mattered. Her mind was not truly on me.

"You're coming with me, Sofi, to the Casa de Campo," she called from her velvet close stool. "I am meeting the King there after Mass." She came to us when she had finished, and held out her hands for Francesca to pour water over them. "Francesca, you needn't go with us this time. I am not having any of my other ladies. It is to be a private meeting."

As exciting as an out-of-doors assignation must seem to a seventeen-year-old girl, I was surprised the King had agreed to one, with the Queen's tendency toward illness and his extreme caution with her health. Madrid in December is windy and frigid. Even indoors in the palace of El Alcázar, with room-sized tapestries covering the thick stone walls, braided rush mats on the floor, and braziers burning charcoal in every chamber, you could often see your breath. "Is it not too cold outside for excursions?" I asked.

"You sound just like my old man of a husband," the Queen chided. "What do you think furs are for?"

"To keep animals warm?"

She swatted at me as I helped her to put on her morning robe.

"As for you, *mon petit chou-chou*," she said to Cher-Ami, who stood on his back legs and barked, "you can go with us, too, if you are good."

Soon after Mass and breakfast, we were huddled next to each other in a mule-drawn litter, the Queen wrapped in a lynx robe with Cher-Ami, and I in a robe of squirrel, as around us the scarlet hangings shuddered in the bitter wind sweeping down from the Guadarramas. We jostled from side to side as we descended the road that wound its way from the cliff upon which the palace was built to the gardens of the Casa de Campo in the valley below.

I nestled my chin into the softness of the fur. "You must be very glad for the King to be home."

"Yes, it is good to have one's itch scratched." She opened her robe enough for Cher-Ami to pop out his head.

Her flippant dismissal of the attentions of the most powerful man in the world discomfited me. She had not just his bed but his heart. Woe to her who broke it: as kind as the King seemed in his contentment, I feared that she had not yet fully tested his wrath. I wished to remind her of her good fortune.

"So it is as Don Alessandro said last spring, then—fulfillment is greater in love than desire."

The smile fell from her face. In a moment's time, her expression changed from that of a teasing girl to that of a hollow-eyed woman. "Do not speak to me of such."

She said nothing after that, only sat stroking her little dog as we made the final descent to the Casa de Campo. I drew back a curtain. Ahead, the mules' black manes slapped against their thick brown necks as we passed under a stone arch wound with bare and thorny rose canes. Past clipped juniper hedges we rode, by empty flowerbeds heaped over with dirt, until we came at last to a collection of low brick buildings fronted by wrought-iron cages: the Royal Zoo. From the pointed top of the largest cage, a scarlet and gold Royal banner snapped straight out in the wind.

"There he is," I said.

The Queen leaned forward to peer around me, a red-gloved finger to her lips. Ahead, the King stood talking with two African gentlemen wrapped in striped robes.

The Queen sank back.

The King turned around. When he saw the Queen, his face shed its usual coldly polite expression and lightened with a smile.

The muleteer stopped our conveyance. The King stepped over

to help us down from our couch. He kissed the Queen. "Now hide your eyes."

The Queen pulled back her chin, brightening. "What? A surprise for me?"

"Do as I say, my darling."

She handed Cher-Ami, yapping, to me and covered her eyes, knocking the diamond dangling from her cap with the cuff of her red gloves. He led her by the crook of her arm to the closest iron cage.

"Now look."

She put down her hands. "Oh, Felipe! A lion."

"A lioness," he said. "Like you."

"Oh!" she breathed. "Will she have cubs?"

"You would think the woman would be happy just to have a lioness," he said to me with a contained smile. "But My Lady, I have thought of that, too. I tried to ask that of the gentlemen who brought her here. Unfortunately, none of us can understand them, though apparently they are upset. I believe they are worried about the animal catching a chill." He arranged the Queen's cloak around her chin. "As I am about my lioness."

She used a childish voice. "You will build her a pretty house, won't you? She does look cold." She pulled free of him and waggled her hand through the cage bars.

One of the Africans jumped forward. Two of the King's men held him back as he shouted in his own language. I caught Cher-Ami as he tried to spring, yapping, from my arms.

The King nodded at the African politely. "I believe he is concerned about your safety, my darling." He tucked the Queen's hands under her robe, then turned her around and drew her against him so that she could watch the lion. "Let us not put ourselves within the reach of the beast."

Patting Cher-Ami to calm him, I gazed at the lioness pacing back and forth across the far reaches of its cage. Straw crunched under paws both frightening and endearing in their heaviness.

"What does it eat, Your Majesty?" I asked.

The King lifted his chin from Her Majesty's neck. "H'm? It hasn't touched the beef we've given it. I think we shall have to put a lamb into its cage."

"Oh, no!" said the Queen.

"Sorry, darling. I fear it might eat its food only live."

I shuddered. The lamb would make an easy kill in this cage little larger than a horse's stall.

"Are you cold?" the King asked the Queen. "Perhaps we should go back to the palace."

"No! I swear I cannot bear one more minute within those walls."

"'Those walls' are covered with the most costly tapestries in the world."

"Please, My Lord, do let us walk." Before the King had agreed, she said, "Stay in the litter, Sofi, and keep Cher-Ami warm."

With the assistance of a guard, I climbed back up onto the brocade couch of the litter, trying to keep my balance as the mules, nervous to be in such close proximity to the lioness, jerked the conveyance. Cher-Ami whimpered as his mistress strolled off in the direction of the garden maze, still green at this time of year with its sturdy walls of trimmed juniper.

I huddled under the squirrel fur and occupied myself with trying to interpret the exclamations of the African gentlemen. When that failed in spite of my familiarity with many languages, I listened to the shriek of unseen peacocks in some distant part of the garden.

The confident face of doctor Debruyne flashed through my

mind. It came to me often, as inexplicably and irritatingly as does a niggling melody from a silly song, though I had not seen him since last May. Now, as in the other times, I strived to put the memory of him neatly out of my head. Yet as firmly as I plugged the dam of remembrance against him, new holes sprang forth and out the thought of him burst. What new discoveries might he be making? Was he having new successes with coca or tobacco or the potato? Did he ever think of me and our experiment—of me, the woman who dared try a new herb in the name of science?

Did he have a woman?

I was fooling myself. He would never want me. Tiberio had not. In addition, the last sight he had of me was with green drool running down my chin and an idiot's lumpy grin upon my face. Definitely not the kind of memory to stick in a man's mind, I reminded myself, at least not in the way a woman would want. He must think me repugnant, a woman who failed to know her place. Just as well if I never saw him again. Indeed, he must have been avoiding me. Surely I would have seen him before we had left Aranjuez.

I jumped down from the litter, unable to stew in these thoughts another moment. Giving the lioness wide berth, I set out briskly, Cher-Ami snuffling the air eagerly from under my arm. I was spending altogether too much time around the Queen with her fixation upon rutting. I needed something challenging to occupy my mind—a Latin book to translate, a medical text to read, a painting commission. I did have my studies of Don Alessandro, made at his insistence when I had seen him at Christmas, and had started upon the underpainting of his portrait, but the work had come to a standstill. For even at that stage, with the picture composed in greenish gray, a disconcerting sadness kept creeping into his haughty and playful face, a sadness that troubled me to paint it.

Distracted by this thought, I skirted the maze, wishing, all the while, I had not left the warmth of the furs on the litter. Just then I heard the swish of greenery. Her Majesty's voice came from within the hedges.

"Surely no one can see us here." I could hear her chuckle. "Now, My Lord, how does that feel?"

I held my breath. Did they not know how close to the outer wall of the maze they had wandered?

I heard moist smacking, then the King's muffled voice. "Why do you love me?"

There was a rustling of cloth. A male groan. The Queen whispered, "You know why."

His voice was gruff. "Is that all?"

"Do you need another reason?"

"Yes."

Though his breathing came harder now, her voice was steady. "I just do."

"Say that you love me, Elisabeth. For the love of God—" He broke off with a groan. There was a crackling of greenery being crushed.

I broke for the litter and, finding it, clambered aboard. I buried my face in my robe as Cher-Ami licked the strip of exposed skin below my glove.

To the Magnificent Sofonisba Anguissola,
In the Court of the Spanish King

First of all, I apologize for the lateness of my reply. I fear the
Maestro's mail is being detained, as is mine, as a resident in
his house. I received your letter only yesterday, more than a
year after you had written. The Maestro is under some sort of
investigation, the full extent of which he will not tell me. His
usual critics, he says. I gather it is about the frescoes in the
Sistine Chapel. Even the Pope rails against them now. The
Maestro, ever sarcastic, asked the Pope if His Holiness should
not worry more about putting the world to right than some
pictures. The Pope was not amused. It is dangerous to bait
such a powerful man in this way, especially now that all are
up in arms about the riots against the Church in Northern
Europe. But since when has the old man ever been cautious
about what he says and does?

I do not write, however, to speak about the Maestro. I write
about us, though by the time you get this the King has
probably settled your portion upon a more worthy gentleman.
But truth will out: My dear Sofonisba, you must know that I
wish to be more to you than a recipient of your letters. But do
you not understand that you are a Lady of the Spanish court,
and, in this vaunted role, unapproachable by the son of a
Florentine whose fortune was made on providing vestments for
the clergy? My family has wealth and standing in Florence
and in Rome, but not of the sort which the King of Spain
would consider appropriate for his ward. The Calcagnis are

rich merchants, but we are merchants just the same, and you, now, are a great lady, as the Maestro has so kindly reminded me, over and over. You are no longer the daughter of Count Amilcare Anguissola, a learned man but not a high-ranking one. See—I did look into my prospects with you, soon after you left Rome that spring four years ago. I asked my friend Giorgio Vasari to make inquiries of your family in Cremona while he was there to interview you for his book The Lives of the Artists, but by the time he arrived, you had already left for Spain. You should be honored, by the way, that he included you in his book. He did not include me. Oh, and furthermore—if you need additional proof of your high stature in the world—there is a commemorative medal of you circulating around Rome. The Maestro brought me one not long ago. He made rather a fuss about it, making a point about your great place in the pantheon of artists. Rest assured, there is no commemorative medal of me.

I hate to end this letter, for I fear it will be my last to you. Do not think I shall ever forget you, my beautiful Sofonisba, or that night we were as husband and wife. I shall treasure it forever.

For your own protection, burn this letter when you are done with it. The world is an uneasy place these days.

With love from Rome,
this 23rd day of November, 1563

Tiberio Calcagni

To Tiberio Calcagni in Rome

I send this by the King's express courier, saying it is an inquiry into acquiring a religious picture for the Queen, though I have never before misused my position here in this manner. How easily it is done!

The Queen asks me if I want a husband. Until now I have said no, but emboldened by your letter, I could ask her to settle me upon you. For whatever reason, she favors me and would do this. Are you desirous of this? Should I ask her?

I am gratified to be the recipient of the medal, but I do not understand it. I still have not even the rank of the Painter to the Queen here, nor was I much more than a curiosity in the courts of Mantua and Milan. But these things matter little to me, as long as I hear from you.

From Madrid,
this 3rd day of January, 1564

Sofonisba Anguissola

ITEM: *The fox is a crafty and deceitful animal that never runs in a straight line. When it wants to catch birds to eat, it lies lifeless until birds land near it, at which point they are immediately consumed.*

ITEM: *"Shadow is the greater power than light, in that it can impede and entirely deprive bodies of light."*

—MAESTRO LEONARDO DA VINCI

26 FEBRUARY 1564
The Palace, Aranjuez

It was a chill day in late February. A wind full of the smell of dead vegetation rattled the few withered leaves that clung tenaciously to the elms across the river, and snatched at our veils and cloaks. We were walking through the King's flower garden as our coaches were being prepared to go to the hunt. Besides the King and Queen, Doña Juana, and a few attendants, Don Carlos was there, too, in celebration of Carnival. I myself was in a daze, wondering what Tiberio would say to my letter. Would he say yes, for me to ask the King and Queen to settle my portion upon him? If so, would he come here, or would I go to Rome? And if all this should miraculously come to pass after so much time, how would I behave around him? It has been four years. He is as a stranger to me. But oh, I remember the feel of his body. The firmness of

his hands, made rough by his work in stone. The way his veins
tenderly bulged in the soft skin inside his wrist. The wiriness of
the curls at his neck. Yet it is more than his flesh I remember. I
had felt his tender soul tremble, and he had felt mine.

"Sofonisba."

Doña Juana dropped back from strolling with the King and
Queen. "Thinking about something?" Her lips curled in a knowing smile.

I blushed, fearing she could hear my thoughts. She seemed to
have that power. "Your Majesty, how may I be of service?"

"I have decided to remove the portrait you have done of me
from my convent."

"Your Majesty, would you like me to make some changes to
it?" I glanced at Don Carlos, sidling up next to the Queen to take
Doña Juana's position.

"No," said Doña Juana. "I suppose you have done the best you
are capable of with it. I have given it to Inquisitor-General Valdés. He has always wanted a portrait of me."

"That is most kind, Your Majesty."

"I thought he could hang it in his Hall of Justice, next to the
portrait of the King. After all, I was the Regent for those years
the King was in England with Queen Mary—the people have
come to associate me with justice."

"Yes, Your Majesty."

Conscious of Doña Juana's gaze upon me, I kept my own gaze
fixed straight ahead, to where Don Carlos whispered earnestly to
the Queen. The King laid a languid hand upon the back of the
Queen's neck.

"Well," said Doña Juana, "Inquisitor-General Valdés says your
friend has certainly benefited from his friends in high places, hasn't
he?" She smiled at my puzzled expression. "Michelangelo Buonar-

roti, I mean. If he were not a favorite of the Pope, his punishment would have been greater." She watched my face. "You do know of the decision?"

I concentrated on plucking a leaf bit from my shawl. "No, Your Majesty."

She lowered her broad brow to watch me with those fierce bone-lashed eyes. "His work in the Sistine Chapel is to be destroyed."

Her neck in the King's grasp, the Queen turned slightly, interrupting Don Carlos. "Have you not been speaking of such for years, dear sister?" she said to Doña Juana.

"Actually, this decision was only just made. As busy as you have been, my sister, with trying to fill a cradle, I can understand how you have not been able to keep up with current affairs."

Doña Juana smiled as the Queen returned her face forward. "At any rate," she said to me, "I would venture to say the chapel will be improved by whitewashing the walls. Good-bye to the young louts with their acorns."

The King frowned over his shoulder at her.

We continued our stroll, the ladies' skirts dragging on the damp stone of the path. A knot clenched in my stomach. Adam receiving the touch of life from God; the story of Noah, rendered with understanding and love; the human body celebrated in all its glory; even the curious quiet painting of Eve: all of it, destroyed.

She brushed her slipper against a withered stalk that had sprawled upon our path. "Really, Felipe, you must have your gardeners pull these. I cannot understand why you will not let them. I care not if it came from the New World—truly, it is no better than a weed."

"The seedpods were quite interesting," said the King. "They

are said to be quite nutritious, though they do look a little off-putting."

I gazed at the shriveled brown stalks

"What is the name of the ridiculous weed?" asked Doña Juana.

The King patted the Queen's neck as she turned to look. "I believe," he said, "they call it 'maize.'"

A mule-drawn coach lumbered up at the end of the garden to take us to the hunt. The King and his son, as well as the Queen and myself, took seats in the first conveyance. Off we went with a jerk.

In time we passed through the leafless brown ranks of the mulberry grove to the east of the palace. "How are the silkworms doing that came last year from China?" the King asked the Queen.

The Queen turned slowly from where she'd been looking out the window, stroking Cher-Ami's head. "I have not attended to them, My Lord."

"I thought we agreed that you would tend to the silkworms in the afternoons, when I was working in my office," said the King.

"I have been resting, My Lord," said the Queen.

"Well, I must not argue with that." He kissed her fingers.

Across the coach, Don Carlos slumped against the leather paneling, his blue-veined eyelids fluttering as he fought off sleep. The King sighed. "I have such fond memories of my mother collecting silk. I wish for you only the same contentment that it brought her. I can still see her wide brow—Juana's brow, Juana resembles Mother in that way—crumpled in concentration as she unwound each little cocoon."

Don Carlos didn't bother to open his eyes. "Did she not have servants to do that?"

"Mother enjoyed it. She spent hours at it. It was intense, meticulous work. I believe I have inherited her ability to concentrate on details for long periods of time." The King smiled. "Still, as a young child, I saw not the merits of her concentrating on her work for hours on end. All I wished was for her to pay attention to me."

The King kissed the Queen's fingers again, then put her hand in his lap. "I remember once I climbed up next to her on her bench, trying to get close to her as she unraveled a silken filament from a cocoon and wound it upon a golden spindle. She must have momentarily rested her hand upon the bench—perhaps her fingers had gotten weary. I did not see them. All I knew was that I wished to be close to her." He grimaced. "I could hear her finger crack, just like a stick, as I sat upon it."

Don Carlos's blue lids folded open. "You broke your mother's finger?"

"I did not mean to. There was a crack and she cried out. Then someone snatched me up and took me away. I could hear her sobs all the way back to the palace. I thought, I have done that to her. I am little, and I have done that. I could not believe a little shoot like me could hurt my all-powerful mother." He looked out the window. "It is my earliest memory."

The Queen raised her gaze to him.

"I did not mean to hurt her," he said.

"Whether you meant to or not," said Don Carlos, "the effect was the same. Did she forgive you?"

"Yes. She knew my intentions were good. After all, I acted out of love."

Our coach hurtled down the narrow lane, then through an almond orchard, past black limbs budded with pearls of white. Into a deep wood of naked oak we soon passed, then came upon a raised platform fitted out with cushioned benches. From either side of the platform, a billowing wall of unbleached cloth stretched deep into the forest, forming an ever-widening chute. Alighting from the coach, I could hear hounds baying and beaters hallooing as they whipped the brush to raise deer from their hidden nests.

"Men, take your positions. Women, steer clear!" shouted Don Carlos. His weariness seemingly forgotten, he drew his sword and ran ahead of his father, ducking under the cloth raised by one of the many men stationed along the temporary wall.

The next coach arrived. I tried not to think of the frightened animals that would soon be leaping down the chute and to their deaths.

Doña Juana trudged up the steps to the platform. "I wish they would get this over with. I have more important business than watching menfolk skewer deer."

The King shaded his eyes to look up at his sister, whose loud voice must have been audible from where he stood. "I seem to recall your eagerness to hunt when allowed to shoot deer from a coach."

"Very well! Give me an arquebus, then! I will make short work of this."

Don Carlos leveled his sword at her. "Hush."

"Insolent," she muttered under her breath as she settled into a seat.

"Sofonisba," she said before I could sit. "You did not ask me why the decision was made against your Michelangelo."

The Queen's hand tightened on my arm. A stag was plunging down the chute, its eyes white in their sockets as hounds tore at its flanks. It leapt for the top of the wall. Three huntsmen rushed over and clubbed it down.

"The Sistine Chapel is only half his problem," said Doña Juana. "Several of his poems to a certain young man have come to the Pope's hand. They are sickening. The old man moans of how at his age he was hit by Cupid's arrows, how he thought he could change but could not. He told the Pope their intended recipient never got them, indeed his desired one has no notion of their existence, but no one believes this. Of course Michelangelo is protecting his lover." She saw my expression. "Do you know who this might be?"

"No, Your Majesty."

She kept her white-lashed gaze fixed upon me. "Are you sure?"

The King stepped into the path of the panicked deer. In one last desperate burst, it bounded over the King's head. The King thrust up his sword.

The deer crashed to the ground. Legs flailing, it struggled to rise, then stood, trembling, as glistening ropes of guts slithered from its belly.

ITEM: *The pelican, when its young are hungry, will peck its own breast until it bleeds and will feed its children upon its blood.*

ITEM: *Oil is not as impervious to water as you might think. Water can seep through a fresh layer of paint.*

16 AUGUST 1564
El Alcázar, Madrid

The King's father, the Emperor Charles, was always on the move, tramping here and there across Europe, fighting wars, brokering deals, and marrying off his children to solidify the greatest empire since the days of ancient Rome. Only after he'd passed the burden of his many kingdoms to the eighteen-year-old Felipe did he settle down in a small but comfortable monastery hidden in the Gredos Mountains, where he spent the last two years of his life eating and drinking and gazing upon his illegitimate son Juan when the fancy struck him.

Not wishing to live the nomadic life that had exhausted his father, the King chose to base his courts in the central location of Madrid, limiting his travel to pleasure palaces within a few days' journey, going farther abroad only when political unrest required it. The dim brooding pile of El Alcázar, built over the centuries upon a sultan's fortress, now is the chief home of the King of Two Worlds. But unlike the bucolic Flemish-style palace of Valsaín in the Woods of Segovia, where sweet summers are whiled away in the cool mountain air, or the riverside jewel box of Aranjuez, where spring and fall are savored in an oasis of green in the arid foothills of the Toledan mountains, there is no easy season in Madrid.

It is said of Madrid that there are nine months of winter and three months of Hell—not so far from the truth. Winter blows in from the Guadarramas in late October and has one thawing one's fingers over the brazier in May. But by July, if you are so foolish as to stand in the sun after mid-morning, it feels as though your skull has become a cookpot for your brain. Strength evaporates from your limbs as your brains boil and your blood bakes, making escape all the more difficult each minute you remain exposed in the sun. Francesca says the bodies of three beggars were found on the steps of the Church of San Pedro el Viejo this afternoon, dead from the heat. I do not tell this to the Queen. She is in her sixth month of pregnancy and must not be disturbed in any way.

How the King does dote on her. He has her drinks iced with snow brought by mule train from the peaks of the Guadarramas. He, master of much of the earth, personally fans her as she lies upon her bed. Her mother's weekly letters exhort her to take exercise. "Knowing you, my daughter," the French Queen Mother writes, "you will be inclined to stay in bed, but you must resist this impulse for your good and the good of the child." How well My Lady's mother knows her daughter. Her Majesty wishes to dally away her time in bed, playing cards with her ladies or, if propped upright with a paintbrush in hand, depicting in tandem with me little portraits of her ladies' children with their favorite pets.

But even if My Lady were inclined to exercise, how much could she take when the King will not allow her to leave her summer rooms in the lower part of the palace, let alone the city, fearful as he is of her traveling in her delicate state? This is why we cannot escape to the cool of the mountains at Valsaín, why we must spend our afternoons trapped here in darkened rooms, prostrate amongst the water jugs, touching our wrists to the condensation that beads upon their sides. He demands that we think of nothing but My Lady's health, and perhaps it is for the best. What good does it do to let my mind wander to the identity of Michelangelo's lover, and to how this might possibly be connected to the reason why Tiberio has not replied these six months?

As delighted as the King is with Her Majesty's pregnancy, he seems not to notice the temperature. Only yesterday he strode into her chamber at the end of *siesta*, a spring to his step in spite of the heat that had sapped the life from the rest of us. The condesa and madame de Clermont rose from where they languished on their pillows and straightened their gowns as Cher-Ami waddled forth to greet him.

The Queen raised herself on an elbow for his kiss. "You have spots on your sleeves, My Lord."

He examined his sleeve. "Indeed I do. It is raining mud outside." He saw me look up from the table at which I was idling upon an uninspired sketch of the Queen. "Sometimes in the summer here," he explained, "when it rains there is a bit of sand in each drop. It comes, they say, from the African desert. Quite a way for a cloud to travel."

The Queen gazed languidly at the covered window. "It is raining?"

"Big muddy drops," he said, kissing the top of her head with each word. "It has probably stopped by now."

"Oh." She sighed deeply. "We cannot hear it down here."

He pulled up a stool, then caressed the mound of her belly. "How is my little prince?"

"He kicks me."

"Perhaps he dreams of spurring his horse. He shall be an excellent horseman, our son."

She looked up at him with a small smile.

"He will win all his jousts," he said.

"I do not want him to joust," she said. "My father . . ."

"Pardon me, My Lady. Our son shall never joust. I will command him not to."

"Oh, he will want to," she said bitterly, "just like Father. He had insisted upon running at lists one more time the day of his injury. No one could stop him."

The King looked pained at her vehemence. "I shall outlaw it, then. There shall be no jousting in all of Spain. There will be nothing to stop him from. See, darling? So simple." He kissed her hand. "I am in control of everything."

"Yes. I know."

Cher-Ami jumped up on the bed.

"How is Don Carlos?" she asked, idly stroking the dog. "I have had no news of him of late."

"As a matter of fact, I have just received word from him. He arrives in town today."

She struggled to sit. "He is coming today? And you did not tell me?"

"I was—"

"Why has Toad not come to see me before this? It has been so long."

"It has been only since Easter." He turned toward me. "Doña Sofonisba—"

I laid down my chalk and curtseyed.

He waved his hand to stop me. "I have news you may not have received. I heard it from my agent who just returned from Venice

with the Tizianos I had ordered. Michelangelo Buonarroti died
on the eighteenth day of February."

The air felt squeezed from my lungs. A great light of the world
had been snuffed.

"Your Majesty, thank you for telling me."

"I'm sorry, Sofi," said the Queen. "I know you thought much
of Michelangelo. I'm sure you would have known sooner if Doña
Juana were not on a pilgrimage to Santiago de Compostela. She
would not have missed an opportunity to upset you with sad tid-
ings of your old master."

The King had hardly had a chance to make a small sound of
disapproval when the Queen grasped his hand. "My Lord, we
must have a grand reception for Don Carlos. As soon as possible.
Tomorrow!"

The King laughed. "What is the haste, my pet?"

"How is the Prince's health, Your Majesty?" asked the condesa,
on her way to her embroidery frame.

The King swung his gaze from the Queen. "The reports from
his physician in Alcalá are good. Thank you for asking, *señora*."

The condesa brushed at her gown, trying to hide her pleasure.

"Can we have the reception tomorrow evening?" asked the
Queen.

The King raised her hand and kissed it. "No, my darling. You
know that preparations cannot be made that quickly."

"The next day, then. I shall wear the gown I have been saving,
the one with the purled gilt embroidery."

"Oh, that's what this is about. Your wish to dress up?"

She slid out her lower lip in a pretty pout. "I have been mold-
ering in my rooms, My Lord. Do you not wish me to look nice?"

"I do wish for you to look nice. Very well, then, we shall have
your reception. As long as you do not overexert yourself."

"I shall be a lamb," she said in a child's voice.

The chamber was in an uproar the moment he left. The Queen called for her musicians, for her master of the household, for her hairdresser, her jeweler, her cook. At last, after the splendid affair had been planned down to the last sugared almond, her dressmaker was summoned to add a panel to Her Majesty's undergown, to accommodate her growing belly.

My Lady obediently raised her arms as the dressmaker took measure of the expanded garment, marking it with pins. *"Madame,"* she said to the dressmaker, "please come to the reception as my guest."

The dressmaker, a round woman whose dark complexion was peppered with even darker freckles, took the pin from her mouth. "Your Majesty, I am honored, thank you. It will be a big occasion. I saw the Infante's cavalcade entering the palace when he arrived the other day."

"Cavalcade?" said the Queen. "Were there many gentlemen?"

"Quite a large party—please, Your Majesty, you must be still."

"Did you recognize any of them?"

The dressmaker sat back on her heels, holding together the seam of the dress. She brushed back her sweat-dampened veil with her arm. "Yes, Your Majesty. Some were quite illustrious. There was the Duke of Eboli, the Duke of Mendoza and some of his family, Margarita of Austria's son—"

"Don Alessandro was with him?"

"Yes, Your Majesty."

The Queen glanced at the condesa, stitching on yet another altar cloth at her embroidery frame. "Anyone else?"

"Oh, quite a few others."

"I see." She drew in a breath. "Did you happen to see Don Juan?"

I glanced at Francesca, who was squatting with the other servants, waving her skirts to create a cooling draft on her legs. It was Francesca's opinion that the King had done us all a favor by sending his half brother to Rome. The less the Queen saw of Signore Juan, she muttered, the better.

The dressmaker rocked back onto her knees. "I cannot say that I saw him, Your Majesty." She took a pin from the cushion tied to her wrist. "Is he a cardinal yet?"

The condesa paused in her needlework.

"He may be by now," the Queen said, "though I have not heard from him."

"Such a pity, that gentleman becoming a religious." The dressmaker pushed a pin into the heavy fabric of the seam. "Young ladies across the kingdom will weep at the loss of such a handsome prospect."

The Queen's color heightened. "He would not marry them."

"A shame," said the dressmaker mildly, not noticing the bright, hard look in the Queen's eyes. "He would make a good match."

"He would not have my sister, my cousin Mary Stuart, or the English Queen Elizabeth. He has not a mind to marry anyone."

The condesa stopped stitching. "Not now, at least, now that the King has wished for him to be a priest."

"A *cardinal*." Madame de Clermont spoke up from within her veils as she cooled her hands against a damp water jar. "The highest position in the Church, other than Pope."

"He would not have had them, regardless," said the Queen. She winced, then put her hand to her belly.

"Kicking you again, My Lady?" I said quickly. "*The King's son* must be a fighter." Need I remind her whose son she carried? The condesa did watch her too closely from behind her embroidery frame.

The next day the Queen woke with a headache, apparent from the first glance at her puffy eyes. Her entire face seemed swollen, even her nose and lips. We tried splashing her face with Hungary water and giving her a piece of precious ice to suck, but nothing worked. Indeed, her pain grew throughout the day.

"It is the reception," said the condesa, sponging Her Majesty's brow. "You are too excited about it. This cannot be good for the baby."

The Queen looked up, the brown of her eyes deepened from the pinkness of her lids. "Excitement is good for *me*. And what is good for me, *madame*, is good for the baby."

The condesa frowned. "Not necessarily. You must put this baby before yourself, My Lady."

"Now, now." I took the damp cloth from the condesa's hands. "We cannot have the baby without the mother." I turned the cloth to find a cool side, then laid it across the Queen's forehead. "There now, My Lady."

The King came after *siesta*. His brows contracted with worry when he found the Queen lying on a daybed, her eyes covered with a wet cloth. At Francesca's suggestion, I had been reading Aesop's fables aloud in Latin. I laid down my book in the middle of "The Wolf in Sheep's Clothing."

He knelt beside her. "Are you in pain, My Lady?"

"It is just this heat." She waved me away, then righted herself.

He took her face in his hands and turned it side to side. "You are not well. I will call off the reception tomorrow."

"No!"

"I will not risk your health."

"The baby is fine, My Lord. I am warm, that is all. Are you not warm, too? It is August!"

He felt her brow and glared at the condesa, who had been hovering nearby, fitfully sniffing at her pomander. "Why has no one told me of this?"

The condesa curtseyed. "We have tried to get her to rest, but she will not be bothered."

Outside, thunder boomed. A good omen. Rain would break the heat.

The Queen sank back with a wince. "Just get me some more ice. That is all I need."

"Ice!" the King barked to the condesa, making her start. She swept from the chamber.

The Queen's brave smile only accented the puffiness of her face. "What do you plan to wear tomorrow, My Lord?"

"Shhh, darling, rest. My usual black—if we go."

"Do you not wish to wear something more festive?"

"I tax my people heavily to pay for my wars. I cannot ask them to sacrifice when I myself live a life of luxury."

She cast down her gaze.

"You," he said, kissing her neck, "on the other hand, shall have every gown you wish. The people take pride in your beauty. You give us the courage to go on."

She twisted the lace of his cuff. "You are so good to me, My Lord. I do not deserve it."

"Shhh, darling. What kind of talk is that?"

Rain did not come that night. Thunder rumbled as I sprawled across my bed, trying to find a cool spot while avoiding contact with Francesca.

"Are you wake, *signorina*?"

My hair stuck on my cheek as I turned my head toward her. "Yes."

"I hear something today."

Crickets chirped outside our window. "Yes?"

"Before the King married the mother of Don Carlos, the condesa, she was promised to him in marriage."

"The condesa?" My shift caught under my hip as I raised myself on an elbow. "That cannot be." I tugged my shift free. "She's more than fifteen years his senior. And while she loves to brag about her rank, even she knows she is no princess. She could never expect to marry the son of an emperor. Who spoke this nonsense, servants?"

There was a hurt silence. "The lower the station, the more likely the truth."

"I am sorry, Francesca, I was not questioning you. But it's an impossible scenario."

"All I say, *signorina*, is she serve old Queen Juana, the King's grandmother, and old Queen Juana's son, the Emperor, he treat his mother bad. He take away her crown, call it his, then he tell the condesa she can marry King if she keep her mouth shut."

"This has to be just rumor. The condesa has never said one ill word about the Emperor, the King, or poor mad Queen Juana, and the condesa would not be one to keep quiet if she had not gotten what was promised to her. Why do you tell me this now?"

"She is bitter, *signorina*. She hate the Queen to have what she think is hers, and then for the Queen to not appreciate it—*ohimè!* She want to see the Queen fall."

"But the Queen has done nothing. And the King loves her so."

The thick air throbbed with the crickets' incessant cries.

"Better, *signorina*, to have a husband without love than one with jealousy."

In the morning, Her Majesty's headache was no better, though she tried to say that it was. Her swollen eyes said otherwise, as did the way she clenched her jaw.

I poured water over her hands at her morning toilet. "You can postpone the reception, My Lady," I said in a low voice. "You can have it another day."

Francesca, behind me untangling my short train, nodded earnestly.

The Queen reached out affectionately to Francesca. "Don't worry, I will be fine—better than if I have to wait another day."

The condesa came over with a towel. "Feeling better?"

"Much!"

I watched the condesa as she went to retrieve the Queen's robe. Had she really been promised to the King? No wonder she wished the Queen such ill, when My Lady's only real crimes were to be impetuous and naïve.

"I ask you to reconsider this," I whispered to the Queen, "for your own good."

"My good? You make too much of a little headache."

Truly, the excitement of the evening ahead did seem to buoy her up through Mass and then breakfast, though the day was so stifling it stopped the breath within one's lungs. By the time she was to get dressed for the reception, the only sign of her headache was a certain tension in her eyes and in her knotted jaw.

After we had tied the last diamond-encrusted bow of her bodice, My Lady stepped from our hands to swish her new gown. "How does it look?"

Every inch of her white silk overgown had been embroidered with tight coils of gold wire in the shapes of intertwining vines and flowers. From the center of each blossom winked a perfect diamond. Tiny diamonds glittered from the gossamer lace of her collar, which had been wired upright to cup her face. Be it from fever or excitement, an otherworldly spark burned in her eyes.

Together with her sparkling raiment, she looked every inch an angel from heaven.

"You shall steal everyone's heart," said madame de Clermont, swathed in her usual veils.

The condesa raised her pomander to her nose. "Everyone's."

From the door, a male voice said, "Magnificent."

I snatched up the Queen's train so that she would not stumble upon it as she turned. The King stood in the doorway, his arms folded over his chest.

"You are a vision, my love."

She waited to receive his kiss, then pushed against him with her fingertips. "Your beard is prickly."

"I am sorry, pet," he said, caressing her cheek with the back of his hand. "I came to make sure you felt well enough to attend the reception."

"I am restored by your touch, My Lord."

A crash of thunder cut short his look of bemusement.

"Perhaps it will finally rain tonight," he said. "Our farmers certainly need it."

"Let the rain hold off until tomorrow," said the Queen. "It will ruin people's finery tonight."

Veils a-rustle, madame de Clermont hurried over to the iron-railed window from which the heavy drapes had been drawn to let in the evening air. "The guests begin to arrive," she announced.

The Queen pulled from the King and went to the window adjacent to madame's, Cher-Ami tottering behind her.

"Slow down, slow down!" the King exclaimed, following good-naturedly. "Oh—doña Sofonisba."

I paused on my way over to madame's window.

"I meant to tell you today, but a little bird interrupted me—my agent in Italy said that at the time he was in Rome, the paintings in the Sistine Chapel had not yet been covered. Perhaps the Pope has changed his mind."

I nodded, grateful for his news.

Madame announced, "The Duke of Mendoza arrives."

The King went to his wife. When I joined the condesa at madame's window, she was watching the King and Queen, not the people arriving below.

The King wrapped his arms around the Queen and rested his bearded chin on her shoulder. "Remember the reception he gave us in honor of our marriage?"

"How can I forget, My Lord? It was the first time that I saw you."

"Yes. You found my beard to be gray."

"It was you that said that, not I."

She kept her gaze upon the guests entering the palace as he kissed her ear. "As for me," he said, "I was thinking what a gift God had sent me. I did not think I deserved such an angel."

She drew a sharp breath.

He smiled, thinking it was his words that had moved her, until he followed her gaze below. "What, darling?" he said, frowning.

"Your friend."

I looked in the direction of her nod. On the arm of the young and darkly handsome Prince of Ascoli, to whom she had been this year wed, was doña Eufrasia, dressed in a gorgeous apple-green gown. But as stunning as were doña Eufrasia's clothes and jewels, that was not what attracted the eye. No, one's gaze was instantly drawn to the panel below her bodice, from which protruded her luxuriously pregnant belly.

Both the condesa and madame turned to the Queen to gauge her reaction.

There was a long pause. "Her child looks to be due before mine," the Queen said.

The King's voice was icy. "I did not know she was pregnant."

I glanced over and saw the Queen staring elsewhere.

A lady in russet alit from the next conveyance and was handed down by a fair-haired gentleman. I saw that it was Don Juan.

The Queen's swallow was audible from where I stood. I could feel the condesa's gaze sharpen upon the King and Queen.

"So," said the King. "My brother joins us. Bold, after he disobeyed me and left Rome. A cardinal's hat awaited him, and he threw it away."

"He left the Church?" My Lady turned to him. "You did not tell me."

"I have been too angry to talk about it. And all for a woman."

The Queen blinked.

"He should have come to me first," the King said. "It is not his place to put aside any honors I give to him."

The Queen's voice was faint. "Who is the lady?"

"María de Mendoza, the niece of the duke."

The Queen swayed.

"She is just a foolish young thing." The King shook his head. "She threw herself at Juan when he stayed with her uncle at Easter."

Don Carlos, his heavy gold necklace clinking against his black gorget, loped into the chamber with Don Alessandro. "We came to pay our respects before the reception." His brow puckered. "My Lady? Are you well?"

The Queen put the back of her hand to her nose. When she brought it away, it was bright with blood.

"Elisabeth? Elisabeth!" the King cried, just before the Queen slumped to the floor.

The

Third Notebook

ITEM: *A drink distilled from the tears and the heart bones of a stag is a cure for troubles of the heart.*

26 SEPTEMBER 1564
El Alcázar, Madrid

She lost the baby. It is whispered about Madrid that it was due to her jealousy of doña Eufrasia, that seeing the King's newly wed mistress so wondrously advanced in pregnancy made her lose her own child in a fit of jealousy. Although the King denied repeatedly that doña Eufrasia's child was his—he claimed to have ended his affair with her long before he had her married to the Prince of Ascoli—his protests were received with a wink by Madrileños high and low. What man in his right mind would turn away the dark-haired and delicious doña Eufrasia if he had a chance at bedding her? Certainly a Queen must be chaste—oh, she must be perfectly so—but a King? He was less of a man if he *didn't* stray. All agreed there was no reason for the King to deny himself the pleasure of keeping a mistress and a wife. The Queen, for her part, should have understood that. It was so needless, all whispered, for Her Majesty to lose the King's heir this way. Especially a king who could choose any lady in the world.

Few knew how close she had come to losing her own life. For three hours after she had fainted, she had remained unconscious. Only an emergency blood-letting revived her. When at last she came to, her will to speak had left her. She lay on her bed, oblivious to our exclamations as she stared into the distance.

"Do not worry, my darling, we will have other children," I heard the King whisper to her, the morning after her miscarriage. I was removing her untouched cup of bread soaked in wine. He kissed her pale brow. "Just get better, my pet."

She gave a shuddering sigh, then closed her eyes.

Doctor Hernández was called. Although the King wondered if there might be a miracle herb from the New World that would help the Queen, doctor Hernández would not risk it. Instead, he continued to listen to her pulse music, then to bleed her, drawing out her bad humors to allow in the good. And though I winced to see him nick her wrists with his lancet and then catch her youth's bright blood in a white dish, I prayed that this would restore her. For my part, I spooned broth into her mouth and bathed her face and wrists with Hungary water, as priests led the other ladies in endless rounds of the Rosary. But priests, doctors, ladies—the results of all of our ministrations remained the same. We were losing her.

And then one afternoon, nearly four weeks after she fell, as I sponged My Lady's neck while rosary beads clicked and her ladies murmured in prayer, Cher-Ami rose from where he lay at the foot of the bed, head on paws. His mistress struggled against her covers, then sat up.

"*J'ai faim.*"

The condesa's fingers froze on the first bead of the third decade. "What did you say, Your Majesty?"

The Queen smiled shakily. "I am hungry."

Madame de Clermont whispered a prayer of thanks as her beads fell to her skirts. "You! Boy!" she shouted at a page. "Bring a compote of fruit and a *crêpe*, cooked in the French style!"

The boy blinked at the Queen who had lain senseless these many weeks.

"What are you waiting for?" cried madame. "Go!"

The King was summoned. He broke from a meeting with his counselor to the Netherlands and appeared immediately.

"Everyone, out!" he cried, striding to her side.

The Queen reached toward me. "Let Sofi stay."

He nodded, then eased down on the bed as the ladies, priests, and pages filed from the room. "My pet." He held her face in his hands, his own countenance crumpled with emotion. "I have been so worried."

"I wish to leave Madrid."

Her first words to him in four weeks.

"Of course. When you are strong enough."

"Now. I wish to leave now. I will gain strength away from here."

He kissed her hand. "Then we shall go—to the Woods of Segovia, I think. It is beautiful there, and the air is healthful. But you must eat first, and get better."

Her eyes shone with tears. "My Lord—I am sorry I lost the baby."

"Shhh, pet." He laid her hand against his chest.

"My Lord, I have been unable to speak, but I was not deaf. I have heard what people whisper about you. About doña Eufrasia."

His brow creased with anger. "The Prince of Ascoli should not have brought his wife here in such a state. To upset you—"

She touched his beard. "I do not believe them. I know you have been true to me."

He pulled away. "I did not know she was with child. No one had told me. I am King, and no one had told me."

"I am sorry I lost our child."

"She should not have come." He rubbed his beard, then lowered his fist upon his knee. "Well, what is done is done, and nothing can change it."

There was a tap on the door. The King signaled for me to get it. I let in madame, who swept over to the bed, her exposed eyes bright with happiness. "*Excusez-moi*, but My Lady, here is your compote." She held forth a silver dish.

The King took it from madame. "The sooner you gain your strength, my pet," he said to the Queen, "the sooner we can get you in a litter to Valsaín." He held up the full spoon.

"I shall eat like a pig," she said, then opened her mouth.

ITEM: *A certain nobleman was so smitten by Julius Caesar's wife, Pompeia, that this gentleman dressed like a woman and sneaked into her home while Julius Caesar was away. The man was discovered before reaching Pompeia; a trial was ordered to prove her innocence in the matter. But even though she was cleared, Julius Caesar divorced her. "The wife of Caesar," he said, "must be above suspicion."*

ITEM: *"There are those who would spend much time on a picture's background. Yet if one throws a sponge full of colors at a wall, it would leave a patch in which one might see a beautiful landscape."*

—MAESTRO SANDRO BOTTICELLI

5 OCTOBER 1564
Valsaín, the House in the Woods of Segovia

The King kept his promise. Within a week we were wending our way through the silent rocky passes of the Guadarramas, eagles wheeling in the stark blue sky above us. Streams splashed violently over the boulders along the side of the trail as our mules strained against their harnesses, their necks blackening with sweat. Inside our litter, wrapped in light furs, the Queen and I played endless rounds of cards when she was not resting or chatting with the King, who plodded beside us on his black charger. Behind us, the condesa and madame de Clermont joggled along mutely in their litter, followed by a train of wagons that snaked along the windswept road cut over the mountaintops in times long past. Roman soldiers had made this road, at the bidding of Julius Caesar. Now the man who rules lands more widespread than those of Julius Caesar leaned from his horse to extend his gloved hand to his lady. She blew him a kiss, then trumped my ace in our game of Triumph.

On we traveled in this way, with overnight rests at Royal hunting lodges, until at last we descended into the valley of woodlands and river-crossed meadows that leads to Segovia. In this valley is nestled the House in the Woods—Valsaín.

Ah, Valsaín, my favorite of the King's palaces. While its rows of balconied windows against warm brick, its tall wooden spires, and its courtyards planted with fruit trees and herb knots do delight the eye, it is the surrounding woods and mountain meadows that enchant me. Here the brushy boughs of the *piños de Valsaín* sigh in the wind as if contented, and tuft-eared squirrels scrabble up the trunks of the stately trees. Birdsong brightens the brisk piney air. It is just the place for a person to regain her health. And so the Queen recovers hers, slowly but steadily.

She was napping this afternoon when I stole into the woods. A book pressed to my breast, I walked along the grassy banks of the River Eresma, its shallow waters babbling companionably from its stony bed. I had in mind to read, but after four long weeks shut up in Her Majesty's chamber, I could do nothing but drink in Nature. With each step that I sank into the spongy green turf tunneled by hidden moles, with each touch of the lichen-splotched rocks that held the cool of the mountain winds within them, with each trill of the warblers flitting through the trees, my black cloak of melancholy slipped from my shoulders just a little bit more. I could almost feel my humors balancing within me.

I wished to paint.

In the week since the Queen awakened from her illness, she has kept me by her side at all times, having me read Latin or pick out the stitches she has done wrong in her embroidery or humor her with silly drawings. And while we enjoy each other's company well enough, I notice the effect my constant attendance has upon the King. He cannot have a moment alone with her, and in this manner could not have claimed his conjugal rights even if doctor Hernández had approved of it. It is as if the Queen has taken to using me as a shield between herself and the King.

But at that moment, as I savored the breath of the wind in my hair and the freedom to wonder what subject I might paint, a soft bleating came to my ears. Stilling my skirts, I eased toward the brushy cove from which it came. Slowly, carefully, I parted the tall grass. There, nibbling on the bark of a small tree was a doe, suckling her two half-grown fawns.

I grinned. Greedy fawns. They banged their heads at her bag and tugged at her teats as if each was afraid the other would get its share. How they reminded me of my own sisters when young, grabbing at Papà when he would bring home a new book from his shop.

"They are brothers now, but when they've grown, they will fight each other to the death."

I turned with a start, sending the doe fleeing into the forest, the fawns sailing behind her. Doctor Debruyne stood behind me, an empty basket on his arm.

Fire leapt into my face. "You frightened me."

He flashed me that disconcertingly friendly smile. "I apologize. Forgive me, *juffrouw*." He bowed and turned to go.

I know that he must have thought me foolish, plain, and bold, but I found that I could not let him leave.

"Will they really fight each other?" I called.

He stopped, then turned around.

I swallowed. "Brothers would fight to the death?"

He crossed his arms and considered me more closely. "If they want the same doe, they will. Forgive me, it was a dark thing for me to say when you were trying to enjoy them."

"No. I am always interested in—in nature."

A crow called. Doctor Debruyne cleared his throat, trying to decide how to extricate himself, no doubt.

"Were you thinking of sketching the deer?" He nodded at the book in my arms.

"It's not a sketchbook. It's the Queen's. *Aramis of Gaul.*"

"Reading about knights and ladies, are you? I had not pegged you as a damsel who swooned for romance."

There was no use in pretending I was a fair flower of femininity. "I'm not. But there were no treatises on painting or medicine about." I frowned at the gilt leather cover of the book, while suffering from the disconcerting sensation that doctor Debruyne was studying me.

After a moment, he said, "You must wonder what I am doing out here in the middle of the forest."

"No! I wasn't."

He pulled back his chin.

"I assumed you were here conducting your experiments," I said staunchly.

"And you would be correct." He raised his arm with the basket. "I have resumed my role as root granny."

I gazed toward the basket, only to catch sight of the silky dark hair peeking from the opening of his untied white shirt. Sweetest Holy Mary.

"The King has asked me to start a new garden here at Valsaín," he said, "with specimens from the mountains of the Andes, brought up from Sevilla. His Majesty thinks the elevation and temperature here might more closely duplicate the conditions of the Andes than those of Aranjuez—quite forward-thinking on his part. Our King knows much about much under the sun."

"He does take a very close interest in many things." I thought of the King ordering every last detail of the Queen's care during her illness and, now, during her recovery here.

"I wish more of his subjects appreciated the keenness of his mind. Back in my native Bruges, he is portrayed as the Devil himself. 'The Black Legend,' the slander about him is called, mostly secondhand propaganda coming from England. I do believe most Flemings think that Felipe eats babies for breakfast. It is odd how willing people are to believe what they hear. Just because something is said does not mean that it is true."

"Yes," I said, thinking briefly of maestro Michelangelo, "but sometimes rumors are true. Did we not prove that with coca?" I raised my chin. There. I had acknowledged the afternoon I had drooled all over myself. "What has become of your experiments with the herb, *señor*?"

"I didn't realize you were interested."

"Of course I am," I said stiffly. "It is science."

He frowned. "I am sorry. It is just that I had the impression you were trying to avoid me in Aranjuez."

I could not speak. Had it not been he who was avoiding me?

"I was not so much offended when I came back with the pliers to remove your woman's tooth and found you both gone. I thought perhaps she had lost her courage or one of you did not feel well from the herb—I hoped that wasn't so. I was relieved when she came down to see me when I inquired about her and I was able to do the job. But whenever I saw you in the distance over the next few weeks, and thought of approaching you—"

He had seen me? And had thought of approaching me? Our gazes met and then flew apart.

"Well," he said, "it does not matter. The case for coca is closed. It seems that the stinging tendrils of the Inquisition reach all the way to the New World."

"The Inquisition?" I said, glad to speak of something else.

"When Inquisitor-General Valdés learned of an herb that soothes countless Indians in Peru, he decided it must be of the Devil. How could all those natives worship God with their heads numb with the green slimy stuff? When I told him I had encouraging therapeutic results from my experiments with it here, he accused me of worshipping science. He had me taken into custody for questioning."

"When?" I exclaimed.

"The summer after our experiment."

"Are you well?"

"The dwindling number of Spanish Protestants and heretics gave him altogether too much time to devote to me."

"That is terrible! You were trying to do such good."

"The King had me freed as soon as he heard, but I went to Sevilla to avoid the Inquisitor-General's eye for a while. I am sorry to say that when I passed through Aranjuez last month, on my way up from Sevilla, all the coca had been destroyed."

"All of it? No! That cannot be. Those who need the relief it can bring will not be allowed to have it?"

"Do not worry, *juffrouw*. His Majesty will not fight the Church, but there are other herbs to try and he supports my work in bringing them to the people. The King wishes me to start an experimental garden of New World plants at El Escorial, too. My work will continue there as well as here."

"The King's new Royal Monastery—I have not been to see the construction yet. They say it will be the Ninth Wonder of the World. His Majesty says he will take the Queen when she has fully recovered, to see how the building is coming along."

"Oh, it is a wondrous sight—a magnificent monastery and palace combined, cradled by noble mountains. I hope you can see it soon. I had come here today to harvest some specimens for transplanting there, but as you see"—he held up his empty basket—"I must change my plan. Oddly enough, a great swath of the planting I wished to harvest has been plucked up, roots and all."

"Was it a valuable plant?"

"Not really. I was raising it only for the flowers, which are not particularly noteworthy. But for some reason, the King is quite fond of them. I was growing the specimens at his request."

"Do I know this flower?"

"Perhaps not." He tossed back the wing of shining dark hair that had crept into his eyes. "Moonflower, it is called."

I shook my head in nonrecognition.

"Few know it," he said, "even in my circle. It blooms only at night. By day, it's a fairly plain plant. I can't think why anyone would want to steal it." He used his basket to scratch his leg. "I just hope whoever took it is careful. It is quite poisonous. The cattle of New World settlers who have grazed upon it have died a slow and painful death. Of the flux, it is said. The poor beasts are made to suffer and cramp until they run dry and die."

I heard the crunch of pine needles. I turned to see Francesca marching toward us, her veil whipping in righteous anger. "There you are, *signorina*!"

I blushed, realizing how openly I had been speaking with a man, and how much I had been enjoying it.

She pinned doctor Debruyne with a stern look.

"How is the tooth?" he asked pleasantly.

She flashed her empty gum. "*Bene*. My lady must not be alone when speak to the gentleman."

He laughed, then bowed to me. "You see that I must take my leave, *juffrouw*."

I curtseyed, then watched him go as I fought off feelings of regret. How easy it was to talk with him. How it stimulated my mind. But perhaps revealing my interest in herbs and science threatened him, as my serious pursuit of painting—and his perception of my success—had discouraged Tiberio. I heaved a sigh, then turned to follow Francesca.

Francesca's rough-spun veil grated against the coarse material of her gown as she shot me a look over her shoulder. "I tell you something now so you know to keep it hush. The Queen no need to hear this bad thing now."

"What bad thing?"

"Servants' talk."

"Not more gossip." But when I drew up to her, I saw that her face was troubled. "What is it, Francesca?"

"The Prince of Ascoli, he died."

"Doña Eufrasia's husband?" I thought of the young man escorting the King's former mistress to the doomed reception. As lean and handsome as an Arabian stallion, the prince was the picture of virility. I remember thinking how gracious it had been of the King to reward his mistress with such a healthy specimen of manhood. "But he was so young."

"Twenty-three."

"How did he die?"

Her thick peasant's brows knitted together. "Stomach flux, for long, long time. Three week he is in terrible pain. The cramps, they nearly rip him in two. They say it is from poison, but *signorina*, what kind of the poison take so long?"

ITEM: *It is said that in the ceiling above the studio of the great painter Albrecht Dürer there existed a grated hole. Whenever Dürer fell into his well-known fits of melancholia and lapsed into idleness, his wife, spying from above, would rap the grate to spur him into action.*

ITEM: *There is another famous hole in the floor. In the Royal palace of Saint-Germain in Paris, under the finest Turkey carpet in the French Queen Catherine's bedchamber—a room seldom visited by her husband—there is a narrow shaft that reaches down through the ceiling below. She no longer rolls back the carpet and looks through the hole—not now that Diane de Poitiers no longer stays in the bedroom below it and Henri of France is dead.*

9 OCTOBER 1564
Valsaín, the House in the Woods of Segovia

The first of the October rains came this morning. It fell in a gray curtain outside the window of the King's office, its hiss blending with the strum of guitars and the scratch of the King's quill as he bent over his desk. I stood by the Queen, waiting to stack the documents that she had sprinkled with sand after the King had annotated and signed them.

It is not every day that I help the King in his office. Today, in fact, was the first. Two of his secretaries had taken ill last night, and when His Majesty mentioned to the Queen after Mass that he was summoning a third to help him plow through his daily stack of documents, she had asked to fill the role.

"I am Queen," she said to him, "yet I have not signed a single document other than letters to my mother since I arrived in Spain." We were strolling in the covered arcade around the courtyard— no other ladies were in attendance. The Queen said they tired her, and the King, never one to enjoy the tension between the French ladies and the Spanish, did not insist upon their presence. Now the rain had begun, dampening one's clothes and impregnating the air with the smell of wet wood. "I do feel quite useless, My Lord. I should like to be a help."

The King held her by the back of the neck as they walked. "You would find it very boring, pet. I read and write until my eyes blur and my fingers cramp. Sometimes I can get quite testy."

"I would not mind."

"That is because you are perfect." He leaned in to kiss her. "But wouldn't you two rather be dabbling at your colors?" He looked over his shoulder at me.

I bobbed in a brief curtsey. These days mostly I read aloud while the Queen listlessly stitches.

"I cannot have my office turned into a hen's nest, My Lady," he said to the Queen. "But very well. Since I cannot see you at night."

She slid out her lip in a child's manner. "Cruel doctor Hernández. He must stop thinking of me as an invalid."

I gazed out from the arcade. It had been the Queen who had appealed to doctor Hernández for respite from her marital duties, telling him that she was too weak for coupling, begging him to bar the King from her bed. Doctor Hernández had reluctantly agreed, but warned her that he would have to bleed her thor-

oughly if her weakness continued for more than another fortnight.

I saw the King's hand tighten around her neck. "Do not worry,
pet. He has told me it will not be long until you will be healthy
enough to resume all your activities."

Soon we were in the King's office, where I waited with my
hands clasped as the King wrote. The rain purred outside the window; the King's guitarists played a light gypsy song. The King was
scribbling away at a document when the Queen asked, "Did doña
Eufrasia have her baby, My Lord?"

He looked up, his round-framed spectacles upon his nose.
"¿Cómo?"

"Doña Eufrasia. Was her child born? I have not heard."

"I don't know—yes, I suppose it was. I am working, pet."

She watched him write for a while. "It was a pity she lost her
husband."

His pen stopped.

"I sent her a note of condolence," she said.

He resumed his writing. "That was good of you."

She sprinkled some sand into her hand, then blew it onto the
floor. "Will you not call her back to court, My Lord, now that her
husband is gone?"

"She has got a baby now," he said, not looking up from his
work. "Regardless, that would be my sister's decision. She is part
of Juana's household, not mine."

"Have you seen this baby? Is he—she—"

"She. I think."

"Is she as pretty as doña Eufrasia? Or does she look like her
father?"

"You are keeping me from my work, pet. Shall I call for another secretary?"

Don Carlos marched into the office, followed by Don Alessandro. The Prince went straight to his father's desk without a glance at the Queen.

The King put down his pen and got up to embrace his son. "How are you today, Carlos? Did you try those herbs I gave you for your head pain?"

Don Carlos shrugged free. "No. It tastes foul. I won't drink it."

"Toad," said the Queen, "will you not say hello to me?"

Don Carlos turned slowly, clenching his fists at his sides as she stepped forward and kissed him on both cheeks.

"What have you to say for yourself, Toady? You have not come to see me for weeks."

"My Lady," he said, his voice breaking with earnestness, "I have heard you are not yet well."

"Do I not look well?" She turned this way and that, her gold and black gown rustling. "Oh dear! I have spilt some sand."

Don Carlos struggled for words as she went over to place the shaker on the King's desk. When she saw the Prince's discomfort, she exclaimed, "Look at your pretty new pendant!"

He gazed down at the ruby-studded jewel upon his narrow chest, then raised his chin with resolve. "It is a locket."

She plucked it up, still suspended around his neck, and opened it. "Why, Toad! It's a picture of me. Sofi, did you paint this?"

I did not need to examine it. I had painted nothing in months. "No, My Lady."

Still bound to the Queen by the chain of the locket, Don Carlos returned his gaze to the floor. "Don Alonso painted it, from the portrait Sofi painted of you."

"May I see?" said the King.

Don Carlos's eyes flashed with hatred. "Why don't you just take it? Take it, like you do everything else from me."

The King glanced at his musicians. They remained bent over their guitars.

"We came to take you walking, My Lady," said Don Alessandro. He had been unusually quiet. "May we please borrow her a moment, Your Majesty?"

"I hardly think that is a good idea," the King said, "with it raining."

"It stopped," Don Carlos said flatly.

We all looked to the window. Indeed, the rain had given way to watery sunshine, with the trees dripping in staccato.

"She is still recovering," said the King.

"She would not need to be recovering if you had not used her for your base desires," said Don Carlos.

"Carlos!" the King said harshly.

A page entered with a tray of pomegranate slices.

Don Carlos marched to the door and, with a jab of his elbow, knocked over the page's tray on his way out. Porcelain smashed. Pomegranate slices, trailing seeds and rosy pulp, slid across the tile floor.

"Better watch him," the King said to Don Alessandro.

"Let me go with them, too, My Lord," said the Queen.

"Absolutely not. He is unpredictable."

"My Lord, Toad would never hurt me. And I can stop him before he hurts himself. I have a power over him. Please let me go, My Lord. It will be good for me to get outside. I shall get stronger in the fresh air."

His face weary, the King pressed his lips to her hand. "I do want you to be well."

"I will be. For you, My Lord. I promise!" She pulled away and fairly skipped to the door, Cher-Ami tottering after her. "Come, Sofi!"

We caught up with Don Carlos in the arcade around the court-yard, where the quince trees, their branches heavy with fat yellow fruit, still dripped from the rain.

"May we come with you?" the Queen asked.

"Wouldn't you rather be with my father?" Don Carlos pulled at a quince branch, showering me in his wake.

"I want to be with you now." The Queen took his arm. "Tell me about yourself, Toad. What have you been doing of late?"

It did not take her long to soften him. By the time the guards were raising their halberds to allow us leave of the palace, he was telling her what he had been doing since her last illness, and about the many expensive things he had acquired.

We were past the meadows and the river and were deep within the woods when Don Carlos turned the subject to My Lady.

"Has it been a trial, Doña Elisabeth, keeping to your rooms so much during this time of year?" he asked. We padded along on the grass, which grew so lushly in the mellow light shining through the pines. Our footsteps sent squirrels skittering up the scaly rust-colored trunks of trees. "I love the fall, with all the riding, hunting, and falconing."

Don Alessandro laughed. "That falcon yesterday nearly took you with it when it set off. Truly, my friend, you must gain some weight, or we shall see you in the skies of Segovia."

"I stumbled," Don Carlos said crossly, "and so released my bird awkwardly. Now Don Alessandro will not let me forget it."

"Do not worry, Toad." The Queen smoothed his hand. "I know he is cruel."

"Now, now," said Don Alessandro. "Is that any way to talk?"

"You are cruel," the Queen insisted, "of the worst sort. You laugh when you thrust the knife."

"Me? Where do you get this thought? Did you dream some-thing up in your illness?"

Don Carlos grabbed her hand and pulled her forward. "Do not mind him. He is harmless enough. It is my father who is the cruel one."

"For what, for trying to get a child on his wife?" said Don Alessandro.

Don Carlos's pale, watery eyes bulged with incredulous fury. He pummeled Don Alessandro's muscular arm with his bony fist. "Take that back! Take that back!"

The Queen flashed Don Alessandro her own look of anger, but as she caressed the Prince's back, her expression softened into weariness. "Carlos, please, both you and I know I must bear the King's children. What other reason is there for me to exist?"

He stopped pounding Don Alessandro. "Oh, My Lady." His voice broke with pain. "You are so much more than that."

The Queen kissed the padded shoulder roll of Don Carlos's doublet. "You are so kind. But you are so, so wrong."

A squirrel jumped onto a branch directly above us, sprinkling our party with raindrops and sending Cher-Ami into a frenzy. Don Carlos scowled up at the offending creature, then, tenderly, wiped the Queen's face with his sleeve. "Oh, Elisabeth, how I wish you were mine. I would treat you so much better than he."

She sighed. "He treats me well enough."

"No! I mean it—I would spend every single moment with you, every minute of every day. I swear, I would never let you out of my sight."

"Oh," she said, "he's quite good at that."

She commenced to walk again. I followed, face forward, not letting Don Alessandro catch my eye. I would not be his ally in provoking Don Carlos.

"If you were mine, we would have fun," said Don Carlos. "How could we help it? We are the same age. How can you stand being with an old man?"

We started down a wooded slope. The soft roar of rushing water marked a turning of the Eresma somewhere below. "He is hardly old," she said, laughing. "Thirty-seven."

"I am nineteen." He straightened, only bringing attention to his frail frame. "In my prime."

She patted his arm. "Then you should think of marrying my sister. It is my mother's fondest wish. She is prettier than I."

"No one is prettier than you, My Lady," he said vehemently.

"Excuse me, Don Carlos," said Don Alessandro, "but let me recount: Our Lady's sister is young and pretty, and your father, whom you dearly love to cross, doesn't want you to marry her because he has already made a French allegiance with Our Lady and wishes to use you elsewhere." He slapped an outcropping of stone embedded in the hill. "Now, tell me again why you will not wed her? I would think you'd run off in disguise and carry her away."

"I don't want to."

"Consider yourself lucky. Your father has asked that I marry our cousin in Portugal, to hold together our realms. The rag picker's mule has a lovelier face than my future bride."

"I hear something," said Don Carlos.

We paused to listen. There was a distinct splashing below, but the source was obscured by a tumble of boulders.

"Maybe it's a beaver," whispered Don Carlos. "Or an otter. Where is my gun when I need it?"

"I like beavers," the Queen whispered back. "*And* otters. Why would you want to kill them?"

"Shhh," said Don Carlos. "Silly. That is just what men do."

We climbed onto the lichen-covered boulders, the *caballeros* helping the Queen and me, hampered by our skirts. A low waterfall came into view, its descent broken by a series of boulders. A few more hard-won steps revealed a pool at the base of the falls. There, swimming in waters clouded by the rain, was neither otter nor beaver but a man. His sinuous arms rhythmically sliced the gray surface. He raised his head to breathe, revealing blond hair darkened by the water.

"Good Lord—Juan!" called Don Carlos. "What are you doing out here?"

Don Juan stopped mid-stroke, then treaded water. His grin grew as he looked over our group, Cher-Ami barking excitedly at pond's edge. "Swimming."

"I can see what you're doing, but why?" said Don Carlos. "You must be freezing."

"Don't discourage him," Don Alessandro said. "He is having a bath, country-boy style."

Don Juan laughed. "Just so. My Lady—please forgive me for not addressing you properly."

Don Alessandro held up a pair of breeches from a pile of clothing on a rock. "I believe I have the reason why."

The color heightened on My Lady's face. "Oh, I think that is not the reason. I think he is afraid."

"Afraid?" Don Juan's grin deepened, his dimples accentuated by his water-slicked hair. "Is that what I am? And why so, My Lady?"

"My husband is very angry at you. You turned down the chance to be cardinal. Do you know how hard he had to bargain for that?"

"Very hard, I would imagine, knowing what a poor candidate I made."

"Easy for you to jest, but he was quite determined for you to have a high position. You took the honor he wished to give you and threw it in his face."

"I am sorry, My Lady. I could not become a cardinal."

"Yes, because cardinals cannot take wives."

Don Juan splashed the water with his hand. "That was not why."

"Oh? Shall I tell that to the Duke of Mendoza's niece? Is she not your lady?"

"I regret that she misinterpreted my stay at her uncle's house. It was necessity that drove me there—I had no place to go after I left Rome. I was not exactly welcome in Madrid."

I saw Don Alessandro's watchful eyes, and Don Carlos's rumpled brow. Did the Queen forget their presence? Had she forgotten the terror she had felt after being discovered by the King at the river in Aranjuez?

"Shall we not walk on?" I said, affecting a playful voice. I addressed Don Alessandro and his smirk directly. "I thought My Lady was the liege lady for you all. Do you errant knights not wish to accompany her?"

"We have stopped playing that game," said Don Alessandro. "We are all a little older now."

"Speak for yourself," said Don Carlos. "I am still your knight, My Lady."

"How about you, Juan?" called Don Alessandro. "Do you still play the game?"

Treading water, Don Juan regarded Don Alessandro. He swung his gaze to me. "Doña Sofonisba, when I was in Rome, I met someone who knew you. He said you were both students of Michelangelo Buonarroti."

My heart stopped. I had known only one student of Michelangelo's in Rome.

"He wondered if you had ever spoken of him, or of Michelangelo."

Don Alessandro snatched up the rest of Don Juan's clothes. "Let it be said that Juan is a knight without his armor."

Don Juan paddled closer to shore, then stood, naked to the waist. Water streamed down his lean body. "Hey!"

At that moment, I should have whisked the Queen from the scene, but I was too stunned by Don Juan's announcement to move. Of her own volition the Queen turned away. "If a cardinal's hat is not good enough for you to wear," she called over her shoulder, her voice reedy with spirit, "perhaps nothing is."

Don Alessandro shoved the clothes into her arms. "Go!"

She held the clothes away from herself as if they were tainted.

"Run!" Don Alessandro exclaimed. "Back to the palace!"

With a giddy yelp, she hugged them to herself and scrambled onto the rocks.

"Behind you," cried Don Carlos with a horsey laugh. "You dropped his shift!"

"Keep going, Elisabeth!" shouted Don Alessandro.

Seeing his chance, Don Juan sprang through the water and halfway onto the shore. His hand was on the shift at the same time Don Alessandro stomped his boot upon it.

An angry voice rang from above. "What is this?"

My heart shot against my chest. Flesh prickling, I looked up. The King stood at the top of the boulders, hands on hips.

Don Juan lowered himself back into the water.

The Queen dropped the clothes as if they had burst on fire.

I held my breath, waiting for His Majesty's rebuke. But instead of shouting, his face relaxed into a mask of *sosiego*, as cool as the dark water lapping around Don Juan's neck. He stretched his hand down toward the Queen.

She worked her way over the boulders. I knew—everyone knew, even Cher-Ami—not to follow.

When they were gone, Don Alessandro tossed Don Juan his shift. I began my own climb over the rocks, my stomach churning.

"I hate him!" cried Don Carlos. "He has got no right to bully her around. He treats his horses better."

"He's her husband," said Don Juan. He caught up to us, buckling his breeches, then scooped up Cher-Ami. "You are blameless, doña Sofonisba. Do not worry, I will make that clear."

"Do you jest?" exclaimed Don Alessandro. "Do you think anything you say to the King will have value?"

When we returned to the palace, the King and Queen were not to be found. I paced up and down the arcade, my brain a puddle of contrite terror. Once again I had failed to rein in the Queen's impetuous behavior. Once again I had brought shame to her, to myself, and to my father, too, if I were lucky enough to be sent home.

What seemed like hours later, the King and Queen swept in from out-of-doors. I fell nearly prostrate into a curtsey.

"Attend to the Queen," said the King, the high color in his face not matching the calm in his voice. "She will need you now."

She smiled briefly as he kissed her hand then left her. Stiffly, she began to walk. Only when I fell in line behind her did I notice the pine needles caught in the back of her braids, and the dirt upon the shoulder of her gown.

ITEM: *Although many pigments benefit from liberal grinding, take great care when preparing pigments like smalt, bice, and the blue, ultramarine. You may think to make them fine by much grinding, but doing so only makes them starved and dead.*

25 APRIL 1565
The Palace, Aranjuez

Immediately after the King found the Queen stealing Don Juan's clothes while he swam, His Majesty launched a serious program of family leisure, a behavior he continues to this day. He wishes to hunt or picnic or boat with his family every day, even though you would think his capacity to frolic would be diminished by the troubles mounting in his lands. Perhaps it is in response to these troubles that he seeks diversion. Perhaps it is better to shoot deer than to worry about the people rising up against the King's rule and the Holy Catholic Church in the Low Countries, threatening to destroy the churches in their towns. Perhaps it is more restful to eat grapes under a spreading oak than to address the problem of the Turks now gathering a fleet in the Mediterranean to sail against Spain. Perhaps it is more peaceful to float down the muddy waters of the Tajo than think of the English pirates, Drake and Hawkins, prowling the waters of the Atlantic under orders of their Queen Elizabeth, eager to steal the gold shipped from the New World—the gold desperately needed to pay the King's restless armies.

I suppose I should enjoy these outings. How much more pleasant they are than contemplating the great and terrible emptiness that I feel these days. If only I could lose myself in planning a painting—an epic subject from mythology, something complicated, something worthy of a *maestra*—but the Queen needs me now, more than ever. For though she has the full attention of the King, even being made to work daily alongside him in his office as she had once lightly requested, she has become as a wild thing—quiet while others are gay, easily startled, given to inexplicable laughter when others are silent. And though she cares little for her appearance now, letting her brows and hairline grow back to their natural state, leaving her hair undressed and her skin unpowdered, she is all the more beautiful for it. Yet she does not enjoy her beauty—I think she is completely unaware of it. How can I think of painting Greek gods when she is so unwell? I must play along at the King's games, hoping to cajole her into health, though we have all been kept so busy at group idleness that even Don Carlos has complained.

"Can I not just go hawking by myself?" the Prince exclaimed just this morning, after Mass.

We were taking a family walk in the flower garden. Dew still clung to the spring-bright greenery along the walkway, dampening the edges of the ladies' skirts. It was the usual cozy gathering of Royal blood—the King and Queen, the King's sister Doña Juana, Don Carlos, Don Juan, and myself. The only one missing was Don Alessandro, who had recently left, grumbling, to wed Princess Maria of Portugal. I was allowed to accompany the family with the idea that I should sketch pictures of them as they ambled. Strolling guitarists and attending servants, Francesca included, completed our little group.

"I have got a headache," said Don Carlos. "I just want to hawk."

In the woods across the river, the cooing of wood doves, the ever-present spirits of Aranjuez, could be heard over the soft strumming of the guitars. The King studied his son. "Have you tried the powders I sent you?"

"I liked the new herbs doctor Debruyne gave me. At least they didn't dry out my throat. Why did you send him to Sevilla with doctor Hernández? I liked him. You're not a doctor!"

I made myself peer into the woods. Doctor Debruyne had been sent to Sevilla? Although I had not seen him these past months, I had thought he was at El Escorial or Valsaín or one of the King's other experimental gardens, and that we had only just missed each other as the court had traveled from palace to palace in the King's new search for pleasure.

Don Carlos kicked a rare Turkish tulip, heavy with moisture, sprawling from its bed. "It would do me more good to let Striker catch wood doves than to drag around these gardens."

"Thank you for coming along and humoring me in my wish for us to be close as a family," the King said in an ironic tone, "even with your dry mouth."

Doña Juana snapped her fingers and pointed at a red tulip standing upright in its bed. Francesca, the closest of the servants, bustled forth and with a grunt plucked the flower, sending off a shower of dewdrops. She gave it to Doña Juana.

Doña Juana took a whiff. "Stinks." She dropped the bloom.

Don Juan, carrying my easel next to me, drew in a quiet breath.

The King slid his hand around the Queen's neck. "I mean not to torture you, Carlos. My most treasured memories as a youth were when traveling with my family—I only wish that for you. Remember visiting Aunt Mary's palace in Brussels, Juana?"

"Yes," Doña Juana said flatly. "Her chambers stunk of over-ripe jasmine and fried garlic."

"I don't remember that," said the King, frowning. "But I do

recall her showing us her works of art. It is where I first saw the work of El Bosco."

"Oh," said Doña Juana, "is that whom we have to blame for your heretical tastes—Aunt Mary?"

"I cannot help that you refuse to see the spiritual message in El Bosco's work, Juana," said the King. "How he must have suffered, imagining Hell so vividly on earth."

"Hell on earth," said Don Juan. "Imagine." He threw a stick for the reddish-furred mongrel he had recently found in the woods. The dog raced Cher-Ami to the prize.

"These are dangerous times to speak lightly of Hell, little brother," said Doña Juana, her harsh voice discordant with the music of the guitars. "The Pope has asked Inquisitor-General Valdés to step up his vigilance in Spain now that the Protestant Huguenots are making such deep inroads into France. In this new atmosphere, men might go to the stake for saying"—she shrugged—"just about anything."

The King stroked the Queen's neck as they walked. "Juan is amongst friends—he need not watch his words here."

It would seem this was true. Instead of censoring his brother since the incident at the pond last fall, the King has treated Don Juan like a dear friend, including him on all his journeys and at every family gathering.

Indeed, he has scarcely let Don Juan out of his sight.

"Heresy is not a problem in Spain now," said the King. "There has not been one *auto-de-fé* this year."

"A mistake," said Doña Juana. "Father left it to me to keep Spain pure and—"

"I think you may rest now," the King said. "The Inquisitor-General, too. I wonder if he might grow too fond of the power that has been given him."

Doña Juana lowered her brow, white-lashed eyes flashing. "Some of us take the sacred charge that has been given us by Father with all due seriousness. If you think for one minute we take it on for our own personal gratification, when some of us could be sitting back instead, wearing new gowns daily and playing with little dogs—"

The Queen broke in, unaware, it seemed, of the ill feelings rising around her. "My Lord, may I take a painting to my mother?"

The King gazed upon her, a slight frown penetrating his mask of *sosiego*. After a separation of more than five years, My Lady is to meet the French Queen Mother in June, at the border between France and Spain. Queen Catherine is on progress with her son the young King Charles, her wish being to show him the full extent of his kingdom. In all his nearly fifteen years, the boy has not been much beyond Paris. But even Francesca mutters that the French Queen Mother's true reason for coming to the border is to meet with our King to remind him of his allegiance with France, and as for seeing her daughter—here Francesca spits before continuing—well, that is just an afterthought.

"Which painting do you think she would like?" the King asked.

"How about one of those El Boscos?" Doña Juana suggested sweetly. "I think she would like *The Garden of Earthly Delights*."

The King glanced at her, unamused. For him to offer the French Queen Mother any of his precious paintings at all was generous. Truth be told, his relationship with Queen Catherine is on poor footing that grows ever poorer. Whereas the King had long ago nipped in the bud the problem of civil unrest by allowing Inquisitor-General Valdés to crank up his rack, Queen Catherine shores up the power of the French Crown by entering into secret agreements with every monarch in Europe. Against the Protestants threatening her from within her own country, she gathers up foreign allies like so many chess pieces, going so far of late as to make an accord with the Turkish Sultan Suleiman, who plans to sail against Spain at any moment. The King had reluctantly been planning to meet with her, but after learning of her alliance with someone with whom he is at war has broken off all plans. Only My Lady's most heartrending pleas caused him to allow her to join her mother still, and even that was on one condition suggested by Doña Juana: that no French Protestant nobles accompany Queen Catherine at the reunion.

Now, for the first time in my memory, the Queen agreed with Doña Juana. "I would like Mother to have an El Bosco. She has nothing quite like them. But *The Garden of Earthly Delights* is too frightening. Even I cannot look at that one, with its strange beasts and monstrous fruits and skewered men. Could you possibly spare the tabletop with the Seven Deadly Sins painted upon it, instead?"

The King drew in a breath. It was well known that of all the Boscos save for *The Garden,* the King favored the tabletop painting especially. He keeps it in the Queen's bedchamber and allows not even the smallest cup or book of devotions to be placed upon it. "If you truly think, my darling . . ."

"I think she would be edified by its many lessons, My Lord. The little dogs fighting over a bone in 'Envy' will delight her— she is as fond of dogs as I am."

"As I recall," said the King, "she has a Leonardo—the one of the woman with the haunting smile, you had said."

"*La Gioconda*, Sofi said it is called."

"Yes. Precisely. Perhaps your mother would like one of his contemporary's works, a Botticelli, perhaps. Or if she likes something a little older, I have several beautiful van Eycks from the collection of my great-grandmother Isabel."

"Are we not yet finished with this walk?" Don Carlos said. "I am tired."

Doña Juana ignored him. "Too bad you don't have a Michelangelo to unload," she said to the King. She lifted her brows in my direction. "I suppose we shall never know the whole truth about him, shall we? Sofonisba, did I ever tell you that I learned the name of the man after whom Michelangelo lusted?"

Francesca's short veil swished as she glanced at me. Don Juan looked at me as well.

"Does the name Tiberio Calcagni sound familiar?"

Guitar music swelled into the damp river air as a thudding filled my ears.

"My Lord, you are always so generous," said the Queen. "I should not have asked you for one more thing. Forget I asked for a picture."

"I will give her the tabletop—I wish for you to be happy."

Doña Juana's bone-lashed gaze traveled from me to her brother.

"Then you will go with me to see my mother, My Lord?" said the Queen.

The King looked grieved. "You know I cannot do that. As much as I'd like to please you, she has pushed me too far with her accord with Suleiman. I am sorry, darling."

I walked along numbly. This is why I had not heard from Tiberio. He was the Maestro's lover. But this could not be.

I took a deep breath for courage. "Your Majesty," I asked Doña Juana, "how do they know it is Tiberio Calcagni?"

Doña Juana's face lit. "Oh, you do know him? H'm. You may not recognize him now, not after his stint in the Castel Sant'Angelo. He has been held there for some time now, and will continue being held, at least until he confesses to his relationship with Michelangelo. Once he has confessed, he will find what is left of himself rowing on a galley. Truly, the prison might be preferable."

The Queen sighed, not listening. "Then, My Lord, will you not mind if at least someone of the Blood accompanies me? May Don Carlos go?"

Don Carlos's pale eyes opened wide. His frail frame jerked upright. "Oh, Father, may I?"

"Do not tell me you would consider letting your heir go to those French!" Doña Juana said incredulously to the King. "Father would never have considered such a thing. If I still ruled . . ."

His Majesty drew in a breath, then exhaled slowly. "You can go, Carlos."

I felt Don Juan's touch upon my elbow. He slid me a look of concern. I struggled harder to master my mask of calm.

"Thank you, Father!" Don Carlos grabbed the Queen's hand and swung it. "Thank you for asking me! Oh, we shall have such fun!" He gasped. "What do French men wear at court? How shall I dress?"

The Queen laughed. "If you wish to look truly French, my Toad, you must dangle the biggest pearl you can find from your earlobe."

"A pearl?" He felt his ear.

Doña Juana glared at her brother, her mind, it seemed, no longer on toying with me. She would have been gratified to know how much damage she had done. "Why don't you lend him La Peregrina, Elisabeth?" she said in a friendly voice.

The Queen's mouth tightened. She looked to the King for support, but he was staring, cross-armed, at his sister.

Doña Juana met his gaze with a lowered brow. "Why don't you let Don Juan go too, then, Felipe? He's such a help to Carlos." She smiled. "You have no objection, do you?"

ITEM: El Diablo sabe mucho, porque es viejo. *(The Devil knows much, because he is old.)*

—SPANISH PROVERB

14 JUNE 1565
Saint-Jean-de-Luz, France

It is unusually hot here in the South of France for mid-June. I have always wished to travel to France, and today, in accompanying the Queen, I have finally done so, though Francesca will not stop grumbling about the heat. By the eleven-o'clock bells, our fine clothes hung on our bodies like wet sacks. By twelve, clouds of gnats rose from the river as if exhaled by the water. By one, the gnats were melting into our eyes as we crossed into France. We heard later that six French soldiers standing guard on the riverbank expired within their armor, cooked like snails in their shells. An inauspicious day, then, for My Lady's reunion with her mother, a fact surely not lost upon that most superstitious of queens, Catherine de' Medici.

New pearl earrings a-swing, Don Carlos and Don Juan came this morning after Mass. They were to escort us to the reception hall in the moldy little palace at which we stayed in Irún. The Queen's brother Henri awaited us, come to fetch his sister and to cross the river with her into France. We were dressed in the richest clothes, as the King had given the Queen an unlimited purse to spend upon the preparations for meeting her mother. Although

English piracy and keeping peace have bled the King's coffers dry, it is far more important to look rich than actually to be rich.

"Look at you!" My Lady cried when the two *caballeros* entered her chamber, her face turning a deep pink. Though the twelve-o'clock bells had just rung, the braids wrapped around my head were already heavy with sweat. The maids of the condesa and madame de Clermont were pouring cool water over their mistresses' wrists—the guards at the door could have benefited from such treatment. The pungent odor of overheated, unwashed flesh oozed from under their armor.

"Look at you, *mon chéri*!" cried My Lady. "You look so French." She threw her arms around Don Carlos, then kissed him soundly on both cheeks. He kissed her back, lingering on the second kiss.

"You look so pretty, My Lady," he said, withdrawing tenderly. "No, not just pretty, beautiful. More beautiful than any woman in the world."

"My dear little Toad. You are always so sweet."

She lifted her gaze to Don Juan, standing back with his arms folded. He came forward and quickly kissed her cheek, the sweat-darkened ends of his blond hair dragging against the cords of his neck.

The Queen smiled brightly at Don Carlos. "Have you seen my brother? How does he look? It has been five and a half years—he was just eight when I left."

The condesa marched from behind the screen. "My Lady, are we ready?" With a scowl at the guards, she took one last fortifying whiff of her pomander, then let it drop on its chain from her girdle before plucking up the long train suspended from the Queen's pearl-encrusted gown. Cher-Ami scampered forward to trot self-importantly before us.

"*Hombre,*" the condesa addressed a guard. "Get the dog."

"No!" exclaimed the Queen. "Cher-Ami goes with me."

The condesa conceded reluctantly, and our party complete, we made for the reception hall.

Henri, Duke of Orléans, sprang forward to embrace the Queen the moment we entered. "Sister!"

The *caballeros'* earrings might have outweighed the French Prince's own dangling gem, but the rest of his spare personage glittered with more jewels than the three of theirs combined. The diamonds sewn into glittering fleur-de-lys on his doublet winked as he kissed his sister. Although she was the taller of the two, being six years older, the monstrous plume on his hat bobbed over her jaunty little cap like a chicken pecking at seed.

"Dear, dear sister." His voice was precociously suave for a youth of almost fourteen years, especially one whose face bloomed with purple pimples. "Did you ever learn to master the guitar? When last I saw you, you were making one wail like a dying cat."

"I see you have not yet learned to master your tongue."

"Who says I want to?"

The Queen's voice was thick with affection. "Still Mother's son, I see."

"That is me." The olive-toned skin of his cheeks folded in vertical creases when he grinned, accentuating the narrowness of his face and the pustules upon it. His eyes were as small and dark as raisins and his lips were leathery and thick, but still you would not call him unattractive. Maybe his glamour was in his jolly confidence, the kind of confidence that comes from knowing one is Mother's favorite child, a fact the French Queen Mother takes no care to hide. I would see this for myself today, long before Francesca had brought it to my attention with her dark mutterings. It was to become abundantly clear that My Lady was beloved by her mother for what she could do for the French crown, while Henri, the golden child, was beloved solely for himself.

This morning, though, I saw only My Lady's joy at being re-united with her family. With Henri chatting self-assuredly at her side, we left the dark of the musty palace for the stultifying bright-ness of the out-of-doors, where more than a hundred Catholic French nobles and their retainers, and the Spanish grandees chosen by the King to accompany the Queen into France, awaited with our litter. Once homage was paid and rank was estab-lished, off we set on the cracked mud road in a cavalcade of lords and ladies and servants that stretched for a quarter-mile, not in-cluding the baggage train that had gone before us into France.

We came to the wide waters of the Bidossa. We were clattering across the bridge, a temporary construction of boards nailed atop two rows of boats, when Henri said to Don Juan, "I do like your earring."

I looked up from where I was leaning over the edge of my litter, batting gnats away from my eyes as I watched silvery schools of fish dart in the clear mountain water of the river. My thoughts had strayed, once again, to Tiberio, imprisoned in the Castel Sant'Angelo. How long had he been in the Pope's prison? Had he had to endure the strappado under interrogation? The torture often dislocated people's shoulders when they were jerked high in the air with their hands behind their back. Too many applications of the strappado's rope, and Tiberio might not be able to sculpt ever again. Then there is the torture of applying fire to the accused's feet, a torture reserved for those suspected of more serious crimes against the Church, as sodomy is considered. I weep inside for him, and then remember that he was Michelan-gelo's lover when he took me that night in Rome. What kind of false thing was he?

Don Juan put his reins in one hand and took the earring from his ear. "For you."

Henri laughed. "Truly? I did not mean——"

The Queen spoke up from next to me. "That was a gift from me."

"Then it's his to give." Henri took out his own earring, threw it into the water with a *plonk*, and hooked the larger pearl in its place. "It looks better on me, don't you think?" He turned his head for us to admire, then noticed the Queen and Don Juan, locked in a cool gaze.

He raised his lips in a lopsided smile. "Do I miss something here?"

Our litter jostled as our mules left the bridge and gained the French bank of the river. Over the blare of trumpets announcing our arrival into France, the condesa shouted for the French nobles to take care of the Queen's skirts; My Lady was helped down from our litter and seated upon the horse provided by her brother the King. As I mounted the mule made ready for me, I saw a soldier slump to his knees at the water's side, one of the victims of the heat.

I bobbed through the town gates on my foul-tempered mule, my vitality sapped by the temperature and my renewed thoughts of Tiberio. Just ahead were the condesa and madame, and in front of them, the Queen, looking fresh and young and glorious in spite of the sweat trickling from her hairline. Townsfolk cheered from every window and door of the half-timbered houses that lined the hard dirt street upon which Her Majesty's sleek white palfrey pranced. Each time the horse shook its harness, it tossed 400,000 ducats' worth of jewels, but the people had not eyes for gems and finery—their love was for their Elisabeth.

At last we arrived at the squat stone château of the French

Queen Mother. My Lady bit her nails through her gloves as she was lifted from her mount.

"How do I look?" she asked her brother when she was set beside him.

"Sweaty, but gorgeous—almost as gorgeous as me." He offered her his arm. "We have kept Mother waiting two hours in this heat. She will have our hides."

Behind the Queen's chief ladies—the condesa stoically erect as she held My Lady's train, though her own neat bodice was thoroughly sweat-soaked, and madame de Clermont, sagging beneath her veils—I advanced through the stifling halls, the tapping of my feet upon the marble floor muffled by the dampness of the air. We passed ranks of beautiful curtseying ladies whose brilliantly hued silks made me, in my embroidered Spanish black, feel like a beetle crawling amongst the company of butterflies. Gentlemen bowed, their earrings a-swing, musicians strummed lutes, singers sang odes to the French Queen Mother and her daughter. There was even a shaggy bear, groaning, to Cher-Ami's petrification, as it lolled on a golden chain, its misery poignant even in this miserably overheated crowd.

My amazed sights wandered to the end of the hall, where My Lady had come to a stop before a dais. There, beneath a filmy web of black gauze wafting in a breeze created by two fanning dwarves, sat a glittering black lump. Trembling, My Lady waited as this brilliant heap rose, laid back the sheer black veil covering its head, and opened its arms. My Lady rushed forward.

Catherine de' Medici, daughter of a duke, niece of popes, wife and mother of kings, drew her daughter to her breast.

As they rocked each other and exclaimed, I could not help comparing the mother with her child. Every feature I so admired in My Lady was swollen and coarsened in her mother. Whereas

My Lady's eyes were endearingly large, the French Queen Mother's orbs bulged like a garden toad's. Whereas the slight puffiness and impish curl to My Lady's lips afforded them a playful pout, her dam's lips, when set together, were as thick and florid as a plum. While My Lady's pretty chin receded only when she tucked it back in jest, her mother's chin appeared to be fastened upon her neck. Truly, Queen Catherine, mother of my dear Lady, was but a puffed frog in a French hood.

Now she pulled away from her daughter and examined My Lady's face. "Where is your makeup? You look so Spanish."

"I am French in my heart," said My Lady.

"Are you?"

The Queen turned to smile upon Henri as he sauntered forward. My Lady, seeing she had been put aside, stepped over to a second figure lounging on a divan on the dais, a hollow-chested youth perspiring in ermine: the King of France. As My Lady's eminent brother received his sister's embrace, the French Queen Mother's highest-ranking noble introduced his Queen to Don Carlos. Queen Catherine let him kiss her hand, then allowed Don Juan to take his turn.

She pursed together her Damask-plum lips. "So, you are the brother."

Don Juan raised himself. "Yes, Your Majesty."

"It seems you sprang into this role full grown."

He smiled. "Like Athena from her father Zeus's brow, Your Majesty."

"Oh, you think it humorous?"

Don Juan became still, as does a buck when sensing danger. My Lady pulled from her brother's arms.

"Her Majesty is correct," said Don Juan. "To claim kinship to the King is deadly serious. I do not mean to make light of it."

The French Queen Mother scooped up the ivory-handled fan attached by a black ribbon to her considerable waist and began to fan herself languidly. "And how do we know you are not a pretender?"

"Mother!" exclaimed My Lady. "Why do you say these things?"

"He can answer for himself." Catherine's lips deflated into a smile. "He is probably used to such questions."

"I am, Madame. But my kinship was thrust upon me. I did not ask to play this role."

"Indeed?" Fanning, the French Queen Mother scanned his well-cut doublet and hose. "You look quite comfortable for someone forced into such a dreadful position. But we do not truly doubt your claim. We had you thoroughly investigated before we offered our youngest daughter to you. You shall tell your brother to reconsider our offer, yes?"

She waved him off before he could answer. "Enough of this now. We are here to celebrate. Elisabeth, do introduce young Juan to your brother the King."

We sat to dinner soon after that, just an intimate family group of fifty-four kinsmen and their attendants. Before we were seated, a small squabble broke out between the French Queen Mother and My Lady over who should take place of honor at table. The Queen Mother insisted that My Lady, as Queen of Spain, outranked her, while she, with a modest sigh, claimed only to be Queen Mother. My Lady argued that her mother should take precedence, but Catherine would have none of it. The Queen Mother lost her place at head of table but emerged the clear victor, as she did, I guessed, in all her encounters.

Dinner, though, was pleasant, with My Lady and her mother

catching up on family news over courses of fowl and beef and fish. My own enjoyment of the food and wine was marred by Francesca's gaze boring upon me from the servants' table, taking in each movement of my glass, and by thoughts of how Tiberio might be faring that very moment in the Pope's prison. How had I not guessed he was Michelangelo's lover? Hanging on the Maestro's every word, following him like a puppy, emulating him in all things—of course he was. There was poetry written to him that proved it. What a fool I'd been, unaware of their relationship in the face of so much evidence. But that night in Rome, Michelangelo had not reacted with the fury one would expect from a lover who had caught his dear one with another. Why had he not shouted and slapped me and thrown me out like a whore? Instead he let me quietly leave, and in my absence sang my praises to Tiberio, making my achievements even greater than they were. Indeed, he'd had a medal made of me. It did not make sense.

I watched the short after-dinner play acted out by the Queen Mother's troupe of dwarves, then afterward withdrew with My Lady to her chambers, with her mother and the other chief attendants. I did not expect the outburst that came as soon as doors were closed and the condesa was removing My Lady's sleeves to prepare her for a rest.

The Queen Mother plucked her ivory fan from its ribbon and threw it to the tile floor, shattering the handle. "Explain, daughter, why you are not pregnant."

My Lady drew in a startled breath.

The French Queen Mother's bulging eyes flashed at the rest of us. "Leave us!" she commanded, then slumped into a cross-legged chair.

The condesa patted at her throat, aghast that she had been shouted at like kitchen help. Madame, perhaps from prior experience at the French court, was already gliding out the door.

I stepped back as the condesa wheeled around stiffly and left the room. I knew I was to go, too, but could hardly bear to leave My Lady looking so distressed, with one sleeve off and the other hanging half untied from her shoulder.

"Go." Queen Catherine waved at me from her chair. "Shoo."

I summoned all my courage. "Please, Your Majesty, may I finish helping My Lady with her gown?"

My Lady folded her hands in supplication. "Please, Mamma, she is—she's Italian like you."

Queen Catherine's protuberant eyes moved up and down over my person in a leisurely fashion. I felt each flaw Francesca tries so hard to scold out of me.

"Big eyes," she said at last.

"Mamma!"

"And we trust no Italian farther than we can throw one. Calm yourself," she said when My Lady started to protest. "We know who she is. She studied with Michelangelo. The old lecher got himself into hot water, didn't he?" she said to me. "Lusting after a man a quarter of his age. Now his lover is in trouble."

The French Queen Mother saw my look of surprise. "Don't you know we know everything? We've seen the poems by Il Divino, mooing like a lovesick cow over his lover. Some loyal friend this boy turned out to be. Of course he denied knowing of the existence of the poems. But he finally admitted he knew of Michelangelo's leanings and denounced him and his work, which might almost have been believable had the boy not been hoarding a large unfinished statue that contains the likeness of his lover. We suppose he's rowing on a galley as we speak. Lucky for him bodies are much needed at the oars to fight the Pope's wars at sea, or his would be swinging from a gibbet." She thinned her lips at me, clearly enjoying my efforts to hide my shock. "She can stay. She's harmless enough."

My Lady grimaced in apology, though not knowing how profoundly her mother had wounded me. Ill, I resumed untying her sleeve.

"You have failed us," the French Queen Mother snapped.

My Lady flinched.

"You have been wed five years. You are comely enough. Our reports say the Spanish King has no physical impediments. He sired one child upon you, though you could not bring it to term, and he has sired other children."

"Child," My Lady whispered, as I pulled the sleeve from her arm. "He only has one child, Carlos."

"Correction: children. There is the daughter he got upon his sister's attendant."

My Lady blinked. "Eufrasia de Guzmán? But she was wed to the Prince of Ascoli. The child is Ascoli's daughter."

The Queen Mother ignored My Lady's look of confusion. "At least our sources say Felipe is no longer dallying with the sister's attendant. They assure us that you are regularly in his bed. Are you?"

My Lady's hands trembled at her sides as I began work on the buttons of her overgown. "Yes."

"Do you please him?"

"Yes."

"He hasn't guessed your"—the French Queen Mother glanced at me—"condition?"

My Lady's hand went to her throat, upon which bloomed the rash that so often bedevils her. "No."

"Where's our fan? You," the Queen Mother said to me, "stop fidgeting with her gown and fan us. It is too bloody hot."

I had no choice but to leave My Lady's overgown hanging open. The Queen Mother waited until I had picked up the broken-handled fan and was waving it over her fleshy face.

"We stopped to see Nostradamus on the way here," she said, "to see if he could predict when a child was to be produced from our contract with Felipe. He would not say, though he was full of news about the boy of your father's Protestant cousin, Jeanne. Forecasting that her son, that puling little Henri of Navarre, would be king! Why in Heaven's name would he think we would want to hear that? Though Nostradamus did say that our Henri was to be King, so we eventually forgave him."

"Charles is already King," said My Lady. "How could Henri—" She stopped as the answer became clear: Should Charles die, Henri would become King.

The French Queen Mother shrugged when she saw her daughter's mouth ease open. "It was Nostradamus's crystal ball, not mine."

"Charles is your son! Does Henri matter so much more to you that you would wish Charles dead?"

The chair groaned as the Queen Mother repositioned herself. "Don't be preposterous." She snatched at the fan. "Give us that."

I relinquished the fan with a curtsey, then, my head pounding, went back to my Queen to help as she stepped out of her overgown.

"We are not speaking of Charles here," said the Queen Mother, "but you. Do you please your husband?"

"I said I did." My Lady's voice was now more angry than fearful.

The Queen Mother fanned herself, making the false curls

bunched to either side of her black French hood bounce. "How often?"

"You tell me, since your spies seem to know so much."

"We are alone together fifteen minutes and already you take that tone with us, and in this foul weather. We cannot bear it."

My Lady tucked in her chin in anger. I began to undo her bodice, willing her to take solace in my presence.

"We do not understand it," said the French Queen Mother. "If you couple every night, where is the child? Come here."

I released My Lady. She drew her arms against herself and, scowling, took a step forward, her bodice open.

"Bend down."

She tipped toward her mother.

The Queen Mother reached with her free hand into My Lady's bodice and felt around. "Where are the amulets we have sent you?"

My Lady withdrew. "The frog charm stank, as did the dried stag's testicles. Felipe threw them out."

Queen Catherine smiled slightly. "We wonder if he does not want you to be pregnant. Perhaps he wishes to cast off you and his alliance with France."

"That's not true. He loves me."

"We remember well when he announced to the world that he loved that ghastly little English queen, Mary."

"He loves me, Mother. I know it."

"You *know* that he loves you." The Queen Mother laughed.

My Lady returned to my side. "I know it will come as a revelation to you, Mother," she said as I lifted off her bodice, "but sometimes people do care for each other with no other motive than love."

"You surmise that he has this so-called love for you because he takes zest in bedding you? Your father would bed us at night, and after we poured our heart and soul into pleasing him, he would wear that Poitiers bitch's colors at the tourney the next day. After all our tenderness, we were just a bucket to collect his seed." The Queen Mother watched as I unlaced My Lady's corset. "Well, regardless. Something is not working here—you should be pregnant. You must make Felipe bed you twice a day. It should not be so difficult a task, as much as he 'loves' you."

"Mother, I am doing enough!"

The Queen Mother reached out and snatched her arm, jangling the neck-strings of My Lady's shift. "Look at me!"

My Lady raised a furious gaze.

"We have heard rumors."

My Lady said nothing.

"Don't think we don't know about your inappropriate relationship with the youngster."

"I have done nothing with Don Juan."

The French Queen Mother paused, then let her daughter go. She sat back with a smile. In a honeyed voice, she said, "We were speaking of Don Carlos."

My Lady turned away. I busied myself with folding her clothing.

"We could always read your face, from the time you were a little child. We wonder—can the King read it, too?"

"There is nothing to read!" My Lady went to the window.

"Quit playing games with us! You are wed to the most powerful man in the world and still you lust after another man. Oh, you are your father's foolish daughter through and through."

"I tell you, it is not what you think."

"Come away from that window. Quickly! People will hear."

My Lady turned toward her mother. "There have been no improprieties."

"We thought we taught you better than this. Don't you know how jealous Felipe is? Just your thinking about another man can cost my alliance with Spain and *your* life. You must give up this brother now." She clicked her tongue. "He's not even full-blooded, just a bastard. We would not waste your sister on him if we did not need Spain so badly."

My Lady closed her eyes. "How can I give him up when I have never had him?"

"Mother of God, girl, quit this pretense! Do you think we jest? How do you think a strapping young man like the Prince of Ascoli died? From a little bellyache?"

"He had the flux. It was very tragic. The King and I were both sad."

"Sad! The two of you could have been as sad as a pair of stiffed whores—that does not mean that your husband did not have him removed."

Fear crept into the Queen's face as she digested this thought. "How can you even suggest such a thing?"

"This is no suggestion, child. The fact is, the foolish Prince could not keep his hands off his wife, and that, you see, was not part of the agreement. He was not to touch what was the King's."

"Why would Felipe care? He told me he had broken off relations with her."

"That may be. We suggest you examine the daughter for his likeness to be sure. But regardless: Once a king's mistress, always a king's mistress. Doña Eufrasia is his property. Oh, it is disgusting, we know, but it is the Spanish way. They treat their horses likewise. The Prince of Ascoli was Spanish. He knew the rules."

My Lady covered her eyes. "This cannot be."

"You are our child. We tell you this for your own good." The French Queen Mother slowly lifted her bulk from her chair and opened her arms. Reluctantly, My Lady came to her. "Wear your charms," she crooned in her daughter's ear. "Stay well. Get yourself pregnant. Stay in his good graces. It will keep you out of the grave."

My Lady laid her head on her mother's rounded shoulder.

"Be glad," the French Queen Mother said. "At least he has put his whore aside. We tried everything in our power to sever your father's connection with that Poitiers bitch, and still, only death finally did the trick."

15 JULY 1565
Valsaín, the House in the Woods of Segovia

When in Genoa to make my crossing to Spain, I saw a French war galley making ready to sail at the docks. The filthy, naked men chained to its rows of benches were hunched over their oars, gobbling the bits of bread thrown to them by their master, while the other crewman made ready with the sails. Then a drummer began his beat, a whip cracked, and with a collective groan, the oarsmen bent to their work. How long can a man survive such a life, made to toil past exhaustion in the blazing sun by day and to sleep exposed to chill winds by night?

Now Tiberio is on such a ship.

Condemned for sculpting his lover's visage: how cruel the irony! The statue that was to make his career had destroyed him. Had it not been found, would the judge have let Tiberio free? He had denounced Michelangelo and his works, the French Queen Mother had said. Had Tiberio born witness against the homosexual leanings in Michelangelo's works and in the man himself, thus shredding the Maestro's reputation to save his own skin? Yet with fire to his feet, even a son would denounce his own father. Who could blame Tiberio for saving himself?

But there is still the matter of the poems Michelangelo had

written to him. The French Queen Mother had said that Tiberio had denied knowing of their existence. Under the pain of torture, wouldn't he claim to know of them just to get his inquisitors to stop?

With these thoughts swinging to and fro in my mind like a bell on a rope, the trip to France passed in a blur. Yet in my troubled state, even I could see that Don Carlos's condition was worsening.

At first on our visit, he had behaved surprisingly well. He had done all the things the heir to the Spanish crown should do: honoring the French Queen Mother by taking her colors at the lists; cheering enthusiastically (perhaps more so than his father would approve) at the many spectacles celebrating the Spanish and French alliance; allowing a draw in a mock battle during a masque, when he really wanted to win. Even when young King Charles insisted on driving his sister, My Lady, on a tour of the countryside, and Don Carlos was already at the helm of her chariot, ready to drive, Don Carlos merely bowed to the boy King and handed over the reins, though his face had turned most red.

The condesa de Urueña thought the improvement in his behavior was due to the break in the terrible heat the day after our arrival in France. Indeed, most were relieved. At least soldiers were no longer dropping in their armor like felled timber.

Madame de Clermont had a different opinion. She insisted that Don Carlos's more chivalrous leanings were due to his wish to impress My Lady's sister Margot, whom the French Queen Mother continues to put forward as another possible prospect to strengthen her alliance with Spain.

But even though the twelve-year-old Margot is nearly as lovely as My Lady, Don Carlos, I fear, has not eyes for her. Indeed, at the French Queen Mother's ball, he backslid momentarily in all the strides he had made in decorum by slumping under the canopy of state between Mademoiselle Margot and the Queen Mother while everyone else danced. The French Princess tried her best to engage him with her winsome child's smile, but his pale gaze remained fixed upon the dance floor, and more specifically upon My Lady, until at last her sister gave up and slouched in the opposite direction.

Don Juan, brooding over by the musician's stand, must have seen Mademoiselle Margot's downcast looks, for he stepped forward and begged the pleasure of being her partner. From where I danced nearby with My Lady's ten-year-old brother, a thistledown bit of a prince incongruously named Hercule, I could see the glow spread over young Margot's cheeks as they took to the floor. Don Juan gently led her through the stately steps of a pavane, his calm attentiveness a contrast to her desperate adolescent chatter.

My Lady and her partner, one of the brothers from the powerful French family of Guise, paused by the pair as the next pattern formed. "Do watch your feet," she told her sister. "Your partner has been known to tread upon slippers."

Mademoiselle Margot gazed up at her partner. "My Lord Don Juan," she breathed, "would never step upon a lady's foot."

"Oh," said My Lady, "he would, and he has."

"You are cruel!" Mademoiselle Margot exclaimed. "I like dancing with you, Don Juan."

"You are kind, *mademoiselle*," said Don Juan.

"Perhaps you would like to wed him, then," My Lady said, addressing her sister but looking at Don Juan. "He has no plans for marriage. Or so he says."

Don Juan returned her gaze. "No, *mademoiselle*, I do not. I am a bastard, you see. I would never have the honor of marrying a daughter of France, no matter what."

"That's not true!" Mademoiselle Margot cried. "Mother said

we could marry." She scowled at Don Carlos, draped in his chair next to the French Queen Mother. "*He* won't have me. I think there is something wrong with him."

The music swelled, setting the dancers in motion. Don Juan led Mademoiselle Margot away. The French Queen Mother, watching from under her canopy, turned to her son Henri. Deep in conversation with a handsome boy, Henri did not see her look of displeasure. Nor did he see the growing expression of outrage on the face of Don Carlos, now on his feet on the other side of Queen Catherine.

I danced on uncomfortably, through no fault of young Hercule, who tried his best to be a manly partner though the cards were against him, as his eyes were level with my bosom. It would not matter if he had the stature of his namesake. My mind was on Tiberio. As I performed the steps of the pavane with this child, he could be rowing under the sting of a whip, his muscles burning, his belly groaning, his tongue swelling in his mouth. Even if he loved the Maestro, he did not deserve this punishment. But why had he taken me that night in Rome? To convince others—himself—that his leanings were like other men's?

I was dispiritedly trying to keep up with my spritely companion, when I noticed My Lady had taken a new partner: Don Juan. As Don Carlos stewed under the dais, My Lady and Don Juan stepped and hopped, not speaking, though a current flowed between their bodies, a current I could feel across the crowded floor, a frisson that raced between their lips and eyes and breasts. With dread that others might be watching, too, I watched as they stopped at the end of the pattern and, with a terrible slowness, lifted their gazes to each other. And as the dancers around them made meaningless talk and straightened their dress, their yearning swelled into the breach between them, jangling, jangling, jangling in a silent cacophony of desire.

The lute struck up. Dancers leaned into their moves, and with them the Queen and Don Juan, their connection broken, though its reverberations sounded in my head even when the music stopped and the gnat-weight Hercule was leading me, shaken, toward his mother. For I knew their desire. And with me, Tiberio had known it, too. Our bodies had not lied. No matter what was said, he desired me that night.

Don Carlos jumped from his seat, startling My Lady, who approached the dais with Don Juan.

"Why do you avoid me?" he demanded of her. "Do you not care about me?"

Don Juan released My Lady's hand. She glanced at her dam, whose fleshy lips were pursed in grim expectation.

"Toad," said My Lady. "Dearest. You know I care about you."

"You haven't spoken to me all night, when I am the one who truly loves and esteems——"

The Queen's fool, a Spaniard called Cisneros, shook his rattle. "Crowns, crowns, King Felipe loves crowns! The new horns on his head—they fit him—zounds!"

Don Carlos's mouth dropped open. He lowered his face with a guilty frown, then burst into a noisy guffaw.

A wave of discomfort passed over the crowd. Did Don Carlos actually think the fool referred to him as the Queen's lover?

"What?" said Don Carlos. "It was just a jest. I have been brought up too well to do anything untoward with a lady."

I felt Francesca's gaze boring into me from a group of servants spilling out from behind a painted screen, questioning my countenance, still unsettled from my memory of Tiberio.

After that evening, Don Carlos seemed to regain his newfound equanimity. For the rest of the visit—at the masques, at the tourneys, at the dinner where two thousand lords and ladies sat down to sup, he behaved as a gentleman, with a minimum of braying laughter or pushing about of the servants. He showed a mature level of compassion toward the Queen on our way home, leaving his own dinner to comfort her that miserable evening in the mountain village of Covarrubias, a day's journey south of Burgos.

We had been happily dining upon a feast of the local fare—trout from the river at the foot of the town, venison, and *morcilla*, the black blood sausage stuffed with rice—when our host, the lord of the village castle, let slip that the tower in which the Queen would be staying had once housed, long ago, a princess who was in love with a shepherd.

The Queen had paused, the point of her knife piercing into a tender cut of venison. "Was she allowed to leave?"

"Your Majesty, no," said our host, a lean, black-haired gentleman whose rough face showed every black pore. "Never. They say her father had the church bells rung to drown out her cries. But even if the villagers could not hear her, they could see her. She would put her face to the bars of the window at the top of the tower."

With uncharacteristic unselfishness, Don Carlos left his own meal to jump up from the table to join My Lady, who had excused herself, claiming a sudden need for air. They went outside, where My Lady paced along the river's edge, Francesca and I and a phalanx of the King's German guards trailing behind.

"What trouble you?" Francesca whispered to me.

I gazed up at the little castle, at the barred opening at the top of its square tower. Had Tiberio had such a window out of which to gaze in the Castel Sant'Angelo? Or had he been in the darkest dungeon, the scapegoat for the Pope's campaign against Michelangelo? Now he was dying at the oars of a ship because someone had been needed as evidence of the Maestro's illicit leanings, and

Tiberio, working in the Maestro's house and subject of the Maestro's poems, had been convenient. But there was proof that Tiberio, as much as he esteemed Michelangelo, was not his lover. Living proof that he had given his naked soul in the act of love to a woman. Me.

Later, Don Carlos rode at the Queen's side as we made our way through the mountains, then crossed the endless arid expanse of the Castilian *meseta*, our train raising a plume of ochre dust soon dispersed by the bone-dry wind. Too overwrought to entertain the Queen myself, I was grateful for his ability to speak to her day after day of his exploits in France and his great knowledge of the world as she sat in her litter with Cher-Ami in her lap, the silver tassels of the litter curtains swaying to the rhythm of the plodding mules.

Finally we neared Segovia, journey's end. The Queen sank back onto her divan, her strength flagging. We were amongst the flat green fields just north of the city; the golden towers of the castle, just now visible, crowned the plains. Behind the towers, the pale blue peaks of the Guadarramas rose in a jagged wall.

"The Camino Real that we take to Madrid runs along that ridge." Don Carlos pointed toward the mountains. "Way up there to the left—see? Can you believe that we get up so high there on our mules?"

My Lady nodded listlessly, then glanced behind our litter, where with a crowd of Spanish nobles rode Don Juan, smiling at his companions' talk, though his mirth did not reach his eyes.

"See the Mujer Muerta?" said Don Carlos.

The Queen looked startled. "The dead woman?"

"That's what they call those peaks. Look—she's lying down." He pointed to the distant blue ridges toward the right. "See the peak that is her head? You can see the profile of her forehead, nose, and chin. Way over there are her feet. She's got her hands folded on her belly and there, above her belly, are her——" He coughed into his fist.

I could hold it in no longer. "My Lady," I whispered into her ear. "I wish to talk to you."

She kept her eyes upon the hazy blue mountaintops. "What, Sofi?"

I darted a glance at the condesa, dozing across from us, her chin on her breast. Who could tell if madame, next to her, was listening, as wrapped as she was in her veils? I kept my voice low. "There is a man I wish to marry."

The Queen glanced at me, distracted, then returned her gaze to the Dead Woman. "What?"

"You wish for me to have a husband. Well, there is a man I desire. He is from Rome."

When she did not respond, I whispered urgently, "Your Majesty, please, you must ask the King to send for him, as quickly as possible. His life is in danger, unjustly so, when I know he—he is a good man."

A single black horse streaked down the dusty road from Segovia, tail straight out, its rider leaning low into the horse's mane.

"Who the devil approaches us like that?" snapped Don Carlos. "Guards!"

"I believe it is your father, Your Majesty," said one of the nobles.

Don Carlos squinted. "He's moving awfully fast." He raised his hand to halt the soldiers.

My Lady sat back in our litter.

The fore guards spurred their weary horses off the road, making way for the galloping rider. In a swirl of yellow dust, the King pulled his horse to a halt.

The cavalcade came to a ragged stop; all the gentlemen dismounted. Trumpets blared as the guardsmen called, "His Majesty the King!"

His Majesty, still mounted, paid no heed. His intense gaze sought the Queen. "My Lady."

She put out her gloved hand.

Don Carlos remained on his horse. "Father! What are you doing out here alone?"

The King brought his own steed near to kiss his Lady's hand. "How was France?" he said to Don Carlos, though gazing at the Queen. "Was it to your liking?"

Don Carlos shrugged.

"Your son acquitted himself well there," said the Queen.

"Good. Good for you, son. My Lady, would you be too weary to ride with me a ways? Valsaín is but a few leagues away."

The Queen took back her hand. "I should like that, My Lord." She gave me her dog.

Upon the King's orders, two guards lifted the Queen from our litter and, her skirts billowing around her, set her upon His Majesty's horse. The King locked his arms around her. She cast down her gaze as he whispered in her ear.

"Father—" Don Carlos began.

The King put spur to horse; they were away.

The condesa drew heavily upon her dust-coated pomander as the gentlemen remounted. "A happy ending."

Don Juan urged his horse forward; he touched the Prince's arm.

"Happy?" Don Carlos shrugged away from Don Juan and yanked on his reins, reeling his horse around. "Happy?"

The condesa sniffed as if slapped.

"She was exhausted!" cried Don Carlos. "He'll hurt her. *Fucker!* I'll kill him!"

A hush fell upon the cavalcade, broken only by the breathing of our mules and the creak of saddles.

"What are you gaping at?" Don Carlos shouted at the crowd. "Have you never seen an old *pincho* fondle his wife?" He jabbed his spurs into his horse, making it scream before it plunged across the verdant plain.

The cavalcade slowly stirred to life. As the muleteers cracked their whips and men chirruped to their horses, the tired beasts strained forward with their burdens. Those of us remaining in the Queen's litter kept private company with our thoughts as our conveyance swayed into motion. The condesa sniffed her pomander; madame twisted her veil. As for me, I searched the empty plains, trying not to think of what the King would do once his son's treasonous words were whispered into his ear, and of Tiberio, rowing away his life under a ship's flapping sail.

ITEM: *The Spanish King Pedro the Cruel earned his title not only for quickly dispatching his enemies, but also for imprisoning his Queen, Doña Blanca, from their wedding night until the day of her death. Her crime? She did not please him.*

18 JULY 1565
Valsaín, the House in the Woods of Segovia

Thirty-eight hours after the King had ridden off with the Queen, she returned to her chambers, ravenous. I stood back in startled awe with the other attendants as My Lady, dressed in the clothes she'd been wearing when I'd last seen her, fell upon the platters of melon and meat and cheese like a man just released from Inquisitor-General Valdés's prison, with Cher-Ami yelping with joy. I wondered if she had eaten in the time during which she had disappeared with the King, but she offered no explanations of where they'd gone or what they'd done, and left no openings for one to ask. Without so much as a word about the previous day and a half, she cleaned the platters, downed a small jug of watered wine, then retired to a *siesta* from which she did not wake until the following morning.

She kept her own counsel about what had transpired with the King as her ladies dressed her in the morning. She said so little as we readied her for Mass that I wondered if she was ill. Indeed, the rash at her throat was inflamed. But upon returning from chapel, as we were following her through the arcade around the court-yard, she announced, "I should like to go on a walk in the woods."

"Are you sure?" said the condesa. "Would you rather not rest?"

"I would like to walk," the Queen said quietly.

The condesa frowned. "Very well. Inez," she said to her servant, "please get my black silk mask. There is enough sun, even in the woods, to mar my skin." She threw madame de Clermont a mournful glance, as if to say she was sorry the French lady would need no mask with all those veils. "And get the Queen's green mask," she added. "The green is good, is it not, My Lady?"

"Thank you, doña María," said the Queen, "but I think it best if only Sofi attends me. The King would like a new portrait done of me, and I want Sofi to do it. She needs quiet in which to consider how she might attempt it."

I let the leather-bound prayer book through which I'd been fitfully flipping drop on the cord around my waist. Although I had scribbled off hundreds of sketches during our trip to France, I had not put together studies for a portrait. Even if the King was interested, I had not yet been asked. But I could keep up my end of the charade if needed.

The condesa smiled stiffly. "Who is to carry your train?"

"Sofi. Or Francesca, if Sofi is busy drawing."

Francesca smiled at Her Majesty as lovingly as a mother at her infant.

"Then—" sputtered the condesa, "then Your Majesty must wear a mask!"

"Certainly," the Queen said sweetly. Her skirts swished against the floor tiles as she left the chamber.

"Dinner is at two!" the condesa called after us.

My prayer book thumping against my leg, I hung on to Her

Majesty's train as she glided through the cloisters. Moving in and out of the shadows cast by the arches, she nodded at the nobles lingering about in hopes of getting the King's ear, at the German guards posted at their stations, at the servants falling into low and loving bows. I wondered how I was to work on a drawing without chalk or pen, but held my tongue, and she said nothing, either, about any subject, as we left the palace and its square pointed towers and entered the meadow on the south side of the estate. Save for the quiet pat of My Lady's slippers, the footsteps of myself and Francesca, and the snuffling of Cher-Ami as he explored a patch of crimson poppies, we walked silently, our skirts catching on the long bent grass.

Francesca and I held our tongues as we passed into a pasture where cows grazed, their bells languidly clanking. I kept my own counsel in the hope of encouraging the Queen to share hers. Once she had unburdened herself, I could remind her about my request for a husband. But on she sailed, over a humped stone footbridge and past a vegetable patch tended by gardeners who rose on their knees from their weeding like rabbits sniffing the air.

At last we gained the wild woods. Our footsteps now deadened by the fine grass sprawling between the pines, we pressed forward, until deep within the forest Her Majesty came to a stop. I was stunned to see her shoulders quaking.

She kept her back to me as I held on to her train, trembling in my hands. "My Lady, what is it?"

She shook her head. A breeze picked up, sending the pine boughs hissing.

"My Lady?" I whispered.

"It was terrible."

I took a careful breath.

"If he would have just given me time . . ."

The wind whipped a lock of hair from my braids and across my mouth. I dared not move.

"I know I should be glad." Her back still turned to me, she wiped her eyes with her hand. "A child can come of it."

I glanced over my shoulder at Francesca.

"But I hate him, Sofi. I hate him!"

"Shhh, My Lady!" I whispered. "You do not mean this."

She shook as she quietly cried.

I raked my mind for words of comfort but could find none. She had no rights to her body—it was the King's to claim. And he was not such a bad man, surely, not as bad as other kings have been.

Francesca stepped forward and took her hand. "Think how lovely is a child, *cara mia*. Your own little child."

"A son," I said.

Her hand still in Francesca's rough grasp, My Lady exclaimed, "I do not want a son! I want a daughter, a daughter I can love and keep and hold to my heart. I will never be like my mother, forcing her to marry just for my gain."

"No, *cara mia*," said Francesca. "Of course you no will. What name you like to give your little girl?"

She sniffed. "Diane. After my governess."

I drew in a breath: Diane de Poitiers may have been her governess, but she was also her mother's mortal enemy. My poor Lady, forever torn between the governess who had shown her love and care, and her natural but distant mother.

"Diana," Francesca said, her rough peasant accent caressing the final *a. "Bella."*

"Why am I always to hate whom I love and to love whom I hate? Why, Francesca? Why am I never free to love whom I love?"

I let go of her train as Francesca gathered the Queen to her breast, clucking her tongue. "*Cara mia*, hush. Hush."

"Tell me the truth, Francesca—he killed the Prince of Ascoli, didn't he?"

Francesca stroked Her Majesty's cheek, shaking her head.

"He has no one to answer to," said the Queen. "He can kill whomever, whenever, however he wants."

"He is mostly a good man," said Francesca. "You must believe."

"And the part of him that is not good?"

Francesca stroked her again. "That part, you keep happy, *cara mia*. Make sure you keep it happy."

ITEM: *A trapped lynx will chew off its own foot to make an escape.*

ITEM: *An amethyst placed in wine will cure the ills of having drunk too much wine the night before.*

27 DECEMBER 1565
El Alcázar, Madrid

Let no one claim I have stopped painting. My most recent subject—done tonight—is a reworking of an old painting of myself, standing at the clavichord. I made Francesca stand behind me and, with the aid of a mirror, added her to the picture. I do believe I have made her into a grimacing brown ghost. What do I expect under the influence of drink?

Items, items—more items for the notebook of the great and magnificent Sofonisba Virgo.

Note: Don't paint over underpainting while it is wet, unless you desire mud.

Note: Wine from along the Duero River is quite good.

Note: The Queen is again pregnant, perhaps two months so.

Oh, the King is thrilled. He dotes upon her with renewed vigor, taking time from his hectic schedule to be with her each day, though war is closing in from all his distant worlds. The Turkish navy has struck in Malta. Protestant mobs have stormed churches in the Netherlands, smashing everything in sight. Spanish troops have massacred French settlers in the New World land of Florida against his express orders to leave them alone. Yet in spite of his mounting worries, he asks the Queen to remain with him during his audiences though she is ill. So patiently, patiently, he waits for her to retch into a basin before he grants entrance to his emissaries.

For while this pregnancy has already much weakened my Queen, it has made a new man of her husband. He dresses with unprecedented thought to fashion, wearing a different doublet most days, not always a black one as before, but perhaps a dark gray or brown. He is growing his hair and mustaches longer, in the style of an adventuresome soldier. He takes more exercise at horse, and has the muscles to show for it, too—I have seen him flex them for the Queen.

This morning the King claimed her directly after Mass. He excused me and the rest of her attendants from duty. I strode, immediately afterward, down the steep brick road to the gardens of the Casa de Campo. As frigid as it was, I had to get outside. But I did not escape. My thoughts of Tiberio caught up with me.

I had asked the King to send a man for him, but what if, when found, Tiberio agreed to marriage only to escape his deadly bonds? What if he had no love for me, just a desire to be free? A man would marry a mule to be released from certain death.

"*Signorina!*" Francesca called from behind me.

I kept walking, letting the downward pull of the hill carry my feet.

"*Signorina!*"

I turned. Francesca was holding her side, trying to catch her wind. I waited until she paddled forward, her footsteps ringing on cold brick.

"What the hurry?" she asked when she caught up.

I shook my head.

"You worry about the *scultore* you ask the King to find for you."

Francesca was aware of my request to wed Tiberio, though I had never elaborated on our night together. I still feared her unfavorable judgment. "Of course I do," I said. "How can I help it? Why should I not think he would take the King's offer just to save himself?"

"What happen between you in Rome?"

I would not answer.

"You no have to tell me. I give up after all the years. I just ask you to think what happen there. What you know in your heart"— she rapped on her chest, making the fringe of her shawl shake— "is the truth. The heart knows what the head do not."

I looked down toward the garden and sighed.

"I think you should paint, *signorina*."

"Paint," I scoffed. "What do my paintings matter? They are just portraits—if don Alonso doesn't get the commission for them first." I resumed walking.

"Who say to do portraits is bad? Nobody. Just you." Francesca drew her rough shawl more tightly about her broad shoulders as she stumped next to me. "I know you since you are a baby, *signorina*. When you learn to walk, you no hold my hand. You pull away, you rather fall than to take help."

"I am not asking you or anyone else to help me."

"*Bene*. But do you help yourself with the painting? No. You like to do the portraits, so do you try to make best there is? No. Yet you want to be the big *maestra*." She spat onto the road. "Just by say 'honey, honey' do not make the sweetness come to the mouth."

A commotion arose from the animal house at the bottom of the road ahead.

Don Carlos's high voice rang out. "I said loose her! I am your Prince and you *will* obey me!"

Francesca's thick brows dashed toward her nose. "What do he want now?"

Although I knew I should have turned back, perversely I walked on toward the pens. There, through the iron bars of the lioness's cage, I saw Don Carlos struggling to free himself from Don Juan, though Don Juan looked to be having an easy time of holding him. Behind them sat Don Juan's long-legged red mongrel, Rojo, scratching behind its ear.

"Believe me, Carlos," Don Juan said. "I am for the creature's freedom as much as you are, but where would she go if she were loosed?"

Like a small child pulling from its nurse, Don Carlos strained toward the lioness padding along the brick wall on the far side of the enclosure. "I don't know—she'll find her way. I don't care! My Lady wants her loose, so I'm letting her go."

"My Lady wants her freed?"

"Ow, Juan! You hurt me! Yes! She told me when I went to see her this morning. She was freeing the canary in my father's office in the French tower when I came in." He stopped struggling and smiled. "When he asked her what she was doing, she said it gave her great pleasure to see it go free, such pleasure that she would have all the caged creatures loosed in the land. You should have seen Father. For once it wiped that maddeningly calm expression off his face."

He broke free of Don Juan with a burst of energy. "Touch me again," he said, rubbing his wrist, "and I'll have you arrested!" He peered through the bars of the cage. "Sofi—are you and your woman just going to spy on me all day?"

"Your Majesty." I came around and curtseyed before him. "Your Excellency," I said to Don Juan.

"Tell Juan he must let me do what I want."

In spite of my troubled mind, I smiled sympathetically at Don Juan. Why he has taken it upon himself to be his nephew's keeper all these years, I do not know. It is a hard job that grows more difficult by the day. Perhaps Don Carlos awakens Don Juan's natural compassion for injured creatures. For Don Carlos is as wounded a creature as any, his damaged brain given increasingly to fantasy and rages.

A clopping of hooves drew our attention. Down the road from which I'd just come trotted the King on a gleaming black stallion. The Queen's mule-drawn litter jostled just behind him, its brocade curtains closed against the December chill. A troop of burly German guards, mounted on mules, followed at a discreet remove.

"Here comes the old billy goat now," Don Carlos muttered under his breath.

The King's horse clattered up then reared back, hooves flashing, as His Majesty pulled the reins sharp. His horse still dancing, the King reached down and touched Don Carlos's shoulder. "My son."

Don Carlos knocked away his father's hand as the Queen's litter came to a halt before us. A slim gloved hand drew back the curtains; My Lady peeked out. Her blink acknowledged Don Juan's presence before she smiled at Don Carlos.

"Toady."

"My Lady!" Spots of color appeared on the Prince's pasty cheeks.

The King retained his pleasant calm as he sat back into his saddle, a bracing wind ruffling the feather in his cap. "Juan," he said coolly. "Nothing better to do today than to admire the animals?"

"That is exactly what I am doing. I am studying patience from this one." He nodded at the lioness, treading in her enclosure.

The King's smile was all coolness. "You believe she has feelings? Thoughts, even?"

"I believe she thinks of her escape, yes."

"Oh, does she?" The King gazed at him a moment. "I suppose my horse is scheming, too. Planning to throw me, perhaps?"

"Perhaps," said Don Juan. "One cannot always know what is on the mind of the creatures around us."

The brothers stared at each other, the King settling his horse.

"My Lady," said Don Carlos, "I hope you are feeling better than when I saw you last. How is your headache?"

"Much better, Toad. You are sweet to ask."

"We would not be out if she did not feel well," the King said mildly.

"Oh," said Don Carlos, "so you do notice when she's ill, then?"

A slight cloud passed over the King's calm features. He sat forward in his saddle to peer into the cage before him. "I hope my lioness does not plan to escape soon. She has a surprise coming for her—" He looked at the Queen. "A mate. Perhaps a cub can come from it."

"A cub," she said flatly. "I should like that."

Don Carlos looked his father up and down. "Why are you letting your hair grow? It is longer than Don Juan's."

I could not help glancing between the King, with his graying hair drawn back beneath his fur hat in a tidy queue, and Don Juan, his carelessly tousled locks catching in the wind.

"The King tells me that the camel in his collection has given birth," said the Queen. "Would you please show me, dear Toad?"

The King's hand went toward his queue. He frowned. "Yes, do show her."

"I will, but not because you asked me. Come, Elisabeth."

"I should like to walk," said the Queen.

"Help her down, Juan," said Don Carlos. "I'm not that strong today. Tomorrow I shall be better."

Don Juan stepped to the edge of the litter. The wind picked up, rippling the scarlet hangings. My Lady closed her eyes and leaned into the waiting arms of Don Juan.

She opened her eyes and beheld him as he set her on the ground.

"Don Juan," said the King. "May I have a word?"

Don Carlos snatched at the Queen's hand. "Come! You don't have to tag along, Sofi," he said when I started to join them. "Just hold on to Cher-Ami."

The remainder of us watched them go, Don Carlos's pale countenance lit up with eagerness as he chatted, Her Majesty's face, already fuller even this early in her pregnancy, alert as she glanced at us over her shoulder.

"Walk with me," said the King to Don Juan.

They strolled past the bars of the enclosure, Don Juan's red dog padding behind them. I stared as if transfixed at the far side of the lioness's cage, where the poor shaggy beast trod the straw-strewn earth. Francesca gazed, too, adept at becoming invisible.

The King and his brother had gotten only as far as the other corner of the cage when His Majesty said, "May I ask you something?" He watched, expressionless, as Don Juan made a soothing sound at the lioness.

Don Juan straightened. "Of course."

"Does my son seem worse to you?"

"Does he to you?"

The King opened his mouth, then closed it. He started again. "I have had reports. I need not remind you that his pages are sons of important people. They cannot be cuffed about like peasants."

"I have spoken with each of the young men," said Don Juan, "when it was necessary. They understand the situation."

"My son, the 'situation.'" The King sighed deeply. "How did it come to this? I remember when he was a babe in the cradle. I had such high hopes for him—such a beautiful child. He was all I had. I lost his mother at his birth."

Francesca's chin drew up closer to her brow. It is commonly said that the King had ignored his first wife, bedding her only enough to plant his seed. It is reported that he had shed no tears at her funeral. She had been just seventeen, and he eighteen.

"I must have respect," said the King. "My position—the security of my kingdoms—requires it. How am I to ask men to give their lives for a man who cannot control his own son?"

"I will work with him, but the problem is not dire. Those around him know his generous side, his natural sweetness. We know he means no harm. He is given to his emotions, good or bad—we all understand that."

"He cannot be ruled by emotions if he is to be King. My father—*our* father taught me that." The King pushed away from the cage. "Why do you care about my son so?"

Don Juan smiled calmly. "He is like a brother to me."

"I am your brother."

They stared at each other, two dogs with a bone lying between them, sizing up their opponents.

"And so I trust you," said the King.

"My Lord!" called the Queen. She approached hurriedly, Don

Carlos lagging behind her. "The newborn camel is pure sweetness! Such long lashes, like a human child."

"I am glad you like it." The King gathered her against himself. "Do you feel well, my pet?"

Her gaze traveled to Don Juan.

The screech of rusty metal rent the air. Shouts went up from the King's German guards just as the lioness streaked past us, her tufted tail arched like a monkey's.

"Look at her go!" Don Juan banged closed the cage door. "Fly, birdie, fly!"

The lioness bounded toward the maze. A German guard chopped the air with his halberd, blocking her way. The beast changed directions, surprisingly light on heavy paws, then changed direction again when charged upon by a pitchfork-waving keeper screaming in Flemish. Her exits cut off, the animal lowered into a crouch, switching her tail.

Don Juan put himself between the beast and the advancing keepers. "Everyone," he ordered in a quiet voice, "allow her room."

The lioness's great bony chest heaved as she glanced left and right, considering her options.

"Shh, my beauty," Don Juan whispered. "I promise, we will not hurt you."

The big cat stared, her ears pivoting to pick up the excited murmurs in Spanish, Flemish, and German around her. She swallowed in nervousness.

I felt the intensity of another gaze close by. I peered past Francesca, her fist balled at her mouth, past Don Carlos, hands on hips, grinning, until my sights caught upon the Queen. Her chin tilted up as if fighting against the invisible bonds holding her from within, she beheld Don Juan with a yearning so naked I had to look away.

When I did so, I noticed the King.

He was watching her, too.

He snatched an arquebus from a guard and slapped it to his shoulder.

A scream scorched my throat: "No!"

The gun went off. The lioness spun around and bounded past the maze.

The guards gaped at the King, still pointing his gun upward, the direction in which he'd shot it.

"Get your nets," he said serenely. "Be sure you capture her well away from the Queen."

He waited until they ran off in a din of clanging armor.

"Doña Sofonisba," he said.

My heart banged my chest like a fist. I had publicly challenged the man responsible for the Queen's—for my—for most of the world's—well-being. A man who could and would do anything he pleased.

I could feel Francesca's frightened look upon me.

I curtseyed low and long. "Your Majesty."

When I arose, his calm expression was almost puzzled. "So-fonisba, did you truly think I could hurt such a beautiful creature?"

"No, My Lord."

He regarded me for a long moment. "I have word for you. From Rome." His calm eyes lingered on my face. I fought back the panic rising in my gut. "About the man you asked the Queen and me to make inquiries into."

He handed the arquebus back to the guard.

"I must tell you, he is dead."

I write this tonight with the aid of a full goblet. Francesca has not stopped me each time I have refilled it. They have not yet captured the lioness, though the King's hunters have tracked her into the hills to the north of Madrid. They will catch her soon and bring her back safely, or so I heard the King promise My Lady, before he shut himself in her chamber for the night.

ITEM: Tactus eruditus *(Latin, "learned touch")* refers to a doctor's ability to glean information about a patient's condition by applying his fingers to the patient's pulse. The rhythm, strength, and tempo, considered together, are called pulse music.

15 AUGUST 1566

Valsaín, the House in the Woods of Segovia

Isabel Clara Eugenia she is named. She was born to the Queen at Valsaín on the twelfth of August. Oh, what a little beauty she is, with a tuft of dark hair and her mother's dark eyes and gossamer ridges where her father's arched brows will appear. Her lips and chin resemble her mother's thus far, a happy victory, at last, of Valois over Hapsburg. Her grandmother will be pleased by this, if not by her lesser sex.

Today we celebrated her baptism. To that end, we met in the main courtyard in the early morning, to wait for the carriages that would take us to the nearby town of Segovia, to the ancient Cathedral being rebuilt there at the King's command. Bees droned in the dewy hedges, birds cheeped from their nests in the palace walls, and cowbells clanked from the meadows nearby until horses and carriages burst onto the cobblestones, drowning the morning music in the rumble of wheels and clatter of hooves. I alit in my assigned carriage, a conveyance far back in the queue. Without the Queen, who was dangerously ill and abed, my rank was much reduced. Indeed, I did not want to go. I wished to stay with My Lady, for the birth had nearly killed her and her life hung in the balance yet, a fact not readily apparent from the festive dress and air displayed by the men and women now packed inside the carriages.

Wedged between two ladies smelling strongly of jasmine, I braced myself against the rocking of our vehicle as it hurtled through the woods toward Segovia. In less than a turning of an hourglass, the high arches of the famous aqueduct from Roman times came into view. Its weed-sprouted pillars, towering over the wall encircling the town, were a jarring reminder of the great civilization that had flowered and flourished and then withered into silence. The line of carriages, reduced to child's toys at its granite-block feet, came to the yellow stone gates of the city and thundered inside, where they were greeted by cheers from the people lining the streets. From their brick and timber houses, the people strained for a view while singing thanks and praise for their Lady and her child.

At last the carriages reached their destination, and the Court assembled within the bare marble walls of the unfinished Cathedral. We stood at the base of the massive stone piers of the aisle and waited for our King to enter.

He arrived to loud fanfare, with the crown of Fernando upon his head and no expression on his face. Was he worried about My Lady? We had left her in a state of near-unconsciousness. She might not be alive when we returned, but to save the soul of her child, the baptism had to go forward. Yet how I wished to flee the place, a place made no less distressing to me even with the sweet voices of choirboys echoing from the arched stone vaults above. My Lady hated this church. Once, several years back, we had come with the King to see his new alterations. A bird had flown in and could not find its way out, its screams growing ever more frantic as it flew higher and higher and found itself more trapped. A workman flung a stone. The bird plummeted to the floor. Cheers went up from the workers on scaffolds and pushing wheelbarrows. My Lady had rushed out into the bright light of day, swearing she would never come again.

I fear that might be true.

Now the King, in his crown and ermine, stopped before the altar and turned. With a rustle of hundreds of rich silks, the crowd turned, too, and beheld, delicately carrying a bundle of ribbons and lace, Don Juan, his handsome face pinched with contained emotion. The King had chosen his brother as godfather.

The bishop entered, resplendent in crimson encrusted with tiny pearls from his miter to the hem of his chasuble, and Mass began. After the bishop had swung his censer, wafting incense over us penitents, he started the spoken rite, intoning in Latin that broke in waves from pier to ceiling to the marble floor, the reverberations punctuated with an occasional echoing cough or scrape of a slippered foot. The King and Don Juan were bidden to the alabaster baptismal font, an ancient piece carved with the shields of long-gone kings.

The bishop raised his voice, his words lost in the crash of echoes. He stared expectantly at Don Juan. Don Juan gazed into the baby's pink face, then held her up to receive her holy sprinkling, the white ribbons of her gown shaking as he did so.

In sonorous Latin, the bishop asked for her father to make the sign of the cross upon the child's forehead. Slowly, the King took his gaze from his brother and transferred it to his newborn daughter, and there it remained, rapt, for the rest of the service.

Not soon enough, the rites were over, and deafened by clanging bells, I waited for my carriage to return me to Valsaín and the Queen. A golden carriage rattled up; its curtain was pushed aside.

Doña Juana's face, framed in black and white by the nun's habit she has taken to wearing, appeared at the window.

"Sofonisba, will you join us?"

A footman opened the heavy golden door. Inside sat Doña Juana and doña Eufrasia, no less beautiful now that she has returned to court. Across from them, like a great sow settled comfortably in a mud puddle, sat Inquisitor-General Valdés, a sweet smile on his fleshy face.

He patted the cushioned seat with heavily ringed fingers. "Sit, my dear. Sit."

I sat, immediately sinking toward his spicily perfumed bulk.

"We were just speaking of you," said Doña Juana.

The Inquisitor-General nodded. "I have been to see the Pope."

I stared. Michelangelo was dead, as was Tiberio. What could they possibly want? Had the King told his sister that he had inquired into Tiberio for me? What harm could she do to me and to the Queen with this information?

"His Holiness much admires the portrait you have done of our Queen," said the Inquisitor-General. "He wishes to commission you for another."

I tamped back my astonishment. "I would be honored. As soon as Her Majesty is well."

"Oh, her mother assured us she would be well soon enough. Good breeders run in the family." He folded his hands over his belly, his slow respirations whistling through his nose. "Catherine had a brood of what, seven? My Lady should be able to have a son soon."

I glanced out the window as we passed the city walls and turned onto the road that ran alongside the aqueduct. My Lady could not eat or drink or sit up in bed, and they had her pregnant with a new child.

With a grunt, the Inquisitor-General shifted in his seat, sending me sliding even closer. "Did you ever hear what became of the Sistine Chapel, my child?"

I caught my breath.

Doña Juana smiled mildly. "I believe she has not."

"They decided not to destroy it." The Inquisitor-General massaged the flesh bulging over the back of his collar. "At least not until it is decided if the changes sufficiently improve the work."

"Changes?"

"A painter was commissioned." The Inquisitor-General quietly burped into his fist. "To paint clothes upon the nakedness of the men in *The Last Judgment*. The ceiling is next."

"Someone is going to tamper with the Maestro's work?"

"Tamper?" Doña Juana raised her brows, noting the rise in my voice. "Improve it, most of us would say. Michelangelo was too stubborn to do it on his own, endangering the entire painting. And so was that lover of his. He said he would die rather than lay a brush to it."

I opened my mouth and then shut it before Tiberio's name could escape.

She gazed at me, filing away my reaction for future use. "And this was after the judge had been good enough to let him go after he'd denounced Michelangelo's homosexual leanings. Bold, considering they still had evidence against him. What became of that unfinished statue, Inquisitor-General? Do you know?"

"I could not say. It was of no value, ruined as it was. Ground up for paving, I suppose."

I stared at my clenched hands.

Doña Juana chuckled. "They have a nickname for the painter they found to do the work on the Sistine Chapel—'Il Braghettone.' Now remind me again what that is Italian for?"

I swallowed. "The Breeches-maker."

Doña Eufrasia tittered.

"Do you remember the name of this man?" I asked.

Doña Juana shrugged. "Someone unimportant. A Daniele somebody. A friend, obviously, who cared little about his own reputation, since painting loincloths does not exactly further one's career."

Was this "Braghettone" Daniele da Volterra? I had met him at the Maestro's house—a self-effacing, kind man, and faithful follower of the Maestro. Tiberio said he had been one of those who had stopped Michelangelo from destroying the statue. Poor signore Daniele. He would be a laughingstock amongst the other painters in Rome, known for daubing breeches onto naked men, yet he had done this to save the frescoes.

A bee flew in through the window. The Inquisitor-General paddled the air, squealing, as Doña Juana swung at it with her Bible. She killed the offending insect, but not before it had stung doña Eufrasia on the hand. By the time Doña Juana pulled out the stinger and the Inquisitor-General had kissed the pink swelling and doña Eufrasia had finished sniffing back her tears, the subject had changed to how Doña Juana would have remodeled the Cathedral in Segovia had someone had the intelligence to consult her.

To Sofonisba Anguissola,
In the Court of the Spanish King

I trust you are well. Today I received the greatest treat—a
copy of The Lives of the Artists *by messer Giorgio Vasari,*
with a mention of you in it. It was personally delivered by the
author himself, he being on business in the area. When Count
Broccardo heard about him, he hurried over and proceeded to
reminisce about you as if you were his own child. Messer
Vasari seemed to enjoy Broccardo's tales, though they were
mostly made up. Messer Vasari is quite a congenial fellow
and seems to know everyone. He regaled us with stories about
all those he knows, including your friend Michelangelo. Did
you know that Michelangelo never painted a portrait of
himself? The closest he came to recording his own features
were on the face of the flayed skin held by Saint Bartholomew
in the painting of the Last Judgment. The likeness is hideous
to behold, said messer Vasari, but quite recognizable. Greatest
artist in the world, but the poor man must not have thought
much of himself to paint himself thus.

Please thank the King again for sending the large sum of
money. We never looked for this windfall, and are grateful
beyond words. It has eased your mother's crippling burden of
worry, at least temporarily, and hence mine, and I have been
able to settle both Minerva and Anna Maria upon wonderful
husbands. Europa, I am sorry to say, eloped this May past
with a Florentine soldier and returned to us as a mother. She
has named her little daughter Sofonisba.

*One last item. Signore Vasari said that he left the
miniature portrait of you that I gave him with a friend who
insisted upon keeping it. Someone in Rome. The name escapes
me now. It seems you have admirers everywhere, my dear. I
am not surprised.*

*From Cremona,
this 29th day of November, 1566*

Your loving Father

ITEM: *Note when painting that the surface of every dark object takes on the color of the bodies placed against it.*

23 JANUARY 1567
El Alcázar, Madrid

Slowly, My Lady grows stronger. By the time the storks had flown for Africa in October, she was sitting up in her bed. On All Saints' Day, she was able to ride by litter to Madrid. Now, in January, she takes walks down the halls of the palace on the arm of the King.

It is touching to see how tenderly His Majesty attends her. While other husbands might be frustrated or even angry with their wives for not assuming their wifely duties more quickly—My Lady is still not strong enough to receive him in her bed—each day the King comes to her chamber before Mass and closely questions her ladies as to her activities during the night. He is anxious to hear, he says, how well she has slept. He attends his own private chapel for Mass while we take her to the main chapel for services, after which, if she is well enough, he then sets her up in his office. With much gentleness and care, he personally settles her onto his red velvet divan and provides her with a special strengthening cordial made of his own devising. Only after she is comfortable, blanket up to her chin, goblet in hand, does he proceed with his work. Even then, he pauses with his pen from time to time, watching over his spectacles as My Lady takes a sip. No Queen has ever been so coddled by her King.

What the French Queen Catherine would have given for even half this attention from My Lady's father. I should be sorely glad for My Lady.

But she is not happy. Yes, My Lady smiles, she talks, she fusses over her pretty baby when it is laid upon her arms. But something is wrong with her. Something is desperately wrong. Her smiles do not connect with her eyes. Her voice is lifeless. Her caresses for her child are cold. She had settled into a closed silence during her pregnancy, but I thought she would be better after she had the child. She is worse. It is as if her soul has taken flight, leaving only the shell of her behind.

I have voiced my concerns to Francesca. *Signorina, you no meddle,* she tells me. *You do her no good by meddle.*

But My Lady is miserable, and I am not the only one who sees it.

This morning I was braiding My Lady's hair when I heard footsteps at the chamber door. My Lady's lips formed a ghost of a smile when she looked into her mirror and saw who it was. "You are up early."

Don Carlos strutted in, swishing his sword like a sorcerer's wand, Don Alessandro shaking his head behind him. Don Alessandro has recently brought his bride back to Madrid, where he took her to her own rooms in the palace, then promptly forgot her. Now, smelling overwhelmingly of perfume—he must have drenched himself before leaving his chambers—he kissed My Lady on the cheek as the Prince sheathed his sword with a zing.

"I have to come early, My Lady," said Don Carlos. He helped himself to the sugared almonds in a dish on her dressing table. "It is the only way I can talk to you without Father lurking around."

She stared at her silver-framed image in the mirror. "He is my husband, Toad."

"He doesn't have to claim every minute of your time."

I hung on to her hair as she smiled up at Don Carlos. "I shall be better soon, then I shall go out with you."

"Soon!" He crunched on the almonds. "It has been months since you had the baby. You should be well by now."

Francesca and I exchanged glances as she handed me a comb. Just yesterday Francesca had muttered how strange it was that a woman as young as the Queen still has not gained her strength after childbirth and is given so to fevers. My Lady is only twenty-one—a mere spring pullet—too young to be withering away.

The Queen sighed. "Don't remind me, Toad. Believe me, I wish I were better."

Don Alessandro picked a bit of fluff that had fallen from his plumed hat to his sleeve. "Cousin, this is not the best way to cheer her up, you know."

Don Carlos ignored him. "Come with me after Mass, My Lady! Then we shall go to the zoo. I know you are fond of the lioness there, that you send her special treats. Or we could go riding about town disguised as—as—monks."

"Monks?" scoffed Don Alessandro.

"I know it will make you feel better, My Lady. You just have to get away from—*things*," he said darkly.

Footsteps echoed in the hall outside. Metal clanked against armor as the guards stationed before the door lowered their halberds in salute and the King entered the chamber. Francesca sagged into a curtsey, and I swept into my own.

Don Carlos frowned as Don Alessandro kissed the King's hand. "I want to take My Lady riding this morning, Father."

"In winter?" he said mildly. The Queen lifted her chin for the King to kiss both cheeks, then gazed again into her mirror. He placed a hand upon her shoulder.

"It's not that cold," said Don Carlos. "She'll be in a litter. We have robes! It would do her good."

The King smiled apologetically, as if sorry to point out his son's poor thinking. "Even if exposing her to chill breezes did not go against all medical wisdom, she would not want to leave her child." He lifted a finger to stroke one of the Queen's cheeks.

"It wasn't so hard for you to leave me," said Don Carlos, "when I was a baby. Eight whole years of my childhood you were gone. Traipsing around Europe and marrying the English hag was more important to you than I was."

The King lifted a brow. "It was my father's wish that I tour our lands and wed Mary, and being a dutiful son, I put all my personal desires aside to do what he asked. I did not realize you held this against me."

"I did not say that. It's just that—you could have taken me with you."

"Self-pity is not attractive, Carlos."

"I am just telling you how I feel!"

"I did not know you 'felt' so bad. I thought Juana raised you in my stead quite well. I won't let her hear how unhappy you are with her."

"I am not unhappy with her! Why do you twist things around?"

The King assessed him calmly with his heavy-lidded gaze. "Is the pain quite bad in your head today?"

"What are you doing?"

The King kissed the top of the Queen's head. "What do you mean?"

"You are trying to make me sound insane!"

"Carlos, I am not trying to 'do' anything."

"You are evil," Don Carlos said, backing away.

"Carlos, please——"

Don Carlos rushed from the room, knocking into the nurse carrying in the Infanta. A cry went up from within the bundle of satin and lace in the nurse's arms.

"Go with him, Don Alessandro," the King said wearily. He took the child from her nurse, then motioned for the serving man standing by the door. "See if my apothecary can mix my son a stronger elixir. He'll know which one."

Having finished My Lady's hair, I drew her girdle around her waist and fixed her prayer book to it. We went soon after to Mass.

Not the sweetly acrid smell of frankincense nor the jingling ring of the altar bells at the Elevation of the Host nor the calming chant of the priests could dispel my uneasiness over Don Carlos. The Prince was only trying to voice what I myself was thinking, that the Queen's recovery might be hastened by letting her venture from within these walls. Regardless, dismissing Don Carlos's suggestion out of hand was sure to set him off. Why could the King not bend for his son, even if the King was right?

At least *I* could get out of the palace. The moment the King claimed My Lady after Mass, I grabbed my shawl and, with Francesca muttering behind me, set out to get some air. Past the flagstones of the palace courtyard I wandered, down the steep Calle de Balien, then through the Plaza de la Villa with its ancient tower. I was glad for the sharp winds from the Guadarramas that tugged my skirts and stung my face. I was alive and well, and as soon as the Queen could safely be left, I was going home.

For I have decided. I need to be back again in Cremona, painting in my room as the bells clang so stolidly out of pitch in the tower of San Giorgio across the piazza and the hens cluck in our courtyard. Once surrounded again by familiar things—Papà, my sisters and brother, the servants gathering around our well, chatting as the bucket lowers once more from its squeaking pulley—I might find again the stillness in my mind into which God can whisper. I might glimpse once more that gossamer connection to the other world that resides in each of us, that essence so rare, so beautiful, so completely true that we can bear to comprehend it only for the briefest of moments. At home, God willing, it will come again to my brush.

It shall never come to me in the stifling atmosphere here.

Thinking how I might broach the subject of my dismissal with the Queen, I began the steep climb up the Costanilla de San Pedro, stopping for breath in front of the Church of San Pedro el Viejo. My hand to my heaving breast, I gazed up the apricot-colored brick wall of the bell tower. Above the Moorish arches of the belfry, upon the red-tiled roof, sat the empty nest of a stork, its tumbledown pile of sticks outlined by the stark blue sky.

"No storks for two months, my lady."

I looked down. An elderly woman held out a bowl from the shadows of the covered church porch. "Alms," she croaked, in a voice as rusty as the gate to a family crypt.

I nodded to Francesca, who took a coin from the purse at her waist.

"Already I feel better," I told Francesca as the coin clinked in the beggar's battered tin bowl. "I could not stay in that palace another moment."

Francesca rejoined me, pulling closed her purse.

I stopped to rearrange my shawl upon my shoulders. "Poor Carlos. I wish he could have convinced the King to let My Lady have an outing. But he spoiled any chance of it by arguing with his father. His rashness undoes him every time."

Francesca tightened her shawl around her head. "The Prince, he have a kind heart."

"If only that were enough to see him through. As fond as I am of him, I shudder to think of him as ruler of half the world. I fear that it is only a matter of time before he goes completely raving mad like his great-grandmother Juana."

From the shadows, the old woman rasped, "Doña Juana was not mad."

I drew in a sharp breath. What was I thinking, speaking so freely in public? My words were not ones that should get back to the King.

The woman's voice came again. "It only suited her son to make her seem that way."

I picked up my skirts, a signal to Francesca that we should leave.

The woman stirred within the dimness of the porch, her coins—precious few of them, by the sound of it—swishing against the sides of her bowl. "My mother was a servant to Queen Juana. I grew up in the convent where she was kept. And I tell you—her mind was clear."

"Come, Francesca!" Why did she tarry so?

"The Emperor stole her crown, then made his son keep it. What a different place Spain would be now if she had ruled. Instead, what did we get? Wars. Fighting for a piece of dirt. Kings and their pride! They would have us all dead before giving an inch."

"Francesca! Now!"

The woman quickened her speech as if afraid we would get away before she finished. "I am not the only one who loved her. Did not Juan Bravo and the other rebels lose their lives in trying to rescue her from prison? But her own sweetness was used against her—she had not the stomach to fight her own son. She went to her grave grieving over him and her grandson."

Francesca regarded the woman, her peasant's face cautious. "You say like you know her."

"Francesca! I am leaving."

"I was the playmate of her daughter. We were the best of friends until Catalina was sent to marry. She was more useful to her brother as a bride than as her mother's only companion."

I caught Francesca's sleeve. Most people are well versed in who was who in the Royal Family—this knowledge was not exceptional. The woman had delusions, claiming to be the friend of Queen Juana's daughter.

Francesca pulled away from me. "Why are you here in Madrid?"

"Thank you for listening, *señora*. When Queen Juana died, my mother and I were let go, too unimportant to be thought a threat to the King. I married a guard who had served the King in the Indies. He joined a regiment and went to France, where he died fighting at Metz. But he did not widow me before giving me something he got in Mexico." She came out of the shadows.

I drew back with a gasp. Above her twisted lips was a gaping hole that had been her nose.

"See what the conquistadors brought back from the New World besides silver and gold."

"Leprosy," Francesca whispered.

"No," said the woman. "The French Disease. And my wounds are not the worst of it." She shrank back into the shadows with a sigh. "I passed the curse to my child at birth. Poor weakened thing, given to fevers and rashes. She did not live to see her eighteenth birthday."

"Give her another *maravedí*." I turned away, gagging into my glove.

A coin clanked upon the woman's metal bowl. "God be with you," said Francesca.

I hurried off, though not before the woman's ghastly image had been engraved upon my mind.

ITEM: *In seeking an answer to a quandary, one must consider the Law of Parsimony, proposed by the English monk William of Ockham. Translated from the Latin: "All things being equal, the simplest solution is the best."*

29 JANUARY 1567
The Palace, Aranjuez

I write this as fast as I can while everyone sleeps. Even Francesca has fallen into a restless slumber, thinking I am asleep. I am not. Too many thoughts rumble unchecked through my head.

Five days ago, just after the Infanta's nurse had brought the baby to the Queen's chamber after Mass, the King surprised us all by announcing that we were to travel to Aranjuez. I could see the Queen's blank stare at the King as she rested upon the divan.

The King nestled the Infanta in the crook of his arm, then looked up. "Do you not wish to go, darling? We do not have to."

"We can truly leave Madrid?"

"Of course we can. If you are up to it. I know it is not the season, but perhaps it is warmer there than——"

She sat up. "How soon?"

He let the baby wrap her fist around his finger and pull it to her wet mouth. "Not so very long. Tomorrow, if you wish."

The Queen paused, eyes alert. "Who else goes?"

The Infanta latched on to a lock of the King's hair as he pretended to nibble on her pudgy fingers. He looked up, making her chortle as she hung on. "Those in the family who always go with us to Aranjuez. Is there someone specific you had in mind?"

The Queen shook her head.

The condesa swept in with madame de Clermont. The little Infanta stared at them, bright-eyed, maintaining her grip on her father's hair as the ladies made their greetings and the King announced mildly that the Queen wished to go to Aranjuez on the morrow. Would it be possible to make ready her things?

In moments, servants were running to and fro, flinching as the condesa shouted a stream of orders from behind her pomander. Her whip-cracking produced the desired results. By morning the next day, I was swaying in a carriage beside the nurse with the baby Princess; the King and Queen were seated on the tufted velvet bench across from us.

"Tired, darling?" the King said.

The Queen lay back in his arms, her head against his shoulder. "Not so very much."

"You can rest when you get there."

She nodded, then sipped from the goblet he held to her lips.

At that moment, little Isabel Clara reached forward from her nurse's lap and grasped the leather curtain at the carriage window. With a baby's spastic movement, she jerked a corner of the stiff leather sheet toward her mouth, eager to gum it.

The late morning sunlight poured through the uncovered opening. My Lady turned her head, shielding her face with her hand, but not before I noticed her eyes. Only the thinnest rim of light brown ringed her pupils. Her eyes were as dilated as a cat's.

I caught my breath. I had noticed that her eyes seemed darker of late, glittering, as eyes do, from fever, but in the gloom in which the King kept her rooms, I had not realized how great a part her enlarged pupils played in the changed appearance of her gaze. Altogether the effect was unnerving.

His Majesty took away the cup; My Lady let her head fall back upon his chest.

The King lifted his gaze and caught me staring. Although I looked away quickly, I could see him frown.

He pressed the Queen's face to his heart. "Doña Elena," he said coolly to the nurse, "do you think it good for Isabel Clara to put that curtain in her mouth?"

The morning after we arrived at Aranjuez, after Mass, when the Queen was settled in the King's office and resting, I went to her mulberry grove, knowing that she would never cause her litter to go there. Although the King had ordered the mulberry trees be planted specially for My Lady, to encourage her in the pastime of tending silkworms, the thought of coddling a worm, let alone one that entombs itself in its own guts, repulses her. Even if she were well and capable of visiting the grounds with the King (for he no more lets her out of his sight than Francesca lets me out of hers), the mulberry grove is the last place in Spain one would ever find her.

Confident of my temporary solitude—save for Francesca muttering within her shawls—I paced among the young trees. The winter sun shone steadily through their naked limbs, creating a lacework of shadows upon my skirt. I hardly marked their pattern. I was desperately trying to recall my lessons on the four humors. Which of them in imbalance is implicated by dilated pupils? Black bile? Phlegm? Blood?

I kicked at the dead, bent grass of the grove. Even if I could recall which imbalance had caused the Queen's pupils to swell, I was not a physician. Indeed, even if I had the answer, who would listen to a mere lady of the court? Why was the King's new physician not acting upon this, bleeding her, cupping her, sampling her urine? How could he—and the King himself, as learned as His Majesty is in medicine—stand idly by when My Lady exhibited this symptom? It seemed a clear clue to her unshakable weakness. Something was wrong, I could feel it in my bones.

I was turning these thoughts over in my mind as I trod, Francesca's heavy step crunching in the long grass behind me, when I heard a man's voice.

"Juffrouw Sofonisba?"

I started.

Doctor Debruyne raised himself from a patch of tall grass by the trunk of a mulberry tree and dusted off his breeches. The cloud of his breath dissolved in the chill air before him. "I am sorry, *juffrouw*, I am afraid I have found none."

Francesca cleared her throat loudly.

Doctor Debruyne smiled at her. "Oh, yes, *mevrouw*. Thank you for reminding me." He gave me a quick bow. "Good afternoon, *juffrouw*."

Having dispensed with court formalities in one swift move, he resumed his train of thought. "I have not found a one."

"A one?" I was confused, flustered, and embarrassingly glad. I had given up hope of ever seeing him again since he had been sent to Sevilla with doctor Hernández, though I hardly hoped doctor Debruyne would ever miss me.

"Cocoons," he said.

"Cocoons?"

"For the Queen." He tossed back the hank of shining brown hair that had fallen in his eyes. "Forgive me, juffrouw Sofonisba. It was foolish of me to presume that because I was sent here to look for any cocoons that might have survived the winter, you had been sent here for the same purpose. There was a bit of logic to my thinking, though. The King said the Queen might wish to expand her industry amongst the silkworms, and you being the Queen's favored lady, I thought she'd sent—" His high forehead rumpled in a frown. "Perhaps my line of reasoning was not so logical after all."

"Oh, I see the logic now," I said quickly, "but no, it has no bearing on why I am here. As a matter of fact, the Queen would never send me here on such a mission. She despises silkworms." I closed my mouth. A simple 'no' would have done.

"She does? Why?"

"Well, they are worms."

"I see. Perhaps it would ease the Queen's mind to know they are not truly worms, but caterpillars—young moths, that is. Who would ever think such a beautiful thing as silk would come from the efforts of a lowly caterpillar?"

Francesca shifted on her stocky legs, seemingly torn between cutting short an unsanctioned private meeting between her mistress and a gentleman, and making allowances for the man who had removed her bad tooth.

I could not help it. My curiosity got the best of me: "I thought you were in Sevilla."

A corner of his mouth lifted in a surprised smile, as if he had not expected me to have made note of where he had gone. "I was. Receiving shipments of herbs directly from the New World as they came into port there. Doctor Hernández and I have been able to keep a few more specimens alive that way, as opposed to waiting for them to reach Aranjuez or El Escorial. The King was quite right to suggest that we station ourselves there."

"The King had sent you?"

He nodded. "I have just now come back to Aranjuez to transplant some of my Chile pepper specimens." He smiled more fully. "Have you made any interesting discoveries since we last met?"

I frowned at the grass, ashamed of letting my studies, my art, my own self-worth, run to ruin over these past two years. I had blamed my situation, my worry about the Queen, even my hopes for Tiberio, for my inability to pursue my dream, but at that moment, as the lacy net of shadows danced upon my skirts, it suddenly became apparent: However I reacted to what life dealt me was my own damnable choice.

Doctor Debruyne's gaze wandered to the tall grass. "I apologize. I must keep searching, though why the King thinks I should be the one to look for cocoons, I do not know. I have much work to do before I leave."

My heart sank most irrationally. "You are leaving?"

"*Signorina,*" said Francesca, "we must go now."

"I believe you are being ushered away, *juffrouw.*"

I looked away, composing myself. "*Señor*, may I inquire where you are going?"

His teeth shone white in his tanned Flemish face. "The King has agreed to send me to Peru."

My breath stopped. Peru? It was on the other side of the world. I made myself smile. "Your dream. Congratulations."

"My goal of gathering native specimens will finally be realized—how well you understand me, *juffrouw.*" He held my gaze. "I wish we had gotten to know each other better."

I willed myself not to look away, even as I stored away his small compliment as a squirrel tucks away a nut. How long it had been since I had savored even the smallest bit of attention from a man.

He sighed. "I believe I am still getting over the shock of being sent. I don't know what persuaded His Majesty to finally send us—I have been a pest about it for years. Well, I shall not look a gift horse in the mouth. I jumped at it when he told me yesterday."

"Yesterday?"

"It is a marvel, isn't it? My ship sails from Sevilla in nineteen days. That is hardly time to gather supplies for two years, let alone to get there."

"You will be gone for two years?"

"Possibly longer. He said to take all the time there I needed."

I fought to keep a pleasant countenance.

He ran his boot over a patch of weedy grass. "I shall think of you, *juffrouw*, when I locate the native coca."

"Yes, please do think of me when you see green streams of saliva trickling down a chewer's chin."

"I will," he said readily. He saw me cringe. "But only in the very best way."

I fought back the smile that threatened to take over my face. "Good luck," I said. "With your experiments."

He paused as if reluctant to leave, unsure, I am certain, of what to make of such a strange person.

"You missed an interesting one," he said after a moment. "Experiment, I mean. You would have laughed. I boiled down moon-flower leaves into the weakest of teas, then drank it. The weakness and lethargy it produced kept me bed-bound for a week."

I frowned as I nodded. "Why would you wish to try it, when it is known to be a poison? Did you not say it caused the deadly flux?"

"True. But in small doses, it is said to bring sweetest euphoria. I had to see for myself. I know, I know, I shall never try that again." He laughed. "My pupils were as dilated as an owl's."

"Your pupils were dilated?"

He nodded. "Painfully. I could not bear light."

I glanced at Francesca, who was frowning most fiercely.

"What is it?" he asked.

I shook my head. Mentioning the Queen's ailment in the same breath as moonflower—I would sound delirious. Treasonous, as well.

Francesca touched my arm. *"Signorina."*

"I think she means for you to go," he said to me.

"Yes."

"I shall miss you, juffrouw Sofonisba, you and your beautiful eyes."

I knew not how to remain there gracefully. He would miss me? He would miss these eyes? With a sudden rush of disbelief mixed with joy, I curtseyed and hastened away.

"Good-bye," he called after me and my tottering black shadow. *"Mevrouw*, I hope your teeth stay strong. And *juffrouw*, if I do not see you for a while—do keep painting!"

I rushed over the long, dry grass, my skirts catching on sticks and brambles. Within sight of the palace, I stopped. Tears flooded my eyes when I leaned over to catch my breath.

Francesca caught up, panting. *"Signorina,* I see what is in your face. No! You can no fall in the love with this one! You hear him, he go across the sea. You never see him again."

"I am not in love, Francesca!"

Fool. Fool! How could I grieve for the loss of this man when I never really had him? Yet my heart was being wrenched from my chest. I could not bear Francesca's probing me about it. "It is not doctor Debruyne who troubles me. It is— It is—" I wiped my face with my arm. "It just strikes me as odd, that is all, that the King should send him away now, after he had requested leave for so many years. Is it purely coincidental that the one man who knows the poisonous properties of the plants from the New World is now being sent to the far side of the sea?"

"What?"

"Who else but him would notice that the symptoms the Queen now displays are the same he himself experienced after drinking moonflower tea? Does anyone else know that the moonflower specimens had once gone missing?"

Francesca's upturned chin quivered. "*Signorina*, do you say— do you say that the King, he poison Madonna Elisabetta?"

I regretted my careless words the moment I heard her accusation. The idea, confined within my imagination these months and years, grew terrifyingly real when voiced aloud. "Never speak of such again! Do you know what a dangerous thing you say?"

"You say it first, *signorina*."

"Yes, and I am sorry. Terribly sorry! Just because the King grows moonflower does not mean he would dream of feeding it to the Queen. Why would he ever do such a thing? He loves her."

Francesca drew her shawl closer, shaking her head.

"Stop it," I said. "If she'd been receiving moonflower tea, surely she'd have the flux by now. A fatal dose of the herb brings death by flux."

I paused. I did not like the look on her face. "What is it?"

"You remember how the Prince of Ascoli die?"

We stared at each other.

"Coincidence," I breathed.

Francesca wagged her head in remorse. "I say it ignorant for the other servants to say the King, he poison Signore Ascoli. I tell them, 'Hush your mouths!' when they say he angry that Signore Ascoli made a child upon signora Eufrasia, when Ascoli supposed to be the husband in name only. '*I* know the King myself,' I say. '*I* know he never do such thing.'"

"He wouldn't. We must not think this."

"You saw Signore Ascoli at the palace reception before he die—Signore Ascoli, he strong as the bull."

"This is absurd. A king poisoning his kin, let alone his wife."

"*Signorina*, name a duke of Milan who has live to be the old age. How many Italian gentlemen die before their beards have turn white, killed by their sons or nephews? Poisoned, all of them."

"That is Italy. They are poison-mad there."

"They poison-mad everywhere."

"Even if the King poisoned Ascoli—and I'm not saying he did!—why would he poison the Queen? He loves her."

We stared at each other. My heart beat faster, as before me flashed the King's face when he observed the Queen and Don Juan playing in the river, and when he watched the Queen stealing Don Juan's clothes in the woods of Valsaín. And how many times had the King seen the Queen gazing longingly at his brother? More times, many more times, than he'd seen her looking longingly at himself.

I gazed at the palace, rising up from the river, its scarlet and gold pennants snapping in the wind. I choked down the knot of fear swelling in my throat. "What do I do?"

"*Do? Do?* You do nothing, *signorina*! I not raise you from the baby to have you burn on the fire of the Inquisitor-General! You *do* nothing but go back to My Lady and work on the embroidery. Paint if you want! Draw the dogs from life! Chisel the statues out of the butter! But for you to do one thing about this"—she spat—"I forbid you."

"My poor little Lady . . ."

"You do not hear me, *signorina*?"

I nodded silently. I set forth, my shawl flapping.

"Where you go?" she cried.

"I don't know. To think."

She followed, moaning as I marched along the south arcade of the palace, reviewing my warring thoughts. Only in a state of unbalance would I question the King's intentions. It was not rational to think our quiet King could poison his own beloved wife. But how could I ignore the possibility of a connection between the Queen's inability to recover from childbirth and the "health-giving" elixirs the King was feeding her . . . if there was evidence.

"*Signorina*, where you go now!" cried Francesca.

I left the arcade and made for the courtyard before the main entrance of the palace, my slippers padding against the flagstones. When Francesca saw where I was headed, she bustled in front of me to block my way.

"No, *signorina*, you let it be! You follow this, it bring you harm."

"And what of the Queen if I do not?"

"*Signorina!*"

I dodged around her and broke into a run. To the far end of the courtyard I dashed, and at last into the King's flower garden, where leaf-heaped beds awaited the distant spring. The thorny canes of roses snatched at my sleeves as I ducked under the trellis. I stopped, panting. Where in seasons past brushy stands of moon-flower had flourished now stood a mound of rotting debris.

Francesca chugged up, holding her side. "See?" she said, gasping for breath. "Nothing. No leaves for him to make the bad tea."

I ran my slipper over the pile, uncovering the withered nubs of stalks.

"*Signorina.*"

The terror in Francesca's whisper jolted me upright. My heart dashed against my chest: Just across the river, under the alley of elms, the King approached carrying the Infanta, wrapped in a fur of ermine.

He leaned forward with a squint to ascertain who it was.

Francesca and I froze as do deer before an arquebus.

We waited as His Majesty paused to point out a nesting wood dove to the Infanta, who reached for it from her cozy wrap. He crossed the bridge before strolling to a stop before us. I curtseyed deeply, wishing never to rise.

"Looking for something?" said the King.

He watched as I rose, his perfect brows arched. In his arms, the six-month-old Infanta watched, too, her own faint brows poised exactly like her father's.

My heart pounded in my throat. "I look for signs of spring."

He switched the Infanta to his other arm. "You won't find many here. By the end of March, things will start to stir."

"Yes, Your Majesty. Thank you. I shall come back then."

He gazed at me, then at the dormant bed. He smiled briefly. "Are you interested in moonflowers?"

My blood froze within my veins.

"I thought you might be, as intent as you were on this bed."

I shook my head.

The Infanta leaned across her father's chest to latch on to his pointed beard, then chortled as his chin moved when he spoke. "If you wish to see it growing," he said, "I have a pot of it near the south window of my library. I have found that by bringing it indoors, I can grow it year-round."

I glanced away, my head light.

"Maybe you can explain to the Queen why I am so taken with the flower."

I looked up. He was studying me coolly, his expression mirrored on the baby's plump face.

"My wife thinks the plant looks like a weed."

My brain seethed with fear, even as my mouth boldly spoke. "Why do you grow it, then, Your Majesty?"

Behind me, Francesca stopped breathing.

A faint smile penetrated the King's calm features. "My mother had morning glories trained around her window at the palace where I grew up. It reminds me much of those."

The Infanta bucked in his arms.

"Isabel Clara, I see a horse. Do you see a horse?" He lifted the child so that she might see the beast being walked from the palace to the stable yard by one of the palace grooms. "Horse. *Horse.*"

She watched, the whites of her widened eyes the moist pale blue of the very young.

"The Queen is resting now," the King said to me. "She will want you when she rises." He kissed the top of the Infanta's head, then walked away.

I curtseyed to his retreating figure, then stood, my heart pounding as wood doves cooed serenely from the elms.

"*Ohimè, signorina,*" Francesca whispered. "We go home to Cremona, before you get in the trouble. Promise me you will do nothing—promise!"

I watched, ill, as the King strolled into the palace.

"If he want to hide the poison," Francesca whispered, "why he tell you where he grow it?"

"What better way to remove himself from questioning than to hide in plain sight? And what cares he about the suspicions of a poor count's daughter? He is King. He can do anything."

"*Ohimè!*" she groaned. "That is the terrible talk. Do not say again!"

But I did not have to say it again. The thought circulated unspoken between us for the rest of the evening. It festered in the air as we ate dinner, when we went to prayers, and as we readied the Queen for bed with the King. I could not meet Her Majesty's eyes. I had promised that I would never keep the truth from her, and now I was withholding information on which her very life might depend. How was I to live with myself? Yet what if I was missing something? What if I was reacting only to the colored pigments on the surface of the picture, ignoring the true basis of the picture—the underpainting beneath? I had to be misinterpreting appearances. In my years in the Queen's service, the King had been only the most loving of husbands.

I shall not sleep tonight. I must figure out a plan, a scheme—some way to keep My Lady alive while I seek the truth.

ITEM: *All rivers run to the sea.*

30 JANUARY 1567
The Palace, Aranjuez

I awoke to the sound of barking dogs. It had taken me all night
to drift into slumber, and now, soothed by the roar of the river
outside my window, my weary mind floated. I imagined the
King's mastiffs finding an intruder in the rose garden—a ragged
vagabond. The dogs leapt, knocking him onto the thorny bushes.
Something silver thudded on the frosty ground—a knife, meant
for the King.

Bells clanged into my dream . . . Five. Six. Seven. Eight.

Eight?

I opened my eyes. The palace bells were ringing, calling all to
eight-thirty Mass.

I sprang upright. "Why did you not wake me?" I cried at Francesca's sleeping form. "The Queen is waiting!"

She did not answer.

How could she sleep so deeply after what we'd learned? Had
I truly found evidence of the King's desire to poison My Lady?
Such is the stuff of books and legends, not of the quiet Paper
King's court. Let Francesca tell me it is all a fantasy, a dreamer's
whim, a chimera that dissolves upon waking.

"Francesca, get up! We're late." Panicking now, I gave her a
prod.

My fingers sank into the bulk. It was but a pillow under the blanket.

I jumped out of bed, knocking the bed-warmer to the floor with a thud, spewing ash and charcoal into the rush matting, then went to the window and opened it a crack. Icy air rushed in with the daylight. A guard's call drifted over the low roaring of the river.

Softly, I pulled the window shut, my guts rolling with guilt though I had done nothing wrong.

I began to dress myself as quickly as I could. Without Francesca, putting on my corset was maddening work. The bell rang the quarter-hour after eight, urging my fingers to move faster on the laces behind my back. Several frustrating minutes later, my bodice lopsided and gapping and my skirts askew, I hurried to the Queen's chambers.

"Hello?"

No one answered. I examined My Lady's dressing table. Water was still in the pitcher, the bowl dry, Her Majesty's towel untouched.

Surely Francesca was with the Queen. She must have arisen late herself and rushed My Lady's toilet and now they had gone to Mass. I glanced around the room. Where was the Queen's nightgown? Nothing made sense.

The halls were empty because of the commencing service. I ran to the chapel inside the palace, my pace checked only upon reaching the door. What would the condesa say when I arrived so late?

I eased my gaze through the stone arches of the windows that opened from the chapel into the hallway, as the priest sang the Kyrie Eleison: Mass had just started. On her pew, the condesa sat rigidly straight, her pomander to her nose. Next to her slumped madame, fingering her beads. On the other side of the crowded chapel, Don Alessandro sat with his chin upon his doublet, sleeping.

The Queen was not there.

I dropped into a crouch, fearful of being discovered. At that very moment, the door to the outside opened at the far end of the hall, letting the cold morning sunshine come pouring inside. Sparked by an urging inside me, I ran for the light, discovering upon passing through the portal the reason for its open state: The man on the other side was polishing the iron straps of the door. He had stopped to chat with a guard; neither man marked the exit of a panicked woman in disheveled dress.

I ran through the garden and over the wooden bridge and into the elm woods. Had My Lady escaped once more to the freedom of the woods? Oh, but the condesa would be harsh with her for missing Mass. Doña Juana would file it away for future damning use. Why had Francesca not stopped My Lady? Where was she?

I raced down the sandy trail, mentally scolding the Queen, berating Francesca, hectoring myself, when I was startled by a further thought: What if the King had ordered My Lady to be taken away?

I hurried on, my stomach burning with anxiety, when around the bend I spied two beggar women in layers of ragged clothing. I drew back, fearful of discovery, even as a ball of white threw itself from within the cloak of the smaller beggar and charged toward me.

The larger beggar woman whirled around, her upturned chin trembling above her wimple. *"Signorina!"*

I gasped. "Francesca?" Cher-Ami bounded into my arms. "My Lady?"

I ran forth to embrace the Queen. Beneath her layers of rough black rags, she wore a simple cowl of fine ivory wool, added protection against the morning chill, but not enough for someone in her weakened state. "What are you doing, My Lady? Why are you dressed so?" I felt her forehead. She was feverish.

"You were not to find us!" Francesca groaned. "Go, *signorina*, while you can."

"I will not! What are you doing?"

"Go back! No one will have to know."

A low whistle came from the direction of the river. Cher-Ami leapt down and scrambled through the underbrush. Before I could make sense of it, Francesca helped My Lady limp after the dog.

"Francesca, what have you told her?" I demanded, following.

"I mean it—go!"

"I am not leaving!"

Moaning like a wounded bear, Francesca gathered up the Queen, then crashed through the greenery. She broke out at the river's edge, where Don Juan waited in the water, holding the reins of a single mule and his great bay horse. His dog, Rojo, loped over to greet Cher-Ami.

With a last groan from the effort, Francesca relinquished the Queen into Don Juan's arms. Wordlessly, My Lady melted against him. It shocked me to see her do so, she who had for so many years scrupulously avoided his touch.

Don Juan drew back and looked searchingly into her face, so pale within her coarse black shawls. "Are you well, My Lady?"

She drank in his gaze. "Yes."

He cradled her to him, tenderly resting his chin upon her shawl-covered head. "Did anyone see you?" he asked Francesca.

She scowled at me. "No."

"I did not know you were coming," Don Juan said to me.

"She not!" Francesca exclaimed. "We go!"

"Let me be the one to decide!"

With his free arm, Don Juan steadied the sidestepping mule and handed its reins to Francesca. "There is a stream that branches from the river just around the bend. We will follow that as far as we can toward Toledo to cover our tracks. Then we will have to ride hard for the Gredos."

She nodded.

"I know places to hide there," Don Juan told me. "When it is safe, we will ride to Portugal, then set sail for the New World."

He pulled over his own horse and lifted the Queen upon it. He grasped her hands. "Elisabeth, this puts you at great risk. Speak now and we abandon the venture."

She gazed toward the palace. "My baby child. She won't even know me."

"We won't go. I will think of something else—kill the brute if I have to."

"No! Juan! He will kill you."

"Wouldn't he love an excuse? But there has to be a better way than this."

The Queen's eyes filled with tears as she searched his face. "Don't you know that I cannot stay?"

"Let me up!" cried Francesca. She struggled to mount the mule.

Don Juan left the Queen to hoist Francesca onto her mule, which she straddled like a man. "Thank you, friend, for alerting me," he said. "You have the heart of a noblewoman."

She frowned darkly. "We go now."

"I am sorry, Sofi," he said. "This is not of your choosing. Stay—I understand."

I gazed at the Queen, drooping over her horse. She spoke the truth. As rapidly as she was failing, she would die if she stayed, whether by poisoning or from entrapment within her gilded cage. I had not acted quickly enough to save Tiberio. I would not make that mistake again.

"I won't fail you," I said.

Don Juan lifted me up behind Francesca, seating me, too, in the more secure style of a man. He touched my arm. "I won't forget this."

The bell rang from the palace signaling the transubstantiation of the bread into the body of Christ. Mass would be ending soon.

Don Juan leapt up behind My Lady and whistled for his dog. The animal bounded through the undergrowth. Cher-Ami yapped at the feet of My Lady's horse. The Queen reached down, her dog sprang into her arms, and thus our ragged band started off.

We followed the bank a short distance toward the palace, then doubled back in the water to muddle our track. Our steeds galloped along the shallow edge of the river until we came to the stream of which Don Juan had spoken. We had not gone far when we heard trumpets calling.

Don Juan tightened his arms around My Lady, then spurred his horse. Francesca's feet bounced from the barrel sides of our mount as she kicked it into action. The blasts of the trumpets were lost in our splashing.

When we stopped some time later, drenched, our steeds blowing hard, the horns sounded no more. We let our mounts drink the very water against which they'd been straining, then pulled up reins and set forth again. I breathed shallowly, listening, listening. The cessation of a call to arms did not rule out a silent ambush.

The air resounded with the wet clopping of our steeds' hooves upon the shallow rocky bed of the stream. Birds darted in the tall browned grasses that grew up between the boulders on the banks.

A single buzzard stirred the relentlessly blue winter sky. The Queen, who for so many months had languished on a divan, leaned against Don Juan's chest, speaking animatedly of her childhood, of playing hide and seek with her brothers, of crouching behind heavy carved furniture in the cold, musty rooms of the family palaces, of strolling hand in hand with her beloved governess, Diane de Poitiers, through gardens ringed with red-and-white-striped poles. She told of her favorite dog, a spaniel named Fitzhugh, that fit inside her sleeve, and of her sister, Margot, singing a nursery song during the solemn occasion of Hercule's baptism. Don Juan, son of the country, listened, his smile a mix of contentment, adoration, and worry.

We skirted Toledo, the spires of its cathedral and the towers of the palace blue in the far distance. The landscape grew more stark. Except for an occasional grove of gray-green olive trees hugging the hills, scrubby shrubs, or a single stunted oak, the terrain was unrelentingly dry and lifeless, a sea of bent bleached grass. Our valley had opened onto a vast plain, exposing us to the eyes of anyone who would come looking.

"Should we have gone to France?" I asked Don Juan, my voice vibrating with the trotting of my mule. "My Lady's mother the Queen would welcome us there, I would think."

"And have her marry me off to some prince?" said My Lady. "No, thank you. And once she hears that I was poisoned, she will wage war on Spain, and thousands will die, thousands who could be home, smoking their pipes and doting on their children. No, let her believe I shirked my duty as Queen and ran away. It will be easy for her to imagine. I have always been a disappointment to her."

I lowered my face. How could she think that her mother, let alone the King, would let her go, as valuable a piece of property as she was? They would never rest until they found her, and then what would they do to those who had helped her to escape? I wiped my brow with the back of my hand. I could not destroy her hope of making it to Portugal and thus across the Ocean Sea, not when I had no other plan.

At last Don Juan steered us into an arid valley blanketed by a flock of grazing sheep. We rode amongst them, sending the herd flowing and eddying, the bell of the lead ewe clanking. Rojo padded beside us, grinning as if apologizing to the rough-haired brown and white dog working to control the panicked flock, now chasing at their heels, now crouching in the dry grass.

The smell of garlic frying in olive oil came from a low mud hut. A man ducked out the door, sending an icy spear of fear through my innards. But with a glance and a nod, he withdrew, leaving his dog to silently escort us away.

Who knows how long we kept plodding? As the winter sun festered overhead, My Lady fell asleep against Don Juan, Cher-Ami tucked in her lap, the strength she had borrowed from the excitement of escape finally abandoning her. More than once, exhausted from worry and a sleepless night, I slumbered, too, only to blink awake with my head against Francesca's back. Then my scalp would tingle anew with fear each time I saw the silent, naked hills and remembered how I had come to be there.

But Don Juan had chosen our route well. Other than the shepherd in his hut and a farmer plodding down the dusty track, his empty olive basket wrapped around him like a bulky straw blanket, we encountered no living persons. Our only accomplices were the sheep grazing silently on the hills, the small birds that swooped from shrub to shrub, and an occasional soaring buzzard. An ember of hope caught heat within my breast—could we truly have escaped?

I was staring at the dun-colored rocks, trying not to think or feel, when I heard murmuring from the horse in front of me. Don Juan bent over the Queen as she reached up to whisper in his ear. I saw his arms tighten around her, her closed-eyed smile. If only Tiberio and I could have had our chance together. He confessed his love for me too late, kept by pride from pursuing a woman he thought to be above him. It seems the Maestro purposely planted seeds of doubt in Tiberio's mind about his worthiness to have me—how clever of him to use Tiberio's pride against himself. But cleverness is the recourse of a man bound by shame and fear to never be able to confess his love outright. No wonder Michelangelo chose to portray himself as Nicodemus. Like Nicodemus, fearful of the consequences of having an unacceptable yearning, Michelangelo had been forced to hide his true feelings while teaching and caring for Tiberio, even giving him to complete what could have been his greatest sculpture.

Yet even as I hated what the Maestro's love for Tiberio did to me and our happiness, I began to pity the old man. What if Tiberio never knew Michelangelo's great love for him, at least while Michelangelo was alive, mistaking the Maestro's brusqueness as unconcern, when in truth it was only roughly masked desire? How it must have tortured the Maestro to find Tiberio and me together that evening, the scene of his heartbreak lit by the candles flickering on his pressboard crown.

"Let us rest for a moment," Don Juan called out.

We stopped and went off privately to take care of our natural needs, then shared a wineskin and some cheese brought by Don Juan. No convincing was needed to return us to our steeds. We rode on, single file, a small and weary train, until the sun edged its silent way below the mountains to our right, leaving a pink-gold sky in its wake and burnishing everything—Francesca's shoulders, the hills, the rocks, the brush—in gold. And then, like melancholy, a grayness felted over the golden light, until at last all was blanketed by a velvet starlit darkness.

Our mule stopped.

I leaned low in the saddle, my heart thumping. Don Juan's horse was not moving.

"What is it?" I whispered.

Don Juan jumped down, leaving My Lady upon the saddle. Taking the reins of his horse and our weary mule, he led us up off the trail, our mule braying in protest as it followed, to where Rojo sniffed at a stone hut.

Don Juan let go of our reins and helped Francesca and me down. Then, with a sigh that could be felt more than heard, he reached up for the Queen. She slid down into his embrace.

They stayed like that for who knows how long, the throbbing cry of a nightjar breaking the still, cool air. He cradled her against himself, then, as if in pain, released her. Their heartbeats audible—no, perhaps it was my own—she lifted her chin. Slowly, he leaned down until their lips met, trembling, to kiss.

Francesca grabbed the reins of their horse, of our mule as well, then marched stolidly away. "I go to sleep," she said gruffly.

With a look over my shoulder—they were pressed together as one—I hurried away.

I woke beneath an oak tree with a halberd at my throat.

"Don't move," the soldier ordered me.

Next to me, Francesca started from behind the halberd that pinned her down. "Do not hurt her!"

"Shut up, old woman!" the soldier barked.

I eased back. My gaze darted wildly from the blade of the halberd shining silver in the growing light of dawn, to the red hairs in the beard of the soldier holding the halberd, to the single horse standing outside the stone hut with Don Juan's dog, sniffing at its foreleg. Why had Rojo not barked?

At that moment, the Queen ducked under the rough wood door frame of the hut, her eyes flashing fire. She had on only a shawl thrown over her shift, and her cowl pulled over her head, but even in this simple garb, gone was the frivolous young girl who had come to play Queen those seven years ago.

She angrily tugged at her shawl as behind her Don Alessandro stepped from the hut. She whirled around to face him. "I thought you were my friend!"

"Kill him if he gives you any trouble," Don Alessandro said over his shoulder to someone in the hut. "He is a dead man, anyway."

The Queen spit at Don Alessandro's face.

He blinked, his expression flashing from shock to rage and then, at last, to icy amusement. "You always did make bad decisions, Elisabeth. Do you think we would have gotten caught if you had chosen me?"

"Why would I choose you?"

"Come now, who could better help you cross the King? I was just a boy when Felipe took me from my home and made me his ward. Could he have thought of a crueler punishment for my father for starting a war? I think I might hate His Majesty just a bit more than you."

"I do not act out of hate!"

"Oh. Lust, maybe?"

She raised her hand against him. He grabbed it, then smiled.

"So cold." He took off his lynx cape and wrapped it around her shoulders. "There now. Better?"

He ignored her look of hatred as he leaned down to pat Rojo's back. "Oh, and My Lady, next time you decide to take a jaunt, don't leave your gossip behind." He shook his head at me. "She broke my concentration on my prayers at Mass."

A man pushed Don Juan out of the hut, his hands tied. Another man held a dagger to his neck. His left eye was swelling shut; his lips, so recently tender servants of his heart, were bloodied.

"Elisabeth," he said. "I am sorry."

And then, as a rooster called, My Lady's face softened into something both pained and beatific, as if she had snatched a glimpse of heaven before falling to earth. Like shadows from a tree waving in the wind, across her calm features played desire and fulfillment, pain and joy, sorrow and peace; things not of this earth, yet part of the very air we breathe.

I drew in a breath: I could see her fragile soul, trembling within her.

A breeze picked up, loosing a dark strand from her cowl. It flew free as My Lady herself would never be, as she lifted her chin proudly from the shimmering silver fur of the wrap. "My Lord," she said, "I shall never be sorry."

ITEM: *Painting is concerned with each of the ten attributes of sight, namely darkness and brightness, substance and color, form and place, remoteness and nearness, and movement and rest. With these in mind, the painter may seek to imitate nature, though she might never fully understand what she sees.*

ITEM: I grandi dolori sono muti. *(Great griefs are mute.)*

—ITALIAN PROVERB

30 APRIL 1568
The Palace, Aranjuez

There. I have put one more stroke on the painting. I have been working on it since I finished the portrait I had started after being placed in the King's custody more than a year ago.

It was that first portrait, of My Lady, that had given me courage. I was compelled to produce it, even if I'd had to scratch my vision upon the dank, cracking walls of a dungeon. A glimpse of heaven had been etched upon My Lady's face as they had led her and Don Juan away that morning, and I had seen her delicate soul, yearning from within. And although the portrait that resulted had not the grandeur of a painting of Christ being taken from his Cross, or of Prometheus being chained to his rock, or the victory of Hannibal over Rome, nor a clever display of pattern, or of contrast, or even of warm color, it was honest, and true, and for that I deeply rejoice.

Although it is odd to be rejoicing during one's imprisonment.

We had been returned to the King immediately. The five of us— Don Juan, Don Alessandro, My Lady, myself, and Francesca— stood before him in his study.

The muffled roar of the river outside mingled with the measured taps of the King's feet as he paced before the window. His voice was as controlled as his footsteps. "You are to act as if nothing happened. If anyone asks where you were, do not say. Invent something. And it had better be brilliant." He turned to the Queen, all emotion chased from his face. "You may tell the condesa de Urueña and my sister that you were with me all the while. How they would love to see you fall."

"What about the men who were with me?" asked Don Alessandro. "What do I tell them?"

The King considered him calmly. "There is a galley ship sailing in three days from Valencia, with four new rowers."

Don Juan's chest rose in a silent inhalation. My Lady lowered her face.

"And Don Carlos?" said Don Alessandro. "He will be asking. I had a devil of a time trying to shake him before I set out. It cost me two good hours—time I could have used to keep these two apart."

The King's wince was almost imperceptible.

"Carlos must never know. It would break his heart." He swung his gaze to the Queen. "He thought you were good."

A knock came on the door. All gazes went to it. Before we would be interrupted, I fell to my knees, my skirts spreading on the floor in a puddle of black. "Your Majesty, thank you for forgiving us."

The King looked down his nose, studying me as if I were a new and possibly dangerous specimen from Peru. Into the long silence poured the sound of the river, rushing urgently to lose itself in the sea.

"I thought, *señorita*, that I knew you."

The knock came again. The King signaled to Don Alessandro to open the door. A guard entered and glanced at me on the floor.

The guard straightened as if he had not seen me. "Your Majesty, the Infanta is here with her nurse."

"Send her in," the King said pleasantly.

He turned away. And for one moment, as the river roared and the wood doves called and the golden workings of the King's German clock clicked and whirred on their endless rounds, His Majesty's mask of cool civility dissolved into bleakest anguish.

When he turned back to us, his face was composed once more. "Get out. All of you. Except my wife."

Fifteen months have passed. As surely as a prisoner in the Inquisitor-General's dungeon, I am held captive, though we may travel from palace to palace. My prison walls are hung with tapestries; my rack is an endless round of following My Lady from her chambers to Mass to her chambers once more; my fire is knowing that I might never leave Spain and see my family. All I have is time. A long, languidly unwinding swath of it. Perhaps it is true; perhaps Time and the King truly are allies. Who better than he knows the quiet power it has.

My Lady grows weaker by the day now, after giving birth seven months ago, in October, to her second child. The Infanta Catalina Micaela is a beautiful baby, though she looks not at all like her sister. She cries very little, unlike her sister, who never holds back the smallest felt slight. It is as if she knows innately not to call too much attention to herself. The Queen's new doctor suggested that the little Infanta was weakened at birth by the French Disease. He questioned My Lady at the delivery, asking if she herself had received the disease at her own birth, and if she had always been plagued by the fevers and sores associated with it. Incensed at such an idea, My Lady dismissed him before the day was out, but not before I heard his conjecture. That would explain the fevers, the rash, and My Lady's growing weakness—but so does poison. Yet could something other than moonflower have caused her pupils to dilate, perhaps some other, well-meant ingredient in the King's special elixir?

I cannot dwell on this now. I cannot bear to think that because I judged the King wrongly and then spoke so rashly to Francesca I have ruined so many lives. Who would think that mere words could affect so many? I meant the best, and so did Francesca, who now drifts around our rooms, murmuring to herself and wringing her hands.

"I make mistake keeping you away from the *scultore*," she blurted one morning as I painted. "I make you leave fast that morning in Rome—I am afraid what people say. If he come, I want you gone."

"But he didn't come, Francesca."

She closed her eyes.

"Did he?"

When she opened them, her eyes were pools of pain. "I did not want the *signorina* to make my mistake. I had give myself to the man I love, just like you. But he leave me, *signorina*, in the end he leave me, with the baby girl and no ring. He never make me a promise."

I stared at her, trying to digest what she was saying. "I understand."

"No, *signorina*. You do not. My girl, they send her away from the convent when she is young. I have not see her for many years. *Signorina,* I do not know if she happy." She took a shuddering breath. "A mother need to know if her child happy."

I took her in my arms. "Oh, Francesca."

"I never want you to feel this way."

"Shhhh," I whispered, smoothing her hair. *"La dimenticanza è il miglior rimedio dell'ingiuria."* The best remedy for an injury is to forget it.

She pulled back, searching my face, then shook her head. "But how, *signorina? How?"*

We could never have known what would happen to Don Carlos. Although we might have guessed that Don Alessandro would leak some of the details about My Lady's unsuccessful escape from the King, and that Don Carlos, upon hearing it, would fly into a fit, we could never have known he would swear to his father's face—in front of a gathering of nobles in Madrid—that he would kill the King as soon as he got the chance. With the respect of his people and hence the security of his kingdoms hanging in the balance, the King acted on Christmas Eve. He entered Don Carlos's chamber at midnight; the doors were sealed off by a team of German guards; the knife Don Carlos hid under his pillow was pried from the Prince's hand.

Don Carlos now languishes in a tower of the palace in Madrid, a danger only to himself, one day imagining himself to be so hot that he begs to freeze himself on a bed of ice, another so cold that he demands to overheat his slight person with fire. His life does hang by the frailest filament of silk. Don Juan is no longer here to protect him. Soon after our capture, the King made Don Juan a knight, gave him a navy, and sent him to fight pirates off the Barbary Coast. Few return from such a mission.

Often, my thoughts return to Tiberio and Michelangelo, to

Don Juan, the Queen, and her King. Will I ever understand the workings of the human heart? Will I ever know why we so often love those whom we cannot possess, and why we do not cherish those whose love we do possess? We are as thistledown twitching and turning in the current, captives to feelings we cannot control. How are we to understand those persons who mean the most to us, when we cannot truly understand our own blind and hapless selves?

Too late, it seems, I began to understand Tiberio. Not long after our ill-conceived attempt at escape, the King, finding me painting on the Queen's portrait, stopped to study my work. Alone and filled with the remorse and shame that his presence now evokes in me, I painted in silence, the hushed dab of my brush against canvas mingling with the moan of the river outside.

I heard his pained swallow behind me. "You have captured her."

I turned my head, just enough.

He held out his hand. My youthful image smiled from the miniature painting on his palm. I saw the emblem Tiberio and I had devised those years ago in Rome.

"This was found by my agent in Tiberio Calcagni's studio in Michelangelo's house. It was the only item in a velvet-lined coffer, on a table next to an unfinished statue."

I looked up into his face, so calm with its mask of *sosiego*.

"Take it." He gave it to me, its smooth copper back still warm from his hand.

And then he left, his fine kid shoes tapping quietly against the rushes.

Now I know the power of the spoken word. Now I know how deeply it can ruin. For the consequences of my own ill-considered speech, I must make amends, and so I paint, here in my tower, with a purpose. I paint for my sisters. I paint for my Queen. I paint for

all the women of the world who, burdened by caring for their fam-
ilies, by the expectations of others, by unbreakable chains of love
or gold, can never go in search of their dreams. How often we cautiously receive our lives, pale, uncertain Eves, as in the Maestro's
painting. If only we can be so brave as to love and accept the fragile spirit residing within each one of us, then, only then, we might
take the gift of self-knowledge offered in its shy and trembling
hands.

I wish doctor Debruyne could see my efforts. I think of him
often. He writes to me from the mountains of Peru, where he
seeks precious herbs that can free man and woman from pain,
from sickness, from the ebbing away of our lives with each breath
that we take. I like to think he will find them, and will tell me of
them someday.

Now, here in my tower, my hands have calmed sufficiently at
last. Once more I may return to my painting. Again I will lift my
brush, and screwing my courage to the sticking point, peer into
the mirror.

This time, maybe this time, I will see the one inside who is me.

Meanwhile, just the toss of an olive pit away, a man stands in
another tower of the palace. As the river below his window roars
on its painful journey to the sea, he tenderly shows an unopened
moonflower blossom to his darling. She touches the fragile closed
trumpet, then looks up, her chin tucked in, to see if she has done
wrong. He shakes his head no and kisses her dimpled knuckle.
How he does cherish her—his heart, his hope, the child Isabel
Clara Eugenia.

Author's Note

Sofonisba Anguissola became the governess to the two-year-old Infanta Isabel Clara Eugenia and her one-year-old sister, Catalina Micaela, after Elisabeth of Valois died from a miscarriage in the fourth month of her fourth pregnancy, on October 3, 1568. In 1570, King Felipe (Philip) chose the thirty-eight-year-old Sofonisba a husband, don Fabrizio de Moncada—a Sicilian, since Sofonisba said that if she must be married, she was "inclined to marry an Italian." She was allowed to leave Spain with her husband in the year of her marriage and was reunited with her family in Cremona. The couple traveled extensively in Italy and Spain, with Sofonisba painting at each stop, until don Fabrizio died in 1579. Newly widowed at age forty-seven, she immediately set sail for Cremona.

During the voyage home, Sofonisba met and fell in love with the ship's captain, Orazio Lomellino, a Genoan more than a decade younger than she. By the journey's end, she had promised to marry him. Sofonisba married, at last, for love.

The devoted couple moved to Genoa. Sofonisba kept in touch with Isabella Clara, Catalina Micaela, and King Felipe, who, until his death in 1598, granted Sofonisba a generous income. In Genoa, she inspired the many young painters who sought her out, among them Peter Paul Rubens and Anthony van Dyck. She lived until the age of ninety-three, painting, always painting, until blindness finally stilled her brush.

All these things are true, yet the story of *The Creation of Eve*, while based on a solid foundation of research, is a work of fiction. However, the most fantastical elements of the story tend to be the true ones.

After Michelangelo abandoned it, his beloved and talented follower, Tiberio Calcagni, worked on the unfinished statue now called the *Bandini Pietà* or *Florentine Pietà*, until his own death (cause unknown) in 1565. It is likely that Tiberio and Sofonisba met when she visited Michelangelo in Rome, as Calcagni, Tommaso Cavalieri, and Daniele da Volterra, the self-sacrificing friend who painted loincloths on the nudes in *The Last Judgment*, were in frequent attendance to the great artist. These three men were at Michelangelo's side at his death in 1564.

As for Michelangelo himself, although during his lifetime he was known as Il Divino, the Divine One, and was sought out by the most powerful men in Italy to decorate their palaces and churches in works of stone and paint, it is true that the only traces he left of himself in his art were as the flayed skin in *The Last Judgment* and as Nicodemus in *The Florentine Pietà*. Neither depiction is flattering. When the sculptor Leone Leoni was to strike a commemorative medal of Michelangelo in 1561, the artist asked to be portrayed as a blind pilgrim leaning on a staff and led by a dog. One wonders whether Michelangelo was deeply humbled by the irony that while he was a revered figure of superstar proportions for his emotional rendering of religious themes, he was attracted to men at a time when homosexuality was a crime against the Church, punishable by death. He must have been very much aware of how his public would hate him for his sexual nature, even as he penned poems to or about the men he loved, including one that he wrote in the 1550s about being shot with the arrows of Cupid at his advanced age. At times he loathed himself for his feelings. He wrote:

> *I live in sin, dying to myself I live;*
> *Life is no longer mine, but belongs to sin;*
> *My good is from heaven, my evil I give to myself,*
> *From my own unbound will, which has been*
>   *stolen from me.*

Yet he also asked:

> *For if of our affections none find grace*
> *In sight of Heaven, then wherefore hath God*
>   *made*
> *The world which we inhabit?*

That he wrote poetry to men was not a great secret in the exalted circles in which he moved, but soon after his death those who wished to protect Michelangelo's reputation in a climate unforgiving toward homosexuality altered his poetry and claimed it was addressed to women. Only relatively recently have historians acknowledged that the subjects of his love poetry were men.

On to the facts about another tormented soul: Don Carlos. It is true that the Prince, always high-strung, became unstable after a head injury that required trepanning. His unpredictable and sometimes violent behavior culminated in threats on his father's life, which brought Felipe to put Don Carlos under house arrest in December 1567. The prince died in a tower of the Alcázar of Madrid in July 1568, after months of rash behavior such as swallowing large gems and freezing himself on blocks of ice. Some readers will be familiar with Don Carlos through the eponymous play by Friedrich Schiller, or through the opera of the same name by Giuseppe Verdi. Both works romanticize the relationship between Don Carlos and Elisabeth, taking great liberties with the historical record.

From what I have read about Don Carlos, I have a difficult time picturing him as a romantic lead. Sickly and erratic, he was hardly a ladies' man. His love for Elisabeth is a matter of record, though, and given that she died a few months after he did, I can understand how a fiction writer might fantasize about them sharing a fatal love. I, however, preferred to take my liberties in imagining the Queen with Don Juan of Austria. As Don Juan was known to be charismatic in real life, and the Queen spent as much time with him as she did with Don Carlos, I thought their romance more believable. I was also intrigued that when Elisabeth died, Don Juan, distraught, raced back from the Barbary Coast (where he had been tucked away by Felipe) and publicly quarreled with Felipe at Elisabeth's funeral. Contemporaries often observed the friction between Felipe and Don Juan. It does not seem a far leap to imagine the jealousy Felipe must have felt when he watched his handsome young half brother interact with the vivacious teenaged Elisabeth. Nor is it implausible to think that Felipe may have noted the startling resemblance between Don Juan and the younger child, Catalina Micaela, and wondered why that might be, as I did, as I wrote our story.

But back to the record: Elisabeth of Valois's father, Henri II of France, did indeed die from wounds received at a tournament celebrating her wedding to Felipe. Several years before the event, the famed soothsayer Nostradamus had warned Catherine de' Medici:

The young lion will overcome the older one,
On the field of combat in a single battle;
He will pierce his eyes through a golden cage,
Two wounds made one, then he dies a cruel death.

When Nostradamus repeated his prediction at the tourney, Catherine was frantic for her husband's safety, but in spite of her pleas for him to stop, Henri ran at the lists three times against a young Scot named Montgomery. The third time, Montgomery's lance broke, sending a splinter through Henri's golden visor and into his eye.

Almost every other bizarre thing I wrote about Elisabeth's mother is true, also. Catherine de' Medici is a figure whose life defies belief, from her consultations with Nostradamus to her use of sorcery to undermine her husband's mistress Diane de Poitiers. The "hole in the floor" recorded in Sofi's notebook is a matter of record, as is Catherine's clear preference for her third son, who later became Henri III. It has been recorded that Catherine de' Medici warned Elisabeth to keep hidden from her husband her "condition," possibly the disease that plagued French kings since François I—the Great Pox, or syphilis.

Contemporary rumor held it that Henri II's father, François, quite the connoisseur of women, suffered from the disease; hence Europeans called it the French Disease. (The French, on the other hand, called it the Italian Disease.) Then, as now, syphilis could be passed to children of infected mothers at birth. This would mean that Catherine de' Medici had the Great Pox, contracted from her husband, Henri II, who had gotten it from his own mother, Claude, the long-suffering wife of François. I leave it to medical historians to decide whether Catherine and the others might have had latent cases that developed into tertiary-stage (final-stage) syphilis late in their lives. I myself wonder about the cases of "gout" from which François I, Henry VIII of England, and Felipe II died; all three of these kings ended their days with terrible abscesses on their thighs—a symptom found in tertiary-stage syphilis. Elisabeth herself was weakened by some chronic physical ailment, be it syphilis or otherwise. She suffered from fevers and weakness her entire married life, and had episodes of hemorrhaging through the nose, as in the true-life incident when she saw Eufrasia de Guzmán in advanced pregnancy, an incident recorded in contemporary accounts. No matter the cause of her fragile health, Elisabeth's repeated pregnancies, so necessary for orderly succession of the crown, undermined any chance for her recovery.

It is true that Don Juan de Austria was plucked from his quiet life as a country boy when his father, Emperor Charles V, the most powerful man in the world, decided to legitimize him, although the Emperor already had a faithful son in Felipe. The relationship between the brothers was predictably prickly—had the Emperor never heard of Cain and Abel when he commanded that Felipe treat his newfound brother well? Don Juan went on to become the most famous war hero of his time, leading the Spanish to an important naval victory at Lepanto. He was also known to have an affinity with animals, even adopting a lion as a pet. He never married.

Felipe, meanwhile, was stuck in his office with the unglamorous task of plowing through mountains of paperwork, thus earning from his contemporaries the title "The Paper King." Always conscious of the impossible amount of money needed to maintain an empire that stretched around the globe, he avoided war whenever possible—hence his association with the Inquisition, which he allowed the Roman Catholic Church to conduct in Spain, as it

had done since the time of Isabella and Ferdinand three generations earlier. Felipe followed his father's line of thinking that
stamping out protest early saved loss of lives (and money) later,
and indeed they both were inflexible in prohibiting the practice
of Protestantism in their realms. Yet Felipe is always associated with the "Spanish" Inquisition, when in fact most European
countries had their own, even more virulent, Inquisitions at the
time. More lives were lost under the forms of the Inquisition in
France, Italy, and England (under "Bloody" Mary Tudor's rule)
than under the Spanish Inquisition. Protestants such as Elizabeth
I of England practiced their own purges of heresy, persecuting
Catholics and racking up death tolls higher than those in Spain
under Felipe II. Our modern-day horror of the Spanish Inquisition and its association with a vilified Felipe are the products of a
smear campaign waged against him by the Dutch and the English.
Their effort at defamation is still effective today, more than four
hundred years after his death, each time he is depicted in books
and movies in English as a half-crazed despot. The image of
him as an avid gardener, devoted father, and devotee of art, science, and architecture is much more in line with the actual man.
His relationship with his daughters, Isabella Clara Eugenia and
Catalina Micaela, was exceptional in its tenderness, particularly
with Isabella Clara, who as a child liked to work with him in his
office. Proud of her intelligence, he renounced his rights to the
Netherlands in favor of her just before he died. She ruled the
Spanish Netherlands with her husband from 1601 to 1633. Don
Carlos, kept from ruling by a father who knew exactly the depth
of his son's failings, would have been envious. Catalina Micaela
married Charles Emmanuel I, Duke of Savoy, and bore ten children before she died in childbirth in 1597, having just turned
thirty.

About Sofonisba's place in the court of Felipe II: It is a matter of record that she was invited by the King to the Spanish court to teach the teenaged Queen to paint, and to attend Her Majesty as a lady-in-waiting. Less verifiable is the contemporary rumor that Sofonisba accepted her position at court after a betrothal offer had fallen through. Could this be when she first developed her stated preference for Italian, perhaps Roman, men? She was accompanied on her trip to Spain by two ladies, two gentlemen, and a staff of six servants. I like to think that once at court, she kept the same faithful servant she had recorded in *The Chess Game* and in *Self-Portrait at a Clavichord*, our Francesca.

Soon after her arrival in Spain, Sofonisba was sought out by others at court to paint their portraits, and she found herself in the unprecedented and uncomfortable position of being both painter and lady-in-waiting. Authenticating her works today is especially difficult; because she was a lady-in-waiting, it was not proper for her to sign her works. Her role as the Queen's lady always took precedence over her role as a painter, so her high position as one of the Queen's favored ladies was likely a mixed blessing to her.

In spite of the demands put on her time at the Spanish court, Sofonisba became the first woman painter to rise to prominence in the Italian Renaissance, and she was praised by Vasari in his renowned book *The Lives of the Artists*. Yet Sofonisba Anguissola's fame faded over time, in part because there were few signed paintings by her done after she arrived in Spain. Fortunately, her work is being rediscovered, in studies by Sylvia Ferino-Pagden and Maria Kusche, and Ilya Sandra Perlingieri, for instance, on whose books I based my research. Sofonisba's unsigned works, long attributed to such artists as Alonso Sánchez Coello and El Greco, are slowly being recognized as hers. One of the rare signed works that has come down to us, indicating its creation

before her time at court, is Sofonisba's self-portrait in miniature, in which she holds a shield containing curiously intertwined
initials—the miniature self-portrait described in this book.

In the last few decades, several of Sofonisba's portraits of Elisabeth of Valois have finally come to light, though none of those
portraits of the Queen was done from life during the three-year
period before Elisabeth's death. Into this breach of pictorial history comes my use of the painting *Lady in a Fur Wrap* in our story.

Lady in a Fur Wrap is a mystery in the world of art, with both
its creator and its sitter as the subjects of debate. Some scholars
attribute the painting to El Greco, but the style is nothing like his
and very much like Sofonisba's. The attribution to El Greco appears to have begun as a cataloguing error when the painting was
exhibited in the Louvre in 1838, hailed as a portrait by El Greco
of his daughter. A little fact-finding at the time might have exposed this as a mistake: glaring stylistic differences in the portrait
from El Greco's oeuvre aside, the artist didn't have a daughter.

Filling in the origins of *Lady in a Fur Wrap* is just the kind of
challenge a novelist craves. After examining Sofonisba's portraits
of Elisabeth of Valois as an adolescent fresh from France, with the
plucked eyebrows and hairline *en vogue* at the French court, I tried
to imagine how this child bride would look as she matured. *Lady
in a Fur Wrap*, which I'd fallen in love with since I had seen it in
Henry Kamen's celebrated biography *Philip of Spain*, immediately came to mind. Kamen attributed the painting to Sofonisba
Anguissola—my first acquaintance with the painter—and identi-
fied the sitter as Elisabeth's younger daughter, Catalina Micaela.
As I researched Sofonisba and her connection to Elisabeth, I
wondered why the woman in the painting couldn't be Elisabeth
herself, now mature at age twenty-two and wearing her eyebrows
more naturally in the Spanish style. The rest of the facial struc-

ture is similar to that in Elisabeth's earlier portraits. Our story, based on fact and filled in with fiction, began to take shape.

But without the real-life, sometimes ridiculous, sometimes tender, and always flawed characters from history, our tale would not exist. It is their portraits—their fragile and elusive inner selves— I hoped to capture on my own canvas.

Acknowledgments

First, I would like to thank my agent, Emma Sweeney, who since reading an early draft of this manuscript has given me confidence, hope, and great suggestions every step of the way. Her enthusiastic support means the world to me, and I will always be grateful to her for finding the perfect editor for this project, Peternelle van Arsdale.

I fear there aren't sufficient words to thank Peternelle. I may have lost track of the number of drafts this book required, but I will never lose sight of my debt of gratitude to her. Her unflagging energy and patience and, most important, her understanding of my story, buoyed me during the arduous months of revision—all this, and with a sense of humor. She made hard work fun. I am thankful for—and amazed by—how much effort she put into every aspect of bringing my dream book to print.

I wish to acknowledge, too, those at Putnam whose support and efforts are crucial to this book: Ivan Held, Catharine Lynch, Kate Stark, Marilyn Ducksworth, and Meredith Phebus. Leslie Gelbman and Susan Allison at Berkley were early and enthusiastic supporters, and for that I am very grateful. I would also like to thank the Putnam sales force—you are my heroes! A round of thanks goes to Marc Yankus for his gorgeous cover collage, to John T. Burgoyne for the lovely map reproduced on the endpapers, and to Lisa Amoroso, Hyunhee Cho, Andrea Ho, Claire Vaccaro, and Nicole LaRoche for making this book so beautiful. Sincere thanks, also, to Lucia Raatma and Anna Jardine for their meticulous work on the manuscript. And a hearty thanks goes to the indefatigable and indispensable Lauren Kaplan for pursuing various details to the far ends of the earth.

Thanks are in order to Teresa Antolin, at the Centro Nacional de Educación Ambiental (CENEAM) in Valsaín, Spain, for sharing her time while enlightening me on Felipe II and the natural and human history of the area. I appreciate the insight into Spanish history afforded to me by Rosa Guillén over a memorable dinner at the Posada Monasterio Tórtoles de Esgueva hosted by José L. Ardura. My education was also tremendously advanced by the prodigiously talented painter and instructor Chris di Domizio, of Atlanta, who opened the world of figurative drawing and painting to me, helping me understand the myriad decisions a painter must make in composing a work. His class changed my life.

I am grateful for my early readers, Ruth Berberich, Brandy Nagel, Lauren Lynch, and Carolyn Koefoot, whose suggestions and encouragement have meant so much to me. Thank you to Grzegorz Filip for his translation work and for his time so generously given on my behalf; to Richard Hooker for allowing me to use a portion of his translation of Michelangelo's unfinished Sonnet 32; and to Steve Berberich for sharing the driving duties with my husband while I was chasing down facts in Spain. I would also like to thank Karen Torghele Anderson, Jan Johnstone, Sue Edmonds, and all the other brilliant members of the book club that has enriched my mind and soul for the past twenty years, for their kind wishes and enthusiasm.

And at the center of my heart, you'll find my family, whose love and pride keep me going. To my daughters, Lauren Lynch, Megan Cayes, and Alison Cullen, and my husband, Mike, I owe my greatest thanks.

Artworks Mentioned in

The Creation of Eve

SOFONISBA ANGUISSOLA (c. 1532–1625)

Portrait of the Artist's Sisters Playing Chess, 1555. Oil on canvas, 72 x 97 cm. Muzeum Narodowe, Poznań, Poland.

Boy Bitten by a Crawfish, c. 1554. Black chalk and charcoal on brown paper, 32.2 x 37.5 cm. Museo Nazionale di Capodimonte, Naples.

Self-Portrait (with Emblem), c. 1556. Oil on parchment, 8.3 x 6.4 cm. Museum of Fine Arts, Boston.

Portrait of Amilcare, Minerva, and Asdrubale Anguissola, c. 1557–1558. Oil on canvas, 157 x 122 cm. Nivaagaards Malerisamling, Niva, Denmark.

Self-Portrait at an Easel, c. 1556. Oil on canvas, 66 x 57 cm. Muzeum Zamek, Łańcut, Poland. (Reproduced on page vi.)

Juan Pantoja de la Cruz, after Sofonisba Anguissola, *Portrait of Isabel de Valois* (Elisabeth of Valois), 1606. Oil on canvas, 119 x 84 cm. Museo del Prado, Madrid.

Self-Portrait at the Spinet, 1561. Oil on canvas, 83 x 65 cm. Earl Spencer Collection, Althorp.

Attributed to Alonso Sánchez Coello, but here to Sofonisba Anguissola, *Portrait of Don Carlos*, c. 1560. Oil on canvas, 109 x 95 cm. Museo del Prado, Madrid.

Portrait of Juana of Austria and a Young Girl, 1561. Oil on canvas, 194 x 108.3 cm. Isabella Stewart Gardner Museum, Boston.

Portrait of Alessandro Farnese, c. 1561. Oil on canvas, 107 x 79 cm. National Gallery of Ireland, Dublin.

Portrait of Isabel de Valois (Elisabeth of Valois), c. 1565. Oil on canvas, 205 x 123 cm. Museo del Prado, Madrid.

El Greco, attributed here to Sofonisba Anguissola, *Lady in a Fur Wrap*, 1577–1580(?). Oil on canvas, 62 x 59 cm. Culture and Sport Glasgow (Museums). (Reproduced on page 443.)

HIERONYMUS BOSCH (c. 1453–1516)

The Seven Deadly Sins and the Four Last Things, 1485. Oil on wood, 120 x 150 cm. Museo del Prado, Madrid.

The Garden of Earthly Delights, 1504. Triptych, with shutters; oil on panel, central panel 220 x 195 cm; wings 220 x 97 cm. Museo del Prado, Madrid.

LEONARDO DA VINCI (1452–1519)

Portrait of Mona Lisa (1479–1528), also known as *La Gioconda* (portrait of the wife of Francesco del Giocondo), 1503–1506. Oil on wood, 77 x 53 cm. Musée du Louvre, Paris.

ALBRECHT DÜRER (1471–1528)

Study of Praying Hands, 1508. Brush and ink heightened with white on blue-tinted paper, 29 x 20 cm. Graphische Sammlung Albertina, Vienna.

MICHELANGELO BUONARROTI (1475–1564)

Sistine Chapel ceiling, 1508–1512. Fresco, 40.23 x 13.4 m. Sistine Chapel, Vatican City.

The Last Judgment, 1531–1541. Fresco, 137 x 122 m. Sistine Chapel, Vatican City.

The Bandini Pietà (*The Florentine Pietà*), c. 1550. Marble, height 22.6 m. Museo dell'Opera del Duomo, Florence.

David, 1501–1504. Marble, height 5.17 m. Galleria dell'Accademia, Florence.

Brutus, 1540. Marble, height 9.5 m. Museo Nazionale del Bargello, Florence.

RAPHAEL (RAFFAELLO SANZIO, 1483–1520)

Portrait of Baldassare Castiglione, 1514–1515. Oil on canvas, 82 x 67 cm. Musée du Louvre, Paris.

The School of Athens, 1509–1510. Fresco, 550 x 772 cm. Stanza della Segnatura, Apostolic Palace, Vatican City.

TITIAN (TIZIANO VECELLIO, c. 1488/1490–1576)

Danaë and the Shower of Gold, 1553–1554. Oil on canvas, 129 x 180 cm. Museo del Prado, Madrid.

Pope Paul III and His Nephews Alessandro and Ottavio Farnese, 1546. Oil on canvas, 210 x 176 cm. Museo di Capodimonte, Naples.

Venus with Organist and Cupid, 1548. Oil on canvas, 148 x 217 cm. Museo del Prado, Madrid.

The Creation of Eve

DISCUSSION QUESTIONS

1. Were you surprised to learn that Sofonisba Anguissola, a Renaissance woman in a male-dominated culture, was a renowned portrait painter? How much of her fame do you think was attributed to her talent, and how much to other factors?

2. In the novel, we see (to varying degrees) the private lives of a servant, a lady, and a queen. How did their lives differ, and in what ways were their lives defined by their gender or their rank?

3. How might Sofonisba's life story have changed if she had married Tiberio Calcagni?

4. As stated in the Author's Note, Michelangelo was attracted to men at a time when homosexuality was a crime against the Church, punishable by death (page 446). In what ways did Sofonisba's attitude toward him change over the course of the novel, in part because of what she learns about his personal life, and in part because of the twists and turns of her own fate?

5. One of the themes in *The Creation of Eve* is how people make judgments of others and how fallible these judgments can be. The author has stated that she purposely gave her characters both good and bad traits. Did your opinion of any of the characters change over the course of the novel?

6. In her Author's Note, Lynn Cullen points out how effectively the Dutch and the English manipulated the legacy of Felipe II as well as their own reputations (page 451). As a result, slander from the 1500s is still accepted as historical fact. Have you seen examples in your own life in which events as reported on the news differed from a scene you actually witnessed?

7. When Elisabeth of Valois was growing up in the French court, titillating questions were debated such as: "Which is better in love: fulfillment or desire" (page 220). Which of those would you champion?

8. Court intrigue, capable of dooming a queen to death, is a potent force in *The Creation of Eve*. Certainly, public opinion can affect the lives and careers of public figures today. Are women still more vulnerable than men?

9. The novel poses the question: How well do we really know those closest to us? Is it sometimes better not to know them too well?

10. At the end of the book, Sofonisba asks: "Will I ever know why we so often love those whom we cannot possess?" (page 441). Is what she questions here universal to the human condition?